The Earth
And
The Flame

The Shadow Drawn Series

Book 2

R D Baker

For Rachel
This story wouldn't be what it is without you

Trigger Warnings

Please be aware of the following potential triggers within this book:

Explicit depictions of sexual acts
Graphic Depictions of violence and death
Sexual Assault, both on page and discussed as a past event
Torture
Kidnapping
Amnesia
Age-Gap relationship
Suicide discussed as a past event
Child abuse discussed as a past event
Loss of a loved one
Discussions of infertility
Occurrences of Trauma and PTSD

Be Kind to Yourself, Always

1
Tallesaign

"**W**hen the fuck did it start doing that?"

Amryn turns to see what I'm looking at, stepping away from the deer we just killed. He stands beside me, gazing across the valley. There's white smoke curling from the top of Arax, the tallest peak of the mountain range that borders the valley Ocario is nestled in.

"Arax is a volcano?" Amryn frowns at me.

I shake my head. "It's not. I mean, it's not anymore. I've never seen it do that before."

A rumbling growls below us, far under the surface of the earth, and the ground begins to shake, loose rocks clattering down the nearby cliff face. Snow falls from the boughs of the trees above us, dumping down on us as we wait for the earthquake to pass.

"Ok, that felt a little odd." Amryn says once the rumbling subsides.

I look back at the mountain, at the swirling smoke that

keeps rising into the mist above it. "This is fucking strange."

"Come on, brother." Amryn hoists the dead deer up over his shoulders like it weighs next to nothing. "Let's get back before any more weird shit happens."

He walks off ahead of me, down the snowy path along the base of the cliffs, back towards Ocario. I follow along behind, listening to him whistle and sing to himself as we go. He's in way too good of a mood for a man who has 300 pounds of deer on his back.

As we cross the open fields, the twinkling lights of the village come into view in the fading afternoon light. The warmly illuminated windows of the houses and the strings of fairy lights sparkling everywhere make it very clear that it's a special day. The square in front of the Great Hall is lit up and decorated, ready for the Winter Solstice party.

"Gonna be a good night," Amryn says as he carries the deer into the barn behind his cabin.

"Yeah, looking forward to it," I reply, wrapping a thick rope around the deer's legs. We attach it to the pulley and Amryn hoists it up, the deer dangling from the barn roof so it can drain.

"Meat for the winter," Amryn says with a grin. "He's a big one too." He turns to look at me thoughtfully. "You going to disappear from this party too or are you actually going to have some fun? Because you always say it but..."

"When you get to my age we'll talk about staying up til 3am for parties, OK?"

Amryn laughs. "The way you always talk you'd think you're 100 or something."

I'm not much of one for big celebrations, but the Winter Solstice night is always a bit different. It's more muted and cozy than the heady, sweaty dance parties that erupt around here every Summer.

We stomp back out into the snow, the light fading around us as we cross the yard towards Cora and Amryn's cabin. There's music coming from inside, candles burning in the windows.

Amryn opens the door, and Cora is dancing around the lounge room with Phoenix, who is bouncing around, squatting and throwing his hands over his head. His green eyes light up as he sees his Dad and me walk in.

This kid is the best. He looks so much like Amryn did when he was little, and he definitely has Amryn's attitude - wild and fearless, but tempered with Cora's sweetness.

"Daddy!" Phoenix cries, his chubby little arms up in the air. Amryn scoops him up with a laugh, swinging his son up over his head.

"How's my little monster, huh?"

"Momma and me is dancing." Phoenix's red cheeks glow as he jigs in his father's arms.

"Yeah I can see that." Amryn smiles widely at Cora. "Has Momma already been hitting the whiskey?"

Cora laughs as she walks over to him and gives him a kiss. "I haven't actually, I've been saving that for later." She grins up at him. "And then maybe you and I can try and make another one of these, huh?" She strokes Phoenix's back.

"Hey, hey," I say from the door, "some things I don't need to know."

Cora blushes and waves me over to the kitchen table. "Can I get you a drink, Tal?"

"Sure." I walk past Amryn and run my hand over Phoenix's soft black curls.

"Uncy Tal!" The little boy exclaims, and stretches out his arms to me. I love this kid. I take him from Amryn and cuddle him tight, and he giggles, winding his little fist around my long black hair.

"How's my favorite little guy, huh?" Phoenix giggles as I kiss his cheek.

"I had a book today, bout butterfies!" Phoenix tells me, his eyes wide.

"Oh yeah?" I give him a big smile. "Do you know, I used to take your daddy out to hunt butterflies when he was little."

Phoenix turns to look at his father. "Daddy like butterfies?"

Amryn laughs and nods. "I sure did, buddy. Uncy Tal knew the blue ones were my favorite."

I look up to see Cora looking at me dreamily. "And what's that look for?" I ask, sitting down at the table with Phoenix on my knee.

"It just looks so good on you." She shakes her head as she pours me a bourbon. "You'd make a great dad, I've always said it. When I think back on you carrying around Phoenix when he was this tiny little baby..." She trails off with a sigh.

"Watch out, brother," Amryn says, punching me in the arm lightly as he passes me. "She'll have you married off before the end of the night. Well, I'm going to shower!"

4

He ruffles Phoenix's hair before he pads down the hallway.

Phoenix reaches up and touches my cheek, running his fingers along the scar that Morgan's magic strike left behind. "It hurts?" He asks, his little face full of concern.

I smile at him and shake my head. "No, kiddo, it doesn't hurt at all."

Phoenix's eyebrows knit together. "The bad lady hurt you?"

My eyes flash up to Cora, and she frowns. "He's been doing this a lot," she says quietly. "He - he knows things. Things he can't know."

I look back down at Phoenix and kiss his forehead. "It's OK, buddy, the bad lady is gone." My stomach drops as he shakes his head sadly. He's just a kid. He can't know this stuff. He's just got a wild imagination.

Cora rushes over and brings me my drink, a wide smile on her face. "Hey Nixxy, Aunty Elise is going to be here soon and you get to have a sleepover!" She widens her mouth in excitement and Phoenix copies her, clapping his hands. "You go and get Mr Umble to take with you?"

Phoenix scrambles down off my lap and his chubby toddler feet pat along the wooden floor to his bedroom. "I be right back!" He calls as he goes.

I look back at Cora, and the smile dissolves from her face. "He's been saying things like this a lot, for like a month now. Things he can't know, things we saw in Nilau. He even asked Amryn about..." She breaks off, and takes a deep breath. "He had a nightmare and he asked why the lady had a mouth in her neck."

"Oh fuck," I say with a sigh, and nod. "Anya."

Cora nods. "Amryn doesn't know what to do about it, every time it comes up he sort of just goes pale and tries to distract Phoenix. But -" she glances over her shoulder in the direction of Phoenix's bedroom. "He keeps saying Morgan isn't dead. And it's freaking me out."

I take a sip of my bourbon and put my index finger to the scar on my face, tracing it slowly. "We saw her die, he's probably just saying things because he's a kid and can't make sense of it."

"Did you feel that earthquake today?" She asks me.

"Yeah, Amryn and I were about to head back in when we felt it. Arax is throwing white smoke, it must just be something to do with that."

Cora chews on her lip. "Yeah... It still all feels... weird."

We look at each other for a moment, and I feel her flash of anxiety like it's my own. Cora can sense things about this place more deeply than I can, and she looks worried. But it can't mean anything, right? It can't all be connected. It's just a little earthquake and a smoking mountain.

And a little kid seeing women with their throats sliced open in his dreams. Fucking hell.

I give Cora a big smile, trying to alleviate her worries. "Come on now, it's Winter Solstice, and we're going to have fun tonight, and try and keep you away from the whiskey, huh?"

Cora returns my smile and nods, tossing her curly hair over her shoulder. "Yeah you're right, it's going to be a great night. I've been looking forward to this all week."

The door to the cabin opens to reveal Elise standing

there, snow dusting her black hair and the shoulders of her red coat. "Hey family!" She says with a wide smile, kicking the snow off her boots.

At the sound of her voice, Phoenix comes barreling out into the room and flies at her. "Leesy!" He calls, and laughs out loud as Elise scoops him into her arms.

"My baby boy!"

I can't help but smile. She's called us all that, and still does. No matter how big we got, no matter that we tower over her now - we're all her baby boys.

Elise talks animatedly to Phoenix, expressing enthusiasm for every detail of his day he's sharing with her, and I think for the millionth time how sad it is that she's not a mother, even though she desperately wanted to be.

I remember my Mom telling me about Elise's husband, who left before I was old enough to remember him. He got tired of waiting and hoping they'd have a baby. Asshole.

Phoenix starts to tell Elise about the butterflies, and when I look back at Cora, her meaningful gaze tells me she's read my fucking mind again. She feels the same way about me that I do about Elise.

"Shut up," I mouth, and grin at her. Being her Draw sure does come with some interesting side effects.

Cora walks over to Elise with Phoenix's backpack. "Everything he needs is in here. Thanks so much for taking him."

"Not a problem at all," Elise says, kissing Phoenix's cheek. "We're going to have the best time."

"You a double, Leesy!" Phoenix announces happily, his chubby fists grabbing Elise's face. "I see your double."

Elise's brow furrows for a moment, and she looks over at Cora. "My double?"

My heart sinks a little. Shit.

Cora chuckles awkwardly. "I think he means Elspeth."

Elise's eyebrows lift slightly, and she smiles as she looks back at Phoenix. "Did Momma show you a picture of your grandma, did she?"

Phoenix takes Elise's hair into his hand, threading it through his fingers, and shakes his head. "No, she sit on the floor, and she sings."

Goosebumps break out over my arms, and the three of us eye each other silently. Amryn wanders into the room, a towel wrapped around his hips, and he looks at us all questioningly as we stare at him in silence. "What did I miss?"

"Nothing," Cora says quickly.

"Y'all look like a ghost just walked in," Amryn says with a crooked grin.

Elise smiles at him and shakes her head, waving her hand dismissively. "Oh no sweetheart, just getting Nixxy ready to go to my house." She bends down to put Phoenix on the ground. "Come on, baby boy, let's get your boots and your jacket on, and we'll walk to my house, yeah? You can come help me feed the goats before dinner."

"Yeah!" Phoenix cheers, offering his little foot to Elise to have socks and his boot put on. "Goat goat goat goat." He chants, bobbing his head back and forth.

Amryn laughs and walks over to Cora in the kitchen, kissing her neck and putting his arms around her waist. I look away, and feel a little pang in my stomach. I'd like that, too. Someone of my own. I sip on my bourbon, and the sweet liquid burns my throat, warming my chest. I hear them giggling as they talk to each other in that secret way couples have.

Yep. I'm lonely again.

I'm not lonely often, most days I can ignore it even when that heavy feeling does creep up on me. Life is busy, and I try not to give myself too much time to think about it. But since Cora and Amryn have been back, since our family has been complete again, I feel it.

I feel all the things I've missed out on, all those years I pushed everyone away, so afraid to lose anyone else I loved. And now I'm probably too old to start all that. Cora always scoffs when I say so - "You're not even 40 yet!" She says it all the time. And she's right, in demon years that's not very old. But I can't shake the feeling that I missed my chance.

"Ok," Elise says, straightening up and taking Phoenix's hand, "we're all set to go, and you all have a great night, yeah?" She looks down at Phoenix, who looks like a little gnome in his pointed hood and his big yellow boots. "Say bye bye everyone!"

Phoenix waves. "Bye bye everyone!"

"Bye sweetheart!" Cora blows him a kiss. "We'll see you tomorrow."

I rise from my chair as Elise leaves, and down the last of my bourbon. "I better go, too. Gotta get ready for tonight."

9

"We'll see you there." Cora says, swatting at Amryn's arms as he hugs her tighter.

As I leave, I hear them laughing together, Amryn growling, no doubt as he nuzzles into Cora's neck. I jam my hands into my pockets, and walk across the courtyard, rounding the edge of the barn, headed for my cabin. The windows are dark as I approach, and it's quiet. No one is waiting for me, no wife or kids or music to welcome me.

Get a fucking grip. I give myself a shake. Why is this bothering me so much today? God, I'm such an idiot.

When I walk into my cabin the air is heavy, the fire in the hearth reduced to glowing embers. I stoke it up, throwing more logs on, then head for the shower.

As I wait for the hot water, I look in the mirror. It's Amryn's face, just older, a few more lines around the eyes, though I do note that these days those lines are laugh lines. So that's nice.

The hot water over my shoulders feels good. I lather myself up with soap, my hands running across the scar on my chest. It still bothers me some days, even though it's been there 20 years now, along with the long white streak in my hair that runs from my left temple.

20 years since this all started. It feels like forever, and it feels like yesterday. Time is weird.

Once I'm clean, I dry off and wrap a towel around my hips. I sit down on the couch, the fire that is now leaping high in the hearth warming me. I light myself a cigarette, the sweet scent of tobacco filling my cabin. I watch the flames absently, water from my wet hair dripping down my chest.

10

In an instant, I can't breathe. I lurch forward onto the floor, on my hands and knees, and it feels like there's an anvil on my chest. I cough and splutter, the cigarette rolling away from me across the wood floor. I clutch at my throat, willing it to open, willing myself to breathe, to just suck in some air, and I can't.

Fuck, fuck, what the fuck is this? My vision goes dark, and I cough and splutter, gripping onto the armrest of the couch to try and haul myself up, but something jerks me back to the floor. And then there's screaming, distant, like an echo, ringing in my ears.

As quickly as it starts, it's over, leaving me doubled over on the ground, gasping for air.

My veins are glowing orange, my whole body on high alert. And then a rumbling sounds, the earth underneath me shaking gently. It sounds like a truck driving right past my porch, and it feels like it, too.

I sit on the floor, leaning back against the couch, waiting for the rumbling to subside. It only lasts about 30 seconds. The still-glowing cigarette is smoldering on the rug, leaving behind a black scorch mark. I pick it up and toss it into the fireplace.

I put a hand to my chest, where my heart is still beating wildly. The echo of that scream reverberates through my head.

What the fuck was that?

2

Tallesaign

The party is in full swing by the time I walk to the Great Hall. Music is playing in the background and bonfires have been lit, people standing around drinking mulled wine served from giant pots that steam in the bitter cold. It's snowing lightly, and I get myself a drink. My chest still feels tight.

The other demons smile and greet me as I pass, and it still feels a little odd to have a position in the clan. Sure, I was the son of the Striker. That meant next to nothing.

Then I was a warrior, but in a broken-up clan that had no ability to fight for years, that also didn't mean a whole lot. Now, I'm one of the Draws of the Shadow Queen, and people look to me. What for, I still don't always know. But they do.

Amryn and Cora are sitting by a bonfire, drinking and laughing. Cora is curled up in her big red coat, and Amryn has his arm around her. She leans her head against his shoulder and gazes up at him lovingly as he says something with a smile. Amryn plants a kiss on her forehead, and then his eyes move over her head, landing on me as I walk towards them.

"Hey brother," he says brightly, raising his glass to clink it against mine as I sit down beside them.

Cora eyes me carefully, her brow furrowing ever so slightly. "What's wrong?"

I meet her eyes and shake my head. "Nothing, why?"

Her eyes narrow. "Something happened."

"I'm fine," I lie, pulling my cigarette case from my pocket. "Just a little tired."

"Are you having nightmares again?"

I chuckle as I put the cigarette between my lips, lighting it with the orange flame that I summon in my palm. "Cora, I'm fine," I say, blowing out a cloud of smoke. "Stop worrying so much."

"Got one of those for me?" Amryn asks. Cora glares at him, and he laughs. "What? It's the Winter Solstice, babe."

I light a cigarette and hand it over to him. "It's not going to kill him, Cora."

"But it tastes like ass." She crosses her arms over her chest with a pout.

"There's one way to keep you two apart for longer than five minutes," I tease. I take a swig of my drink as Amryn laughs heartily. "I swear, you know I can sense your emotions right?"

Her eyes widen. "You mean you can feel it when we -" She breaks off and shakes her head. "No, I'm not even going there."

I shrug as Amryn begins to laugh uncontrollably. "I just feel that you're both happy." I take a drag of my cigarette.

13

"Very, *very* happy."

Cora flushes bright red. "Oh god fucking dammit."

"And that you're happy a *lot*," I go on, laughing as Cora grimaces.

Amryn is laughing so hard tears are rolling down his cheeks. "Brother, I tell you, the shit we nearly got busted doing in Nilau."

"Ok, that is not a laughing matter," Cora says indignantly, "that was life or death."

Amryn leans back and wipes the tears from his cheeks, and gives her a wide smile. "Baby, if I don't laugh about it, I'll cry." He takes her hand and kisses the back of it gently. "I'm sorry, come on, I'll stop."

Cora rolls her eyes and looks back at me. "We nearly got busted on the porch of mine and Finn's house one night."

I nearly choke on my drink and burst out laughing. "You what?" I splutter.

"So you get to talk about this?" Amryn teases her. He looks back over at me. "This one, two weeks without me and what did she do? Threw me down into a garden chair and was on me like -" Cora slaps him in the stomach and he theatrically sucks in a breath. "OK, OK, I'll stop."

"*You*," Cora says, grabbing his hair, "told me to use your outdoor shower like it was all innocent and then you had your mouth on my-"

"OK, *OK*," I exclaim, laughing into my drink, "I get it, you two fucked a lot, goddamn, *enough*."

Amryn pulls Cora close and kisses her, both of them

14

smiling and looking into each other's eyes.

Someone plops down in my lap suddenly, and I'm overwhelmed with the scent of sweet vanilla and a mass of strawberry blonde hair.

"Hi babe." Lorelei sits on my knees, her big blue eyes gazing at me.

I see Amryn suppressing a laugh over Lorelei's shoulder. "Speaking of fucking," he says quietly, but definitely loud enough for me to hear. He sniggers as I shoot daggers in his direction. "How are you, Lorelei?" He asks, raising his eyebrows at me.

Little brothers.

"I'm great, Amryn," Lorelei says, but her eyes stay on me. "Where have you been, Tal? I haven't seen much of you lately."

"I've been busy," I say. "You missed me, huh?"

"Mhmm." She nods.

Amryn rises to his feet with a grin. "Come on babe, let's go find a garden chair," he says with a laugh, pulling Cora away with him.

Lorelei watches them go, then turns back to me. She grins, tracing a finger over my cheek.

"You look good tonight," she says.

"So do you," I reply. She looks too fucking cute, that pretty hair hanging down her back, wearing a blue sweater that's cut way too fucking low for it not to be intentional.

I raise my cigarette to my lips, and she grabs my hand, directing the cigarette to her own lips, taking a long drag, her eyes on mine the whole time.

"I have missed you," she says quietly.

I know I shouldn't, but I put my arm around her, my hand running up and down her back.

Lorelei is too young for me, she's barely 20 years old, but she's been pursuing me relentlessly for months. I know I should be more responsible, but fuck, tonight she's smelling so good and her pretty blue eyes just stay fixed on me, like she's seeing right through me.

Lorelei giggles, wrapping her arms around my neck, and it's not lost on me that she's giving me a really good view of her cleavage.

"Did you miss me, too?" She whispers in my ear.

"Yeah." My mouth brushes against her jawline, breathing in that heady scent of vanilla. "I did miss you."

She wiggles her ass on my lap, and she knows exactly what she's doing. There's a flood of heat in my groin, and my hand sits low on her back, just above her ass. I should probably push her off, right? Except that's the last thing I want to do right now.

"You're being a bad girl," I mutter, leaning back and eyeing her carefully, taking another drag of my cigarette.

She flutters her eyelashes at me. "Do you want to punish me?"

I brush a kiss against her shoulder. "Maybe you need a bit of punishing, huh?"

Her eyes widen a tiny bit, her lips parting as she gasps. Then she gives me a little smile, leaning closer to me. Her breath washes over my lips.

"Am I interrupting?" A man's voice asks. *Oh shit.*

I look past Lorelei, and her father, Elias, is standing there, looking at us critically. He's about five years older than me, and he doesn't look happy to see his daughter wrapped around me. I give him a nod.

"Hey, Elias." I keep my hand on Lorelei's leg. "Party's pretty great, huh?" I take another nonchalant drag of my cigarette.

Elias looks at his daughter, crossing his arms over his chest. "You behaving yourself?"

Lorelei sighs and rolls her eyes. "We're just talking."

"On his lap?"

"Yes, on his lap," Lorelei snaps, "I'm not a kid anymore."

"He's old enough to be your father," Elias counters, his eyes moving back to me.

Lorelei laughs out loud. "You're trying really hard to find a problem here, aren't you?"

I rub her back and gesture for her to get up. She slides off my lap, and I rise to my feet, towering over Elias.

"You got a problem?"

He takes a deep breath, considering his words carefully as eyes around us turn to see what's going on. "No, no problem," he says finally.

"You want me to stay away from your daughter?" I'm not looking for a fight, but I'm also not about fathers treating their daughters like property.

Elias's eyes blaze. "I don't want her to make a mistake."

"She won't." I clap him on the shoulder and take Lorelei's hand. "Come on, babe." I pull her away, towards the bonfire at the far end of the Hall.

Lorelei giggles, and clutches on to my arm. "He's going to be mad for days."

"Let him be mad." I know she's too young for me. I know I should be responsible. But I don't want to be alone tonight. I stop walking as we round a corner of one of the houses, and push her back against the wall. I lean down over her, and her arms wind around my neck.

"You want me to kiss you?"

"Yes," she says with a sigh.

I brush her mouth with my lips, and grin. "I got a feeling you want a whole lot more than that."

She gives a little gasp, and smiles back abashedly. "I do."

"So, what is it you want?" I brush my mouth along her jawline, and feeling a fucking thrill as she shivers.

"I - I want you to take me back to your place."

"Mmmm," I growl against her collarbone. "And then?"

She giggles, pressing her hips against me. "You know what I want."

"Are you getting shy on me?" I ask, smiling at her.

"No." Her voice is suddenly full of sass, and she grabs my collar pulling me closer. "I want you to take me home and fuck me." She pulls my face towards hers, and I kiss her, and I feel kind of stupid for not doing this sooner.

Why have I been saying no all this time?

I pull back from her, and kiss the tip of her nose. "Let's go then."

We walk hand in hand back to my place, and I barely have the door open before she jumps on me, kissing me hungrily. I put my hands under her perfect little ass, holding her up, carrying her to the bedroom blind, because she will not let my mouth go.

I feel around for the light switch, and click it on when I find it. I want to see every inch of her while she's in my bed.

We fall on to the bed together, and she's tearing at my clothes, crazed, and I laugh, throwing off my coat and pulling the shirt off over my head. I lean back over her, and her eyes widen as they fix on my chest.

"Oh fuck," she says, looking up at me, her lips all red and full from kissing me. "What happened?"

I shake my head, smiling. "It was a long time ago."

She pushes herself up on her elbows, and traces her lips along the scar, kissing it gently, looking up at me with those pretty blue eyes. *Fuck.* She's so sweet, she's so pretty, and she's here kissing my chest. My cock is straining in my jeans, and I exhale heavily.

She lies back down, unbuttoning her shirt, pulling it open to reveal her lacy blue bra. I lean down and kiss the mound of her breasts, tracing a hand down over her belly to the waistband of her pants, opening the buttons. I push my hand down, underneath her clothes and into her panties, and she gasps, grabbing my shoulders as my finger moves over her clit.

"Tal," she says with a sigh, her hips writhing under me. "Please fuck me."

I rise over her, pulling her pants down her legs, and

taking off my own. I kiss my way back up her body, tracing my lips over her smooth pussy, her hips, her stomach, her breasts. The thrill I feel as she gasps and quivers is intoxicating.

I lie over her, and her legs open for me. She gazes up at me with slightly widened eyes. "Can you turn off the lights?"

"I wanna see you, baby," I say, stroking her cheek with my hand.

"It's just... I..." She blushes, covering her eyes with the back of her hand. "I've never done this before."

Fuck. *Fuck. You fucking idiot.* I sit up quickly, and she looks at me from under her hand, hurt flashing across her face.

"I'm sorry," she says quietly.

"No, no, come on." I take her hand. "Don't apologize, don't be silly."

"You don't want to sleep with a virgin, huh?" She asks, sitting up and pushing her hair out of her face.

"That's not it, I just don't want to, I don't know. I don't want to take advantage of you."

She shakes her head adamantly. "You're not. I want you. Why can't it be you?"

"Why do you want it to be me?"

"Because you're good-looking, and you're sweet, and I like you." She eyes me shyly. "I like you. I like your arms."

I laugh, and the tension in the room seems to release. "My arms?"

She nods, and reaches out to run a hand down my

bicep. "They're big, and they look like a safe place to be." Her eyes move back to my face. "You make me feel safe. And that's a good thing for my first time, right?"

I can't really disagree with her there. "Yeah, it is. Of course it is."

"I want it to be you. Just, turn out the lights first. I'm nervous." She gives me a small smile, and reaches behind her to unhook her bra.

The sight of her completely naked has my cock immediately hard again. Fuck it. She wants me, and I'm done saying no to her, to everything.

I get up and turn the lights off, climbing back onto the bed, over her. Her arms go around me, and I kiss her, taking my time, tasting her mouth, feeling her tongue play over mine.

She's grasping at me, her legs hooked around mine, and I pull back from her. "Be patient, baby," I say, and start kissing my way down her neck, over her breasts.

"What are you doing?"

"I want to hear you come," I murmur, and I work my way back down the bed, kneeling on the ground, and she yelps as I pull her towards me.

She giggles, and then her back bows and she cries out as my tongue moves over her pussy, pushing it open, finding her clit. Her skin is soft and smooth against my mouth, and I roll my tongue around her, and the sounds she's making are going to send me over the edge right here on the fucking floor.

She rakes her hands through my hair, grabbing a fistful of it and thrusting herself against my face. I grip her ass tighter, holding her to me, and she yanks on my hair, crying out.

"Tal, oh my god, Tal, I'm going to come."

Yep. That's the point, baby. I keep licking and sucking, and she gets wetter and wetter, her thighs trembling. Both her hands are in my hair, her nails raking against my scalp.

She whimpers, and her back arches so hard it feels like she's about to bend herself in half. "Fuck, oh *fuck*!"

I dip my tongue lower, almost to her opening, then lick back up over her clit. She lets out a choked scream as her body quivers violently, and then her hands drop from my hair. Her legs flop to the bed as she breathes rapidly.

I keep licking and she gasps, giggling as she scrambles away from my mouth.

"Oh god, stop," she says breathlessly. "I'm going to pass out if you do that again."

I climb over her, kissing her neck. Her arms are thrown up over her head, her eyes closed.

"Good?" I ask, nudging her jawline with my nose.

She nods. "Uh-huh. So good. *Fuck*."

I chuckle, and run my hands over her stomach, down between her thighs, and she moans. She's dripping wet now, just how I want her to be.

"You want more?" I whisper in her ear.

"Yeah." She shivers a little. "I want more."

I reach over to the nightstand, yanking the drawer open. I reach around blindly, retrieving the foil packet. I tear it open with my teeth, and Lorelei props herself up on her elbows, watching with widened eyes as I roll the condom down over my length.

"Will you fit?" She asks in a small voice.

I lean over her, kissing her neck. "That's why I wanted you to come first, baby."

"OK." It's not a word so much as a little breath, and she opens her legs, letting me settle between her thighs.

I push my cock into her slowly, feeling her open for me. Her body tenses under mine as a gasp escapes her, and I move to catch it with my own.

"Are you OK?" I ask against her mouth.

She squeezes her eyes shut and bites her lip, nodding.

"Baby, look at me." I stroke her cheek with the backs of my fingers. Her eyes open slowly, and I smile at her. "I've got you, OK?"

She arches gently under me as I claim her mouth again, easing further into her. God, she's so fucking tight. She squirms underneath my body, and I groan against her neck as I seat myself fully inside her slick warmth. *Fuck.*

"Does that feel good?"

"Yes."

"Do you want me to do it harder?"

She nods, and she cries out as I thrust again.

"Did I hurt you?"

She pushes her mouth against mine, kissing me hungrily. "Just fuck me," she pants, "stop worrying and just fuck me."

I grin, and fuck her harder. She doesn't want me to

worry, she doesn't want me to hold back, so I don't. And from the sounds she's making, that's exactly what she wants.

Goddammit this isn't going to last as long as I want. She feels too fucking good. Her hands are on my ass, urging me to move, and I can feel myself rising already.

She pulls me down to kiss her, giving me an excuse to slow down, to try and draw this out. And then she wraps her legs around me and holy *fuck*. Not even wearing a condom is going to save me from this being embarrassingly quick.

"Can I get on top?" She asks suddenly, her hands against my chest.

I smile down at her, and clutch her in my arms, rolling on to my back with her. She rises up on top of me and whimpers a little as she lowers herself right down on to my cock.

"Tell me if I do it wrong," she says in a small voice.

I run my hands along her thighs. "Baby, there is no wrong. You feel fucking incredible."

She lets out a small, breathy laugh that turns into a moan as she begins to ride me. The moon has started to shine, and the light illuminates the room, so I can see her moving, see her breasts bouncing as she starts to roll her hips on me.

She's so wet, every move she makes sends my nerves firing, and the heat and tension builds in my thighs. I grip her hips with my fingers, and I groan.

"Is that good?" She asks shyly.

"Baby, it's fucking amazing."

She giggles, and rides me harder, and I inhale sharply. I don't want to come yet, I want her to get off again first, but *fuck* she's so tight and this angle feels too damn good.

All of a sudden, I can't breathe. The room goes black and the weight on my chest is fucking unbearable. Someone's screaming. It's like they're dying, sheer terror that's almost palpable, striking so deep that it feels like my own.

Pain shoots through my hands, my fingertips feel raw, as if they've been dragged against stone. I feel like I'm suffocating. The air is thick and I can't breathe. It's hot. Everything tastes like dirt.

I lurch up in the bed, and Lorelei cries out, springing off me. I gasp for air, crawling for the edge of the bed. I'm going to be sick. The weight on my chest. What the fuck is this? The screaming reverberates around my skull, and I hammer against my temple to try and make it stop.

Just like before, it's over as quickly as it began, like a door slamming shut. It's just me and Lorelei in the room, the moon is shining, and I can breathe again. I stumble to the window, tearing it open, gulping down the frigid night air. My hands are fucking shaking.

"Are you OK?" Lorelei asks in a tiny voice.

My shoulders are still heaving, and I can't fucking get my voice to work, so I just nod then turn to look at her. She's curled up on the bed in a protective little ball, her eyebrows drawn up. Shit. What a great first time.

"What happened?"

I shake my head, and push the window closed. "I don't know." My voice is hoarse, and my chest still aches.

"Was it me?" Her voice is almost inaudible.

I sit on the bed beside her and take her hand. "No, it wasn't you, you were great, that was - I don't even know. It happened to me today, and it's like - I can't breathe. I don't know why."

"I thought you were going to die."

"I didn't mean to frighten you." I take her in my arms, and she nuzzles against my chest. She starts to cry quietly, and I curse whatever is fucking causing these blackouts right into an active volcano. "I'm so sorry I ruined this for you."

She looks up at me and dashes her tears away, smiling through them. "It's OK, I'm being stupid. You just scared me so bad."

Yeah, I scared myself too. "I'm OK, I promise." I kiss her gently. I feel so fucking bad for her.

Yeah OK, and for myself too.

"Do you just want to cuddle for now?" She asks.

"Yeah, that sounds good. Just let me clean up first." I climb off the bed and head to the bathroom, peeling off that condom I didn't fucking need after all. God fucking dammit.

I rinse my face with cold water, trying to erase that hot feeling of stale air and dirt, mixed with a fuck ton of disappointment. I look in the mirror, and sigh. *Good one, Tal. You got a hot girl in your bed and you nearly die. Life's over, man.*

I give myself a shake, kicking my self-pity into a dark corner of my brain, and soak a washcloth in warm water. I take it back to the bedroom, where Lorelei is sitting on the bed, knees drawn up under her chin.

"You OK?" I ask, sitting beside her.

She nods, then looks at the wash cloth with a small frown. "What's that for?"

I can't help but chuckle. "Thought you might wanna clean up, too."

"Oh." Followed by an embarrassed little giggle. "I thought because you hadn't... I mean, I guess... Thank you." She takes hold of the cloth, her eyes flickering up to mine when I don't let it go.

"Lie down," I say, "let me do it for you."

She regards me with disbelief. "You want to clean me up?"

"Baby, it's the least I can do after I nearly died on you." I laugh when her eyebrows shoot up. "Hey now, come on, it's OK. I'm fine. I promise. Just let me do this for you."

She shuffles back on the bed, her knees jerking together a little as I move closer, and she clutches a hand to her face as she laughs.

"Do all men do this?" She asks as I gently wash between her thighs.

"They should."

She scoffs. "Yeah, they don't though, do they? You're definitely not like other guys, Tal." She bites her lip. "Am I bleeding?"

There's a few pink streaks on the washcloth, which I throw into the corner of the room. I'll deal with it tomorrow.

"A little." I lean forward to stroke her cheek. "Are you

sore?"

She shakes her head. "No, I'm OK. It felt good. Just... *full.* It's weird." She gives another one of those sweet, shy giggles. "Have you ever had sex without a condom?"

I shake my head. "Nope."

"Do you want to?"

I shrug as I take her hand. "Yeah, of course. But it's safer this way."

Her brow crinkles for a moment as she considers those words, and then she lets out a long sigh. Her fingers run up and down my arms.

"I'm ready for that cuddle now." She smiles at me.

"Of course, baby."

I click the light off and we lie down together. She backs against me, cradling into the crook of my arms with a happy little moan. She's incredibly warm, and smells so damn good.

She falls asleep within minutes, but I lie awake for a long time. Every time I close my eyes, the air becomes thick and hot, and the screaming comes back.

When I do finally fall asleep, I dream of bloody fingertips, nails torn from the flesh as they claw violently, desperately at slabs of rock.

When I wake in the morning, my fingernails have dirt under them.

3
Tallesaign

hoenix comes running across the snowy garden towards me, smiling widely. "Uncy Tal!"

"Hey buddy." I scoop him up as he reaches me, and his little arms go around my neck.

Cora smiles at us as I walk over to her. She rubs her hands together, trying to warm them. "Hey, you." She says. "You OK?"

"I'm fine, why?"

"You look tired."

I try to keep my expression even. "Just had a few bad nights, I think it must be the full moon or something."

"No, no, no," Phoenix says in a sing-song voice.

"No?" I grin at him. "What's no, kiddo?"

"You sleep in the dirt." He says, grabbing a strand of my hair and twirling it around his fingers.

I look at Cora, and her expression changes from one of confusion to concern. "Tal, what's going on?"

I don't want to scare her. And I don't really want to talk about the fucking nightmares, the... the... I don't even know what to call the attacks when I can't breathe. Scrubbing dirt out from under my nails every morning is getting old, too.

Since the Winter Solstice, since Arax started throwing that white smoke, it's happened every day. But I can't explain it, and Cora looks so damn scared right now, I don't want to make her feel worse.

"Nothing's going on." I assure her. "Like I said, he's just babbling. He's a kid." Phoenix taps my shoulder and wriggles in my arms, so I put him down on his feet, and he runs back over to the snowman he's working on.

Cora steps closer to me. "This isn't the first time he's said it, Tal. Phoenix keeps talking about the dirt, about you sleeping in the dirt."

I gesture to the garden around me, trying to keep my expression light. "Hey, his momma loves gardening, of course he's talking about dirt."

Cora puts her hands on my chest and her green eyes burn into mine. "Tal, sleeping in the dirt?"

"Cora, it's just -"

"No." She grabs on to my jacket and shakes me gently. "Stop it. You and Amryn keep acting like all this stuff doesn't mean anything. Phoenix keeps talking about you sleeping in the dirt, and you think that doesn't mean anything?" She clenches her eyes shut, and she puts her head against my chest.

"Hey." I put my arms around her. "Honey, come on now. I'm right here. I'm fine."

She shakes her head, and when she looks back up at me, she's crying. "I have this weird feeling, like - like something's coming. And then Phoenix talked about you being asleep in the dirt, and I... I don't want anything to happen to you."

I stroke her cheek, wiping away her tears, and shake my head. "I'm not going anywhere, honey. I promise."

"Momma?" Phoenix is toddling over, his face full of concern as he looks at his mother. "Momma sad?"

Cora quickly wipes her tears away, and smiles at Phoenix as she steps away from me. "Momma's alright, little bug. I just love Uncle Tal a lot, you know?"

"Me too." Phoenix says, and he looks adoringly from Cora to me.

My heart swells, and I run a hand over his head. I look back at Cora, and press a kiss to her temple. "Come on, no more tears."

Her eyes shift, looking at something beyond me, and she gasps. I turn around to follow her line of vision, and I see she's looking at Arax, which is still violently spewing smoke. Except now that smoke isn't white anymore.

It's red. Thick, violent, crimson red.

"What is that?" Cora murmurs.

Suddenly, the ground beneath us begins to quake, and I grab Phoenix, holding on to him tight as Cora clutches on to my arm. It's stronger than it has been before, enough for us to lose our balance. Cora looks up at me, and she's gone pale.

Amryn comes running towards us from across the field, kicking up snow as he goes. The rumbling subsides as he gets closer. "You OK?" He calls out. Cora runs to him and he throws his arms around her. "That one was a lot stronger than the others."

"And look." Cora says, pointing at Arax and its crimson whirl of smoke.

Amryn frowns, looking at us both. "What is going on?"

"Awake." Phoenix says suddenly. "Awake, awake, awake."

"Who's awake, buddy?" I ask him.

He points to Arax. "The double."

We don't have time to ask him any questions, as screams start to come from the village. Amryn and I exchange a look, his eyebrows shooting up in alarm.

Phoenix jerks in my arms. "Momma!" He reaches out for Cora, who takes him from me.

"You two, go and see what's going on," she says, starting to run back towards her cabin. "I need to get him safe. I'll be right there!"

Amryn and I pelt across the snow, towards the screaming, our flames at the ready.

A rush of fire erupts from the southern end of the village, and we head for it. Demons are running past us, their eyes wide with terror. What the fuck has them this spooked?

We come upon a group of demons standing around an enormous crack in the ground, a dark crevasse in the white snow. It takes me a second to realize what they're firing at, and what that rushing sound is - snakes are pouring out of the earth, thousands of them, dark green and slithering.

"What the fuck is this?" Amryn's eyes are wide as he looks at me, and we quickly step forward to help, firing on the creatures that just won't stop coming.

They get closer and closer to our feet, their mouths torn open to reveal long white fangs. The sound they're making is positively unearthly, a high-pitched hissing shriek. It hurts my ears, and I wince as it gets louder, as more and more of them continue to pour out of the ground.

One of them lunges at Amryn's leg, and he kicks it away, only for another ten to make their way directly at us. The ground shakes again, sending another wave of serpents out of the canyon forming in the snow.

"Step back!" Cora's voice sounds behind me, and everyone around us scatters.

There's the familiar tingle in the air, the hairs on the back of my neck standing up as Cora summons the Inera. The shock wave rushes over us, a bright flash of white. The serpents scream in a sickening crescendo, writhing as they are reduced to ashes.

When the light dims, the crack in the earth is empty, a wide, yawning abyss of black.

Cora steps forward between us, and looks down into it. "How did serpents make it to sacred ground?" She gazes up at Amryn.

He shakes his head. "I don't know, but I don't like this." He looks over to Arax, which is spewing more and more red smoke.

"There are protections in place here," Cora says slowly, shaking her head, "there's barriers, why aren't they holding anymore?"

There's a rush of wings above us, and an angel lands on the other side of the crack. He's wearing a black cowl over his head, and when he looks up at me, his eyes flash silver, like mercury. His skin is so white I can see the blue veins underneath it, even at this distance.

"Azrael," Cora calls, "what are you doing here?"

"I need to speak with you, my Queen," he replies, his eyes unblinking. "Urgently."

Angels make me uneasy. I remember my father meeting with two of them when I was a child, and their red eyes freaked me right out. The humans always think angels are beautiful, with white wings and long white gowns - nothing could be further from the truth, for some of them at least.

Demons all look like humans. Lots of angels look like monsters that crawled straight out of your worst nightmare. I haven't really trusted any of them, except Zadkiel. And this one, with his silver eyes and his translucent skin, makes my skin crawl.

He sits on a chair in the Great Hall and leans on his scythe like it's a cane, pushing back his cowl to reveal a chalky bald head. His gaze on Cora is intense - well, as intense as it can be when he has no fucking pupils and you can't read his expression.

"There has been some trouble, I hear." He says in a high, rasping voice.

Cora nods. "Yes, there has been. There have been

earthquakes, and red smoke above Arax."

Azrael scratches his cheek with a long black talon. "I see."

"What did you need to tell me?" She asks him.

"Gabriel has attempted an uprising in the Halls," Azrael replies. "He has tried to incite a revolt against you and the Old God."

"On what grounds?"

"On the grounds that you have violated the Fate set down for you, as did your parents before you."

The council behind Cora murmurs softly, and she takes a deep breath. "I can't violate a Fate that was decided through corruption."

Azrael nods. "I agree, majesty. But there are those who do not see things as I do."

Amryn shifts beside me, and his hand rolls into a fist on his thigh. "So, what exactly is Gabriel calling for?"

Azrael's gaze shifts to Amryn - I think - and his jaw flexes from side to side, as though considering what to say next. "He is calling for the death of the Shadow Queen, and her heir."

The council explodes into protests, and Amryn springs to his feet, both hands up in flames. "Tell Gabriel to come down here and say that to my face," he snarls, the veins on his neck glowing bright orange.

Azrael calmly raises a hand. "Please, I am merely here to inform you of what is being said. I do not agree, and neither do many of the others. All those that side with the Old God have sworn to leave the Earth Realm to your

Queen, and they will stand by that oath."

"How do I know that for sure?" Amryn demands. "That son of a bitch Michael seemed pretty eager to come down here and side with the rival clans."

"No one wants another war," Azrael says.

"We're not the ones who keep starting the goddamned wars," Amryn replies.

"You said there are those who wouldn't agree with you," I interject. "So, if it's not the angels, who?"

Azrael's gaze shifts over the council, towards the doors of the Great Hall. "There are always those who will dissent," he says slowly, "and sometimes they are closer than we could ever suspect."

Cora's eyes snap over to meet mine, and I can see the fear in her face.

"In our own home?" Amryn asks. "No one here agrees with the ways enforced by the rival clans, that's why they're here."

Azrael nods. "Indeed." He's not making any sense and it's pissing me off.

"Are the serpents significant?" I ask him. "The mountain smoking, and the earthquakes, all of that - is it significant?"

"Oh yes," he says, rising to his feet. "Everything is connected, sometimes it merely takes some time to discover how." He walks over to Cora and Amryn, who are both on their feet now. "I have claimed each of you under my scythe," he says quietly, "and I do not doubt there are those who would see you there again. I do not wish for that to happen. Be aware that your enemies may be closer than you think."

I feel sick, and I see Cora grasp for Amryn's hand. They both died. They were both dead, once, and the thought of them being dead again... I rise to my feet as well, and we watch as Azrael walks out of the Great Hall, taking off into the wintery sky in a rush of black wings.

Cora turns to Amryn and puts her hands on his chest. "I need to be with Phoenix right now."

He nods and kisses her forehead. "Let's go." He turns to me and nods. "You OK, brother?"

I merely nod. I can't talk yet. Amryn's face flashes with concern. I manage a weak smile and dismissive wave of my hand. He hesitates, but then puts his arm around Cora, and leads her out of the hall.

I watch them go, and the council disperses around me, frowns and furrowed brows passing me. Everyone's worried. We all know this won't be good. It can't be good. Amryn's right; the angels claim to want peace and then they start another fucking war.

I'm all alone in the hall when my hands begin to ache. It's more than pain though. It's a deep, wearying emptiness, as though they're searching for something. It hits me in my gut, like the deepest loss I've ever experienced. It takes my breath away for a second. I clench my eyes shut, willing myself not to black out again. But my chest keeps rising and falling with every breath I take, even as that bolt of grief remains.

It's not my grief. I can sense that much. And it's not Cora's, or Amryn's. But it's hollow and consuming, sharp and worn at the same time. It rolls over me in waves, and I flex my hands, willing for it to stop.

I gasp as it washes off me, I can feel it running down my arms and draining from my fingertips. It leaves me shaking, and it's just another thing to add to the weird fucking pile of shit that's happening to me right now.

There's movement out of the corner of my eye, and I look up to see Lorelei standing in the doorway of the Great Hall. She smiles shyly, her hands tucked into the back pockets of her pants.

"Hey." She sidles towards me slowly. "All alone in here?"

"Yeah," I say with a heavy sigh, "I just needed a minute, you know."

"Are you OK?"

I nod. "Yeah, just dealing with..." With what? I shrug. "Just dealing with some weird shit." She stands right in front of me, and puts her arms around my waist. I stroke the hair out of her face. "You OK?"

"Yeah, just those snakes really freaked me out."

"Me too." I raise a hand to her face, tracing my thumb along her lower lip. "I hate snakes."

"Maybe I can come to your place and we can try to cheer each other up?" She says, pressing herself against me.

I smile down at her, and plant a kiss on her full red lips. "Sure."

We walk back to my cabin, our arms around each other. I will the ache in my hands to go away as her warmth seeps into me. I will it to go away as her arms wind around my neck, as she pulls me down into bed with her. I will it to go away as I peel off her clothes, as she moans and writhes and shakes underneath me.

But it doesn't.

The cold air burns my lungs, and my chest hurts as I gasp for air. I put my head between my knees, willing the sick feeling of fetid, heavy, hot air to leave me, for the smell of dirt to go away.

"Tal?" Amryn's voice sounds in the darkness, and I hear the porch creaking as he walks towards me. "Hey, you OK?" He sits down beside me, putting a hand on my shoulder as I continue to heave and retch, unable to speak. "Tal, what's going on?"

I shake my head, and suck in a breath, my lungs finally expanding again. I grasp his hand on my shoulder, and he just sits with me, waiting.

"I'm OK," I rasp finally. "I just... I just had a bad dream."

"That must have been one hell of a bad dream. You're a wreck."

"Just... dreaming of suffocating," I reply. I lean back against the bench, and my sides ache from the exertion of trying to breathe. "I wake up and the feeling's still there, like, I don't know, like I'm trapped somewhere." The ache in my hands is unbearable, and I stretch them in front of me.

"How long has it been going on?"

"Since the Winter Solstice." I look at him in the dark. "I can hear a woman screaming, and I feel stone. I keep thinking maybe it's a memory, maybe I'm remembering Mom, or something. But it doesn't sound like her."

Amryn leans back beside me, crossing his arms over his chest. "Phoenix keeps talking about you being in the dirt."

"I know, Cora and I talked about it."

"It's really freaking her out." Amryn goes on. "She's got it in her head that someone's going to die, and then Azrael showing up, and throwing suspicion on to the whole fucking village, it's made things a little tense." He looks over at me. "And now you're out here choking and throwing up, dreaming about women screaming and suffocating."

"Yeah, things are a little weird around here right now."

The ground rumbles beneath us, and we both look up to see Arax glowing red across the valley, the smoke luminous above the mountain range. We wait until the rumbling subsides, and I sigh. "Real fucking weird."

"Are you going to be OK?" Amryn asks me. "Did you want to come and crash on the couch? I don't really want to leave you alone."

I shake my head. "No, that's OK. I got Lorelei inside."

"Oh, right." He hesitates for a second, I can practically hear him considering his next words. "How's things going with her?"

"Yeah, uh, good."

I hear him snort a little. "Yeah, uh, good?" He repeats. "That's it?"

"She's sweet," I say, "but... I don't know."

"You seem to like her a lot."

"I do. I do like her a lot."

"And she really likes you," he says

"She does, I know she does. I just..." I'm not sure what I'm actually trying to say. "I like her a lot. It's just not the same."

"The same as what?"

I look over at him. "You and Cora."

"Hey, man, that's not, I mean, every relationship is different."

"You sure about that?" I ask, rubbing my hands together.

"Of course." He assures me. "I mean, me and Cora, that's a whole thing, there's a history there. You can't put two couples next to each other and expect those relationships to look the same."

I nod. He's right. I know he's right. And yet...

"You ever lie awake at night, and your hands just ache, because you need to touch... someone?" I ask him, flexing my hands in front of me. "Like, you feel physical pain because they're not with you?"

"Tal, I could write a book on that feeling." He puts a hand on my shoulder. "You feel that way about someone?"

I shake my head. "No. There's just an ache, and no matter how many times I touch Lorelei, no matter how many times we..." I clear my throat quickly. "You know... But the ache, it just never goes away."

"Give it time." Amryn gives my shoulder a squeeze.

"These things take time."

"Sure."

"I gotta get back inside," he says, rising from the bench. "You should go in, get some rest."

"I will. Thanks for checking on me."

"Anytime." He goes to walk away, then stops, turning back towards me. "You know... You know that it's OK, right? To not be sure about things. And to break it off if it doesn't feel right."

I attempt a small laugh. "Yeah, I know that."

"You deserve to be happy, Tal. And not in a way people tell you to be happy. In a way you want it to be." His footsteps crunch across the snow, and I hear the door to his cabin closing in the silence of the night.

I get up and lean against one of the posts on my porch, and look up at the moon, floating above Arax, above the swirling, glowing red smoke. I mull over Amryn's words, but my brain is too foggy, and I suppress a yawn.

I should get some sleep.

I head back inside, and climb into bed next to Lorelei. She rolls over when she feels me next to her, and cuddles up to me, shivering.

"You're like ice, babe." She whispers. "Did you go outside?"

I put my arms around her, and kiss her forehead. "Yeah, I just needed some air."

"Another nightmare?" She asks, tracing small circles on my chest.

"Yeah, it's OK, it passed."

"I was thinking..."

"Oh yeah? What were you thinking about?" I ask, twirling a strand of her hair around my finger.

"Do you want to have a baby?"

The question catches me off guard, and a laugh escapes me. "A *baby*?"

Lorelei leans up on one hand, looking down at me as she pushes her hair out of her face. "Yeah, a baby. You keep talking about how you're old, *so* old," she says cynically, "and well, I was thinking, if you want a baby, maybe we could start trying to have one now."

I sit up and take her face in my hands. "Darlin, why don't we just enjoy things now, just the two of us, and see where it goes, huh?"

"Do you love me?"

Fuck. Fuck. This is why you don't sleep with a young woman who's never been with anyone else and think it'll just be some casual thing, you arrogant fucker. I don't want to lie to her. I don't want to hurt her. And I sure as hell don't want her to think I used her.

"Baby, I like you, a whole lot." I say to her, and press a kiss to the corner of her mouth. "I really do. Love takes time, right?"

"I love you." She says quietly.

I'm a fucking asshole.

"Thank you." *I am such a fucking asshole.* Her head drops a little, and I pull her back down onto the bed with me. "Baby, come on, I care about you. I do. A lot."

"I see the way Amryn looks at Cora," she says, and her

voice is tight, like she's about to cry, "and I want you to look at me like that."

I guess I'm not the only one who's been watching them and feeling a stab of envy. "Give it time, baby." I say, hugging her close to me. "Let's just give it time."

4
Tallesaign

'm about to go to bed when there's a frantic knock at the door. When I open it, I find Cora standing on the porch, her arms wrapped around herself, tears streaming down her face.

"Cora." I stumble forwards and grasp her arms. "What's happened?"

"Phoenix is really sick," she says, her voice strained from crying. "H-he spiked a fever, and we can't get it down." She swallows hard. "Amryn's with him now, and I need to go get Fenella to look at him."

"Ok." I shrug on my coat, stomping into my boots. "Come on, I'll come with you."

We rush across the village to Fenella's cabin. She's a powerful healer, but I know Cora wants her for another reason.

Fenella is a witch.

Her cabin is at the edge of the village, where she generally keeps to herself, partially because she's a little reclusive and eccentric - but mainly because she still gets too many nasty looks from the demons.

Many of them still don't trust witches, even though Fenella has lived here since well before I was born. She was granted refuge when she saved some demon kids after one of the wars, but even that act of goodwill hasn't stopped the demons being skittish around her.

I reach up and touch the scar on my cheek without really thinking. I wonder if Fenella has similar powers to the evil witch who had her throat torn out by Amryn in Nilau. From what I've been told, Fenella has strong psychic abilities. And that's exactly why Cora wants her to see Phoenix.

Cora raps on Fenella's door, shifting on her feet, her arms hugged around her. After a minute there's no movement, and Cora knocks again.

"Come on, come on," she murmurs.

I'm about to tell her to just go and get Elise, but then the large brass handle clicks down, and the door creaks open.

Fenella is a pleasant looking older woman, chubby and round-faced with wiry white hair which is always sticking out from underneath the blue silk turbans she wears. She's wrapped in a bright orange dressing gown as she smiles at us through the gap in the doorway.

"Good evening, majesty," she says quietly. "The *bebe* ill, is he?"

Cora is speechless for a moment, brushing her hair out of her face as the frigid breeze catches her curls. "Y - yes, Phoenix is running a fever, and I -"

Fenella steps through the door, her bag in hand, big

black boots already on her feet. "Let's go then." She takes off at a surprising speed across the snowy ground. Cora and I follow her back to Cora and Amryn's cabin.

Amryn is sitting on the couch with Phoenix lying against him when we walk in. Phoenix looks up at us without moving his head, his cheeks bright red, his little mouth squished open, pressed against his father's chest. Amryn's face is filled with concern, and for a moment I'm reminded of what an excellent father my little brother is.

I can't help but wonder if I would be a good father, too.

Fenella sits down beside Amryn, and rubs Phoenix's back gently. "Now, *papillon,* how are you?" She asks in a soothing voice. Phoenix merely looks at her, his eyes glassy, his breathing shallow. Fenella tuts quietly, and puts a hand to his forehead. "What happened before he became ill?"

"He was asleep," Amryn replies, "and then I heard him crying, so I went to check on him, and he - he said -" His eyes flash to me.

"What did he say, *mon cher?*" Fenella asks.

Amryn looks back at her. "He said his uncle was dead."

I hear Cora inhale sharply next to me. That's why she went to come and find me. Not because she was scared of Fenella being a creepy witch, Cora's too tough for that. No, she was afraid she was going to find me dead in my cabin.

"Oh dear," Fenella says, and turns to reach into her bag. "Has he been saying things like this a lot lately?"

Cora nods, clasping her hands together. "Yeah, all the time. But it's never made him sick."

"Mmm." Fenella pulls out a small vial of purple liquid, and tips it against her fingertip. She rubs whatever it is against Phoenix's temples and under his jaw. "This will help the headache you have, *papillon*." She puts her hand on his back, and her veins glow, a faint lilac.

Phoenix's little eyes close, and he snuggles into his father. Amryn puts a hand to his son's forehead, and relief floods his face. "He's cooling down," he says to Cora.

"Oh thank god." She rushes over to him, putting her hand on Phoenix's back. "I was so worried."

She sits down beside Amryn, and he gently places Phoenix on her lap. "Here, you stay here with him, I just need some air."

"Sure," she says, and Fenella takes her hand as Amryn pushes me outside onto the porch.

Amryn is stalking back and forth, raking his hands through his hair.

"Hey, hey," I put my hands on his shoulders, trying to stop him, but he pushes me off, and keeps pacing. "Amryn, what's going on?"

"What if this is my fault?" He says, not looking at me, still pacing, pacing.

I frown at him. "What if what is your fault? Phoenix is sick, that's not anyone's fault."

"What if he's got this - this premonition stuff because - because -"

"Because why?"

"Because -" He sputters and claws his hands into his thighs. "Because of what happened."

I grab him and force him to look at me. "Amryn, stop, you're not making any sense. What are you talking about?"

"The witch," he gasps, and I see he has tears in his eyes.

"Fenella?"

"No." He says through clenched teeth. "Morgan. When she -" He sucks in a breath. "When she..."

I shake my head. "Amryn, I don't know what you're talking about, you need to calm -"

"When she fucking raped me!"

I feel like someone punched me in the gut. "Holy fuck." I grasp his shoulders tighter. "Amryn, she did *what?*"

He can barely get the words out, his whole face crumpled with pain. "That witch crept in to my cell, pretending to be Cora and she... she fucking raped me." He grits his teeth, a strangled sob catching in his throat. "She said she made it so I couldn't have kids. I thought... when Cora got pregnant I thought she must have been bluffing. But what if... What if she did something else?" He swallows hard. "What if there's a part of her, in me, and I passed it on to him?"

He collapses against me, trembling violently. I put my arms around him, around my little brother, and fury courses through me. I wish I could dig that fucking bitch up and murder her all over again.

Cora had told me, vaguely, that Morgan had

glamoured herself to try and trick Amryn while he was captured. But she'd never told me exactly what Morgan had done.

I should have known. All those weeks after Amryn got back, after we got back to Ocario. The hollow look in his eyes, the silences, the excessive drinking.

"Phoenix has no part of that witch," I tell him, "no part. He's yours, and he's Cora's, and he's got some powers we haven't seen before, that's all. He's your son." I pull back and look at him. "He's *yours*, and he's amazing *because* he's yours, and because you're an incredible father, OK?"

"I just can't help but think -"

"That witch was fucking with your head, she would have said anything. This has nothing to do with her. He's a special kid."

Amryn nods and wipes his face with his hands. "You have a cigarette?" He asks. I pull the case out of my coat pocket and offer him one, lighting it with my hand. He inhales deeply, and leans on the porch railing, looking out at the night sky. "Sorry you had to find out like this.

"Do not apologize to me for anything to do with that," I say, lighting my own cigarette. "You don't owe me anything." I lean back against the porch railing so I can see his face. "You OK?"

He nods, inhaling again. "I am now." He exhales, flicking ash onto the snow. "I was messed up for a long time. I - I kinda went crazy. I was waking Cora for sex, every night, sometimes a few times, I was just..." His eyes flash up to me. "Sorry, you probably don't need to hear this."

"I'll hear whatever you need to tell me. You don't need to be ashamed."

"I wanted to be close to her," he says with a sigh. "I just - I wanted her all the time, because I wanted to feel *her*, because I needed to be reminded that she was there. I'd ask her to talk to me, during the whole thing, because when I couldn't hear her voice, I'd be - it would be like I was suffocating."

I suck deeply on the cigarette, noticing my glowing veins. Seeing my brother in this much distress, all these years later... I try to steady my breathing, and listen to him as he goes on.

"I got better, slowly. Cora got me through it. I should have talked to you about it."

I shake my head. "Listen, I told you, you don't owe me anything. Of course I want to be there for you, but... The important thing is that you're alright."

"Thanks, Tal." He rubs the back of his hand across his eyes. "I am, really. Just, tonight with Phoenix getting sick and everything he's been saying, I started to wonder, you know?"

"Well, stop wondering." I say to him, pointing my finger at him. "That's an order."

He smiles weakly. "Yeah, I will. You're right." He looks in through the window of the cabin. "I don't want him to be scared, or sad. I just want him to be OK."

"Of course you do. And he will be. He's a sensitive kid, and with the snakes and the earthquakes and all the other weird shit going on, he's probably picking up on some things he normally wouldn't."

Amryn nods. "You're right."

Fenella walks out onto the porch, her bag in hand. "The *papillon* will be fine in the morning, he needs a good sleep." She eyes my cigarette. "Ooh, you have one of those for me, *mon cher*?"

"Sure." I offer her one, and she giggles as I offer my hand to light it.

"*Merci*," she says, exhaling with deep appreciation. "Mmm, the tobacco here is really very good, so sweet and clean." She looks at Amryn as she inhales. "The boy is beautiful."

Amryn nods. "Yeah, just like his mother."

"And his father." Fenella says with a wink, and Amryn chuckles. She puts a hand on his shoulder. "Her magic cannot do what you fear. Do not worry. She has not left a trace on you." She pats his shoulder, and walks away into the darkness, toward her cabin.

Amryn leans heavily against the porch railing, sucking on the cigarette which is nearly spent. "She knew."

"And you heard what she said." I say with a smile. "See? No trace of that bitch, nowhere. She's dead and gone, and that's all there is to it."

Amryn runs a hand over his head. "Yeah, yeah, she is." He stamps his cigarette out in the ashtray on the table, and smiles at me. "Thanks for coming. Sorry to get you out of bed."

"Anytime. Glad I was here."

He grabs me in a hug. "I'm really glad you're my brother."

"Me too."

I touch the scar on my cheek as I head back to my cabin, and something Phoenix did comes back to mind. When I'd assured him Morgan was dead, he shook his little head. A flicker of fear passes through me.

I push the thought away. Fenella just said there was no part of her in Phoenix, or in Amryn.

But as I look up at Arax, spewing crimson smoke, glowing in the dark, I can't suppress the feeling that maybe Phoenix meant something else entirely.

I scrub the dirt from under my fingernails over the basin, and feel arms around my waist. "What were you doing this morning?" Lorelei asks. "Gardening in this weather?"

I laugh awkwardly. I don't know how to explain this. It's starting to drive me a little crazy.

"I, uh, had to fix something outside, in the barn." I reply, watching the grimy water wash down the drain. I dry my hands on a towel and sigh.

Lorelei kisses my back, and her hands move down over my hips. "You need to be somewhere this morning?" She asks in a low voice.

I grip the edge of the counter as she moves her hand over my crotch, rubbing my cock, making me hard.

"No, no plans."

Her hand moves into my pants, and I keep swelling. Her fingers feather up and down my length, the light touch of her hand sending my nerves on edge.

I tip my head forward, breathing in heavily, and it feels good. I wonder if I'm just being stupid about all this. She wants me, she wants a family, maybe I should just stop resisting, like I'm waiting for something, something that might not even be real.

She puts her other hand on my cock, and she's licked it or something because it's wet and fuck, both her hands sliding up and down my length...

I groan, and she giggles.

"Is that good?"

"Yeah," I gasp. "Fuck.Yeah."

"Turn around." She says, taking her hands off me.

I turn around, leaning back against the basin, and she drops to her knees. She pulls my sweatpants down in one quick movement, and her strawberry blonde hair bobs back and forth as her mouth works my cock.

If she's never done this before, then she has really good fucking instincts. Her tongue swirls and moves and she pulls me so deep into her throat, knowing exactly how to get me to moan.

I'm an idiot. This woman, she's sweet, pretty, has a perfect ass, and she loves me. And I'm here questioning it.

Fuck it. She wants me to love her? Fine. I'll love her. If she wants a baby, I'll give her one. If she wants to blow me like this a few times a month, I am happy with that. If I get to sink my mouth into that pussy of hers a few times a week, great. Life will be good. I'm not going to push this away anymore. I'm too old for games.

I thread my fingers through her hair, and she rolls her tongue over me, one of her hands fisting the base of my cock. Heat rises in my head, in my thighs, in my groin, and she pulls me out of her mouth, looking up at me as her lips press against my shaft, her fingers running over my head rhythmically. Her eyes stay on me as she takes me back into her mouth, and fuck, she takes me in deep.

I feel myself rise, then all the heat she's built up, all the nerves she's sent firing, they all explode as my cock pumps down her throat. She stays still on me, swallowing everything I give her as I hold her head and try to catch my breath.

When I stop trembling she releases me, gazing up at me with her big blue eyes, and she grins as she wipes her mouth with the back of her hand. I can't help but laugh, and run my hand along her jawline, under her chin.

"You look pleased with yourself." I say, and help her to her feet.

She puts her arms around my neck. "I want to make you feel good, and that seemed to feel good."

"Good is not the word for it." I stroke her cheek with my hand. "You're so beautiful, Lorelei." I kiss her gently, but when I pull back from her and open my mouth to speak, she quickly puts a finger to my lips and shakes her head.

"I won't believe it if you say it now," she says, and there's a hint of sadness behind her eyes that makes me instantly feel guilty. "Don't say it now. Say it when you mean it."

"What makes you think I'd say it and not mean it?"

She shakes her head again, and leaves me standing in the bathroom, and I feel like a fucking asshole all over again.

5
Tallesaign

"What are you doing up here?"

I roll my eyes. "Being your Draw fucking sucks sometimes, just so you know."

Cora chuckles as she walks to my side at the cliff's edge, and hugs her arms around herself as the breeze blows across the frosty valley. "Did you want to be alone?"

I give her a sideways glance and sigh. "No."

"Well, then," she says, tipping her head to gaze at the gray sky, "good to see my instincts aren't off." She tilts her head to look at me. "What's going on?"

"I don't even really know. Just up here, feeling like a jerk."

"Is it the thing with Lorelei?"

I exhale heavily. "You don't want to know."

"I wouldn't ask if I didn't want to know."

I shift on my feet, unable to look at her. "She - she did something to me this morning, and it felt great, and then she stopped me from saying something to her and..."

"Tal, will you stop talking in riddles?" Cora interjects. "Just tell me what happened."

"She blew me and I wanted to say I love you and she stopped me because she said it'd be a lie if I said it right then." I blurt the words out before I can think about it too much, and when I turn to look at Cora her eyebrows are raised. "See? Told you you didn't want to know."

She shakes her head. "It's fine, I'm just - why would she think you wouldn't mean it?"

"Because she told me she loves me and I said fucking *thank you*, like a total asshole." I turn back to look over the valley.

Cora sucks on her teeth. "Ouch."

"Yeah."

"I mean..." She nudges me gently with her shoulder. "Do you love her?"

"No," I reply, too fucking quickly. "I - I don't know. I just, I don't know." I jam my hands into my pockets, and snowflakes start to fall from the sky. "She wants a life with me, and she wants babies, and I want those things too. I just..."

"You don't want those things with her?"

I shake my head. "It's not that. I like her, she's beautiful, she's sweet, the sex is good. It's just - I can't explain it." I struggle to find the words, to explain this feeling in my hands, this deep feeling of need that has become way too distracting. "I feel something, I feel an ache for something that I've never had. That I've never even known, and it's driving me crazy."

"Like, love?"

I shrug. "Like... a missing piece."

"Amryn said you've been having nightmares." She fixes me with those green eyes of hers. "Said he found you basically choking on your porch the other night."

"Yeah," I say with a sigh. "I keep dreaming I'm trapped, under stone or something, like I'm in a tomb. My hands hurt all the time." I stretch them out in front of me. "I keep scrubbing dirt out from under my fingernails, it's always there in the morning."

Cora links her arm through mine and leans her head against my arm. "Maybe you should go and talk to Fenella," she says. "She knows things. It's a little creepy."

"I don't know how much bad news I could handle," I joke, and Cora gazes at me critically. "I mean it. Maybe I'm just..." I sigh heavily. "Maybe I'm not meant for all this, to be happy with someone. Maybe I spent too many years shutting myself off, and now I wouldn't even know what it felt like."

"I don't believe that for a second," Cora says, rolling her eyes. "You'd be a great husband, and an amazing dad."

I shift on my feet. "My Dad, he was..." An asshole. I don't want to say it. It's unfair. I'm not a teenager anymore. He was loyal, a good Striker. He adored my Mom. But he was a shitty parent, especially to me. "He was difficult," I finally say, "and I wouldn't want to be like that."

"What did he do?"

I clear my throat. "He was harsh. Strict. He didn't like

my mom hugging me too much, he said it would make me soft."

"Oh my god."

"Yeah. And then when you were born, he was all about protecting you, making sure I never let you out of my sight. That was my job, to keep you safe." I clench my eyes shut for a second as the memory of Cora and Amryn screaming for me comes into my head. My mother, crying as she watched my father die while I stood by, frozen, the blood magic seeping into my skin, eating away at me. "He expected a lot of me, and I don't think I was ready for it. I was just a kid."

"I'm sorry, Tal." She presses her face against my arm.

I smile down at her. "I love you, kiddo."

She smiles back, and reaches up to me, planting a tender kiss on my lips. "I love you too." She presses her forehead against mine, her eyes closed. "You deserve all the things you tell yourself you don't deserve, all the things you were afraid to lose." When she opens her eyes, they're shining with unshed tears. "And I really, really hope you find them, one day." Her brow furrows suddenly, and she steps back from me. "What's that sound?"

We both look out over the valley. There's a rushing sound, like an approaching rain storm, but the clouds above are a soft gray, releasing a gentle shower of snowflakes. There's no wind. Everything is still and peaceful, except for this rushing sound. It gets louder and louder.

"What the fuck is that?" Cora says again, looking over the cliff edge at the treetops below.

And then I see it. A black cloud, winding and twisting across the valley, undulating towards Ocario. "There," I point, and as I do, I realize it's not a cloud. It's a flock of birds, enormous black birds.

Before I can say another word, Cora leaps off the cliff edge, her white wings unfurling behind her, and she shoots through the sky towards the village. I launch myself off the cliff after her, my black wings extending out behind me soundlessly. The distant flock comes closer and closer as Cora and I race to beat them to the village. The wail of the siren sounds, and people start running for shelter.

We land outside the Great Hall, and everyone's taking cover around us as the sirens continue to drone. Cora dashes off through the buildings, her eyes on the sky, and I follow her, looking upwards, trying to see where the flock has gone. I can hear them, rushing, sounding like a wave about to crash over us.

I nearly collide with Amryn as we round the barn. "What is it?" He asks me as he runs alongside me.

"A flock of birds, big black ones," I reply, and we both stop short as Cora comes to a halt, looking directly overhead.

"Oh my god." She turns and pushes us both under the nearest roof before we can look ourselves. We get under cover just as the enormous black creatures begin to plummet to the ground.

It takes me a moment to realize what's happened, and I summon my flames, ready to burn anything that moves. But they're dead.

They're all dead.

They lie on the ground, their beady black eyes wide open, their claws curled up under them, their wings lying limply on the ground. They've all just dropped out of the sky. Dead.

"It's a Purge," Cora says as the sickening thud continues on the rooftop above us, glass shattering in the distance. "My mother - I mean, Anya, she told me about it, years ago when I was a kid."

"What does it mean?" Amryn asks her.

Cora sighs. "It's a warning. The last time it happened, the war broke out shortly after."

As she says it, I remember it. I remember seeing the dead birds being thrown onto bonfires, the sickening smell of burning feathers filling the village. One month later, we were under attack.

We wait a few minutes, and Amryn peers out from under the roof. He scans the sky, then waves us both out. "It's over," he says, stepping over some of the black birds.

They're twice the size of a cat at least, their wingspans immense. There's no movement in them at all, they're just... dead.

"Come on," Cora says, starting off towards the Great Hall, "we need to check if everyone's OK."

There are smashed roof tiles on the ground. Windows are smashed, dead black birds hanging on the sills, their beady eyes fixing us with their death stares as we pass. I can hear some children crying, and I turn to Amryn.

"Where's Phoenix?" I ask.

"He's with Elise," he replies. "I'd just taken him there when this all started."

62

Good. He's safe.

The other demons are starting to emerge from their houses, following us towards the Great Hall. It seems the sirens did their job - the streets are clear, we haven't found anyone injured yet.

There's a group already outside the Great Hall, talking animatedly. I spot Elias in the middle of the group, gesticulating wildly as he argues with the others.

As Cora approaches, his eyes narrow and he crosses his arms over his chest. He gestures to the sky with a jerk of his head. "You have an explanation for all of this?"

Cora shakes her head. "Of course not, I have no idea why this happened."

He scoffs, and looks around him, looking for support. "I think I can guess why, if you can't, your majesty." He nods. "Oh yes, I have a theory."

"Why don't you share it with us then?" I say.

Elias's gaze becomes poisonous as it brushes past me. "We've all heard what that angel said when he was here," Elias says, and murmuring breaks out behind him.

"And what's that?" Cora asks.

"That they're calling you and your son an abomination in the Halls," Elias replies, and Amryn moves so quickly I barely even see it. He towers over Elias, who takes a stumbling step back.

"I would choose the next words you speak about my wife and my son very, very carefully, my friend." Amryn says, his arms glowing, his voice low.

Elias splutters, and shakes his head. "Is that a threat?"

"Yes it fucking is." Amryn raises his hand, a small flame erupting.

The group behind Elias disperses quickly, and he looks from side to side, realizing he's all alone, facing off against the Draw. It's not a great place to be.

"I can't be the only one questioning things!" Elias cries, looking past Amryn, at me, to Cora, to the other demons gathering in front of the Great Hall. "Not one of you is wondering why this is all happening?"

"Of course we are," Cora replies, going to Amryn's side and putting her hand on his shoulder, telling him wordlessly to stand down. "We're all worried, and scared. But -"

"Maybe Fate has finally had enough!" Elias replies, stumbling back further, away from Cora and Amryn. Lorelei appears at my side, clasping on to my arms, and Elias's eyes flame. "Maybe Gabriel is right!"

Loud protests erupt from the other demons, and several of them leave the square, but Elias isn't stopping.

"Maybe, just maybe, the abomination of Fate has run its course."

Amryn seizes Elias by the collar. "You call my wife an abomination one more time and I will tear you in fucking half." He spits in Elias's face. "She is your Queen, and you better start showing some respect."

Elias scoffs. "Respect? What does your family know about respect?" His eyes move over to me, and Lorelei clutches my arm tighter.

"Hey!" Amryn barks, and Elias's eyes snap back to his face. "You don't look at them, *I'm* talking to you."

"Or what?" Elias sneers.

Amryn raises Elias off his feet, and Cora rushes forward.

"Enough!" She calls. "Amryn, put him down." Amryn keeps Elias in the air and looks down at Cora. "Amryn, put him down," she says again, "this isn't the way."

Amryn looks back at Elias, who is struggling in his grasp. "I won't warn you next time," Amryn snarls through gritted teeth, and lets Elias go, who almost loses his footing as he hits the ground.

Cora looks down at Elias with a raised eyebrow, every inch the Queen as she sizes him up. "The last war broke out because we were tired of the Line being corrupted. Because Fate had been twisted by dark magic. I gladly go against that Fate, as we all do, because we won't be bound by laws that weren't created by us, by our traditions, and were instead created by those that sought to advance only themselves."

Elias darts his finger in her direction. "Times have changed, and maybe Fate has, too." He points up at Arax. "The world is angry. It is sending us warnings, and we need to heed those warnings before we all end up in ruin." He looks around at the others. "Snakes? Earthquakes? And now all this?" He gestures at the dead birds around him. "If it isn't Fate, then what is it?"

I've had enough of this. I step forward, and Elias's eyes flash with fear. "I didn't lose my family for you to be the angel's mouthpiece. If you agree with Gabriel, go." I point towards the cliffs. "Go on, go and find a rival clan who thinks like you. Go and seek out Gabriel, and see how he treats demons wanting to ally themselves with him."

"So, that's what you do with anyone who disagrees, is it?" Elias asks cynically. "Cast them out?"

"No one is casting you out. I'm telling you that if you think there's some violation going on here, you're free to leave."

Everyone turns to look at Elias, whose eyes dart around, his resolve faltering with every second that passes without a supporting voice. Realizing it's fruitless, he throws his hands into the air and storms off.

Cora exhales heavily, and turns to look at me. "Thank you." She says quietly.

I nod, and make a split second decision. "I'm going up to Arax."

Amryn and Cora's eyebrows shoot up in alarm, and Lorelei's head snaps up to look at me. "Tal, why?" Lorelei asks.

"To prove that this isn't some message from Fate," I say, gesturing towards Arax. "To prove that it's just a mountain spewing some smoke."

"You don't need to prove anything to anyone." Amryn insists.

"Yes I do, because shit like what Elias is talking about, it spreads. It poisons people. The rival clans, that's what caused them all to splinter off and decide they knew better. That's how the Line was corrupted."

Cora shakes her head. "Tal, what do you think you'll find up there?"

"Nothing." I reply with a shrug. "That's the point. No Old God sitting up there plotting our downfall, no angel army ready to take us out. Nothing. And that will at least allay any fears that Arax is some harbinger of doom."

"It's dangerous," Lorelei says.

I look down at her and smile reassuringly. "I'll be fine. I won't be gone long, a day at most."

Cora and Amryn look at each other, and I see Amryn nod. Cora turns back to me with a sigh. "Be careful, OK?"

"I always am."

6
Tallesaign

t's just getting light outside as I dress, pulling on an extra layer of clothing for going up to Arax. I don't feel the cold much, but up there the air is thinner and makes it harder for me to keep warm.

I was woken by a nightmare again last night, fetid air in my nose and the taste of dirt in my mouth. The screaming in my head is the worst of it. Terrified, hopeless, desperate. It destroys me every time.

It makes me think of my mother, as she watched my father die. Of Ebony, as she dragged poor Ceili's lifeless body back to Ocario. I've heard too many bone chilling screams in my life, and to be constantly woken by this one... I'm tired.

Lorelei stirs in the bed, her arm reaching across the mattress, as she somehow notices my absence in her sleep. I look her over, at the star tattoos that track down her shoulder, the mass of her strawberry blonde hair splayed across the bed.

I move to bedside, leaning down to brush a kiss on her

shoulder. I want her to make the ache go away. I want this to be enough. She deserves that. I deserve it too. But the ache remains.

She sleeps on as I slip out of the house.

The morning sky is clear, the rising sun illuminating the growing dawn with icy blue and soft peach light. The snow glitters as I walk out across the village, and my breath escapes my lips in thick white puffs.

I break into a run once I've cleared the houses, and open my wings, lifting off into the sky, meeting the sun's rays as they claw their way over the tops of the mountains.

The higher I rise, the colder it gets. The landscape is an almost uniform stretch of white, catching the hanging light of the growing dawn.

I cover the distance to Arax faster than I thought I would, and I find myself flying over its foothills while the sun is still low over the horizon. I land just beyond the treeline, which ends abruptly to give way to gray boulders, square and jagged, surrounded by snow and black volcanic soil.

Some deer scatter down the mountainside as they hear me approach, the clattering of their hooves echoing over the rocks. The sun is bright but the air up here is freezing.

I make my way up the mountainside, closer to the peak, closer to the crater spewing red smoke. I stay alert for any movement in the mountain, ready to leap into the sky. I don't much feel like getting crushed by any falling boulders.

It's oddly quiet up here, no birdsong, no wind movement. I tell myself it's normal for winter, all the way up here, no trees. But no air movement at all? I feel like I'm in a vacuum.

I step on something, and I'm met with an aggravated hiss. I jump back, and a snake rears up at me, its fangs bared. I stumble back against a boulder, and the snake slithers after me. I fire a flame at it, and it squeals sickeningly, its skin blistering as it burns. It takes me a second to register - a snake? Out on the mountain in the snow? I shake my head.

I turn around and look down the mountain, over the hills beneath me. It's a beautiful sight, the snow reflecting the soft peach light, the trees half-shaded as the sun rises. I take a deep breath. I haven't left Ocario in a long time, and it feels nice to have a new view to look at. Change is good.

My mind strays to Lorelei, and I wonder if she's awake yet. Is she lying in bed burying her face into my pillow to smell me because she misses me? Because I wasn't there when she woke up?

I keep asking myself if I love her, when I know damned well that I don't. I can't twist my way into feeling something for her just because I feel like I should.

I've never been in love before. Sex is a completely different matter. I've slept with plenty of women, they always seemed to like me. But it never lasted beyond a few fucks at my place. And usually that was down to me. I cringe a little as I think back to the days after the war, after I lost my family. I used sex as a coping mechanism, trying to ignore the pain and loss I felt.

It was wrong, and I tried to get better, tried to *be* better. But I could never bring myself to take that extra step with someone. Too afraid to lose someone else, too afraid I'd fuck it all up anyway.

Lorelei and I are together almost every day now, and I feel something for her I've never felt before - but it's not what I imagine love to be. Maybe I'm just looking for a feeling that doesn't exist.

Amryn was right when he said that no two relationships look the same, I know that. But with Cora and Amryn, it's palpable, anyone who sees them knows just how crazy they are about each other. They look at each other with something, something I can't describe, something I've never felt.

What is it? Need? Yeah. They need each other. You can see it. Their hands are always looking for the other's.

I look down at my hands, the fingertips raw from being scrubbed every morning. What are they looking for? I wish I knew.

The rocky mountainside becomes steeper suddenly, and I have to climb it now. My fingers grasp onto the sharp, snowy rocks, hauling myself upwards towards the crater. Wisps of red smoke unfurl from cracks in the rocks, and there's a strong scent of ash. There's still barely any air movement, and it's so noticeably absent that it's making me feel a little freaked out.

A rock slips out from under my hands, and I lose a few feet, my fingers grasping at the cliff face to stop myself from falling. My wings unfurl instinctively, and I laugh at myself. I'm feeling on edge. I need to calm down.

I use my wings to propel myself up, carefully. The red smoke becomes thicker and thicker, and it makes me cough. This is probably stupid. I can barely see anything, and the smoke stings my eyes. I pull in my wings, climbing up blindly, and my hand lands on a rock that's searing hot. All the rocks beyond that point are hot, scorching, and I can feel the heat radiating against my face.

Lightning flashes in the crimson smoke above me, but there's still no sound.

Nothing.

Dead silence. Nothing but my breathing, and the sound of my boots scraping against rocks.

I put my hand down on something that isn't rock, something mobile and writhing. I feel the scales under my hands, and then my feet aren't touching rocks anymore, and -

SHIT SHIT SHIT SHIT. I'm climbing over fucking snakes.

I let go and I'm falling back down the cliffside, through the red smoke. My hands grab at the stone, and the feeling of the rock against my fingertips triggers some memory, and I'm under the ground, the weight on my chest, falling blind through darkness, and it's not quiet anymore, the screaming is back, and it's deafening.

My wings aren't out.

I'm not underground, I'm in the air.

LET ME OUT!

Was that real? I blink rapidly, trying to regain my sight. I know I'm going to hit the ground soon if I don't start flying.

Air rushes into my lungs, and I open my wings, which break my fall enough to make the thud to the ground a little less painful than it would have been. I land on my side, pain shooting through my hip, and I grit my teeth.

Well fuck. That wasn't fun. Crimson smoke and a mountain peak covered in snakes. I'm really regretting my decision to get curious about coming up here. I can't even begin to decide what this means. It sure as hell isn't going to make anyone feel any better about what's going on.

LET ME OUT!

My head snaps up, and I look around me. Was someone out there? Was that just more screaming in my head? In the silence out here it was becoming too hard to tell.

PLEASE NO. PLEASE DON'T.

I clench my eyes shut. I don't recognise the voice. It's a woman. She's terrified. I can hear it. I can feel it.

But there's no sound up here. It's all silent. Still all silent. I shake my head, and sit up, putting my hand to my hip, my veins glowing, and the pain subsides. I'm hearing things again. Like the screaming. More bad dreams.

I look down the mountainside, towards the treeline, and decide to go down and see if there's any sound or movement in the forest. The deer were here when I arrived, so there has to be some life beyond that treeline. I'm becoming less sure of what I'm looking for as I get to my feet and walk.

The sun is rising slightly higher in the cloudless sky as I approach the imposing forest. It barely casts any shadows in the trees, and it's unsettling. The forest is icy cold, no air movement.

It takes me a second to realize there's no snow on the

ground down here. The ground around me is black. It must be the soil, I reason, volcanic soil is black. But this is pitch black. And the smell is overwhelming, the same smell as the one from my dream. Bile rises in my throat.

I look up at the treetops, inhaling through my mouth, and the snow really is just dusting the treetops. It hasn't reached down the boughs of the trees, it hasn't reached the ground, like there's an unseen ceiling somewhere in the canopy.

The hair on the back of my neck stands up. Why is there no fucking sound anywhere? I wish the deer would come back. Some signs of life would be welcome right now, some signs that I'm not completely alone.

I continue through the forest, my footsteps quiet on the black floor. It gets darker and darker, and I have to summon my flames to keep going. The canopy seems to close in above me.

I start checking over my shoulder, sure I wouldn't even hear the approach of an enemy in this vacuum. I should get out of here. This is so fucking unnerving.

And then I hear it.

Whimpering. Crying. The crack of twigs, the crunch of leaves.

I move towards it, slowly. I don't call out yet, not wanting to fall into a potential trap. The sound of sobs almost seems to echo in the otherwise noiseless forest, and it surrounds me, making it hard to gauge where it's coming from.

I spy a pile of boulders in a small clearing of trees, and I make my way towards it. That looks like a place someone would seek shelter and try to hide.

I step on a dry twig, the sound of it snapping like a gunshot, and it makes me jump. There's a loud sob, and a figure springs up from the boulders, pale white in the darkness. They break into a run, but they're limping heavily, obviously hurt.

"Wait!" I call, running after them. "It's alright! I'm not going to hurt you!" I mean, I might if you try to kill me.

At the sound of my voice they stop short, and turn slowly to face me. I slow my steps, dimming my flames. They stay still, shivering. I can see long dark hair, hanging past their hips, and their arms clutched to their chest protectively.

"It's OK," I say again. "I'm not going to hurt you." I reach them, and big brown eyes look at me, wide with terror. "It's OK."

She's trembling violently, her dark hair matted to her head, twigs and leaves and dirt caked in it. Her face is filthy, and her forearms are bleeding.

"Wh - who are you?" She has an accent. Russian? Spanish? Idiot, those are completely different accents. I'm really bad with this. It must be Russian, Astrid had a lilt like this to her voice, and Ebony still has it sometimes.

I smile at her. "I'm Tallesaign. I'm not going to hurt you." I take my coat off, and hold it up in front of her. "You look like you're really cold, I'd like you to put my coat on, would that be alright?"

She looks me up and down for a moment, and gives a tiny, brief nod. "Yes."

I step forward, stopping instantly as she flinches. "It's

OK," I say quietly, holding the coat out to her. "You put this on. It's real warm."

She reaches out a hand to take the coat, and winces, snapping her arm back to her chest. Her eyes meet mine, and she whimpers. "My arms, they hurt."

Her chin drops to her chest, and sobs begin to shake her shoulders. As she turns away from me, I see streaks of blood on her back, soaked through the grimy fabric of her dress. She's hurt really badly.

I step forward and she whips around, stumbling backwards from me, shaking her head. I hold my hands up in front of me and stop moving.

"What's your name?" I ask her.

She stops stumbling away, and her chest quivers as she tries to breathe, through the cold, through the pain. "J... Ju... Juno."

I smile. "That's a beautiful name, Juno. Now, I'm pretty worried about your arms and your back. You're hurt badly, and you're cold. I'd like to get you to safety so we can check you over."

She shakes her head, starting to edge away from me again. "No, I... I don't want to."

"I can't leave you out here. My village isn't far away. I can fly us both there, but I will need to pick you up for that."

"Don't touch me!" She turns, breaking into a sprint. She only makes it a short distance before her foot catches on something, and she hits the forest floor hard. She's already turned on to her back, scrambling away from me as I rush towards her. "Don't hurt me!" She screams, her eyes wide.

I stop short, dropping into a crouch 10 feet away from her. "Juno, hey, it's OK. Juno, I need you to listen to me."

"No!" She cries, backing into a tree.

"I can see someone has hurt you, badly. I'm not going to hurt you."

"Who are you? *What* are you?"

"I'm a demon," I say, and hold up my arm, with just the veins glowing, "I'm just a demon, and I'm not going to hurt you. I want to take you to my home, to Ocario, get you warm, and get those wounds taken care of, OK?"

Her breathing is ragged, but she doesn't flinch or move away as I get closer to her. I inch forward, and her eyes start to lose some of the wildness, some of the terror. By the time I reach her, her face is almost neutral.

I show her my coat again, my other hand still raised. "Juno, I'd like to help you up, so I can put this around you, is that alright?"

She looks from the coat to my face and back, clutching her hands together. Finally, she nods, and I reach out to put a hand on her arm. She inhales sharply as I do, but she doesn't flinch. Her eyes meet mine, and I smile.

"It's alright," I say, and I rise slowly, both hands under her arm to help her up with me. Blood seeps through her dress, and I try not to push too hard.

Once we're standing, I put the coat around her. The cotton dress she's wearing is torn, revealing scrapes and grazes on her skin. I can't even begin to guess what color the dress is meant to be, it's caked with dirt and grime. She grits her teeth and whimpers as her arms slip into the sleeves of the coat. Her distress makes my chest ache. She's in a lot of pain.

Now that we're both standing I realize how much taller than her I am, head and shoulders over her. I give her a smile.

"Well, I think I'll be able to carry you easily, Juno." I look down at her bleeding bare feet. "Would you like me to carry you to the treeline? Your feet look pretty sore and I don't want to make you walk any further than you need to."

Juno holds her arms back up against her chest, and I see her fingernails are all ripped, bleeding, torn from the flesh. Fuck. What the hell happened up here?

She considers my words for a moment, then nods hesitantly. "My feet really hurt."

"I bet they do." I move to her side. "I'll put an arm around your waist, and then you need to hold on to my neck OK? I'll put my other arm under your legs and pick you up, is that alright?" She nods again, her eyes staying on my face. I put my arm around her and lean down so she can put her arms around my neck, and her eyes clench as she does. "You OK?" I ask.

She nods, biting her lip.

"We'll get you seen to in no time," I assure her, and with one quick movement I sweep her up in my arms.

I begin to pick my way through the darkness of the forest, back towards the tree line, checking around me for any enemies that might appear in this eerie, noiseless place.

I start to worry that maybe this was a trap, that Juno

was bait. But out here? That's unlikely. Who the fuck else is as stupid as me and wants to investigate a mountain spewing red smoke that's crowned with writhing serpents?

The edge of the forest comes into view, and I breathe a sigh of relief. I look down to see Juno gazing up at me. I give her a smile.

"Have you ever flown before?"

Her brow furrows. "I - I don't know." She shakes her head. "Maybe? I don't know."

"It's alright," I assure her. "Just hold on to me, and don't worry, just keep your head down. It'll be over before you know it."

We emerge into the sunlight, and Juno burrows her face into my chest. "It's so bright." She says, her voice muffled.

"Just keep your head down, it's alright." I unfurl my wings, and launch myself into the air. Juno's grasp around my neck becomes tighter, and I feel her chest vibrate as she makes a sound. I hold her tighter as I fly. "You're safe," I tell her. "You're safe with me."

7
Tallesaign

uno falls asleep as we fly back to Ocario, and the sun is skirting low on the horizon when we arrive. Ebony and Liall are sitting on their porch when I land, and they eye me with surprise before jumping up and running towards me.

"Oh my god," Ebony exclaims, "who did you find?"

"Her name's Juno," I reply, pulling my wings in. "I found her up in the forest on Arax, she's hurt badly." I look down at Juno, who is blinking slowly as she gazes up at me.

"Tallesaign?" She says in a small voice, and something shifts inside me - a sharp jolt in the center of my chest, followed by a flood of warmth. I can't breathe for a split second.

Juno's eyes widen as she sees Ebony and Liall, and she burrows her face into the crook of my neck, clutching on to me with her bloody fingers.

"No!" She cries. "No! Don't let them hurt me!"

"Juno," I say soothingly, "Juno, honey, it's OK. They're my family, they want to help you." I look at Ebony. "Go and get Elise." She turns and runs without another word.

Liall gestures for me to follow. "Come on, let's take her to our cabin."

"Juno, we're going to my uncle's cabin."

Her head stays buried against me, like a frightened kitten. "No. No."

"Honey, you're safe, I swear to you." I lower my mouth to her ear. "I won't let anyone hurt you. I swear it. You're safe with me."

Liall holds the door to his cabin open, and I carry Juno inside. She still won't let go of me, so I sit down on the couch with her in my lap.

"Honey, we need to get this coat off you. I'll be gentle."

Juno whimpers as I let her go, staying as close to me as she can while I peel the sleeves of the coat carefully down her arms. As soon it's off, her arms are back around me. She begins to sob, and I feel like she'd crawl right into my skin if she could.

Liall shakes his head as I look at him, his arms crossed over his chest. "Holy shit. The poor thing."

Juno's chest heaves against me, her fingers digging into my neck. I want to rub her back or something, but I'm afraid of hurting her worse. I rest my cheek against the top of her head instead.

"It's OK," I whisper. "I promise you. You're safe."

The door to the cabin opens, and Elise and Ebony come in. Ebony waves to Liall to come outside, closing the door behind him, leaving only Elise and I with Juno. Elise approaches slowly, sitting down beside us on the couch.

"Hi there. Who's this, Tal?"

"Her name's Juno," I reply.

"Hello Juno," Elise says, "I can see you're hurt pretty badly. May I take a look?"

Juno shakes her head against me. "Leave me alone!"

"This is my aunt, Elise," I tell her. "She's a very powerful healer. She won't hurt you."

Juno's breathing is rapid as she slowly, slowly turns her head to look at Elise, her cheek pressed against my chest. Hesitantly, she extends a trembling hand to Elise.

"Oh dear," Elise tuts as she looks over the slices in Juno's skin. "Those look very sore." Her eyes move up to Juno's, and she extends a hand. "May I?"

Juno sniffles, and nods.

Elise's hands glow a soft yellow as she takes Juno's hand in hers, and the light travels up Juno's arm, over the cuts and grazes. Juno sucks in a breath as her skin knits together.

"It's OK," Elise assures her. "Healing can be a little uncomfortable, but you'll feel much better very soon." The light continues to travel down Juno's other arm, and I feel her back warming up under my arm.

Her breathing begins to steady as her body relaxes against me. I look down at her, watching her lips quiver. Her hair is a deep red, like red wine, I can see glimpses of it through the dirt. Her eyes flash up to mine for a split second, and she blinks a few times before looking back at

Elise.

"Do you know who did this to you, Juno?" Elise asks.

Juno shakes her head. "No. I don't. I... I was alone, up there, and I don't know... I don't know..." She breaks off as she chokes up.

"Don't worry." Elise gives her a kind smile. "You don't need to think about that right now."

I see Amryn through the window on the porch, talking to Liall and Ebony, casting a quick glance in the window at me, his brow furrowed. He nods as Ebony responds, and says something like "Yeah, no problem" and heads off again.

"I'll bet you'd do anything for a nice warm shower," Elise says to Juno.

"A what?" Juno asks in a small voice.

Elise eyebrows flicker upwards for just a second. "A shower. A wash, sweetheart. To get you all clean"

"Oh." Juno shifts in my lap. "Yes. I would like that."

Elise gasps, and pulls her hand back from Juno's suddenly. She puts a hand to her forehead. "I'm sorry," she says quickly as Juno flinches. "Oh I'm sorry, I didn't mean to startle you." She gives Juno a reassuring smile. "One of your injuries is a little worse than I thought, that's all. I might need to get another healer to help me." Her eyes meet mine, and I can see that it's not good.

The door opens and Juno's head shoots up as Cora walks in. "Hi, I heard we might need some clothes?" She smiles at Juno. "Hi there, I'm Cora." She holds up a stack of clothing in her hands. "I brought these, I hope they fit you." She places them on the table and backs to the door, her eyes meeting mine as she nods. "I'll leave you alone, OK?" She heads back out onto the porch.

Elise rises to her feet, and she looks pale. "I'm going to go and get another healer, but for now why don't you get cleaned up, and we'll get some food for you, yes?"

Juno nods. "Yes, thank you." She stretches her hand out in front of herself. "Thank you. It feels - it feels good now."

"Good, I'm glad." Elise looks at me. "I'll go and get Fenella." She hurries out of the cabin, closing the door softly behind her.

Juno is leaning against my chest again, her face tipped up to look at me. I smile at her, and for some insane reason I raise my hand to her face and push aside a strand of her hair. It doesn't even feel weird to do, and she sighs a little.

"How about I show you where the shower is?" I say, and she nods.

Climbing off my lap, she's a little unsteady on her feet. I look over my shoulder as we walk, showing her the way, and she gazes around the cabin as we go, her arms hugged around her.

In the bathroom I turn on the shower, and stand back. "I'll leave you to wash up, but I'll stay outside the door in case you need me OK? One of the women will be back in a second, and they can help you out if you need anything."

Juno shakes her head. "No. Only you."

"Hey, don't worry," I say, "I'll be here."

I close the door, and lean against the wall. What a

crazy day, the poor thing. Who would dump a woman out on the mountain like that? It must have been a sacrifice, I've heard rumors that some clans still do that shit.

"Tallesaign?" Her voice drifts through the door, and I push it open, popping my head in. She's still in the middle of the bathroom, in her dress. "I can't - I can't take it off." She says. "It just won't move, and my arms, they still - I can't lift them without pain."

I hesitate for a second. "I can get one of the women to come help you," I offer again, but she shakes her head emphatically. I guess we're doing this. I step forward and gesture for her to turn around. "I'll have to tear it off, OK?"

She glances over her shoulder and nods, pulling her hair out of the way.

I grab the top of her dress, which is stiff and brittle with filth, and tear it open with my hands, revealing her back. Nausea washes over me. The haphazard map of grazes and gnarled scars on her back looks painful. I realize I'm staring as she begins to shiver. She's huddled over, covering her front, clutching the remnants of the dress to her.

I clear my throat and quickly step back from her. "Call out when you're done, and I'll bring you some clothes," I say. I pull two towels down from the shelf above the sink and put them out for her. "There, you have everything you need now."

I sit down on the floor outside the bathroom, and rhythm of the falling water changes as she steps under the shower. I lean my head back against the wall and close my eyes. Those scars, those wounds. Someone hurt her really badly.

I rub my hand over my chest, remembering how the blood magic burned when it was used on me. I want to tear whoever did this to Juno into tiny pieces.

Footsteps approach, and I open my eyes to see Cora padding toward me. She sits down on the opposite wall, her knees pulled up to her chest. "Is she OK?"

"Hard to say," I reply with a shrug, "Elise said some of the injuries were too much for her to heal. Just then, when I took her dress off, I saw her back and I'm pretty sure she's been hit with blood magic."

"Oh shit." Cora shakes her head. "Who would be using that on her?"

"I thought maybe she was a sacrifice," I muse, rubbing my chin. "I've heard rumors of some small clans still doing that stuff."

"That's barbaric," Cora whispers. "The Old God doesn't ask for sacrifices."

"I don't think that's who they'd be sacrificing to, if you get my drift. If they're using blood magic, there's witches involved."

"Fucking witches." Her eyes flash to mine quickly. "I mean, not all of them obviously. Fenella's great." She cocks her head and narrows her eyes. "What do you mean you took off her dress?"

I gesture to the bathroom door and clear my throat. "I, uh, had to help her take her dress off, it was stuck and it's filthy and stiff and, uh, yeah."

Cora nods. "Right."

"I asked if she wanted one of you to help and she insisted she wanted me." Why do I feel so awkward explaining this? "She keeps saying she only wants me."

"Well, that makes sense," Cora says, tapping her nails together. "You found her, you're going to be the safe place for her until she calms down and knows no one's going to hurt her."

We hear the water shut off, and I get to my feet. "I need to get her some clothes."

"I'll get them, just wait here." Cora heads to the table while I wait. She brings them back, and I knock gently on the door.

"Juno? I have some clothes for you."

The door opens a crack, and she peers around at me. Her skin isn't dirty anymore, it's pale and creamy and her cheeks are bright red from the warm water. Her brown eyes are wide and clear as they dart from me to Cora and back.

She backs up, holding the door in front of her so I can walk into the bathroom. I put the clothes on the counter and head back out with a nod, keeping my eyes averted.

"Will you wait for me?" She asks as I walk out, and I turn back to look at her face. "I mean, will you be just outside here, please?"

I nod. "Of course I will be."

Cora sighs as the bathroom door closes. "The poor thing." She shakes her head. "She's terrified."

"Yeah." I don't know what else to say.

"Well, I'm going to head home and leave her to you

and Elise, there's no point overwhelming her." Cora says. "She needs some rest and maybe she'll be able to tell us more about herself tomorrow."

I nod. "No problem."

She smiles at me. "She's lucky you're such a stubborn ass. If you hadn't gone up to Arax - " She breaks off, and shrugs. "Thankfully she's OK." She turns to head out of the cabin.

I lean against the wall and wait for Juno to come out of the bathroom. I can hear her shuffling around, and then the door opens. She gazes at me, her mass of hair hanging over her shoulder, and she holds up a brush.

"I can't," she says, her voice cracking. "My back, I can't lift my arms. Could you brush my hair please?"

"Of course." I give her a smile as I step into the bathroom.

She turns her back to me, and hands me the brush. I lift the ends of her hair up in my hand, and begin to run the brush through them gently.

"Thank you." Her eyes meet mine in the mirror.

I take in her face properly for the first time. She can't be more than 30, but her eyes have a weariness to them that speaks of wisdom, and battles fought. She has a small mouth with full lips and a deep cupid's bow. Her light brown eyes are lined with long lashes, like a deer.

I smile at her reflection. "No problem at all. You must feel like a new person with all that grime gone."

She nods, watching as I keep brushing her hair. "I can't remember when I was last clean. I feel like I was up on that mountain for years."

"Do you know how you got there?"

"No." Her face is blank. "I don't remember anything."

"Not who hurt you either then I suppose?"

She flinches, and a small whimper escapes her. I put a hand on her shoulder, and her eyes flash to my reflection again.

"It's OK." I say quietly. "I won't ask you again, I'm sorry."

Juno nods, and her head drops forward, her hand moving up over mine on her shoulder. "You said I was safe with you. You said it as we flew. That I was safe with you."

"You are." I reply, and her hand clasps mine tighter.

"Tal?" Ebony's voice sounds at the bathroom door. "Tal, would Juno like something to eat?"

Juno's head snaps up and she spins around, looking up at me with wide eyes. "Who is that?"

"That's Ebony. She's another aunt. It's OK." I give her a reassuring nod. "We'll be right out!" I call to Ebony, and her footsteps retreat.

Juno takes a shuddering breath and gives me a small crooked smile. Her whole face lights up, just from that small shift. "They call you Tal?"

I nod. "Yeah, Tal."

"May I call you that, too?"

"Sure." I return her smile. "Come on, you must be starving."

We walk out into the kitchen, and Ebony and Liall are

sitting at the table. They both smile warmly as Juno walks in behind me, Ebony rising to her feet. "Oh, you look so much better, sweetie."

"Thank you." Juno replies with a shy smile. "And thank you for the clothes." She runs her hand over the soft black sweater that hangs over black leggings. "It is so nice to be warm again."

"We're just glad Tal found you," Liall says. "He must have a sixth sense, he was so insistent that he had to go up that mountain."

Juno looks up at me. "Thank you," she whispers.

I shake my head, gesturing to the table. "Come on now, you need to eat something."

We sit down together at the table, and Ebony brings us both a steaming bowl of rice topped with a thick vegetable gravy. Juno inhales deeply and sighs.

"This smells wonderful," she says.

Ebony smiles and places a basket of bread on the table in front of us. "I hope you like it. You need some good food and a good night's sleep in a warm bed. The world will look a lot brighter in the morning."

"We made up the spare room for you," Liall says, gesturing to the door beside the fireplace.

Juno's eyes widen a little, and she looks at me with alarm in her face. "I want to stay with you." Her brow furrows a little as she puts a hand to her head. "Sorry, I don't mean to sound ungrateful. I'm... I'm being stupid."

I reach out and take her hand, and she sucks in a small breath as her eyes flash back up to mine. "We'll do whatever we need to to make you feel safe, Juno." I assure her. "You've been through something terrible. It's OK."

She eyes me shyly. "Can... can I stay close to you?"

I see Ebony and Liall exchange a glance out of the corner of my eye.

"Of course you can. I can sleep on the couch, out here, if that's what you want." I gesture to her bowl. "Now come on, eat. It'll do you good."

She hesitantly raises the spoon to her mouth,taking a bite of food. Her eyes flutter closed as she chews, and an appreciative hum sounds in her throat. When I chuckle her eyes flick open, and she smiles again, a little self consciously.

"Good?" I ask.

She nods and looks over the table at Ebony. "It's delicious, thank you."

Ebony waves her hand. "Not a problem at all." Her eyes move to mine, and she raises her eyebrows. I shake my head slightly, not understanding what she wants me to do, but she glances away quickly when Juno raises her head as the door opens behind us.

Elise and Fenella walk in together from the gathering dusk, Fenella clutching her leather bag, from which comes the clink of glass as she sets it down on the floor.

"Juno, this is Fenella." Elise gestures to the old woman beside her. "She's another one of our healers, she's here to see if she can help me with the wounds on your back."

My gaze moves to Fenella, and I almost jump when I see her face. Her eyes are fixed on Juno, and they're a violent purple, like Morgan's, almost like Michael's. She's not blinking.

91

"*Merde.*" She says quietly.

"Is something wrong?" Elise asks.

Fenella approaches Juno slowly, her hands clasped before her. "What have we here?"

Juno tenses beside me, and I instinctively reach out to take her hand. "It's OK." I whisper.

Fenella stands behind us, and Juno twists in her chair, her eyes wide as she looks Fenella up and down. Fenella's face is full of sadness as she slowly brings a hand to Juno's face. "*Mon cher,*" she says quietly, "they cut off your wings, didn't they?"

Ebony gasps loudly from across the table, her hand flying to her mouth. My eyes meet Elise's over Juno's head, and her hands are clutched to her mouth, shaking her head.

Fuck. *Fuck.*

Juno's a fallen angel.

Those scars, those grazes, those gnarled and whorled cuts, all over Juno's back. She had wings. And some sick sadistic fucker sliced them off and then threw her down on that mountain, probably as punishment.

Juno gazes up at Fenella, her eyes full of tears. "I don't know. I don't remember."

"I'm so sorry, *mon cher.*" Fenella strokes Juno's cheek. "I am so sorry they did this to you."

A tear runs down Juno's cheek, and her eyes move to me. Her lip quivers, and then her shoulders begin to quake, her hands covering her face as she begins to cry.

"Oh, *mon cher,*" Fenella says soothingly as she puts her

hands over Juno's back. "I will do what I can." Juno slumps forward, the top of her head resting against my chest, and she continues to cry as Fenella's hands move over her back, slowly, gently, her veins glowing a soft purple.

Ebony's hands are still clasped over her mouth, and Liall puts an arm around her. We've all heard the stories of fallen angels before. They usually die pretty quickly once they're tossed from the Halls, their powers taken from them, weakening them.

I've never heard of one having their wings cut off before though. Not even demons were subject to that fate when we were thrown out of the Halls.

"There, there, child," Fenella says after a while. "I think that is enough for today." Fenella looks at me. "She will need more healing, but a good rest is best right now. She has been through so much."

I nod. "Yeah, that's true." I run my hand gently over Juno's hair. "Honey, you need to go get some sleep." I say softly, and her head falls back. Tears are running down her cheeks, and I brush them away gently with my fingers. She doesn't even flinch as I do it.

"It's going to be alright now," I whisper, "I told you you're safe, and I mean it."

The fire crackles, and I hear footsteps behind me. Liall walks around the couch and sits down at the far end, exhaling heavily as he does.

"Well, the light's off in her room and she's quiet, so I

guess she's asleep. Ebony's gone to bed as well." He rubs his chin with his hand, and regards me with raised eyebrows. "What a day, huh?"

"Yeah, pretty crazy." I cross my arms over my chest and settle down further into the couch. My eyes are heavy and I'm tired, all the flying has worn me out.

"She, uh -" Liall shifts in his seat, and clears his throat. "You and her, you seem to be... Close?"

I shake my head, chuckling. "Liall, we met this morning. I don't even know her."

"No, I mean, she seems to trust you, and you two seem to have, I don't know, a bond?"

I shrug as I yawn. "She's scared and she latched on to the person that rescued her, that doesn't mean anything."

"So, the fact that you knew she was up there also doesn't mean anything?"

My eyes snap to his. "I didn't know she was up there," I say quickly. "I went up there to see if anything strange was going on with Arax."

"Are you sure about that?" Liall's mouth twitches pensively. "You fly up there on a whim and just happen to find her?"

"Lucky coincidence." That's all it was, wasn't it? It has to be.

"Incredibly lucky," Liall mutters cynically. He shakes his head, then looks at me, curled up in the corner of the couch. "You must be tired, I'll let you sleep." He pats me on the shoulder as he passes me on his way to his bedroom. "Good night, Tal."

"Night." I reply, stretching my legs out. I lay my head against the soft pillow, and watch the flames dancing, my head beginning to swim as sleep takes over.

Just as I drift off, the unbearable weight on my chest is back, and I sit bolt upright. The smell of dirt fills my nose, and the screaming is back.

But this time it's not in my head. It's Juno's terrified screams coming from the bedroom.

8
Tallesaign

"*J*uno!" I clutch her in my arms as she screams and writhes. "Juno, you're OK. It's Tal. I've got you!"

"Please don't!" She pushes against my chest. "Don't! Let me out!"

"Juno, you're safe, you're safe."

"It's dark," she sobs, "it's dark and I can't breathe."

"Honey, I know. I'm here. I've got you." I cradle her head against my chest. "It's all over, it was just a nightmare."

The light in the hallway clicks on, and Ebony and Liall's footsteps approach. Juno blinks as the dim light washes over us, breathing heavily, her hands still clutching on to me. Ebony peers into to the room, pausing with her hand on the doorframe as she sees us on the bed together.

"Is everything alright?" She asks anxiously.

"She had a nightmare," I say, "it's OK, it's passing. Go on back to bed. Just leave that light on, would you?"

Ebony nods, and the cabin falls into silence again as

she and Liall retreat back to their bedroom.

Juno nuzzles into my chest, and I put my arms around her as she tries to catch her breath, as her sobs slowly subside.

"I'm sorry," she whimpers.

"Don't be sorry," I say. "You had a nightmare."

"I couldn't breathe," she says, "I couldn't breathe and there was dirt everywhere and it was all I could smell." Her breathing speeds up again. "It was so dark."

My stomach drops a little. The same nightmare. We had the same nightmare? "It's all over now," I say, trying to soothe her. "You're safe. I'm here."

She shuffles back a little from me, sniffling and wiping her face with the back of her hand. "I'm sorry, I'm crying all over you and you don't even know me."

"I don't mind at all."

"I feel like..." She gives a small laugh. "It's stupid."

"What's stupid?" I ask.

New tears form in her eyes. "I feel like I dreamed of you." She shakes her head. "It's not possible, I know that. But I feel like... I feel like I saw your face somewhere, and it must have been a dream."

"Maybe you did," I say with a smile. "Maybe we were meant to meet."

"Yes, maybe." She sighs heavily and wipes her eyes. "I need some water."

"I'll get you a glass," I say, rising from the bed.

"No!" She springs up after me. "I'll come with you. I - I

don't want to be alone."

We walk into the kitchen together, and I fill a glass under the tap. She gulps it down quickly, wiping her lips with the back of her hand.

"Thank you," she says, smiling shyly. She inhales deeply through her nose, and coughs a little. "I need some fresh air." Her eyes flash to mine. "Sorry, I know it's cold, but would you come outside with me for a moment? Just for a moment."

"Of course." I pull down a coat from beside the front door and shrug it on, then help Juno into one of Ebony's puffer jackets.

The night is still as we walk out onto the porch, the only sound our muffled footsteps. Mist dances across the icy ground in the moonlight.

I take my cigarette case from my pocket and pull one out, putting it between my lips and lighting it with my hand. Juno watches me curiously in the brief flare of my flame, and she chuckles.

"You smoke?"

"Yeah I do, you want one?" I hold out the case to her.

"I don't know." She lets out a soft laugh, a low, luscious sound that makes my heart flip-flop in the best and most unexpected way. "Maybe not yet. I'll try to remember if I smoke first."

"Well, you have a sense of humor," I say, and inhale deeply. "Can't remember anything but your name, and you're making jokes about it."

Juno walks to the porch railing, leaning against it and gazing up into the moonlight. "I'm just glad to be here."

She sighs. "I can't believe I'm not up on that mountain anymore."

"So am I." I say it quickly, and then catch myself, clearing my throat. "I mean, it must have been so terrifying, being up there all alone."

She nods. "The worst thing is that it's all I remember. I feel like I was up there for years. There's... there's nothing but that mountain."

"It'll all come back, I'm sure of it." It occurs to me as I say it that maybe she doesn't want it all to come back. Fuck knows what happened to her. "You'll heal, you just need time."

"Hmm," she muses quietly. "Time. Time is a funny thing. To know you've had so much of it but to have it all disappear from your mind, to wonder where it went." She looks over her shoulder at me. "I'm probably keeping you from a wife and children, aren't I? I'm sorry."

I shake my head as I draw on my cigarette. "No. No wife, no kids."

Juno's eyebrows shoot up in surprise. "You're not married?"

"No." My mind wanders for a second to Lorelei, who's probably wondering where I am. The news of Juno's arrival has no doubt traveled around the village quickly, so I hope she's put two and two together. "I have a - well, a -"

"A lover?" Juno offers, and her smile shifts. She looks away before I can interpret her expression.

"Yes, I suppose you'd call her a lover."

"What's her name?"

"Lorelei."

"That's nice." Juno says quickly, then straightens up, smiling at me in the darkness. Her hair looks almost black in this light, her pale skin glowing in the moonlight. "I should get some sleep. Hopefully no more nightmares." She pauses in front of me, and hesitantly raises a hand to my face. Her fingers stroke my cheek, running over my scar. Her eyes flash to mine as I inhale sharply at her touch, her fingers jerking back to hover just above my skin. "Did I hurt you?"

I shake my head. "No."

"How did this happen?" She runs her fingers softly along the scar again, her eyes staying on mine.

"A witch hit me with her magic. She was trying to hurt someone I love, and, well, this is all that's left of her."

Juno's eyes wander down my face, over the scar, over my lips, and it's there her gaze pauses and the floor seems to tilt a little. I've stopped breathing when her hand splays over my cheek.

"I dreamed of you." She says it quietly, her eyes moving back up to meet mine. "I know your face."

I heard your voice.

I don't say it, because I don't know what it means. I don't know what any of this means.

All I know is that I want to protect this woman, to kill the creature that mutilated her back and cut off her wings, tear anyone who ever tries to hurt her apart.

A distant echo sounds in my soul, and I push it away. But as I raise my hand to put it over hers on my face, I realize that my own hands don't ache anymore.

They don't ache anymore.

"I'm sorry someone hurt you, but if anyone ever tries to hurt you again, I'll kill them."

She nods. "I know."

Then her hand drops from my face, and she pushes through the door, back into the cabin. I want to follow her. I want to hold her so she doesn't have another nightmare, and if she does, I'll be there to ward off whatever scares her. But I can't. It's not my place. I don't know her.

I throw the cigarette stub into the bucket by the downpipe, and I take a deep breath of frigid night air. I put a hand to my chest, and I feel the distant echo growing closer.

I wonder how long I can push it away.

The sound of someone clearing their throat wakes me. I shift, feeling weight against me, hair tickling my chin. The fire crackles nearby, and I open my eyes slowly. Ebony is standing beside the couch, two mugs in her hands. Her eyebrows are raised, and it takes me a second to realize what the weight on me is.

Wine red hair spills over my shoulder, and Juno's hands rest against me, her cheek pressed to my chest. I don't know when she came out here. But she's sleeping peacefully against me. I glance back up at Ebony, who shrugs.

"I came out this morning and she was here." She says quietly. "She must have had another nightmare."

"I guess so." I run my hand gently over Juno's head, and she frowns in her sleep, turning her face and laying back down on me. "Honey, it's time to wake up."

"No," Juno mutters sleepily, "go back to sleep, *Zhizn Moya*."

Ebony gasps.

"What?" I ask with a furrowed brow.

Ebony shakes her head and puts the cups down on the coffee table. "Nothing, sweetie. I'll just leave these here and let her wake up properly." She rushes off, and a door closes somewhere in the cabin.

"Juno." I jostle her shoulder gently with my hand. "It's time to wake up. Come on, there's hot coffee."

She shifts so that her face is pressed into the crook of my neck, her lips brushing ever so gently against my collar bone. I feel deeply ashamed of the desire that shoots to my groin. *Fuck.* Not the time, not the person, you fucking pervert.

"OK, honey, come on." I sit us both up, and she curls her arms around my neck, frowning. She snuggles into my lap, pressing her face against my chest. Fuck, she's really not making this easy for me. "It's time to wake up." I put a hand under her chin so her face is turned up to mine. Her lips are pursed into a sweet little pout and *goddamn fuck it all.* "Honey, come on."

Her eyes open, and suddenly widen as she looks around and gets her bearings. "Oh Tal, I'm sorry, I was sleeping on you?" She sounds horrified, and climbs off me, backing into the opposite corner of the couch. "I'm so sorry."

"Don't be sorry." I give her a smile. "Really, it's fine. You probably just got scared during the night."

Her eyes move over my bare chest, and her cheeks flush violently red. "I don't even remember coming out. Oh my goodness, how embarrassing."

"Don't be embarrassed," I say, reaching out to pick up one of the mugs and handing it to her. "Come on, it was a crazy day and you just got scared."

She takes the mug from me and sinks back into the sofa. "You must have had a terrible night's sleep."

"I didn't even notice you were there until I woke up."

She raises an eyebrow and scoffs, a crooked grin pulling up the corner of her mouth. "I don't believe that for a second."

"You're tiny, honey, I didn't feel a thing."

"Mmm, such a big strong man and I am just a little feather, *da*?" She smiles, her eyes straying across my bare chest. She must sense me watching her, and her gaze moves back to my face. "Sorry, I don't mean to stare."

"It's OK, the scar scares everyone." I know the scar looks bad, and I run my hand over it self-consciously.

"I wasn't looking at your scar." She takes another sip of her coffee, her eyes fixing me over the edge of her cup.

"What were you -" I break off as I see the flush in her cheeks, and laugh. "*Oh.*"

"Sorry," she says quickly.

"No, it's fine, it's fine." *God fucking damn.* Guess sleeping curled up together has gotten us both into a weird headspace.

She pulls her knees up against her chest and tosses her long hair over her shoulder. "You keep calling me honey," she says with a small smile.

"Sorry. It's a bad habit I have, the pet names."

She shakes her head. "I like it."

"You called me something when you were waking up," I say. "*Zhizn Moya*, or something. What does that mean?"

Before she can answer, the door to the cabin opens, and Amryn and Cora walk in. Juno doesn't jump, she merely turns to look over her shoulder, and I see her smile.

"Good morning," she says, rising to her feet. "You brought me the clothes yesterday." She says to Cora, and extends both her hands to her.

"I did." Cora smiles widely and takes Juno's hands. "How are you feeling? You look so much better today."

"I'm feeling so much better, thank you." Juno looks up at Amryn, then back at me over her shoulder. "Is this your brother?"

"It is," I reply, rising from the couch. "This is Amryn, and his wife Cora."

"You two are so alike," Juno says as she smiles at Amryn. "It's so wonderful to meet you. Thank you for welcoming me and taking care of me."

"Of course," Amryn replies. "We're just glad you're safe."

"The council has asked us to meet," Cora says to me.

I open my mouth to ask why, but she gives me a meaningful glance, and I know it's because of Juno. With all the weird shit going on, they're going to want to know everything they can about this mysterious newcomer, the fallen angel who had her wings cut off.

"Not a problem." I reply. "I just need to head to my place and get changed."

Cora nods. "Great." She looks back at Juno. "I've been told you don't remember anything, is that right?"

"That's right. I remember being on the mountain and that's all." Juno 's shoulders slump a little. "I wish I could tell you more."

"Please don't worry about that now," Cora assures her. "There's plenty of time for all of that." Her eyes flash to mine again, and I can not only see she's worried, I can feel it.

"Juno," I say, taking her hand, "I'll be back soon, OK? You stay here and rest."

Her face falters a little, but she nods. "I'll be alright." She moves back to her spot on the couch.

"Trouble?" I ask Cora as we walk to my cabin.

"Unfortunately, yes. There's a lot of stress about a fallen angel we don't know being here. And the council wants to know what else you found up on Arax."

Oh shit, of course. I found more weird stuff up on Arax. They're not going to like this.

"There's snakes up on Arax," I say to Cora. "The whole peak is covered in them, in that red smoke. And the place is - it's fucking silent."

Amryn frowns. "Silent?"

"Yeah, like it's in some sort of vacuum, there's just no

sound, everything's being swallowed up by something." I reply as we reach my porch.

Amryn and Cora exchange a glance. "Well, this is going to go down well." Cora says. She looks back to me. "Come on then, the council doesn't like to be kept waiting."

"I'll just get changed and meet you at the Great Hall." I spring up onto my porch in one step, pushing through the door into my cabin. I hurry into my bedroom, throwing open the curtains. I jump as the comforter murmurs and begins to move.

"What the -"

"Baby?" Lorelei's face emerges from the bed, squinting at me in the morning light.

"Hey, yeah it's me." I exhale heavily. "Sorry, you startled me."

She blinks in the sudden onslaught of light. "I was waiting for you last night." She yawns, rubbing her eyes. "Where were you?"

"You didn't hear about what happened?" I ask her, pulling my sweater off over my head.

"I heard you found someone on Arax," she replies, "and she was hurt real bad."

"Yeah, she was, I mean, she is, but she's feeling better today." I pull on a pair of black pants and a long-sleeved black shirt. "She was scared, so I stayed with her."

"You stayed with her?" Lorelei tilts her head and pouts. "What do you mean?" Her eyes are still sleepy, but open now and fixed on me.

I feel a twinge of guilt. No, not a twinge. A fucking *mountain* of guilt.

I don't want to tell Lorelei I woke up with another woman in my arms, that she snuggled up to me, called me god knows what as she pressed her face against me. And I sure as fuck don't want to own up to how nice it felt. I'm such an asshole.

"She was terrified, baby," I say quickly. "She had nightmares and she just latched on to me. I didn't want to leave her alone, so I slept on Ebony's couch for the night." I sit down on the bed and reach out to take her hand. "I'm sorry, I should have known you'd be waiting for me."

"It's OK." She smiles at me, and climbs out of the comforter, wearing only panties. She climbs on top of me, holding my face in her hands, and plants a slow, tender kiss on my lips. "You're a good man, Tal."

And those words just make me feel even fucking worse. Right now I feel about as far from being a good man as possible.

"You're beautiful," I say, putting my hands on her back, and she's all warm and inviting from being curled up in bed.

"Can you come back to bed?" She grinds her hips against me as she bites her lip.

"No, baby, the council's waiting for me." I stand up with her wrapped around me, placing a quick kiss on her forehead. "I'll be back as soon as we're done, OK?"

She pouts as I put her back down on the bed, but she lets me go. "OK, I'll see you later then." She watches me, propped up on her elbow, as I leave the room.

I hurry to the Great Hall, and I feel so fucking ashamed of myself. I don't want to admit it, but it felt good to have Juno in my arms. When she curled up against me, pressed her lips against my neck - *fuck. Stop it.*

What the fuck is wrong with me? I shake my head at myself. It's like cheating, isn't it? No wonder Ebony was so shocked to see us like that.

Fucking asshole. Lorelei deserves better than this.

I don't have any more time to wallow in self-hatred, as I walk into the Great Hall to find the council members flinging a million questions at Cora, too caught up in their own panic to listen to the pleas of their Queen to all stop talking at once.

The noise stops when I walk in, as glances are exchanged amid a brief silence. Then the questions start again, all being flung in my direction now, and at an even louder volume.

I hold my hands up. "Hey, everyone, this isn't helpful," I say, raising my voice to be heard over the noise. "You all need to stop, or I can't answer anything you want to know."

"The red smoke." Hannigan, the oldest of the council members, stands up, his arms crossed over his chest. His face is a mass of wrinkles as he frowns at me. "The red smoke, what is it?"

"I don't know," I reply. "It smells like sulfur. It seems to just be volcanic activity."

"*Just.*" Hannigan pulls a face as his tone becomes mocking. "Oh, *just* volcanic activity, nothing to worry about then!"

"I didn't say that." I resist the urge to be disrespectful and roll my eyes. "But I don't know what's causing the smoke."

"So, why did you go up there?" Morag, one of the other elders, stands up and her bony finger darts in the direction of the door. "There's talk that you're linked to this, this thing you've brought back."

"She's not a thing," I snap. "She's an angel and she was badly hurt."

"I won't have an angel in this village!" Morag exclaims.

"Why ever not?" The voice comes from the doorway, and Zadkiel bends down to fit through, smiling widely at us all.

Morag sniffs loudly. "I meant no disrespect, Zadkiel," she says quickly, "but this one, she's not like you. We don't know her."

"From what I'm told she doesn't know herself," Zadkiel replies, walking slowly to my side and placing a heavy hand on my shoulder. "How are you, Tal?"

"I'm fine, thank you."

Zadkiel cocks his head. "You look different."

"Is this the time for small talk?" Hannigan throws his hands up in frustration.

"Oh, you demons are impatient," Zadkiel says with a heavy sigh. "What exactly do you want to hear? That she's a danger, that she's here to burn the village to the ground? She couldn't be here if she meant harm, you all know this."

"With all the harm that we've had here, nothing would

surprise me anymore!" Morag retorts. "The earthquakes, the serpents, the Purge. It's all a warning, Zadkiel."

Cora rubs her hands together, and nods. "Azrael told us Gabriel is trying to cause some trouble for us."

Zadkiel scoffs. "Don't pay him any heed, he's nothing but a criminal. He has no support in the Halls, and the Old God has a close eye on him."

"And what if he's right?" Elias stands up from the back of the group, and I suppress the urge to throw him out.

"What are you doing here, Elias?" I ask him. "You're not a council member."

He crosses his arms over his chest, sneering at me defiantly. "I think the people of this village have a right to know what's going on, and not through the filter of what all you fine people believe we have the right to know."

"Are you accusing us of not telling the truth?" Cora asks him.

"I just want to hear things with my own ears, majesty." Elias replies. *Smug fucking bastard.*

"Well, hear this," Cora says, her voice taking on an icy edge. "I will never lie to you, and I will never keep anything from you, any of you, especially something important to the safety of Ocario."

"Good." Elias shrugs jovially. "So this one -" He points at me, "won't mind telling us what he saw up there and where he found this fallen angel."

Zadkiel gives me a side glance and chuckles. "Floor is yours, dear."

"There wasn't much there," I begin, shifting on my feet

as everyone stares at me. "The red smoke, and silence."

"Silence?" Morag asks.

"Yes, silence. Unearthly silence. It's like someone has sucked all the sound out of the forest, like it's suspended in some sort of other dimension. It was eerie." I take a deep breath, knowing the next bit isn't going to be received well. "And there are serpents. All over the peak."

The council members exclaim loudly, chattering away over the top of each other. Elias looks far too pleased with the unrest exploding around him. Cora raises her hands, pleading for everyone to calm down, but they won't listen.

I jump as Zadkiel lets out a high-pitched whistle, and he grins at me as he pulls his taloned fingers from between his lips. "Learned that watching baseball," he says to me quietly, clearly pleased with himself. It's worked - everyone's shocked into silence. "Perhaps you'd all let Tallesaign finish what he has to say?" Zadkiel says. He gestures to me to keep talking.

I hate speaking in public, but I take another deep breath and continue on. "As I said, the peak is covered in serpents. But they weren't anywhere else on the mountain, just up on that peak, in the red smoke."

"Where did you find the angel?" Morag asks me.

"She was down in the forest. The forest seems to have a spell over it, there was no snow on the ground, and it was really dark." I feel a shiver down my back as I remember the feeling in that forest. Eerie. Fucking weird. "She was badly injured. She was filthy and terrified."

"Who put her there?" Hannigan asks.

"She doesn't remember," I reply. "She doesn't know

anything. She knows her name and that's it, nothing else."

"She speaks Russian." Ebony's voice is small from the front of the group.

"She does?" The question slips out of me before I can think.

Ebony nods slowly. "Yes. I heard her - I heard her speak it this morning when -" Her gaze darts away from me. She knows what Juno said to me.

"So, we have a mutilated Russian angel with amnesia who was retrieved from a snake-covered mountain and we're supposed to be OK with this?" Elias laughs out loud.

"What exactly are you worried about?" Amryn asks him.

"The same thing I was worried about after the Purge," Elias replies. "That this is all a sign that the Fates are unhappy with us, with the corruption going on in this village."

Amryn sneers and rubs a hand across his mouth as he sidles up to Elias. "I think I warned you pretty clearly before what was going to happen if you ever said anything like that about my wife or my son, right?"

"I'm not afraid of you," Elias says, puffing his chest out.

"No?" Amryn's right in his face now. "You fucking should be."

"What're you gonna do, huh?"

Amryn rolls his shoulders, the muscles on his back rippling, and I know this isn't going to end well. I step forward at the same time as Cora.

"Amryn, stop," Cora says. "This isn't helpful."

"He's just being an asshole," I say.

Elias's eyes widen as he looks at me, and his arms unfurl as he leaps forward to rush at me. Amryn slams his fists into Elias's chest, and he hits the floor with a loud thud.

"You stay the fuck down," Amryn says, pointing his finger at Elias. "And you threaten any of my family again, I will fucking end you."

"You and your decrepit fucking family," Elias hisses. "Your depraved fucking brother diddling little girls and -"

Amryn reaches down and seizes Elias by the collar. "What the fuck did you just say, you fucking asshole?"

"Amryn, stop." I call out.

Zadkiel has his hands clutched to his mouth as he chuckles beside me.

"You're sour that your daughter is fucking my brother, is that it?" Amryn asks with a laugh. "Your daughter, who's a grown woman? That's why you're doing all this?"

"She's half his age!" Elias's face is purple with rage. "He's old enough to be her father!"

Amryn lets him go, and Elias's head strikes the floor. "You need to stop this, Elias." Amryn says pointedly. He turns to look at Cora, and dips his head, walking to her side. "I'm sorry."

Cora flashes him a look of mild irritation and shakes her head before she looks back at Elias.

"Elias, there's no corruption here. There are strange things happening, yes, but fighting amongst ourselves won't help. Causing unrest won't help. We fought to have our home be safe, and I won't let you destroy that peace."

"He's to stay away from Lorelei." Elias jabs a finger in my direction.

"That's up to your daughter to decide," Cora says. "She's an adult. If you have concerns about her choice of partner, then you discuss those with her, in private, not here at a council meeting where she's not attending. Do you hear me?"

Elias gets to his feet, shaking his head. He huffs a little, but as he casts his eyes around the hall, his face flushes red, and he storms out without another word.

Morag gives herself a disgraced shake, and her face turns back to me. "If we're quite done discussing what goes on in the bedrooms of this village, maybe we can get back to the matter of the fallen angel," she says.

"What about her?" I ask.

"How has she survived?" Hanniagn asks. "They always die when they fall, and very quickly."

"And if she's fallen, it's for a reason," Morag says quickly. "Who knows what crimes she's committed?"

"Hey." All eyes turn to Amryn. "I don't think any demon in this room is in a position to question anyone thrown from the Halls."

Cora nods. "Exactly. I won't label her a criminal for no good reason."

"We don't know a thing about her!" Hannigan exclaims. "She doesn't remember a thing, who knows what she's done!"

"Is there a way her memories can be retrieved?" Morag

looks over at Elise. "Won't they come back with healing?"

Elise shakes her head. "That's not something we can heal. Whatever happened to her is terrible enough that her own mind is trying to protect her from it, and that's a barrier I can't overcome."

"What about Fenella?" Morag asks. "She's a witch, and she - well, we all know she knows things sometimes, things she can't know."

Elise holds up a hand. "I think we have to remember here that Juno is terrified, and was badly injured when she came here. I don't want to subject her to some form of memory retrieval that she may not be ready for."

"Elise, we need to know." Morag insists, and her eyes move back to me. "Tallesaign, she trusts you, is that right?"

I shift on my feet. "Sure, she seems to, but only because she's afraid." I'm intensely aware of Ebony's eyes boring into me as I speak, and I avoid her gaze entirely, shame welling up inside me again. "I'm not going to try and talk Juno into anything she's not ready for, just like Elise said. Her memories will come back. When she's ready, when her mind's ready."

Hannigan throws his hands up. "Well, I guess there's nothing else to discuss then. We'll have to contact the scholars about the snakes on the mountain, and the silence up there." He shakes his head as he gazes at Cora. "I don't mean to be alarmist, but a part of me is pretty certain that none of this is good news."

"We don't know what it means." Cora replies. "Until we do, there's no point speculating and driving ourselves crazy."

I know she's trying to sound confident, but I can feel her apprehension. What part of this could possibly be good news? And what the fuck is going to hit us next?

9

Tallesaign

sit bolt upright in bed, bathed in sweat. Gasping for air, the pressing weight on my chest dissipates slowly. Fuck. *Fuck.* I feel sick. I could hear Juno screaming again. She's asleep in Liall and Ebony's cabin, she's fine. Right?

I reach down to check if Lorelei is still asleep, then I remember she's not here.

Elias finally put his foot down after the council meeting and told Lorelei she wasn't allowed to be with me. It was ridiculous, with lots of tears and yelling, but then finally Lorelei told me she'd go home and talk to him. I think we both know it's over.

I hate that I'm suspended between relief and regret. Maybe it's better this way. She can go on and find someone she deserves, someone who wants to give her all the things she wants.

I throw myself back down on the mattress, my chest still heaving as I suck in one sweet, cool breath after another. That fetid, hot air makes my stomach churn.

I can't get the sound of Juno screaming out of my head.

117

Why am I hearing it? Why won't it go away, even now that she's safe, now that she's here?

My feet are practically burning, wanting to walk out into the yard. Just to check if the cabin is alright, that nothing's happened to her. It's stupid. But I just have to know. Just a quick check, just to calm my nerves.

I get out of bed, pulling on sweatpants and throwing my jacket on before stepping into my boots. It's snowing when I step outside, the air icy cold.

There's no moon, only the dim light from my cabin illuminating the courtyard. I walk along my porch, right to the very end, where I can catch a glimpse of Liall and Ebony's cabin. It's fine. Of course it is.

I'm an idiot.

"Can't sleep?" Juno's voice sounds from the darkness. She chuckles as I jump, and she walks down the steps of Liall and Ebony's cabin, across the snow towards me. "Sorry, I didn't mean to startle you."

"It's OK." I watch her come closer, a black coat wrapped around her, snow flecking her deep red hair. "I just had a bad dream, and I wanted to - to get some air."

She comes up on my porch, her arms hugged around herself against the cold. "I had a bad dream, too," she says, taking a seat on the bench. "Always the same one, always trying to breathe, and the air is hot and thick and I can't see."

"Yeah, that sounds terrible." I sit down beside her.

"And you?"

I don't know what to say. "Uh, just, you know, falling and stuff."

118

"Hmmm." She stretches her legs out in front of her. "Do you have a cigarette?"

"Decided you do smoke, huh?" I ask, retrieving the case from my pocket.

"I decided I might try it and see if I do."

I take two cigarettes from the case and put them both between my lips, lighting them and handing her one. I watch as she inhales deeply, and she chuckles as the smoke spills from between her lips.

"Oh yes, I smoke," she says with a throaty laugh. "That feels much too good."

"It's the tobacco. It's nothing like that shit the humans smoke. That stuff tastes like pure death."

"Well this is delightful," Juno says, crossing her ankles and pulling her shoulders up against the cold. "I needed this after that fucking dream."

"Sorry I wasn't there for you tonight."

She shrugs. "It's OK, I understand. You can't be there with me every night. They'll stop one day. They have to, right?"

"Sure. And you'll remember everything again too, don't worry."

"It's so strange," she muses. "I keep going through this list in my head of everything I know about myself. I count it over and over in my head, one after another. And every time I reach the end of it, I think to myself - maybe this time the list will be longer. Maybe I'll remember something new." She laughs sadly as she flicks the ash onto the snow. "But I never do."

"What do you remember about yourself?" I ask, turning my body towards her. "Tell me."

"You want to know?" Her eyes are illuminated briefly by the flare of the cigarette as she inhales. "You want to know all the things I remember?"

"Sure. Might help you remember more."

She gives another one of those low laughs that makes my breath catch. "OK, I suppose. Well." Her lips twitch a little. "I know I like strawberries. I like red wine. I hate the feeling of wool socks on my feet. My favorite color is blue. Not just any blue though, cornflower blue."

"What else?" I ask. Her voice is enthralling, almost musical.

"I like the smell of lavender, and I think I used to bathe in lavender oils. I like hot buttered bread, but I always eat the end of the bread untoasted. I like it fresh." She giggles. "All these silly things to remember."

"Not at all. These are all the things that make up a person, right?"

"I suppose so."

"Go on, what else?" I press her.

"I love thunderstorms, and cats. I don't like sour things. Dusk is my favorite time of day, I love watching the sun set."

"So do I."

The curve of her cheek shifts as she smiles at me. "And I like men with dark hair," she says in a low voice.

I laugh a little breathlessly, and suck on my cigarette. "Is that so?"

"Sorry. I shouldn't say such things to a man who's spoken for."

"Oh I'm not -" I catch myself quickly. I shouldn't be this fucking eager to move on when Lorelei was literally crying and begging for her father's approval this afternoon. I clear my throat, shaking my head. "I mean, Lorelei and I, it's, well, her father doesn't approve. He's made it clear he doesn't want anything to happen there."

"Do *you* want something to happen?"

I take an extra long drag to delay answering the question. *I did. Until you came along.* And I have no fucking idea why.

"She's very young," I say. "She's very romantic about life with me, but I don't know..."

"What don't you know?"

"I - I don't know if I can give her the life she wants."

"You don't know if you can or you don't know if you want to?"

I laugh, the sound muffled by the falling snow. "You're rather direct aren't you?"

She shrugs as she inhales. "I feel like, with you, I can be, yes?"

"Yes." I agree quickly. She makes me comfortable. I want to talk to her. I can't explain it.

"So?" Her eyebrows are raised. "Is it because you can't or because you don't want to? Is there something wrong?" She leans a little closer. "Is the sex no good?"

"Fuck," I say with a laugh. "You really don't hold back at all." I lean forward, resting my elbows on my knees.

"No, the sex is fine."

Juno sucks on her teeth. "Fine? Oh dear."

"No, no, I didn't mean it like that. It's just -" I run a hand through my hair. "I don't, I mean, I didn't love her, and I hate that about myself because I should have. She's pretty and she's sweet and she loves me, and she wants a baby and all of that. All the things I want."

"Ah but loving someone because you should defeats the purpose of love itself, doesn't it?" Juno says. "We love for reasons we can't explain, because our souls recognize each other. The echo of a love we once knew and have found again."

I exhale heavily at her words, and that strange warm feeling wells up in my chest. "That's a beautiful way of looking at it."

"Perhaps." She shuffles closer to me, and seems to hesitate for a moment before she leans her head against my shoulder. "How did you know I was up there, on that mountain?"

"I didn't." The lie slips out too quickly, and I'm sure she can sense that what I'm saying isn't true.

"Yes, you did." Her head turns, and she gazes up at me.

I turn toward her, and she lifts her head from my shoulder. I look down at her, barely able to make out much of her face in the dim light. She lifts a hand to my face, her fingertips grazing my skin.

"You found me." She says quietly. "You knew I was there, didn't you?"

I swallow hard. "Tell me more about yourself." I'm

painfully aware of how close her lips are. "Tell me more of what you know."

"I have a birthmark on my lower back." She turns her hand to run the backs of her fingers down my cheek. "It's red and purple, like someone squashed a berry on my skin." Her hand runs down the side of my neck, coming to rest on my chest. "I like the smell of wood smoke, hay, and rain on a summer's day, when the rocks outside are baked from the sun, and the ground is hot."

My mouth is going dry. I swallow again, and lick my lips. I try to ignore the ache to pull her close. I will away the urge to crush those full lips under mine, because it's absurd. My head is swimming. Maybe she's a witch and cast a spell on me, because all I can focus on is her mouth.

"What else?" I just want her to keep talking. *Keep me out here with you, all night. Keep me from thinking about taking you inside, into my bed, to feel your cheek against my chest again, to hear you say something sweet to me again. Just talk to me.*

"I like to go swimming... but only with no clothes on."

Fuck. I suck in a breath, and her mouth turns up into a smile.

"Do you like that too, Tal?"

"Y-Yes."

"Tell me." She lays her forehead against my jaw. "What else do you like?"

"We're supposed to be trying to get your memory back," I say. *Just keep talking. Please keep talking. I'm going to do something I'll regret if you don't.*

And then I lean my face into her hair and breathe her

in, and her hand moves over my thigh. What the fuck am I doing? What the fuck are *we* doing?

A scream breaks through the night, a blood-curdling shrieking from overhead. Juno jumps and clutches onto my arm.

"Oh god, what is that?" She asks, her voice quivering.

A flash of orange erupts over us, reflecting off the windows of the cabins opposite us. It's flames, a fireball. The shrieking above us grows louder, and I can hear a whirring of wings.

Chimera. *Fuck.*

I spring to my feet, and pull Juno up with me. "Go back to Ebony's cabin, now. Go there and stay with them, they'll keep you safe."

"But Tal -"

"You go there and stay with them." Another fireball explodes, closer this time, and terrified screams sound in the night. "Go, now, and stay with Ebony and Liall."

She doesn't protest any further, scurrying down the porch steps and bolting across the courtyard to Ebony's cabin. I run around my cabin, toward the sounds of shrieking, the screaming and the exploding fireballs.

Wings swoop above me, flapping over my head. I summon my flames and send them upwards, and I hit the creature that was about to strike. Its loud scream echoes through the night as it descends towards the snowy ground. I can hear it withering behind me as I keep running.

Demons are racing from their houses, some in a blind panic, others with their flames ready, looking up into the dark, shrieking, whirring night sky.

I see one of the others, turning in a circle as he stares upwards, ready to strike. A black figure plunges from the sky, and he screams as the creature drives a trident into his face. My stomach drops as the demon slumps to the ground. *What the fuck?*

Zadkiel takes off into the sky, green flashes exploding from his hands as he sends his strikes after the armed creatures in the night sky. He takes out several of them, and they fall, scattering across the square outside the Great Hall.

"Tal!" Amryn calls out to me. "Tal!"

A fireball explodes to my right, and I stumble sideways. Straightening up, my ears ringing slightly from the explosion, I look over to see several houses burning. The sounds of running and screaming become audible again.

"Get out of the village!" Zadkiel calls as he swoops overhead. "Out into the fields, away from the houses!"

Amryn is at my side, his flames drawn. "What the fuck are these things?" He asks, looking upwards.

"Chimera. Fucking cherub mutants. They're armed."

One of them swoops down on Amryn, screaming as it brandishes its trident, and Amryn sends his flames into it. It hurtles into the wall of a house, and it shrieks terribly as it burns on the ground.

Pain shoots through my shoulder, and I cry out as I feel the weight of one of these fuckers land on me. I grab it with a flaming hand, flailing at it as it digs its trident into my flesh. It screams as I burn it, but it doesn't let me go.

"Fuck!" Amryn exclaims, and he throws a flame at the thing on my shoulder. He misses, but the thing jumps off me anyway, taking off into the night.

"Where's Cora?" I ask, clutching my shoulder. It's wet with blood. "Where's Cora?"

"She was with Phoenix, she was taking him to Ebony's, I told her to find us." He steps closer to look at my shoulder. "Fuck, that's -"

I wave him off. "I'm fine, we don't have time for that now."

"Incoming!" Zadkiel calls above us, and Amryn and I look up in time to see a ball of electricity hit him in the side. He plummets from the sky, landing heavily in a smoking heap not far from us.

I run over to him, Amryn right behind me. "Zadkiel?" I kneel beside him.

"It smarts a little." He grimaces, clutching a hand to his side. His eyes widen as they meet mine, and he shakes his head. "Tal, it's bad." He points over my shoulder, and I look up to see two enormous black angels swooping over the village.

"Amryn!" I call. "Time to fly, brother."

Amryn's eyes flare with concern for only a split second before his wings unfurl, and I follow him up into the sky. The flames of the burning village below us illuminate the night around us. The two black angels fix us with glowing orange eyes, embers in their otherwise featureless faces.

One of them hisses and flies right at Amryn, who sends a fireball at it. He catches the edge of the angel's wing, and they lose a few feet as they cry out in surprise.

126

"Fool!" The other one shrieks, and between his hands he summons a ball of electricity, lightning bolts snapping and flaring.

"Amryn!" I call out, but he's turning too slowly, still focused on the other angel who is trying to recover in the air. I hurtle towards him, trying to beat this fucking ball of lightning before it hits him. His eyes widen as he sees me coming towards him, and then there's a painful flare in my back as the electricity hits me.

I'm paralyzed, volts of lightning coursing down my limbs. Amryn stretches out his arms to me, trying to catch me before I plummet to the ground. The other angel sets his sights on Amryn's turned back and summons up one of these snapping, flashing balls of fury.

I fight one arm free of the angry sparks holding my body immobile, and manage to throw a fireball, sending it over Amryn's shoulder into the angel's face.

My body feels hot and numb at the same time, the ground growing closer as I keep falling. I try again to free my wings, but it's no use.

"Tallesaign!" It's Cora's voice, from far below. There's a flash of white, and the chimera around us shriek again as they scatter.

I hit the ground hard, landing flat on my back, and my vision goes fuzzy for a moment. I gasp in a breath. Then Cora's standing over me, sending the Inera into the air above us, illuminating the village bright like daylight. There's a rush of wings, and another explosion to our right.

"They're going!" Someone calls.

"They might be regrouping!" Amryn shouts from above.

Cora drops to her knees, putting a hand on my chest. "Are you OK?"

I nod, and push myself up on my hands. "Yeah, just knocked the wind out of me." My back is burning, but I don't have time to think about that now.

Cora swings around, her white flames leaping high as the black angel lands in the village square in front of her. I get to my feet, standing behind her, my flames ready, and Amryn hovers above us, prepared to strike.

"What do you want?" Cora calls, her voice rising to be heard over the fire roaring around us.

"Ah, the Shadow Queen," the angel hisses, his mouth a black expanse that's barely visible in the coal darkness of his face. "You've been in the human realm too long, majesty, you are weak."

Cora sends a shock wave washing over him, the walls of the surrounding houses shaking as she does. "You're not welcome here."

The angel laughs, a horrid high pitched cackle. "Am I supposed to be impressed?"

"What do you want?" Cora asks again.

"Isn't it obvious?" The angel's arms are outstretched as he gestures around us. "Chaos! Anarchy!" Lightning flashes in the sky above us, and the angel tips his head back, cackling louder. "Are you watching us, Father?" He screams into the sky. "Are you displeased?"

"You'll leave now!" Cora commands. "You are not welcome here, this is Sacred Ground!"

"What are you going to do?" The angel jeers, his wings spreading wide behind him.

"Blow this fucker up," I say to her, and Cora glows bright white, summoning her power.

"This is my last warning," Cora says.

"Go on then." The angel challenges from behind gritted teeth. "Let's see the damage a Shadow Queen can do."

The flash is immense, bright white, and the ground beneath us quakes heavily as the Inera's shock wave washes over the earth. The flames around us lessen as they are quashed by the pressure, and I stumble a little as blood pours down my shoulder.

The angel is no more, an explosion of black ash on the ground. The sound of the flames burning is replaced by sobs, screams, children crying. Amryn touches down beside us, his face full of concern as he looks at me.

Cora's shoulders are heaving, and her eyes slowly change from white to green as she turns back to me. "Oh Tal," she says, stepping forward and putting her hands against my chest as I falter a little.

"I'm OK," I assure her. She cries out as I slump against her, leaning heavily on her shoulder.

"Tal?" Her eyes are wide as she holds me up. "Tal?"

"Cora!" Ebony is running towards us, and her hysterical edge to her voice sends an icy sensation down my spine. "Cora, I can't find Phoenix!"

Amryn runs to meet her, grabbing her outstretched hands. "What? What do you mean?"

"Our house," she sobs, clutching Amryn's hands, "they hit it, and the roof collapsed. I can't find Phoenix, or Liall, or Juno."

Fuck. Cora runs off, and Amryn is right on her heels. "Tal, stay here!" Amryn calls over his shoulder.

No chance. Not when my nephew's missing. I force myself forward, fighting the light-headedness that seizes me. They need me.

"Phoenix!" Cora screams. "Phoenix!"

We pelt around the corner of the houses towards Ebony's cabin, and Cora collides with Liall. He's coughing, his face covered in soot. Cora grasps on to him. "Liall, where's Phoenix?"

"I don't know," he says, tears streaming down his cheeks, tracking through the soot as he continues to cough. "I lost sight of him, I heard him crying but-"

Amryn bolts past him. "Phoenix!" He calls, running, running. "Phoenix!"

I stumble around the other side of the houses, towards the barn. "Phoenix!" I call. "Juno! Where are you?"

I can hear Cora and Amryn screaming for their son, and the sound throws me back in time for a moment - my mother, Amryn, Cora, Ceili. Screaming for me. My mother's mournful cries as my father fell.

"Elspeth, stop him!" He calls. "Stop him! He can't come out here!"

My stomach drops for just a split second. I'm remembering it wrong. That's not what he said. But my mother is crying and saying that she can't, that she'll hurt him. That she'll hurt *me*.

"He's your son!" My father cries back. "Do it now!"

I shake my head, stumbling into the wall of the barn. I've lost too much blood, that's all. I'm weak. I'm not thinking straight. I'm mixing things up. I need to find Phoenix, and Juno. They have to be here somewhere.

Cora is screaming in the distance, and Amryn keeps calling for his son.

I throw open the doors of the barn. "Phoenix?" I call, nausea washing over me. I try to blink away the white spots dancing in my vision. I have to find them. "Phoenix? Juno?"

There's silence, only the distant cries and screams of the villagers, but then I hear something. The rustle of hay.

"Uncy Tal?" A tiny voice sounds in the dark, and a figure rises slowly, stepping forward.

Juno carries Phoenix towards me, and his tiny arms reach out to me, his little face red from crying, his green eyes wide with fear. I clasp him to me with the arm that doesn't hurt.

"Oh buddy." I breathe a heavy sigh of relief. "Let's get you to your momma and daddy." I look at Juno, her face smeared with soot, and attempt a smile.

"The lady took me out of the fire," Phoenix murmurs, his little fists grabbing on to my hair.

"The lady did good, huh?" I say, nodding to Juno, who tries to smile back.

"Phoenix?" Cora's voice comes closer, and I walk towards it as quickly as I can, my legs feeling heavy.

"Cora!" I call. "Amryn! I've got him!"

They come flying around the corner of the barn, and Coras' face crumples as she sees Phoenix in my arms. "Phoenix!" She cries, and the little boy bursts into tears, stretching his arms out to his mother. "Oh, Phoenix!" She takes him from me, clutching him to her, and Amryn puts his arms around both of them, digging his face into Phoenix's black curls.

Juno is at my side, looking up at me, and her brow furrows as she sees my shoulder. "You're hurt." She puts a hand under my arm as I begin to sag. "Oh my god, Tal, you need help."

Amryn's head shoots up. "Come on, we need to get you to a healer."

Juno's hand stays under my arm as we walk back to the Great Hall. I cast a glance up to the night sky - no more chimera, no more black angels. Just the glow of fires as the village burns around us.

The Great Hall is full of demons, sobbing and crying. Many are lying on the ground, bleeding, burned. The healers are rushing around, trying to help, but there's so many injured.

I collapse onto a chair, and Juno kneels beside me, her face full of concern.

"I'm going to find Elise," Amryn says, and rushes off.

Cora sits on the ground beside us, Phoenix in her lap. She rocks him back and forth in her arms, tears streaming down her cheeks. Her eyes move to mine, seeing me watching her, and I give her a weak smile.

"Juno got him out of the house."

Cora's eyes widen. "Thank you." She says, her voice

strained as she looks over me, to Juno. "Thank you for saving him."

"Of course," Juno replies, and she reaches up to clutch my hand. "Are you OK?"

I squeeze her hand and nod, even though I'm feeling light-headed. "I'll be fine. Really."

I look up to see Zadkiel leaning heavily on two demons as they guide his enormous, hobbling frame across the Great Hall. He's clutching a hand to his side, and his mouth is twisted into a grimace of pain. When he looks up and spots me, he attempts a smile, but his eyebrows draw together and I see him puff out a heavy breath. Thankfully he's alive.

Liall comes over to us, his hands clasped to his chest. "We have some dead." He tells Cora mournfully in a low voice.

Cora gasps a little, and strangled sob escapes her. "How many?"

"Fifteen so far."

Cora clutches Phoenix to her. "Oh no." She puts a hand over her eyes, and rocks back and forth, to comfort herself as much as the little boy in her arms, I'm sure.

Amryn and Elise cross the Hall, rushing to my side. Elise inspects my shoulder and shakes her head. "This is pretty deep. Those little bastards and their tridents." She looks over my shoulder, at my back, and gasps. "Your back is burned! What happened to you?"

"One of the angels," I reply. "They had this electric stuff, balls of lightning, they were pointing it at Amryn. I intercepted it and it hit me square in the back."

Amryn's face contorts as he looks at me. "I should have had eyes on both of them."

"Hey, what else are big brothers for?" I try to keep my tone light, but I wince and squeeze Juno's hand tighter as Elise's hands warm on me, the glow passing over my skin, healing my wounds.

I cast my eyes over the Hall, the sounds of crying and pain at a constant level. There's a line of bodies at the far end, and my stomach wrenches. Our own, dead. And for what? Why?

I blink as I see a girl covering her face and crying. I recognise her. I know her.

"Tal, hold still," Elise says as I lean forward.

I narrow my eyes, my vision clearing a little. The girl has strawberry blonde hair. Just like -

"Tal, I need you to hold still." Elise insists again.

I lurch to my feet, and Elise protests, but I don't hear what she says. I stumble across the hall. No. It can't be. It can't be.

But it is. The girl is Lorelei's little sister.

I reach the line of dead bodies, seeing faces I know, eyes closed, or open and vacant. The girl is on her knees beside a body and I feel the air leave my lungs.

Lorelei's one blue eye stares up at the ceiling. Her beautiful face is half gone, her skull caved in, wet and red and raw, fragments of bone stuck in flesh. Her strawberry blonde hair is caked with blood. Her hands lie motionless on the floor beside her. Her chest is still, no breath escaping it.

No. No no no no no no.

My legs buckle beneath me, and Lorelei's little sister begins to cry harder. I kneel beside Lorelei, and reach out to take her hand.

Oh no no no. Not Lorelei. Not her. Why her. Not her. Her hand is icy in mine, all the life and warmth already drained from her body.

I'm sorry. I'm so sorry. Lorelei, please come back. I'm sorry. I'm so sorry.

10
Tallesaign

I hear the footsteps approaching but keep my eyes fixed on the funeral pyre. I've kept my distance - Elias made it clear I wasn't welcome - so I sit far away, in the darkness, where no one will see me, where no will notice me. Here I can beat myself up for not shedding a single fucking tear over the woman who shared my bed.

I take a drag of my cigarette, ignoring Amryn as he sits down beside me.

"Hey brother," he says softly.

I don't respond. I take another drag, barely tasting the tobacco, barely aware of the smoke falling from my lips as I exhale. I don't fucking feel *anything*.

"I'm sorry, Tal." Amryn reaches over to me, and I shrug him off.

"Don't touch me."

"OK, I'm sorry." If he's hurt by my response, he doesn't let it show. He's being patient and understanding, and for some reason that makes me, the numbness even worse. "This isn't -"

"Don't fucking say this isn't my fault."

"But Tal, it's *not* your fault."

My head snaps around to look at him. "Do you know where I was?" I ask him. "Do you know what I was doing before the chimera came? Huh?"

Amryn shakes his head, his expression pained.

"I was sitting on my porch with Juno and she had her face against my neck and her hand on my leg and I wanted to take her inside and fuck her," I spit out. I look back at the funeral pyre, rubbing my bottom lip with my thumb, the smoke of my cigarette curling into the cold night sky. "Lorelei didn't deserve this, and I didn't fucking deserve her."

"Tal, come on, that's not why she died."

"Yes it is." I shake my head. "I'm a fucking curse."

"Don't talk like that." Amryn reaches out to put a hand on my shoulder, but thinks better of it, and lets his hand drop. "Tal, you're not a curse. This isn't your fault."

"I couldn't save her." The numbness starts to dissolve, and my chest starts to ache, concave, falling in on itself. A breath rasps out of me, and I throw my cigarette to the ground, stamping it out. "I couldn't save her, or you, or Dad, or Mom."

"Tal, stop." Amryn puts his hand on my shoulder, pressing against it to turn me to face him. "Tal, you can't beat yourself up like this. You wanna feel bad for almost cheating on Lorelei, OK, fine, but that's not why this happened. You didn't fail her. And you didn't fail Mom or Dad either."

"I doubt our father would see it that way." I scoff. "Do you know how often I've gone over and over in my head, like on a fucking loop, wondering what he thought when I couldn't save him? When I wasn't fucking there?"

"Tal, Dad loved you." Amryn insists. "He would never have been ashamed -"

"Do you know who our father was?" I ask. I can feel venom coursing through me. I'm angry. I should stop talking. But the pain that's replacing the numbness is consuming me and I want to hurt more. I want to hurt him too.

Amryn's face twists with sadness. "Tal, I know Dad was difficult -"

"Our father was a *fucking asshole.* He wouldn't let our mother hug me because he said it would make me weak. He had me outside training no matter what, even when I was sick, even when it was raining or freezing or blazing hot. The first time I fucked a girl he beat me senseless, because he was mad I wasn't watching you and Cora."

Amryn's brow furrows, and he squeezes my shoulder. "I'm sorry, I -"

"You fucking idolize him."

"No I don't!" He protests. "I idolized you!"

"Well don't!" I jab my finger in his face. "I'm a piece of shit who couldn't protect his family." My finger darts in the direction of the funeral pyre. "That girl over there is dead and she died loving me, hoping we could be together, and what was I doing? I was thinking about fucking someone else." I rise to my feet, ready to storm off, but Amryn stands in front of me, blocking my way. My little brother, who's not at all little. He's eye to eye with me.

"Tal, you're not a piece of shit." He says, putting his hands on my shoulders. "You're allowed to make mistakes. It doesn't make you weak, or a failure."

"You ever do that to Cora?" I ask.

"What?"

"Think about cheating on her."

Amryn shakes his head and laughs incredulously. "You know what, yeah, I did, strictly speaking. I didn't just think about it. I did. A few times."

I frown at him, and scoff. "I don't believe you."

"Well, it's true. With Ceili as a matter of fact." Amryn says. "And plenty of other girls, in one way or another. Anyone who'd look at me, anyone who showed even an ounce of interest in me. Because I wanted to push away everything I felt for Cora, and because I was fucking terrified of being alone for the rest of my life."

"That's completely different," I reply, waving my hand dismissively. "She was married to someone else, you weren't cheating on her."

"I still thought about being with someone else when I loved her."

"Well I didn't love Lorelei, so... I don't know if that makes it better or worse." The words taste sour as I say them. I didn't love her. What the fuck was I thinking?

"You're not the first man to sleep with someone they don't love." Amryn says. "I did it too. You think I loved Ceili? I cared about her, but she wasn't Cora. It was completely different."

I run a hand over my face. "Lorelei deserved better."

"Well, fuck, Tal, what am I supposed to tell you? Yeah, she did. I'd like to think you'd have done the right thing, but maybe you wouldn't have." Amryn looks over at the funeral pyre. "You and Juno, you've got - I dunno. A thing. Everyone can see it. It's like a thread between the two of you." He looks back at me, his expression earnest. "But that did not get Lorelei killed. You, finding someone, finding someone to - to stop that ache, someone that made you feel something, that didn't kill Lorelei. Those fucking chimera did."

"All I can think about, yeah?" I cross my arms over my chest. "All I can think about now is that it's tainted the thing with Juno. That if something happens now, it'll be wrong."

"It won't be," Amryn insists. "Please don't punish yourself for this. You don't deserve it."

"Yes I do." I jam my hands into my pockets and walk away from him, into the darkness, away from the fires burning our dead, burning the body of a woman who still had a whole life ahead of her.

My cabin wasn't damaged in the fires, but the cabins around it are either damaged or gone. Ebony and Liall are staying with Cora and Amryn now, after their place burned down. After Phoenix nearly died in the fire. After Juno saved him.

Juno.

My heart does that fucking jolt thing in my chest again as I think of her. Fuck this all.

It's like a thread between the two of you.

140

I want her and I don't know why. And I feel nothing but guilt and shame over it.

Of course she's waiting outside my cabin when I get there. I've tried to avoid her since the attack, I couldn't face it. Now she's here, forcing me to face her, forcing me to confront everything I'm feeling.

I hate this, and I love it. I want her to go away and I want her to stay forever. I can't fucking explain any of it.

Juno rises to her feet as I approach the cabin, pulling her coat around herself. I don't say a word as I climb the porch steps, throwing myself down onto the bench beside her and pulling out two cigarettes, lighting them and handing her one as she sits back down. I'm smoking too much, but I don't care.

Juno takes the cigarette, and I can feel her eyes on me. "I'm sorry about your friend. She was so young."

"Too young to be burning up on a funeral pyre, yeah," I say bitterly. I sigh and look over at her, the light from the porch illuminating her from behind, her hair glowing deep red. "I'm sorry. I'm being an ass."

"Please, don't apologize," she says quickly. "What's just happened, it's terrible."

"I should feel more, but I don't. I keep telling myself I feel more, I have to feel more. But I don't. I'm sad but - but I didn't love her."

"You don't have to have loved her to be sad she's gone." Juno inhales on the cigarette, blowing the smoke away, and she puts a hand on my arm. "You cared about her, and that's enough." She sighs. "I feel guilty."

I turn my head to look at her. "Why?"

"Because I was here, with you, and you weren't, well, you weren't -" She takes her hand from my arm. "I shouldn't have been flirting with you, that was wrong."

"I should have stopped you." I rub my hands together and look out into the night, the smell of the funeral pyres still carried on the breeze. "But the truth is, I didn't want to. And that's what's killing me. I was going to..."

"What were you going to do?" Juno asks when I don't continue.

I shake my head. "It doesn't matter."

"It matters to me."

I spin around to face her. "What is this? This - this -" I gesture back and forth between us helplessly. "*This*. What is it? Because since you've been here, you're all I can think about. And I can't explain why. It makes no sense."

"You think it's different for me?" She asks. "I've dreamed of your face, and I knew you. When you told me I was safe with you, I knew you'd said those words to me before."

"That's not possible."

"Don't tell me what I know!" She cries. "I've forgotten so much, I know nothing about myself, but I know, I know it in my bones, in my soul, that you are a part of me."

No. It can't be. I shake my head. "It's not possible, Juno. You were scared and alone and I just happened to rescue you, that's why you feel -"

Her slap catches me off guard, and when my eyes flash to hers I can see she's shocked herself. Her hand flies to her mouth, and she shakes her head. "I'm - oh god, I'm so sorry." She gets to her feet, and scrambles off the porch.

I hesitate for a split second before I follow her. "Juno, wait."

"No, I'm sorry." She keeps walking. "I'll stay away, I will, I'm sorry." She's sobbing now.

"Juno, please stop." I say, but she keeps on walking. I don't even know where she's going. She's just headed into the darkness, away from me, her hands to her face. "Juno, wait."

"Please leave me alone."

"I'm not going to do that." I reach out a hand and grab her shoulder, turning her around to face me. "Juno, wait."

"No." She shrugs out of my grasp but stops walking. "I'm sorry." She says again, her head hanging, her hands to her forehead. "This feeling drives me crazy. I want you, all the time. Being with you is all that makes sense to me. And it's just another thing on my list of things I cannot remember, and I hate it."

I take a deep breath, and reach out to her. She doesn't resist. I pull her closer, and her face tips up to mine. "What you said, about love..."

"An echo of a love that two souls remember," she says, and my eyes have adjusted to the darkness enough to see the sad smile on her face.

"Is that what you feel when you look at me?" I ask quietly, pulling her even closer, so she's against me. I can feel her heart pounding in her chest.

"I - I don't know. I don't know. I feel it, this pull, here." She puts her hand over my heart. "But I don't know. I want to be close to you, that's all I know. And with what just happened, I know - I know the time wouldn't be right for more."

My heart does a little flip at her words. "More?"

"What you wanted to do," she says slowly, "on the porch. With me. I may not have any memories but I'm not stupid." She leans her head against my chest and sighs. "Please just let me be close to you. Maybe, maybe things will make sense again soon. If we just stay close to each other."

"I heard your voice," I tell her, putting my arms around her. "In my dreams. I heard you calling for help. Like you were calling out for me."

"I told you," she says softly, gazing up at me. "I told you that you knew I was up there. You came to find me."

"Maybe I did." I stroke the sides of her face gently with my fingers. "And I did want that. The other night."

"You wanted me in your bed."

I nod. "Yeah."

"Do you still want that?"

I suck in a breath. "I think you know I do. But right now -"

"No, I know." She nuzzles into me again. "Like I said, just let me be close. I don't want to be away from you."

"You can stay with me, in my cabin." I know as I say it that it's probably a bad idea. If she crawls into bed with me again...

"Thank you." She murmurs.

The stars twinkle above us as the clouds race across the navy blue expanse, and I try desperately to push away the guilt I feel - Juno is here, warm in my arms, while Lorelei

144

burns away in a nearby field. I wonder if that guilt will ever go away.

Juno is sleeping on my couch. I stand and watch her, wondering if this is creepy but she's so beautiful I can't look away. Fuck this is all confusing.

She insisted on sleeping out here, insisted she wouldn't take my bed. I heard her cry out once in her sleep, but she went quiet again after that. I was grateful that I didn't have a reason to go and ask her if she wanted to sleep with me after all. I know she wouldn't have said no, and I know... I give myself a shake, and suppress the desire that courses through my limbs.

Juno shifts in her sleep and the blanket falls away a little, revealing that she's naked underneath, the curve of her breast and a soft tan nipple coming into view. *Fuck.* I dig my nails into my palms, and stare, and entertain the thoughts of what I want to do to her right now for way too fucking long. *Stop it.*

In the kitchen I try to make as much noise as possible to wake her up, so she doesn't realise I've been a pervert while she's been asleep. I slam the kettle on the stove, turning the flame on to boil water. I pull out two plates, clattering them on to the counter. I glance back over to the couch, and see her head moving at the end of it, her hair spilling over the armrest.

"Tal?" Her voice drifts across the room as she sits up, blinking at me, rubbing her eyes. "It's morning already?"

"Sure is," I say, grinning at her.

She rises from the couch, the blanket pulled around her, and she shuffles across the wood floor towards the kitchen. She walks up behind me, and lays herself against my back, sleepy and warm. *Fuck. Fuck.* This isn't going to be easy.

Being noble is too fucking difficult.

"How did you sleep?" She asks me, and an arm wraps around my waist.

"Fine, and you?"

"Better, being close to you." She says with a sigh, and the other arm wraps around my waist. The blanket falls around our feet.

Fuck. My hands flex on the counter. Don't turn around. *Don't fucking turn around.* Oh god, she's naked against me and her breasts are pressing against my back and she's so fucking warm, and I'm just a horny teenager who got old, aren't I.

I try to keep my breathing even as I run my hands over her arms. "You should get dressed before you get cold, baby."

"M-mmm," she says, shaking her head against me. "You can keep me warm."

"I thought last night we said -"

"That was last night," she interjects, her hands moving over my stomach, fingers straying into the waistband of my pants. "Today is a new day, *Zhizn Moya.*"

Her hand strays further, and I pull away before she reaches what she's looking for, spinning around to seize her in my arms.

Eyes up. *Eyes fucking UP.*

"Juno -"

She rolls her eyes. "Yes, I know, you're being a noble man, it's good." She sighs. "I'm sorry, I know we agreed the timing was wrong."

"I just want it to be... I don't know. Right. Not like this."

"Can I kiss you?" She asks me, pressing herself against me harder.

Oh fuck, if you kiss me now, when we're like this... But I want to. I want to know that everything I'm feeling is real. "Sure, if you like."

She wraps her arms around my neck, and pushes her mouth against mine, softly, sweetly. Shivers of ecstasy run down my back as her lips part for me, and her tongue runs over mine tentatively.

Oh god. *Fuck.*

Everything I feel sure as fuck is real, right along with her breasts against my bare chest. My hands move down her back, stopping just short of her ass because I know if I cross that line, it'll be over.

She deepens the kiss, becoming more urgent, and I suppress a groan. I want to pick her up and carry her to the bedroom and -

She draws back from me, smiling, her brown eyes sparkling. "That was nice."

"Yes it was." *Would have been nicer if it could go on though.* I don't say that part out loud, not that I need to. I'm sure she can feel exactly what she's doing to me.

"I should get dressed." She says, and steps out of my arms. Walking totally naked across the kitchen, she gives me a full view of her tiny waist, round ass and milky smooth skin.

Oh god I am so fucked.

There's a knock at the door, and I take a deep breath to try and calm myself down. *Shit.* The knock sounds again, thankfully killing the bulge that's grown in my sweatpants. *Goddammit, Tal, get a grip.*

I open the door to Amryn, and his expression has me worried instantly. "What's going on, brother?"

"We have a situation," he tells me.

"What situation?"

"Elias has lost his shit, and I don't think this is going to end well." He jerks his head in the direction of the Great Hall. "Get dressed, we need to go."

Juno looks at me questioningly as I rush into the bedroom. "There's problems in the village," I tell her, "Cora and Amryn need me."

Most of the village is in the square when we get there, and Juno keeps a hold of my hand as we go. Cora is arguing with Elias, whose face is bright red. His other children are cowering behind him, bags at their feet, tears streaming down their faces, clinging to each other as their father rages.

"What's going on?" I ask as I reach Cora's side.

Elias's eyes flash from me to Juno, and he looks down at our joined hands. "Didn't take you long to get over my daughter, did it, you fucking pig?"

"Elias, we know you're upset, you just lost your child, and -" Cora holds up her hands, trying to calm the situation.

"You have no idea how I feel!" Elias screams. "This whole fucking village is falling apart because of you!"

"This isn't what Lorelei would have wanted," Cora says, "this was her home and your kids have their whole lives here."

"Don't take my daughter's name in your mouth, you fucking bitch!" He hisses, jabbing his finger in her face.

"Elias, please -" Cora pleads, and Elias's hand shoots out to hit her.

I drop Juno's hand to lunge forward, and I see Amryn moving out of the corner of my eye, but there's no need for us. Cora has Elias by the throat, holding him aloft, his feet dangling a few inches off the ground. Her eyes have gone blank white as she stares at him.

"Elias," she says in a low voice, "you wanna know what happened to the last man who hit me?"

Elias garbles and gurgles, his hands flailing at Cora's arms. His other children are crying and wailing, covering their faces with their hands.

"He ended up as a pile of ashes that scattered to the winds somewhere in Nilau." Cora lowers him to the ground but keeps a grip on his throat. "Now, I don't want to do that to you because you just lost your daughter, and your other kids are watching. So, you need to calm the fuck down, do you understand me?" Cora turns and glances over her shoulder. "Can someone get these kids out of here?"

Elise and Fenella hurry out of the crowd, and put their arms around Elias's kids. "Come on, *mes filles*," Fenella says warmly, dabbing the tears from the smallest girl's face with the lacy sleeve of her dress. "I have cookies at my house. Let's get you all comfortable, *oui*?"

"You leave my kids alone!" Elias screams, his voice breaking under Cora's grip around his throat. "You stay away from them, you fucking witches!"

"I told you to behave yourself," Cora warns again as the girls are guided out of the square.

"Or what?" Elias hisses.

Amryn laughs out loud and shakes his head. "You're really looking for a beating, aren't you?"

"You think I'm scared of you?" Elias bares his teeth at Cora. "You think I'm afraid of some degenerate fucking bitch like you?"

Amryn takes a step forward but stops short as Cora looks over her shoulder at him. *Stop.* Her command rings through the blood bond to both of us, and her gaze moves back to Elias.

"My Draw is aching to kick your ass," she says in that low, lethal voice that even makes me a little nervous. "And the only reason I'm not letting him is because I'm a parent myself and I cannot even begin to imagine the pain you're in right now."

"Fuck you." Elias spits in her face, and Amryn is positively bristling with rage.

"You will go and calm down," Cora says. "You will take time to grieve and care for your kids, and then you can decide if you still want to be a part of this clan."

"This clan," Elias says with a sneer, his eyes darting around to the other demons. "This fucking clan, what good have you ever done any of us?"

"I said, go and calm down." Cora releases his neck and steps back from him. "Go on."

Elias stumbles backwards, his face twisted in grief and anger. He seems almost drunk, ambling from side to side, as though unsure of which direction to go in.

"I don't want this man in the village anymore," Amryn says quietly.

"We need to give him time." Cora gazes up at him. "He's just gone through something awful and -"

Suddenly Elias roars, summoning a flame and firing it directly at Cora. I reach out to grab her and pull her out of the way at the same time that Amryn leaps into the path of the flame.

Cora slams into me as the flames tear across Amryn's shoulder. Amryn's hand flies to his neck as he staggers sideways.

"Hold him down!" I call, and several warriors rush forward to seize Elias and pin him to the ground, where he's raging and garbling wildly.

Cora spins around and rushes to Amryn's side. He grabs on to her arm, and sags heavily against her.

"Tal, he's hurt badly," she says to me, panic wringing her voice. "I have to take him to Elise."

"Go, go, I've got this." I assure her, watching as she drapes Amryn's arm over her shoulder. I turn back to Elias, who is still surrounded by warriors, and even though he's still sneering, his face is marred by fear as I stand over him and summon a flame.

"You shouldn't have done that." The warriors step back a little. "Attacking the Queen and injuring a Draw, who also happens to be my brother. Not a wise move."

"You're gonna kill me, huh?" Spittle runs down his chin as he laughs bitterly. "Lorelei would love that, what a fucking hero her one true love turned out to be." His eyes move to Juno, and he looks her up and down, his nose wrinkling. "At least you found this piece of ass to replace her quick huh? Although, a mutilated fucking angel like this one should be glad anyone would look at her, even a half breed piece of shit like you."

I bare my teeth and move to seize him, but suddenly a hand is on my arm, in the orange flames leaping from my hands. Juno's eyes meet mine, and the flames aren't hurting her, not even a little.

"Tallesaign." Her voice is soft, soothing and cool. "He's not worth it."

"Fuck you." Elias spits blood at us both.

"I'm all that's stopping you from being a pile of ash right now, you watch your mouth." Juno scolds him. Her eyes soften as they meet mine again. "*Zhizn Moya*, please. This will not help Amryn, or this man's poor children." She puts a hand to my cheek. "They need their father."

I take a deep breath, the well of her eyes drawing me in. My flames extinguish, and I straighten, looking at the warriors standing guard around us.

"Lock him up," I say to them, "the Queen will deal with him later."

"Deal with me, huh?" Elias asks scornfully. "Execute

me, you mean?"

"Listen to me," I say, leaning over him. "You are causing trouble where there's already more than enough and -"

"Whose fault is that?" He's hysterical, almost screaming. "Everyone's scared! Everyone's angry! Look at everything that's going on! And you? The Queen and her fucking dual Draws. What do you do? Nothing!"

Murmurs come up from the crowd, and I turn to look at them all in disbelief. "Who thinks like him?" Eyes avoid me, shaking heads. "Anyone? Because if you do, speak up." The demons begin to disband, leaving the square, giving Elias filthy looks, tutting at him.

"What is wrong with you all?" Elias screams at them all, desperate for agreement, for one voice to validate the rage he's feeling.

"They see sense," I tell him, " they don't want another war."

"We're in another war!" He rakes his hands through his hair. "My daughter, my beautiful daughter, she didn't deserve to die. All those people, they didn't deserve to die. Why? For what?"

"Of course they didn't, but this, all of this?" I gesture to him with my hand. "This isn't going to help." I nod to the warriors. "Get him out of here."

They haul Elias to his feet, who protests for only a moment before he collapses into incoherent garbling. Even through the rage, I can't help but feel sorry for him. He's an asshole, but he's an asshole who just lost his kid.

I know he's right, in a way. Whether or not we want it,

something has it out for us. Something wants to hurt us. Ocario is no longer sacred ground that can't be touched by malice - we seem to be fair game.

I put a hand to my chest, realizing my breath is heaving out of me. A soft hand touches my shoulder, and I look down to see Juno's brown eyes gazing at me.

Amryn. Shit. "Come on." I say, pulling Juno along behind me.

Ebony is sitting outside Fenella's cabin when we reach it, Phoenix perched on her knee, and Elias's youngest daughter playing at her feet with a small tea set. She gives us a weak smile. "He's OK, Fenella is treating him now."

I breathe a small sigh of relief. "Good."

She waves towards the door. "You should go in, Cora was looking a little pale."

I nod, running my hand over Phoenix's black curls before I push the cabin door open. Amryn is sitting on a green velvet chair in the middle of the circular room, Fenella hovering over him, her hands glowing softly as she heals the burn that snakes over his shoulder, down his arm and back. Cora is kneeled beside him, clutching his hand, and she swallows hard as her eyes meet mine.

Amryn's head lifts as I walk in, and he smiles weakly. "Hey brother."

I gesture to his wound. "Hope that ink survives a burn like that."

He chuckles. "I'll be pissed if it doesn't."

Cora rolls her eyes. "Trust you two to be worried about tattoos at a time like this."

"It's either laugh or cry, baby." Amryn reaches out to trace a finger down her cheek. "Come on, I'll be OK. Fenella's got this."

Fenella nods and smiles, her eyes staying on the wound. She begins to hum quietly as she works. The cabin smells of lavender, and it's toasty warm. I walk to one of the round windows and look outside, seeing Ebony, Phoenix and Elias's youngest daughter trying to catch the snowflakes that have started to fall again from the gray sky.

Juno walks in, and Fenella smiles at her, still humming, a little louder now, so I can make out the tune. Amryn's eyes close as his head tips back, and the wound begins to fade, giving way to fresh skin that shimmers under Fenella's hands. Cora lays her head on Amryn's lap, and he gently strokes her hair.

Everything is calm, and quiet, the soft lilac glow of Fenella's hands illuminating the inside of the cabin as the sky outside darkens, heavy snow clouds rolling in.

And then the hairs on the back of my neck stand up. I recognise the tune Fenella is humming.

All those years ago, sitting outside the nursery as my mother rocked my baby brother, my stomach wrenching as I longed for someone to hold me, to show me tenderness, to hold my hand and sing to me.

The tune Fenella is humming is the tune my mother hummed to Amryn. The tune only she knew. The tune I've never heard anywhere else, before or since.

"Fenella," I say, "that song you're humming. What is it? It sounds so familiar."

She smiles, her eyes remaining on Amryn. "An old

tune from the lowlands. I sang it to my children, when they were babies."

"Did you teach it to my mother?" I ask.

Elise springs up from her chair and rushes over to Juno, who has perched on a chair close to me, next to the window. "How's your back, sweetheart?"

Juno nods. "Much better, thank you."

"She's healed really well," I say. "Her back's completely smooth now."

Elise turns to me with a raised eyebrow. "And you know this how?"

A flush rises in my cheeks as all eyes in the room turn to me. "I, uh -"

Elise rolls her eyes as Juno takes my hand, giggling. "Tal, you are incorrigible."

"We didn't do anything!" I feel like a kid again. "She told me it was better!"

"Sure she did." Elise says, shaking her head. Giggles erupt from the others, and Cora covers her mouth with her hand as she looks at me apologetically, trying to hide her grin.

"Where's Daddy?" A voice comes from the next room, and one of Elias's daughters is standing there. She's twirling a strand of her hair around her finger, her eyes wide as she looks around at us all. She can't be more than 12 years old.

"Your Daddy needed to go and calm down," I tell her. "He just needs a little time."

"He wants us to leave." The girl swallows hard, and she

bites her lip. Poor kid. "I don't want to go. This is my home. But Daddy's so angry."

Elise goes to the girl's side and puts an arm around her. "Daddy will calm down, don't you worry." The girl wraps her arms around Elise's waist, burrowing into her, and Elise's face twists with pain for a moment as she puts her arms around the child.

I wonder where Elias will go, where he'll take these poor kids, who've lost their mother and now their sister, and what kind of life they'll have. As much as I want him to go and take his bullshit with him, for the sake of his daughters I can't help but hope he just calms down and focuses on them instead of his rage.

11
Cora

nowflakes flutter from the sky as I walk across the dark field. I only ever see him over here. He doesn't seem to like anyone else. It's strange, he loves the Earth Realm so much, but he always wants to watch from a distance, never get involved, never interact.

My boots crunch in the snow, and I pull my coat tighter around me. Arax continues to spew red smoke. It's almost normal now, it's hardly even worth noticing anymore. I wonder for a moment if it will ever stop.

The scholars have said the serpents on top of the mountain are a sign of trouble, and I had to restrain myself from throwing their ridiculously oversized books out of the window. A serpent-topped mountain - what could be good about that?

My lungs burn as I inhale deeply, the only thing lighting my way out here is the soft glowing light from my veins. I wish he wouldn't make me walk all the way out here, it's dark, cold and late, I just want to go and crawl into bed beside my husband.

My hand strays over my stomach. I haven't told him

yet. With Phoenix, I told him immediately, as soon as I knew, because of his fears of what Morgan had done to him. This time I'm nervous about telling him, and I don't know why. We wanted another baby, we've been trying for a couple of years now.

Amryn loves being a father. Phoenix is the best thing to happen to us, besides each other. And yet...

"You're glowing, Cora." The voice makes me jump.

"Why do you always have to startle me?" I ask, and his white beard twitches as he chuckles.

"You need to be alert at all times." He says, and his eyes twinkle as he looks down at me. "You really are glowing though."

"Thanks."

"Congratulations." He gives me a warm smile.

"Thanks." I shift on my feet. I hate that he knows and Amryn doesn't. It feels so wrong. "Unfortunately I'm not really getting to enjoy it, you know? With everything that's been going on here."

"Yes, you have been having some trouble." He holds up a hand, casting it over him in a wave, and a carpet of starlight strays through the air above us. "That should help."

"What was that?"

"A protection spell, the old one has become weak in the face of the new threats Ocario faces." He puts an arm around my shoulder, and we look up at the night sky. "There is a change coming, my dear."

"Azrael said that Gabriel was trying to stir up trouble in

the Halls." I give him a side glance. "Trying to turn them against me, saying I'm a violation of Fate."

"Well, if anyone had anything to say about that it would be Azrael, being the angel of Fate, and he is on your side." The Old God says, squeezing my shoulders. "He was beautiful once, can you believe it? When the witches corrupted the Line, they weakened him. Uriel healed him, but he remained as he is now. A sign of the corruption that remains."

"Will it ever go away?"

The Old God sighs heavily. "Perhaps."

"You're not filling me with hope here."

He chuckles softly. "I'm sorry, my child. I'm not very good at this anymore."

"I don't want another war." I say quietly.

"Then perhaps you should talk to Gabriel directly."

I can't help the gasp that escapes me. "You are joking."

He shakes his head. "No, I'm not. He can't hurt you, and he won't, believe me. Azrael and Zadkiel will be there, and they will definitely keep him in line. I think it would be best to speak to him directly."

"He's behind all this shit isn't he?"

"Yes." A pause, and he shrugs a little. "And no."

"Will you stop being cryptic?" I shrug his arm off. "I'm cold and tired and I just lost 15 of my people in this village. I thought my son was dead for way too many minutes and I just need to know what's going on."

"Alright." He takes a step towards me, eyeing me carefully. "The chimera, they were Gabriel's. He sent

160

them. But the rest of it..." He shakes his head.

"The serpents? The Purge?" I spread my hands, waiting for an answer. "You're telling me that's something else?"

The Old God looks over towards Arax. "The last time that mountain threw up red smoke was almost 40 years ago." He looks back down at me. "Everything is connected, in ways we do not always expect. The Earth and the Flame will meet again, and when they do, their memories will change this Realm and every other one, in ways we cannot begin to fathom."

I growl in frustration as he disappears into thin air. "Thanks a lot!" I call to the sky, and I am answered with a flash of lightning. "Yeah, you heard me." I stalk away, hugging myself as the chill of the night envelops me.

Fucking cryptic bullshit. My head throbs, trying to figure it all out. *Everything is connected, in ways we do not always expect.* I need to ask Elise about Arax smoking red years ago, what happened when it last did.

And Gabriel coming here? Fuck that. But I know the Old God is going to send him either way. I just hope we have some warning. Angels love just showing up. Ugh. I rub my temple, feeling a headache come on. I just need to get to my warm cabin, and my husband.

Warm light spills from our windows, and I walk faster, eager to get out of these boots and warm my hands by the fire. I hurry up the porch steps, pushing the door open.

Amryn is asleep on the couch, his arm behind his head, his long black hair spilling down almost to the floor. I watch him as I take off my coat and boots. Every time I see him like this, I can't believe how beautiful he is, and that he's mine. I grin as I wonder if this feeling will ever go away, or if we'll still be like this when we're old and grey. I hope so.

The cabin is quiet, and it's so late I'm sure Ebony and Liall are fast asleep by now. I strip down to just my t-shirt and panties, and crawl over Amryn, pressing my lips against his rock-hard stomach. He stirs, a hand straying over my head, and I gaze up at him, his hazel eyes meeting mine.

"Hey baby." He puts a hand against my cheek. "You're freezing." He pulls me up against him, and I lay my head on his chest, breathing a deep sigh of relief at being back in his arms. "You OK?"

I nod. "Yeah."

"Old God being a dick again?"

"Mysterious as always," I say with a sigh.

Amryn chuckles as he kisses my head. "Why does he always have to do this to you?"

"He has more faith in my problem-solving skills than I do evidently." I trace small circles on his chest with my fingertips. "I love you."

He clutches me a little tighter. "I love you, too."

I raise my head to look at him. "Amryn, I have to tell you something."

"What is it, baby?"

Baby. Yeah. Exactly that. But as I look at him, I can't say it. Why don't I want to tell him? What is wrong with me?

"The Old God wants Gabriel to come here to talk to me." I say instead.

Amryn's eyebrows shoot up. "Fucking what?"

"I know, I know." I spread my hands on his chest. "I reacted the same way. But he's said he'll send Azrael and Zadkiel along. Gabriel can't hurt me anyway."

"What the fuck could we possibly have to discuss with Gabriel?"

"The whole Fate thing, set him straight, and with Azrael there maybe he'll just stop."

Amryn laughs bitterly. "Yeah, sure, Gabriel's going to stop because his brother tells him he's being a dick."

"It's worth a try."

"It's not worth shi-"

I smother his mouth with mine. He tenses, considering protesting for a second, and then he melts against me. His hands are in my hair as he holds me to him, his lips opening, warm and inviting. I don't want to think about this anymore tonight. I just want to be with him.

"That's not fair," he says when we part, his eyes closed as he grins. "You know what that does to me."

"Yes I do." I grind against him, feeling him swell underneath me. "That's exactly what I want right now." I kiss him again, deeper, more urgently, and he groans softly.

"What do you want?" He asks, grinning, his eyes still closed.

"I want you to take me to bed and fuck me."

He opens his eyes, his hands still in my hair. "We gotta be quiet."

"Ebony and Liall are deep sleepers," I murmur against

his lips. "Now take me to bed."

"Whatever you say, baby."

12
Tallesaign

I can't sleep.

Every time I close my eyes, there's a wall of stone in front of me, the overwhelming smell of dirt, nothing but hot, fetid air in my lungs. I'm so damn tired of this. My head throbs, and my throat is dry. I just want to fucking sleep.

I stretch my limbs out across the bed, an impossible expanse, wide and yawning and speaking of all the emptiness I feel. I hate lying here alone. I hate lying here, knowing she's right *there*. I want to carry her back to this bed and finish what she started in the kitchen this morning. It's more than lust - it's longing.

Footsteps pad softly down the hallway, bare feet on the wood floor. I raise my head, and Juno walks in, tentatively. Without a word she crawls in beside me, under my arm, and snuggles against me.

"Can't sleep?" I ask her, burying my face in her hair, breathing her in.

"No." She spreads her hand on my chest. "It's lonely

out there."

"It was lonely in here, until a moment ago."

She nuzzles into my neck, and heat floods my groin. I clutch her closer, seeking out her mouth. I know we said we'd wait, I know we said it was wrong, but fuck, this is too much.

I lean over her, and she's flat on the bed, my fingers entwined with hers. She sighs as my lips trace her jawline, her back arching as she presses her body against mine.

The cold sheet startles me awake as I roll over, and my hand reaches across the bed, realizing the space beside me is empty. I roll flat onto my back, exhaling heavily. *Fuck.* I finally get to sleep and I dream of her, of course. This is killing me.

Soft footsteps come down the hallway.

"If you're a dream, I don't want it." I call.

The footsteps pause, and then I hear a giggle. "Shall I come in and pinch you to prove I'm real?"

"Sure, only if you pinch me really hard though."

Juno walks into my bedroom, and she leans against the door frame. "Where would you like this pinch?"

"My mouth." I reply, raising my head.

She walks over and climbs on to the bed, and then she fucking straddles me. She leans down over me, the curtain of her hair blocking the moonlight, cocooning us in. She nips at my lower lip, and I can feel her mouth turning up in a grin as I suck in a breath.

"Am I real?"

"Not sure yet." I reply, feeling like I'm about to

explode. "Maybe give it another try?"

She giggles, and kisses me again, slowly this time. *Fuck.* I'm going to fucking float away. Her lips are soft and warm, her tongue tracing over mine. Goddamn, I love kissing. I love kissing *her.*

"And now?" She asks, brushing her lips along my cheek. "Is it real?"

My hands move down her back to her ass, and my cock is straining underneath her, I know she can feel it. She grinds against me gently, and I groan.

"Tell me something real." She whispers against my ear. "Tell me something about you."

"What do you want to know?"

"Anything. Everything."

"I hate the heat," I reply, moving my hands under the thin tank top she's wearing, over her back, her smooth back that doesn't bear any wounds anymore. "I like the cold. And I like rainy days better than sunny ones."

"Mmmm." She lays her head against the crook of my neck, tracing my collarbone with her fingertips. "What else?"

My head is swimming, clouded with desire. My hands run down her back, around the curve of her waist. "I hate blueberries."

She shakes gently as she laughs on top of me. "So do I." She raises her head, her hand moving to my cheek. "Have you ever been in love?"

I shake my head. "You?" Fucking idiot. "Sorry, that was a stupid question."

"I think so." She replies. "With you. In another life." She grinds against me again, and I exhale heavily. I want her so badly. I need her.

I've never needed anyone like this before in my life.

"My hands," I say to her, my fingers running up her back, into her hair, "they used to ache. All the time. I could barely move them." I brush my mouth against her neck, feeling her pulse quickening. "But then I found you. I held you. And they stopped aching." She sighs as I kiss her throat, her hands behind my head, holding me against her.

"Tell me something else."

"I want to be inside you." My teeth seize her earlobe gently, and she shivers deliciously as a shower of goosebumps courses down her arms. I press myself upwards, against the heat I can feel between her thighs. "Do you want that too?"

She moans, and the sound has me harder than steel. God fucking *damn*.

She kisses me again, hard this time, deep and passionate. "Yes, Tal." Fuck I love how she says my name. "I want that too." She lets out a breathy laugh as I press open-mouthed kisses to her throat, tasting her skin. "I can't even remember if I've ever done this before, it will be almost like my first time."

Her words tear me straight out of the moment, and the anvil of guilt I've been carrying for the past few days lands with a thud in my chest. I throw my arms down onto the bed, and she raises her head quickly.

"Tal?" She asks. "Did I do something wrong?"

"No, I just -" I run a hand over my face. Fuck it all. "I'm sorry, it's just - I don't want to take advantage of you."

Juno shakes her head. "No, no, you're not. I want this too."

"You don't know who you are." I push against her thighs, and she climbs off me. I don't want to admit what's going on, why I really need to get out from underneath her right now.

"What does that have to do with anything? I have no memories so I can't make a decision like this? I can't decide that I want you?"

I pull myself up, leaning back against the headboard. "I don't know, it just feels -"

"That's not it, is it?" She interjects, her body tense, perched at the edge of the bed. "It's the girl, Lorelei. You feel guilt."

I reach out to take her hand, and she yanks it away. I lean back against the headboard with a sigh. "I'm sorry."

"You need to stop being sorry." She rises from the bed, and I move quickly after her as she crosses the bedroom.

"Juno, please -"

"No." She spins on her heel, and her eyes gaze up at me, wide, angry. "I want you. I thought you wanted me."

"I do." I take her hand. "I do, I want you more than anything."

"But this guilt, it stops you." She shakes her head.

"Yes," I say with a sigh. "I'm sorry."

"Stop it." She pulls her hand away from mine. "I don't want you to be sorry anymore. I want you to be happy."

She turns and storms out of the room.

I'm tempted to follow her, but I think better of it, sinking back into my bed. We both need to cool down. After I ruined the moment. I lay flat on my back, the cool air washing over me. I suck in a deep breath and close my eyes.

You're a fucking idiot, Tal.

Somehow, I need to let this guilt go.

Juno is sitting at the kitchen table when I walk out of my bedroom the next morning. She's wrapped in one of my sweaters, her knees pulled up against her chest, her bare feet curled over the edge of the chair. Her red hair cascades down over her shoulder, and she's so beautiful it hurts.

I'm a fool. I could have had her last night, I could have woken up in her arms.

"Good morning." She says, her eyes avoiding mine.

"Morning." I walk to her side, and put two fingers under her chin, tipping her face up to look at me. Her eyes are sad. "You look beautiful this morning." I give her a crooked smile.

"Thank you." In one sudden movement she's thrown her legs down off the chair and her arms are around my waist, her face pressed against my stomach. "I should have been more understanding last night. I'm sorry, that was wrong of me."

"Please don't apologize," I stroke her red hair. "I'm

sorry I hurt you. I really am. It felt so good and I ruined it."

"No, you were right. We agreed and said we would wait and then I - I did that." She gazes up at me. "I just - I was so lonely out here. I wanted to be with you."

"I know, honey." I stroke her cheek gently. "It'll be OK. The right time will come."

"I want you to tell me more about yourself." She says. "I want to know everything I can about you, if I can't know anything about myself."

"What do you want to know?"

Her fingers trace the scar on my chest. "What happened here?"

I sigh, and sink down into the chair opposite her. "It happened the day my father was killed."

She sucks in a breath. "Oh god. You don't have to tell me."

"No, it's OK." I run a hand through my hair. "Our village was attacked, because the rival clans found out about Cora, being the Shadow Queen. The idea was to kill her, and my brother, but one of the clan leaders thought better of it, and decided he'd claim them for himself instead."

Juno's brow furrows. "Why?"

"Power." I say with a shrug. "He married Cora off to his son, and kept Amryn close as his Draw. He knew they'd make each other more powerful, and he wanted to corrupt that."

"And you?"

I frown, reaching across the table, and her hand meets mine. "I was trying to save them." I swallow hard as their screams fill my head. "I was running, trying to catch up to them. Amryn was calling for me, saying he was scared."

Elspeth! Do it now!

I clench my eyes shut. I'm still remembering it wrong. "My father, I was almost in his sight, I was running and then -"

"Elspeth! They'll kill him!"

"I can't!" She's sobbing. I can hear her.

"Tal!" Amryn's crying, and Cora is screaming. "Tal!"

I'm coming, Amryn. I'm coming. My legs won't move faster. I pull my scimitar from my back.

"Elspeth! Do it now!"

I see a flash of flames over the boulder. I'm almost there.

"Tal!" Cora's little voice is shredded with fear. Fuck. I'm coming, kiddo. I'm almost there.

"Elspeth! You have to do it now!"

"I'll hurt him!"

"He's your son!" My Dad's voice is strained. "You have to do it NOW!"

The flash of green hits me in the chest, and my lungs are emptied of air instantly. I can't scream. I can't move. I can't do anything.

What the fuck is this?

The acid burn chews at my skin, at my bones. I'm going to die. Tears run down my cheeks. Fuck, fuck, I'm going to die.

Amryn and Cora are screaming. My mother is sobbing. She screams my father's name as a rush of flames explodes over the boulder in front of me.

He's dead, I know he is. I feel it.

Astrid calls out, assuring the little ones, telling Cora everything will be OK. Her voice is cut off suddenly, and Cora's high-pitched scream sends chills through me.

I try to move.

I have to move.

They need me.

"Tal?" Juno grips my hand tight. "Are you OK?"

I shake my head, breathing heavily. "I don't know."

"You were suddenly gone," she says, her face twisted with concern.

I lean back in my chair, trying to regain my composure, trying to catch my breath. "I keep remembering that day, and I'm remembering it wrong."

"How so?"

I trace a finger along the scar on my cheek. "The witch who did this, she did this too." I gesture to my chest.

And suddenly I remember.

The flashes of deep violet, as Morgan threw her strike at me. The purple shards I found Cora's medallion in, the remnants of Morgan's magic, wasted on the ground.

I look up at Juno. "At least I thought she did."

"I don't understand." She says, frowning.

Me neither. It's not possible. I blink, trying to clear my thoughts, trying to make sense of what's happened. My blood runs cold.

"I need to talk to my brother."

Amryn answers the door with a smile, which quickly falls as he sees the expression on my face. "What's up?" He asks, looking from Juno to me.

"We need to talk." I say.

He raises his eyebrows and gestures for us to come into the cabin. "Sure, I mean, did something happen? Are you OK?"

"Do you remember anything about the day you were taken?" I ask him.

Amryn shrugs. "I mean, flashes of it, impressions. I remember Mom crying, and her holding on to me and Cora, but that's all. Why?"

"Where was I?"

He hesitates for a second. "Uh, you were running towards us."

"Did you see me?"

He shakes his head, an uneasy smile settling on his face as he blinks. "I - I don't know, Tal. I think so. I mean... What's this all about?"

174

"The blood magic strike," I say, stepping closer to him. "The strike that paralyzed me, where did it come from?"

"From Morgan." He's looking at me like I'm crazy. "You know that."

"Do you know that, or are you just saying that because we think it?"

Amryn frowns. "Ok, I don't know where you're going with this but it's starting to weird me out."

I point to my cheek. "In Nilau, the power Morgan used was purple. The strike that hit me the day you were taken, the day Dad died - that was green."

"She probably had a whole range of powers, Tal." Amryn crosses his arms over his chest.

I shake my head. "That's not how it works, their magic is the same as our flames, it's one color, always."

"So whose strike was it?" Amryn asks, shrugging. "There were no other witches there that day."

Weren't there? The thought is tugging at the edge of my consciousness.

"Dad was yelling to Mom," I say slowly, "to do it now. Telling her they were going to kill me. I don't remember seeing any of you, I thought I did but I don't. I was behind a boulder, and then the blood magic just came out of nowhere. And the strike was green."

Amryn's frown deepens. "Tal, what the fuck are you talking about?"

"Amryn, what if there was another witch there that day?"

"What other witch?"

"Mom."

Amryn's eyes widen for a moment before he laughs, shaking his head. "Brother, you need to get some sleep. Our Mom was a demon, you and me, we're full-blooded. Remember?" He summons up his flames, glowing orange in front of me. "And Mom had them too. I remember, they were yellow, just like Elise's. A witch doesn't have flames."

He's right. I know he's right. "What if -"

He claps a hand on my shoulder. "Tal, it's been a shit time lately. You've been through it. Maybe you're looking for explanations for things that just aren't there."

Before I can respond, the door flies open behind us, and Cora storms in, her cheeks flushed. "You all need to come with me right now."

"Is something wrong?" Amryn asks.

"You could say that," Cora replies. "Gabriel's here."

13
Cora

'm always fascinated by how different all the angels look, even now, when my stomach is twisted in terror as I look at the angel calling for my death.

Gabriel is the very image of those angels the humans fawn over. Big white wings, wavy blonde hair, tanned skin, eyes the color of turquoise. His clothing is almost laughable - baggy torn jeans and a tight white t-shirt, showing off his muscles. He looks like a model for a sports brand. He regards me with a wide smile, revealing his mouthful of even white teeth. He's a walking cliche.

"So glad you could make time for me," he says as I sit down opposite him in the Great Hall. Amryn and Tal sit on either side of me, their veins glowing. They're both on high alert. Zadkiel and Azrael sit behind Gabriel, there to keep him in check, supposedly. That's what the Old God said, at least.

I smile back at Gabriel. "I thought it was the least I could do, since you took time out of your busy schedule trying to get me killed."

He throws his head back and laughs. "Oh majesty, it's

177

nothing personal."

"Since I like being alive, I'm going to take it pretty personally." I reply sweetly, and Zadkiel bites his lip, trying not to laugh.

"You have to see, this isn't easy for me." Gabriel sprawls on his chair, one arm slung over the back of it, almost like he's posing for a photo shoot. He's clearly very taken with himself. "It's not much fun when someone is looking over your shoulder, not letting you have any fun."

"Fun?" I raise an eyebrow. "I don't think it's *fun* the Old God objects to."

Gabriel scoffs. "He objects to everything I do."

"Only the things that hurt others."

Gabriel runs his hand through his hair. "I haven't had any complaints so far."

"The little virgin in Bethlehem would probably have something to say about that." A gasp rises from the room. I know we're not supposed to talk about this. But since it's Gabriel's claim to fame, I'm not going to let it slide.

Gabriel looks at me with what I can only describe as admiration. "Ooh, look at you, coming out, guns blazing." He chuckles, running his tongue over his teeth. "That little virgin is hanging on the wall of every Italian Grandmother in the world, she did very well from the fame I brought her."

"Fame?" I laugh incredulously.

"You have to admire her creativity," he muses, inspecting his fingernails. "But then, she needed to come up with a good story by the time I was done with her." His eyes move to mine, and he looks positively evil.

I shake my head. "What do you want?"

His mouth twitches pensively. "You know, I think what I want most is for us to come to an amicable arrangement." His eyes flicker to Amryn, then back to me. "Maybe a fuck in exchange for peace?" Amryn leaps to his feet and Gabriel bursts out laughing, waving his hands dismissively. "Calm down, calm down. She's not my type. Besides -" his eyes move over me, and he cocks his head. "In your condition I couldn't really have fun the way I would want to."

My chest becomes tight and my cheeks flush as Amryn looks down at me. "Her condition?"

"Oh yes." Gabriel rubs his hands together. "Which brings me back to my point. I would like to offer a truce."

"What condition?" Amryn asks me.

Gabriel snaps his fingers. "Excuse me, we're speaking, Draw. Sit down."

Amryn obeys, and sits down slowly. I inhale deeply through my nose, willing my hands to stop trembling.

"What kind of truce are you offering?" I ask him. Please don't let him hear the quiver in my voice.

Gabriel presses his splayed hands together, pursing his lips, as though he's still considering what to say. Fucker. "I offer you peace in exchange for the relinquishment of your powers."

Protests erupt from the council and the villagers, and even Zadkiel's head snaps to look at Gabriel in disbelief.

"And why would I do that?" I ask.

"Because you are a violation of Fate, my dear." Gabriel

replies. "You're not supposed to exist, much less be the Shadow Queen of this Realm."

Azrael rises to his feet, leaning on his scythe. He pushes his cowl from his head, and looks down at Gabriel with a critical gaze. "I am the one who will speak on Fate, my brother."

Gabriel gestures grandly with his hand. "Then please, speak."

"Fate has been corrupted," Azrael says, his voice rasping across his lips. "The witches had created a Fate that deviated from the plan set down, and I have never been the same since."

"Yes it's very sad you lost your pretty black hair." Gabriel rolls his eyes. "But things change, and so can Fate."

Azrael shakes his head. "Not in the way you think."

Gabriel sighs and turns to him. "So, she's meant to be here?" He points at me.

Azrael's gaze moves to me, and he nods. "She is meant to be here. And I shall ensure she is safe for all of her days." He bows his head to me, then pulls the cowl back over his head, taking his seat again.

I bow my head to him. "Thank you, Azrael."

Gabriel throws his head back and garbles in frustration. "You're all so fucking annoying." He rolls his head back and forth, then looks back at me, his eyes narrowing. "OK, so I offer you different terms."

"You have nothing to offer me," I reply. "You have no support, you have no voice, nothing."

He nods. "This is true." He sniffs and gazes at the ceiling. "You know this, this Shadow Queen thing, it's passed down the maternal line, from mother to daughter."

I shift in my seat. "I do."

"So much responsibility," he says, rubbing his chin. "So much danger. Not having a choice in such things." He sucks on his teeth. "What a burden to bear."

"You don't scare me."

"Ah but will I scare your daughter?" He fixes me with his electric blue eyes, and grins, baring his teeth.

"Our -" Amryn breaks off, looking from me to Gabriel.

Gabriel gestures to me, then covers his mouth, his eyes wide. "Oh dear, did I spoil the surprise? Congratulations, Daddy."

I reach over and take Amryn's hand, not meeting his eyes. "Not now." I say in a low voice. "I'm sorry, but not now." I look back at Gabriel. "I told you, you don't scare me, and I will protect my daughter and prepare her for this life in a way that I was not."

Gabriel chuckles. "How touching." He shrugs. "It doesn't matter. All I need is some support in the Halls, and believe me, I will get it."

"Gabriel," Zadkiel begins, but Gabriel turns on him with a dismissive wave of his hand.

"Shut up, little lamb," Gabriel snaps. "We all know where your loyalties lie." He rises to his feet, and casts his cynical grin over the council. "Well, it would appear we are..." He trails off, his eyes fixed on something.

His expression shifts, slowly at first, from smugness to

confusion. He shakes his head, and then his eyes widen in a look of sheer terror. His mouth is open and moving, but no sound comes out.

Then he freezes.

A murmur comes from the council, and Zadkiel leans forwards, his eyebrows lifting. Even Azrael frowns. Gabriel is so stock still I wonder for a second if he's died. Do angels do this if they die? It's like he's turned into a statue.

I turn in my chair, following his gaze. There's the council members, murmuring amongst themselves. One of them leans to the side to speak to the demon beside them, and Juno's eyes meet mine. She shrugs a little. I turn back slowly, and Gabriel's hand is raised, pointing.

Right at Juno.

"What is she doing here?" He asks.

Everyone is turning to look now, and Juno glances around, shrinking down a little as eyes bear down on her.

"What the fuck is she doing here?" Gabriel asks again, his voice rising in pitch.

Tal tenses beside me. "She's taking refuge here."

Gabriel's eyes flash to Tal, and he stumbles backwards a little. "She should have been returned to the Halls immediately." He sputters. "An angel has no business being down here, with you demons. Who knows what you're doing to her."

I put my hand on Tal's arm, knowing he's about to spring to his feet. "She's fallen, Gabriel. Why would anyone return an angel to you that was cast out of the Halls?"

"Fallen?" He sputters. "Fucking *fallen*? She's none of your concern."

"I'm not sending a fallen angel back to the Halls with you," I tell Gabriel. "She's safe here, and we're looking after her."

"You're coming with me now. Gabriel steps foward, curling his fingers to summon Juno to get up. "Now, right now, you're coming with me."

"No," Juno says. "I'm not going anywhere with you, I don't know you."

Gabriel grins, chuckling through gritted teeth. "My dear, you don't want to stay down here, do you? With these feral creatures?"

"I'm not going with you," she says again, "I am staying here."

Gabriel's face goes red, and he begins to advance on the council. "I said come here now!"

Tal shakes me off and springs to his feet, rushing Gabriel, his red flames leaping high from his hands.

Wait, they're red? Since when are they red?

He has a good seven inches of height on Gabriel, and he towers over him.

"You don't touch her." Tal says.

"Get the fuck out of my way." Gabriel tries to push past him, but Tal grabs him by the throat and slams him into the ground.

"You don't. Fucking. Touch. Her." Tal snarls, baring his teeth at Gabriel, whose eyes are wide with terror. "Now get out of this village and don't come back, do you understand?" Gabriel opens his mouth to speak, but Tal presses down on his throat. "I said, get. The. Fuck. *Out.*"

"Or what?" Spittle explodes from Gabriel's lips as he forces the words out against Tal's grip.

Tal lowers his face right over Gabriel's. I feel my jaw drop open as wings explode from Tal's back - but they're not his wings, not black smoke, not the wings I've seen him fly with thousands of times.

They're flames. Giant, towering, red and orange flames.

"I'll kill you." Tal says.

Gabriel sees the wings of flame, and begins to make a sound like a strangled rat. He writhes out of Tal's grip, and scrambles to his feet. Tal straightens up and Juno rushes to his side. Gabriel looks at them both with a look of sheer terror, and flees from the Great Hall without another word.

The council members are on their feet, crying out and talking over each other. Amryn is standing beside me, his veins glowing, regarding the scene with mild shock.

Tal and Juno gaze at each other as Tal pulls his wings in, and he raises a hand to her cheek. "I told you - I'll kill anyone who tries to hurt you."

She nods and presses her lips into the palm of his hand.

I rise to my feet, feeling weak. "I think we can say this meeting is over." I nod to Zadkiel and Azrael. "Thank you for coming, I felt much safer with you both here."

"We'll make sure Gabriel behaves himself up there," Zadkiel assures me. "I doubt he'll be coming back anytime soon, thanks to you." He puts a hand on Tal's shoulder as he passes him. "Well done. That was quite something."

Tal bows his head as the angels leave. The council begins to disperse, their eyes wide and questioning as they pass by Tal and Juno.

A wave of nausea rushes over me, and I feel faint. I turn to Amryn. "I need to get out of here."

"Why didn't you tell me you were pregnant?" Amryn asks as soon as the cabin door closes behind us.

I sigh with exasperation. "That's what you're focusing on right now? Your brother just exploded into flame wings, and held down an archangel like it was nothing, and this is what you're worried about?"

"Why, Cora?" He shakes his head. "How long have you known?"

"Since just after Winter Solstice."

He scoffs in disbelief. "You've known for over a month, and you didn't tell me?"

"Amryn, this isn't important right -"

He slams a hand against the door. "Stop it!"

"Stop what?"

"Stop dismissing this like it's no big deal!" He cries. "We tell each other everything, *everything*, Cora, and this? You keep *this* from me, even though you know, you fucking *know* how scared I was, that Morgan had -"

"We have Phoenix, and you're still scared?"

"Yes!" He bellows. "Of course I fucking am!"

I take a deep breath. "I'm sorry." I take a few steps

towards him, but he holds out a hand to ward me off.

"Why?" He asks, pain etched on his face. "Why didn't you tell me?"

"I - I don't know." I shake my head. "I just don't know. I guess, what Gabriel said today, that was part of it. I was worried, because what if it is a girl, and -"

"Well now we know it is, thanks to him." Amryn leans against the wall behind him, his hands resting on his knees. "What a way to find out." His eyes move back to mine. "And the rest of it?"

"I - I -" I shrug as I stutter. "I don't know. I was being stupid. I was nervous."

"Do you not want any more kids?"

"Baby, that's not it at all." I go to him, taking his face in my hands. "I love having a family with you. I love being a mother. I do."

"So - why?" He asks helplessly.

I put my arms around his neck and hold him close, his arms encircling my waist. "I just don't know. Life, and a family, and all of that, it all feels weird. I'm still struggling with the idea of this being real, and everything I thought was real being a lie."

He nuzzles his face into my neck. "I'm sorry, baby. I shouldn't have yelled at you."

"It's OK."

"No it's not." He draws back to look into my eyes. "I'm sorry. I know all this family stuff, it's still a big deal. For both of us."

"It is." I sigh heavily. "I still... I dunno." Tears sting my eyes, and I try to blink them away. "I still think of Anya as being my Mom, and I see it myself, every day, that I do things the way she did them. And then I feel like I'm somehow letting my Mom down because I'm not doing what she did and..." My voice cracks a little and Amryn holds me close again.

"Your Mom loved you, and she would have been glad to know that Anya loved you and looked after you." He puts a finger under my chin, raising my face to his, and kisses me softly. "I'm sorry. I'm just mad that fucker Gabriel was the one to tell me, and not you."

"I know, I hate that."

He raises his eyebrows. "And then Tal doing whatever the fuck *that* was really kind of nailed the mood for the day."

I feel another wave of nausea wash over me. "Have you ever seen anything like that before?"

Amryn shakes his head. "Nope. That was crazy. And Gabriel was fucking spooked when he saw Juno, that was weird. Like he recognised her."

"You don't think he was just surprised to see an angel down here?" I know this isn't the answer, but I need to get the question off my chest.

"Nah, that was genuine fear."

The door to the cabin opens, and Ebony walks in, followed closely by Liall who is bent down to fit through the door, Phoenix perched on his shoulders.

"Hello family!" Liall says jovially, leaning forward as Phoenix stretches his arms out to Amryn.

"Hey buddy," Amryn says, taking Phoenix in his arms,

187

"you OK?"

"Yeah!" Phoenix exclaims, brandishing a carved wooden dagger. "Uncy Li made me a sword!"

Amryn laughs. "I can see that, very nice. Uncy Tal will have to show you how to use it properly, huh?"

I turn to Ebony, who smiles questioningly as I touch her arm. "Can I ask you something?"

"Sure honey."

"Arax, and the red smoke." I gesture to the window. "Do you remember it happening before? Because the Old God said it last happened 40 years ago."

Liall laughs out loud. "You know, it's funny you mention that, we were just talking about it."

Ebony rolls her eyes as she smiles. "I can't believe everyone forgot, honestly. The entire council was up in arms about it, when we've seen it before."

"Especially because it's such an easy day to remember!" Liall chides her gently, poking her in the ribs.

"Oh stop it," Ebony says, slapping his hand. "I was distracted that day, OK?"

I look from Ebony to Liall hoping an explanation will come, but they're both laughing, caught in memory. "Distracted?" I ask finally.

Ebony looks back at me and nods. "Midwifery duties. I had a lot on my mind that day."

Liall crosses his arms over his chest and smiles wistfully. "He was such a sweet baby, wasn't he?"

"Who?" I feel like I'm going to burst.

"Tal." Ebony sighs happily. "The last time Arax spewed red smoke like that I was helping Elspeth deliver Tal."

14
Tallesaign

inspect my back in the mirror. It doesn't look any different. Not that I expected it to. Those wings disappear just like the smoke. I look at my hands, summoning my flames, and they erupt in the dim room.

Bright red.

My flames have always been orange.

I gaze at my reflection and jump. My eyes are glowing red. Fuck. I extinguish the flames, and everything's back to normal, besides the faint red glow that remains in my veins.

I flex my hand, remembering the feeling of that fucker's throat in my grasp. Remembering the way he looked at Juno. That look was one of terror, of recognition. Gabriel knows who she is. And that worries me. If he's this scared of her, he'll try to destroy her.

I need to protect her.

A gust of wind blows snow against the window pane as I lie back down in my bed. I run my hand over the scar on my chest. I know Amryn is right. I know who our mother was. I know it. But the thought won't leave me alone. The memories of that day keep playing over and over in my head. Are they memories? I'm starting to question myself.

Everything that's happening lately has me questioning myself.

I hear a sound from the other room and sit up. It sounds like Juno, calling out softly. I wait to see if she goes back to sleep, but then I hear it again. She must be having a nightmare.

I pad down the hallway quietly, and see her lying on the couch. She's moving under the blanket, her head tipped back, her mouth open slightly. Her red hair glows in the light of the fire crackling in the hearth.

I stop, narrowing my eyes, trying to figure out if she's awake, and then desire floods my groin when she moans.

Her face turns towards the fire, and her eyes are tightly closed. The blanket shifts enough to let me see her bare chest, her breasts rising and falling rapidly. Her right hand twirls and teases her left nipple, her other hand between her legs. The blanket is still covering her, still concealing that part of her I want to see most.

Her breathy moan steals my gaze back up her body. I'm pretty sure I've stopped breathing. Her back arches as her hands move, her hair spilling over the edge of the couch.

I'm fucking mesmerised, frozen to the spot as another moan escapes her. I watch as her stomach sucks in, her hand moving faster, and I swear to fucking god my mouth is watering as I think of sinking my tongue into the flesh between those thighs.

I should go. I shouldn't watch her like this. But I'm entranced, unable to tear my eyes away from that beautiful, undulating body.

She sucks in a breath, and her brow furrows, her head tipped back as she bites her lip, suppressing a cry. I can see she's about to come, and my hand digs into the door frame as blood rushes to my cock.

Her thighs shake, and she braces one foot against the armrest, the other dropping to the floor, her toes curled and that damn blanket is still blocking me from seeing all of her. Her hips lift off the couch as her body goes still. She clasps a hand over mouth, the hand between her thighs continuing to move as she draws out every last second of her climax.

I watch as she quivers, her chest jerking as one shuddering breath after another leaves her. Her hand drops from her mouth to the floor, and she sighs.

I pick that moment to shift on my feet, finally able to move, trying not to think about how fucking hard I am right now. The wood floor under me creaks, and Juno's head shoots up, looking right at me, lurking in the darkness.

Fuck. "I'm sorry" I quickly turn my back to her. "I didn't mean to -"

"Tal."

I look over my shoulder, and she's raised up on her elbows, looking back at me. My breath catches as I take her in, her cheeks flushed, those perfect fucking breasts still moving rapidly as she subsides.

As if she can feel how badly I want her, she slowly

takes a hold of the blanket around her waist, pushing it aside so it slides to the floor. She spreads her legs open for me, giving me the perfect view of that pussy glistening with her arousal.

Slowly, she trails her hand down her body, my eyes following hungrily, over her stomach, between her thighs, and into the slickness that begs for me to taste. Her fingers part her lips, and one finger slides inside her.

"Come here, Tal." It's a command, one I'm only too happy to obey.

Her finger continues to move in and out of her as I walk to her side, kneeling on the floor. I want to touch her, I'm fucking aching to, but her gaze tells me I'm to wait. Patiently. Even though right now I feel anything but.

"Did you like what you saw?" Her eyes stay fixed on me as her hand continues to move.

"Yes."

"Do you want to know what I was thinking about?" She gasps a little, and I swear I'm going to lose my fucking mind.

"I was thinking about your mouth." She licks her lips as her eyes flutter closed. "I was thinking about your mouth, kissing me, everywhere." Her eyes open a little, and she smiles. "Would you like to do that?"

"Yes." I've lost the ability to form a sentence. All I can think about is crushing those lips of hers under mine, sinking myself - any fucking part of myself - into that delicious heat between her legs.

She withdraws her hand from her pussy, laying it above her head. With her other hand, she traces a circle over her lower stomach.

"Here." Another command.

I try to show some restraint as I sink my lips into the flesh of her stomach. Somehow this feels more intimate than eating her out. I can smell everything I want, it's so fucking close, but kissing her here, doing her bidding - I need this. I *want* this.

I push my pants down as my lips rove over her skin, and fist the base of my cock.

"Uh-uh," she says. "No touching."

Fuck. I inhale sharply, and put my hands over her, on the back of the couch. She reaches out and pushes my hair out of the way, watching as my lips worship every silky inch of her stomach.

"Now here." She runs a finger down the length of her thigh, the one closest to me.

I dive on it like it's water and I'm a man dying of thirst. I've never had a woman do this before, never been directed around another person's body like this - and I fucking love it.

I trace one lustful, open-mouthed kiss after another along her thigh, getting closer and closer to her pussy. I move a hand tentatively up her stomach, further, between her breasts, and she doesn't stop me.

She moans as I almost reach those soft lips, dripping with arousal, and then she grabs my hair, pulling me back. I hiss out a breath, and my cock is straining so desperately for release it hurts.

"Now the other one." She traces her fingers down the thigh that's still hooked over the back of the couch.

I groan low in my throat as I lean over her, and the heat from between her legs burns against my chest. I press my lips into her thigh, my hand hooking under her knee to draw her closer to me. Her skin smells like a fresh fucking meadow, like the sweetest fucking summer breeze washing right over me.

Once again, I almost reach her pussy, when her fingers dig into my hair and pull me away. Something like a growl leaves me as I meet her eyes. She raises an eyebrow as she gazes at me.

"Now," she says in a low voice, "because you've been such a good boy, I let you pick." Her fingers tense in my hair, and I grit my teeth at the sting that feels so fucking good. "Where do you want to kiss me now, Tal?"

I want her pussy. I want to say it. But I'm riding a wave of anticipation that's arching so high it's making me fucking drunk. Some sadistic part of me wants to stay right where I am, stuck in that ache, that yearning for her. I want to drag this out.

"Your mouth," I say, her hands still tangled in my hair, still holding me back.

She pulls me up to her, slowly, still moving so agonizingly fucking slowly. Finally I'm over her, my hands on either side of her head, against the armrest. She relaxes her grip on my hair, gently caressing the back of my neck.

"My mouth is yours," she murmurs.

I've kissed plenty in my life, and not one of those kisses has been anything like this one. It's like coming home. It's like fresh air. She tastes like every good dream I've ever had. Every moment of doubt or fear or longing, every moment when I've wondered if I'd ever feel this way - it's gone at the touch of her mouth on mine.

I draw back from her, my shoulders heaving, and she traces a finger down my cheek. "Now." She takes my hand. "I want you to touch me here."

I groan as she puts my palm to her pussy. She's so fucking wet. I move gently, and she sighs, tipping her head back. I slip one finger between those soft lips, and her chest jerks a little. I move a little further, catching her mouth with mine again as I push my finger inside her. She quivers as I roll my palm over her clit, feeling that slick heat dripping over my hand.

"Those words," I murmur against her lips, "those words you said to me, what did they mean?"

She smiles, gasping a little as I push another finger inside her. "*Zhizn Moya.* It means My Life."

My life.

I kiss her again, ferociously this time, my palm sliding over her wet pussy as she begins to tighten around my hand. She's going to come again, I can feel it in the tension in her chest as she trembles under me. My mind is fucking blank with desire, all I can focus on is her breaths, her moans, every tiny movement of her body.

Her back begins to bow, and suddenly she's pushed my hand away, tangled in my hair again as her teeth seize my earlobe.

"On your back," she says.

I'm so light-headed with lust I feel like I'm going to pass out. I lay down on the rug in front of the fire, watching as Juno rises from the couch. She smiles as her eyes wander over my body, and she lowers herself onto me, straddling my thighs. She looks down at my swollen cock and licks her lips. I'm sure if she does that again I'm going to come.

"Mmmm, you look so good like this, my love." Her hands grip my hips. Her fingers splay out, brushing closer and closer to my groin. "So beautiful." She lowers her mouth to my stomach, and I gasp as her lips move over me. She's claiming me - she's doing exactly what I did to her but under her terms. She's letting me know I'm hers.

My cock is pressed between us, throbbing with need. My hands move to her back, my fingers feathering up and down her spine. Her long hair brushes over me, and every nerve in my body is on fire. Every touch threatens to send me over the edge.

She lifts her head and smiles at me, her eyes hooded with desire. She begins to crawl up my body, but she doesn't stop at my cock - she keeps going, until her knees are either side of my head. She runs her fingers through my hair. Her pussy is inches from my face.

"Now where do you want to kiss me?" She asks.

I pull her down onto my mouth and the hot pressure at the base of my spine swells so violently at her taste that I almost come. Juno cries out as my tongue swirls around her sweet, swollen clit.

Fuck, fucking *fuck*, she tastes good. I pull her clit between my lips, my face soaked in her scent, in her arousal. She's exquisite. She's perfect.

I push my tongue inside her and she moans. I look up her body to see her hands on her breasts, her head thrown back as she rides my mouth.

"Oh Tal," she gasps, her delicate fingers pinching her

nipples. "Fuck."

Her thighs tremble either side of me, my fingers digging into them to keep her steady, keep her on my face. I move my tongue back to stroking her clit, rolling over it. I hear her breath hitch, her body tensed over me, and then with a loud cry, she pulses against my mouth.

She rises off me, her breathing ragged, and she slumps over the couch. I'm pulled so taut I can barely move, and then she looks over her shoulder at me. Her lips pull up into a grin, and she crooks her finger at me.

"Come here."

I don't need to be told twice. I kneel behind her, pressing my cock to her entrance. And then with a loud moan she's eased herself back on to me, and my brain fucking short circuits.

She's so hot and wet. Sinking into her, feeling her around me, completely raw, nothing between us - it's fucking heavenly. My fingers dig into her hips, and I don't want this feeling to stop, but holy fuck I know I can't last long like this.

"Fuck me hard." She braces her hands against the back of the couch.

As if I had any other choice right now. I drive into her, looking down to watch myself sink into her pussy over and over again, my cock glistening with her juices. She's all I can feel, all I can smell, all I can taste - she's consumed me. I'm hers. I'm fucking *hers*.

White-hot desire floods my groin and my thighs, snaking up my back. She leans up on her hands, her red hair tumbling down her back as she arches even more, angling herself fucking perfectly for me. I move one hand to her shoulder, the other still on her hip, keeping up that rhythmic pace that has sent her thighs trembling.

A thin layer of sweat has broken out over her skin, and she's so achingly fucking tight.

"Tal," she moans, "oh fuck, oh fuck."

I groan as I feel myself rising. I want her to come on my cock. I move my hand from her hip to between her thighs, stroking her soaked clit with my finger. Her hands flex, her fingers digging into the couch.

"Yeah," she gasps, "oh god."

It doesn't take much to send her back over the edge, and I can barely think or breathe as I feel her pussy clenching onto me. She bounces herself back against me as I slam into her, and then we're both coming, our cries intermingling as I press my mouth against her shoulder. I move my hand from her shoulder down to her hand, as she slumps forwards, and her fingers entice with mine.

We stay like that, a heaving, sweating tangled mess of limbs as we try to catch our breath. Juno turns her head, her cheek on the couch. Her eyes are closed as she smiles.

"I have been aching to do that," she says after a while. "You have no idea."

"Oh I think I do." I push her hair aside so I can kiss the back of her neck. "I nearly lost my mind, I wanted you so bad."

She giggles, opening her eyes and looking over her shoulder at me. "Well, now you have me, my love."

"It's you that has me now." I lean forward to place a kiss on her lips.

199

"Mmm." Her lips hum against mine. "Such a good boy."

Her words send a new rush of desire coursing through me, and I think she's going to send me to an early grave.

Holy *fuck,* what those words do to me.

She seems to feel me getting hard again, and she tosses her hair as she laughs.

"More already, my love?" She draws back to gaze at me with those stunning brown eyes.

I laugh breathlessly and shake my head. "I think I need a cigarette first."

"Oh yes." She gasps a little as I withdraw from her, wiggling her hips as I move away, as though testing how she feels. She meets my eyes with a satisfied grin. "I like your cock."

"Oh yeah?"

"Mmmm." She stretches her back and sighs. "I like them big."

My cheeks flush a little, and she laughs when she sees. I get to my feet which is not exactly easy since my legs have turned to fucking jelly, but I manage to make it across to the mantlepiece, retrieving my cigarette case and lighting two while Juno climbs back up onto the couch.

I hand her one of the cigarettes as I sit down on the ground beside her, and she tucks a hand behind her head as she gazes at me.

"You're so beautiful," she murmurs. "The most beautiful man I've ever seen."

I lean over and brush my nose along her ribcage,

breathing her in. "I don't know what you've done to me, but I never want it to stop."

"Tal," she says slowly, and I fucking love hearing her say my name.

"Mmm?" I look up at her.

"I don't remember a lot, but I do know the old stories. About our kind."

I chuckle. "Our kind? What do you mean, baby?"

"I mean that this isn't allowed," she replies, and flicks her cigarette into the ashtray I hold up for her. "You, and me. An angel and a demon. That's forbidden, isn't it?"

I suck in a deep drag of the cigarette, blowing the smoke towards the fire. "I suppose so, yes." I don't want the feeling to go away right now, this euphoria. But she's right. This isn't allowed. We've violated the blood covenant, and it never even occurred to me until this very moment.

"So we have violated the laws?" Her voice stays even as she says it.

I lean over her, stroking her forehead with my fingertips. "If we have, I don't care."

She smiles. "You would cause another Downfall for me?"

"Any time." I brush a kiss against her jaw. "Besides, you think the Halls are going to bother about some nobody demon and an angel fucking?"

Juno giggles. "Hardly a nobody demon, my love. You're one of the Draws of the Shadow Queen."

"Still doesn't matter," I say with a shrug. "I'm not letting anyone take you away. This - it's... I've never felt like this about anyone before. Ever."

Juno stamps out the cigarette in the ashtray after I put out mine, and then pulls me up onto the couch, on top of her. I settle between her thighs, feeling that desire for her rising again.

She kisses me, but it's tender, almost as though she's questioning, letting me take the lead. My tongue caresses hers, my whole body tense with need.

"I love you," she murmurs against my lips, and my world tilts on its axis.

I look down at her with wide eyes. "Y-you what?"

She shakes her head, smiling, and I swear I can see tears glistening in her eyes. "I love you. You're a part of me. I can feel it. And I love you."

"I love you too." The words just slip out.

And it's not because I just had the best sex of my entire fucking life. It's because she's right - I'm a part of her, and she's a part of me. Two halves of a broken puzzle piece that never fit in before. I kiss her again, and again, drinking her in.

And then I take her to my bed. Where she belongs.

Dawn is barely breaking at the horizon when Juno's screams tear me from sleep. She's sitting up in bed, her arms cast out in front of her, her eyes so wide I can see the whites gleaming in the half light.

"I killed you," she cries. "I killed you, you told me to

do it, oh fuck, oh god."

"It's OK, it was just a nightmare." I try to hold her, but she's shaking and writhing out of my grasp, clawing her hands against her temples.

"You told me to." She gasps in a breath. "You told me to kill you, and I stabbed you. I watched you die."

"Juno, it's OK," I say, taking her in my arms. "Baby, you're safe, I'm here."

"It was him!" She screams before she collapses against me, her shoulders heaving as sobs wrack through her body. "Oh god, Tal, it was him. I remember. I remember."

"What do you remember?" I cradle her head to my chest. "Juno, you're safe. No one can hurt you. What do you remember?"

She looks up at me, shivering, her hair sticking to her tear-stained face. "Gabriel. He cut off my wings."

My veins ignite almost instantly as rage swells at the base of my neck. He knew her. That's why he looked like that. Because he fucking did this to her. I'm so filled with fury I can't speak. I just hold Juno to me as she cries, as she slowly calms and begins to breathe again.

"He's going to pay for what he did," I say quietly, tipping her face up to mine. "I swear to you, he is going to suffer. And no one is ever going to hurt you again, do you hear me?"

She nods, squeezing her eyes shut. "I know."

"Do you remember when he did it?"

"No, but I remember how it happened."

"Do you want to tell me?" I ask quietly. I don't want to push this.

She nods. "Someone - someone betrayed me. I only have an impression of it, that someone I loved betrayed me. I trusted them, and they delivered me to Gabriel. I think -" Her voice breaks, and she sucks in a breath. "I think someone abused me."

"Abused you?"

She sighs heavily, and pulls back from me a little. She takes my hand, clutching it to her chest. "I have this impression, this feeling of betrayal. Someone I trusted, they betrayed me. They were - angry." Her eyebrows knit together as she tries to place her memories. "Something hadn't worked, they told Gabriel it hadn't worked when they brought me to him."

My stomach constricts violently, I can almost feel her pain, I'm sure of it. I don't know what to say, what to do, so I just keep hold of her hand.

She gasps suddenly, and a hand flies to her mouth. "Someone raped me."

I have to calm down. I'm going to set fire to my damn bed. I take a deep breath, resisting the urge to sweep her into my arms because I don't know if that's what she needs. I don't want to disrupt her memories, even if they're painful. She wants to remember, she needs to.

"Someone raped me," she repeats quietly, "and then they brought me to Gabriel. I was on a hard floor, it hurt when they threw me down. I was shackled. He cut them off. He was -" Her breath hitches in her throat. "He was laughing while he did it." Her voice breaks, and she slumps against me again.

I'm going to kill him. That angel is dead, he just doesn't know it yet.

"I don't know what happened after that," she says after a while, once she can speak again, once the sobs have subsided enough. "After that it is just darkness, and pain." She looks up at me. "And then you. Then there is just you, and your face, and your voice telling me I'm safe."

I smile at her. "And you are safe."

"I know." She nods slowly. "I know I am. But... I'm so angry. I can't remember. I can't remember why, or when. I cannot remember any of it. Why?"

"You're not ready for it yet," I say softly. "You're just not ready yet. It'll come back."

She puffs out a breath. "I'm a little frightened. Of what else there is to remember."

"I know."

She entwines her fingers with mine, lifting my hand with hers, and she looks at my hands. "Your flames, they have changed color?"

I nod. "Yes, they were orange, and now they're red."

"And your wings?"

"That's changed too. They were black smoke." I turn my hand with hers, meeting her eyes. "You touched my flames, and they didn't hurt you."

"I just knew," she says, withdrawing her hand from mine to put it on my chest. "I knew you couldn't hurt me. It didn't even occur to me, for a second."

"That only happens when two people are bonded. Like Cora and Amryn, their flames, they can't hurt each other."

I smile as I wipe her tears away, brushing the hair out of her face. "I am a part of you. I am."

She nuzzles into me and lets out something that sounds almost like a sigh of relief. "*Zhizn Moya*, I am so happy you found me."

"So am I, more than you can know."

15
Amryn

I roll on to my side, watching Cora sleep next to me, naked, beautiful, peaceful. My hand strays over to her stomach, no sign of any bump yet. Our daughter's growing in there though, safe and snug. I lean over, placing my lips on Cora's belly.

"Can't wait to meet you, little bug," I whisper.

Cora stirs, her hands running over my head, holding me to her. "I'm sorry." She murmurs. "I'm sorry I didn't tell you."

"Enough of that." I move up to her mouth, kissing her gently. Her eyes are still closed, determinedly so, as though she's holding on to the last traces of sleep. "I'm not angry. I'm excited."

She smiles. "A girl."

I lay my head on her chest, listening to her heartbeat. "A girl."

Phoenix starts laughing in his room, and we both chuckle.

"Someone's in a good mood." Cora says.

"Granny, stop that!" Phoenix says amid peals of laughter.

I feel Cora hold her breath as I raise my head. "He's doing it again."

I climb off her, swinging my legs off the bed onto the ground, stepping into my sweatpants and standing up to pull them up my legs. "It's fine, he's just playing." I give her a reassuring smile. "It's nothing, really. He's just got a wild imagination."

Cora sits up, eyeing me uncertainly. "Amryn, he's doing this all the time. We should talk to Fenella about it."

"Why?" I try to stay jovial. This is nothing. The gnawing feeling of dread won't go away, no matter how much I smile, though. "What's Fenella going to tell us, hmm? A witch? What could she know?"

"Maybe she could tell us where he got it from?"

Maybe there was another witch there that day.

I shake my head. No. This is all ridiculous. "I'll go and get Nix his breakfast. You get some sleep, you must be tired from all that baby-growing you're doing." She huffs out a breath as I leave the bedroom.

Phoenix is sitting on the floor in his room, playing with his train set, animatedly explaining how it works to the thin air beside him. His eyes light up as I walk in.

"Daddy, Granma and I playing with my trains!" He says brightly, turning to the empty space beside him. His face drops, and he looks around, as though he's lost something. "Granma?" He stands up, looking around the room.

The icy feeling in my stomach is unbearable.

"Daddy, where Granma go?" Phoenix stretches out his arms for me to pick him up.

I scoop him up in my arms and put him on my hip. "Nixxy, I need you to tell me who you were talking to,"

"Granma," he says, his green eyes earnest, "she sings to me."

"Yeah, you told me that, but how do you know she's your Granma, buddy? Did you see a picture of her?"

Phoenix shakes his head. "No, she tell me."

"Is she your imaginary friend?" I lean my forehead against his chubby little cheek. "Are you making her up so you have a friend to play with?"

Phoenix grabs on to my hair and shakes his head emphatically. "No, Granma isn't magiary. Granma's real."

"Sure, buddy. Come on," I say, bouncing him on my hip, "let's go and get breakfast."

"Porridge!"

"No problems, buddy," I reply, laughing as we walk to the kitchen together.

"But Daddy," Phoenix says, grabbing my face, "Granma needa tell you something. For Uncy Tal."

"Oh is that so?" I sit him on the kitchen counter beside the stove. "Does she want Uncy Tal to come play trains too?"

Phoenix giggles and clutches his hands to his mouth. "Silly, Daddy." He shakes his head. "No, Granma said to Uncy Tal that she's sorry."

I open the cupboard to pull out the large glass jar holding the oats. "What's she sorry for?"

"She hurted Uncy Tal."

My eyes move slowly to my son, to his innocent little face as he gazes at me. "Granma hurt Uncle Tal?"

Phoenix nods, pointing to his chest, drawing a line across it. "Here. She said sorry. She didn't mean to."

The hairs on the back of my neck stand up. "What did she hurt Uncy Tal with, buddy? Did she tell you?"

Phoenix nods. "The green."

I try not to show him how shaken I am. He has no idea what he's saying. He's just a kid. He's making lucky guesses. He doesn't know. He can't know.

I pour milk and oats into a small copper pot on the stove, heating them for Phoenix, and I hear him start to hum a song as his little legs dangle over the edge of the counter.

A song I remember.

The song my mother sang to me when I was little. The song Fenella was humming as she healed me in her cabin.

I need to talk to Tal.

Tal takes a long drag of his cigarette as we walk to Fenella's cabin. His hands are shaking, the smoke pouring from his lips in a heavy huff.

I look up at Arax, which has stopped smoking, not white smoke, not red. Nothing. It's just stopped.

Everything is getting too weird.

We both lift our hands to knock on Fenella's door, eyeing each other awkwardly as we both pull our hands down.

"What do we even ask her?" I ask.

Tal opens his mouth to answer, and we both jump as the door opens. Fenella smiles out at us, a silky green turban on her head, wiry white hairs sticking out from under it. Her eyes go from one of us to the other.

"Why don't you both come in?" She opens the door wider. "It's so cold today."

We both hesitate, then Tal walks in ahead of me. The cabin is warm, and smells of lavender. A fire crackles in the rounded cast iron stove in the corner of the room. Fenella gestures to the table.

"Come, boys, come and sit." She crosses her legs one over the other, smoothing her velvet dressing gown with her pale, papery hands. "Now, what would you like to ask me?"

Tal takes a deep breath. "Did you know our mother?"

"Oh, *oui*, I did." Fenella nods, her smile warm.

"Did you know - " Tal's eyes flash to me for a second. "Did you know if she was -"

"*Mon cher,*" Fenella interrupts, "I think it is always best to ask the question that will start the story, not the one that will end it."

Tal glances over at me, and his brow furrows. He looks back at Fenella. "Where did you come from?"

Fenella leans back in her chair. "Do you have a

cigarette for me?"

Tal opens his cigarette case, offering Fenella one. She places it between her lips, taking Tal's hand so he can light it for her. Her wooden chair creaks as she leans back, gazing at the ceiling as she inhales. She rubs her cheek with her thumb, and looks back at us both.

"Many years ago now, I had to flee the Lowlands when war was declared," she begins. "My husband, he was killed in battle, and I had to run with my children. It was a terrible time. Just terrible."

"Where did you go?" I ask, but I can see from her face that she's lost in memory.

"We walked, oh we walked," she goes on, "for so many days, sleeping in fields. Trying to keep warm. It was bitter cold. My children would cry, they would beg for warmth, and I had to listen to them weeping. There was so little I could do." She inhales again, the smoke furling from her mouth with a heavy sigh. "And then, we were attacked by another witch. She wanted to hurt my children, so I had to bind her with my magic." She lifts her eyebrows, blinking rapidly as though trying not to cry. "But I was weak, half-starved, grieving. My magic was not strong enough to stop her completely. She was determined to cause my babies harm."

"Why did she want to hurt your kids?" Tal asks.

Fenella shrugs, flicking her cigarette into the floral porcelain ashtray on the table. "I do not know. She was so very angry." She shudders a little. "Her enchantment, she sent it after us as she was bound, as we ran away. It hit one of my girls, it hurt her. To this day I will never understand why..." She trails off, gazing out the window, her brow crinkling at the painful memories.

"Did she survive?" I ask.

Fenella nods. "*Oui*, she did."

"So what happened to them? To your kids?" I don't want to rush her, but the gnawing feeling of anxiety in my stomach is overwhelming.

"We had been traveling for many weeks," Fenella says slowly, "and I knew we needed to seek help, we needed to seek refuge. My children, I knew no one would take pity on us, I knew we were feared. But I hoped, I so much hoped, that perhaps they could find refuge here. Even if I was cast out, or killed, at least my children would be safe."

I shake my head. "But, if they wouldn't take on witches, I don't understand."

"My children had very fortunate gifts, *mon cher*," Fenella goes on, her fingers tracing the embroidery on the tablecloth. "*Le mimetisme.*"

"*Le mime-*" Tal repeats, stopping as the foreign words sink in. "Mimics?"

Fenella nods, her sad smile casting over us both. "*Oui.*"

"What does that mean?" I ask.

"Mimics," Tal says, looking over at me, "they can copy powers, no one would even know they weren't that race."

My chest is getting tighter and tighter in the warm cabin, my head full of questions and yet I have no ability to verbalize any of them.

"So, what did you do?" Tal asks.

Fenella swallows hard, her eyebrows rising as she takes a shaky breath. "I told them what they were to do. I told them to imitate what they must. To tell the demons I was merely a kind witch who had found them on the road, and had saved them. Perhaps, by some luck, someone would take pity on me." A soft, sad laugh escapes her. "My girls, so very clever."

"Your girls?" I ask weakly. It's all starting to dawn on me.

"*Oui, mes filles,*" she says, "but from that day, no more." She shakes her head slowly, stamping out the cigarette in the ashtray. "From that day, the word *Maman* did not fall from their lips. Never again."

Tal and I exchange a glance, and I feel sweat erupting on the palms of my hands.

"Where are your daughters now?" Tal asks slowly.

Fenella clasps her hands on her lap. "When we arrived here, I was treated with kindness. I was allowed to stay, for being so brave, for protecting these poor demon children. I was given this cabin to live in. I served this village, caring for their sick and wounded." Her eyes crinkle as she smiles at us both. "And I was so very honored to see both my grandsons born."

Tal gasps, and I feel the floor drop out from under me. Blood rushes through my ears.

"You're -" I break off, rubbing my fists along my thighs. "You're our grandmother?"

Fenella nods, tears in her eyes. "And I am so proud of you, both of you. Of the men you have become."

"Our mother," Tal says slowly, "and Elise? They're your children?" He rises from his chair, towards the window. "But that means -" He turns back to look at

Fenella. "That means that Amryn and I, we're - I mean we're not -" He shakes his head, running a hand over his mouth.

"We're not full-blooded demons?" I complete the thought for him. Even though it doesn't feel like it should matter, right now, it does. "We're half witch?"

"*Oui*," Fenella says, nodding.

"Is that why Phoenix can do what he does?" I ask.

"Ah, *le papillon*," Fenella clasps her hands to her chest. "My great-grandson. The most beautiful child." She nods. "*Oui*, he has inherited abilities from our family."

The words hit me like a landslide. *Our family.* I get to my feet, feeling unsteady, clawing my hands through my hair as I try to make sense of everything.

"The day our father was killed," Tal says, leaning on his hands on the back of a chair, "what happened?"

"Your father knew who your mother was." Fenella's face twists with pain as she gazes at him. "He knew her power. He accepted her completely. It was their secret, and he never told another soul. But on that day -" She inhales sharply. "On that day, he asked your mother to reveal her power, to save you." She looks up at Tal. "He loved you so much, *mon cher*. You were his pride, all of it."

Tal's fingers claw into the chair as his head drops, but Fenella keeps speaking.

"Your father knew Lordain and his witch would kill you," she says. "You were young, and strong, a warrior. He could see you coming, he could see you were ready to fight, but you were outnumbered. He knew you would

215

fight to the death. He called out to your mother, begging her to stop you, to bind you in place, where you stood."

The wooden chair creaks audibly under Tal's grip.

"Your mother was terrified." Fenella rubs a hand across her forehead. "She was so scared to hurt you. But she knew it was the only way to save you."

"So she used blood magic on him?" I ask.

"*Oui,*" Fenella says, nodding, her eyes moving to Tal's inert frame. "Your witch blood saved you, it stopped the blood magic from killing you." She looks back at me. "This is how Zadkiel knew when he fired that dart at you, in Nilau, that you would not die. You may be hurt by such things, but not killed."

"Does this have anything to do with Cora?" Tal asks suddenly.

My eyes snap to his face. "What do you mean?"

He gestures back and forth between us, his eyes fixed on Fenella. "Us, being her Draws, both of us. But we're not demons, not full-blooded. What does she have to do with this?"

Fenella's brow furrows. "I do not know what you mean. Cora is a demon, full-blooded, there is no connection."

Tal shakes his head as he looks at me. "I don't believe that."

"Why?" I ask. "What would that have to do with anything?"

"Why were we chosen as her Draws?" Tal asks. "You and me, two hybrids, two half-breeds? Morgan would have known, she had to have known. She would have sniffed us out, they can recognize their own kind."

"Tal, you're not making any sense."

"Why would Fate choose us?" Tal asks, and his eyes become a little wider. "Why us? You and me? Why is there this bond?"

I splutter as I try to find the words, try to make sense of what Tal is asking me. "Tal, it just did, I mean, why are those things connected?"

"Witches corrupted the Line," he says, his eyes moving back to Fenella, "they corrupted Fate. They twisted it to their own ends."

"I still don't get -"

"Fate chose two witches to be the Draws of the Shadow Queen," he says, his eyes moving slowly back to my face. "What do you think that could mean?"

I shake my head. "Tal, I'm going to need you to be a little clearer here."

"Our link to Cora is a corruption of Fate." He looks back at Fenella. "Isn't it?"

Fenella shakes her head, inhaling sharply as she clutches her hand to her chest. "Oh *mon cher,* no, your love for Cora, it is pure. There is no corruption there."

"A witch would say that wouldn't she?" Tal says bitterly, and storms out of the cabin.

Fenella puts a hand over her mouth, tears rolling down her round cheeks. "Oh *non,*" she whispers, "Amryn, I swear to you -"

I go to her, putting a hand on her shoulder. "It's OK, he's just taking it all in."

217

She clutches my hand, pressing it to her lips. "I love you so much, my baby boy," she says softly. She leans against me, her breaths shuddering as she cries. "I am so sorry."

"It's OK, I'll go talk to him." I put my arms around her - around my Grandmother. "I'll be back soon, OK?" I smile at her as she wipes her tears away. "I'll bring Phoenix with me."

"Oh please, yes." She nods.

I rush out of the cabin, following the footprints in the snow, following Tal. I see him up ahead, head down, stalking towards the forest.

"Tal!" I call, breaking into a jog to catch up with him. "Tal. Come on, wait for me."

He storms ahead, ignoring me.

"Tal, come on." I catch up with him, putting my hand on his shoulder. He turns, flinging my hand off him, and as he looks at me, my stomach drops when I see his eyes glowing red. "What the fuck, Tal?"

"You and me, we're meant to do something bad," he says to me, the veins in his neck beginning to glow red. "We're meant to hurt Cora."

"What the fuck are you talking about? Tal, you need to calm down."

"We're witches, Amryn!" He cries. "Witches, the ones who corrupted everything, who twisted Fate, who made it so assholes like Ragnar and Lordain could claim power. But we're the Draws of the Shadow Queen?"

"You're saying the love I have for my wife isn't real?" I ask, fury suddenly coursing through me. "Is that what you're saying?" I shove him in the shoulder. "All those years I wanted her, I longed for her, I risked death every time I touched her, it was just some primal urge to destroy her?"

"Maybe it was," he counters. "You fucked her all those years knowing what would happen if you were found out. Doesn't seem much like a Draw who gives a fuck to -"

I throw my fist without thinking, striking Tal in the cheek. "Fuck you!" I scream as he stumbles, feeling my own veins burst into shimmering heat. "Fuck you and your fucking paranoia! Your fucking self-loathing and -"

Tal turns on me, his fist striking me in the jaw. White light flashes through my vision, pain shooting through the side of my face. I recover quickly, grabbing him by the collar, his eyes wild as I'm face to face with him.

"What is going on?" Cora's voice echoes across the field, and we both turn to look at her. She's running towards us, her face twisted in disbelief. "What the fuck are you doing?"

Tal's jaw is feathering violently as his eyes fix back on me. I shove him away, tasting blood, feeling it pool in the corner of my mouth.

Cora reaches us, looking from one to the other. "I want someone to tell me what the fuck is going on right now."

Tal gestures to me. "He threw the first punch, maybe ask him."

Cora's eyes widen. "You did what?"

I take a deep breath, trying to steady myself, slow my racing heartbeat. "Maybe you should tell her what you said, about us, about how I feel about her."

219

"Oh for fuck's sake!" Cora exclaims, throwing her hands up. "Someone just fucking tell me -"

"We're witches," Tal shakes his head, a bitter smile on his face. "Fenella?" He points to her cabin. "Yeah, she's our grandmother. And Elise is a witch too. So is your son."

Cora sucks in a shocked, stuttering breath, her eyes wide as she looks back at me. "What?"

I glare at Tal, and nod. "Yeah. It's true. She just told us."

"But Elise is a demon," Cora says, shaking her head. "She has flames, and she, I mean, she... No, that's not possible."

"They're mimics," Tal says, "they can imitate powers. They pretended to be demons to seek refuge here."

"And Tal here thinks we're here to destroy you," I say. Tal rushes at me again, and Cora stops him, pushing him back.

"Tal, no!" She cries. "Stop it! What the fuck is wrong with both of you?"

"Get your hands off her!" I step forward, Cora's hand shooting out to stop me. "She's pregnant, you fuck!"

"Yeah, with another fucking half-breed!" Tal sneers, trying to push past Cora.

"ENOUGH!" Cora cries, and the shock-wave of the Inera washes over us, the ground beneath our feet quaking.

When the explosion of light dissipates. Tal looks at me, his shoulders heaving, his eyes back to normal. His face crumples with pain and disbelief as he lowers his gaze to

Cora.

"I'm sorry," he says quietly. "Fuck, Cora, I'm so sorry." Cora puts her arms around him, drawing him close, and he buries his face in her hair. "I'm so sorry. Fuck, what's wrong with me?" He looks up at me, shaking his head. "Amryn. I'm sorry."

I exhale heavily, rubbing my jaw. "Yeah, me too."

Cora releases Tal and her green eyes fix on me. "Whatever this is, whatever you've found out, we can't let it do this to us, OK? We can't let it tear us apart."

"Tal's worried that maybe us being your Draws has something to do with the witches corrupting the Line," I tell her. "Maybe we're meant to destroy you, and we just don't know it."

Cora scoffs, and shakes her head, looking up at Tal. "How many times, how many opportunities have you both had to hurt me, when I was totally unaware?" She strokes his cheek. "You don't think Morgan would have used Amryn before now, to take me out, if she'd had the chance?"

Tal shakes his head, putting his hand over her hand. "I know. It's crazy. It's stupid. I just don't understand..." His eyes are mournful as he looks into her face. "What if everything's connected, in a way we just don't understand yet?"

Cora inhales sharply. "We - we don't know. And until we do, we'll just... We'll just wait and see."

Lightning flashes above us, and Cora's brow furrows as she gazes up at the gray sky. "It can't be." She murmurs.

Footsteps crunch through the snow, and we all turn to

see the Old God walking through the trees towards us, frowning heavily. Tal and I both take a step back at the same time. Neither of us have ever seen him before, not in person, he only ever talks to Cora. His eyes are fixed on Tal, his expression darkening with every step he takes.

"It seems we didn't learn anything from the last time, did we, Tallesaign?" His voice is thunderous.

"What do you mean?" Cora asks, placing herself between them.

The Old God stops walking, clasping his hands over his round belly. "Why don't you ask your Draw here what he's been up to?"

I look over at Tal, whose eyes are fixed on the ground. "Tal?"

"What are you talking about?" Cora asks. "Tal hasn't done anything."

The Old God inhales heavily through his nose, his eyes rising to the sky. "The last time this happened, there was a mutiny that weakened me so heavily it took hundreds of years for Fate to right itself, and I am in no mood for that to happen again." He looks back at Tal, drumming his fingers rhythmically against one another. "Are you going to tell them, Tallesaign, or shall I?"

"Tal?" Cora turns to look at him. "What did you do?"

Tal shakes his head. "Nothing. I don't know what he's talking about."

The Old God scoffs. "Indeed."

Cora sighs in exasperation. "Just tell me."

"He and the fallen angel he rescued," the Old God

says, "have decided to violate the Blood Covenant."

"What Blood Covenant?" Cora asks.

"The one dictating a mingling of the species would not take place." The Old God says.

Tal laughs bitterly. "An intermingling, huh?" He crosses his arms over his chest. "And why is it that two intermingled hybrids were chosen as the Draws of your Shadow Queen?"

"Don't change the subject," the Old God scolds him.

"Is someone going to tell me what's going on?" Cora asks.

"Juno and I," Tal says, not looking at her, his eyes staying on the Old God.

The Old God shakes his head. "The angels always told me your kind were depraved, voracious, unable to control your primal urges. All these years, I looked away, I gave you all the good grace to believe that you would behave yourselves."

"Behave ourselves?" Tal asks incredulously. "I had sex with a woman I love. She gave herself to me willingly."

"It is forbidden." The Old God's voice becomes deeper, bouncing off the trees, the snow, a sickening echo around us. "And she is not just a woman, she is an angel and -"

"And I'm a witch," Tal interjects. "Now, again, I'd like to know why you chose the two of us to be the Draws of your anointed Queen?"

The Old God's eyes flash dangerously. "I do not answer to you."

223

"And I don't answer to you." Tal replies.

Cora's head snaps to look at him. "Tal, enough."

"I'd actually like to know the answer to that, too," I say, stepping forward. Tal's eyes flash to mine, and he gives me a brief nod. Cora's gaze is pleading as she looks at me, and I shake my head. "No, I mean it. Tal's right."

"Demons may do what they like," the Old God scoffs, "but the angels -"

"Oh so this is about keeping the bloodline pure, is it?" Tal chuckles, running a thumb along his lip. "I get it. So down here, we can fuck who we like so long as we leave your precious winged babies alone, is that it?"

"Cora," the Old God says, "get your Draw in line or I will be forced to do it for you."

"Get me in line?" Tal steps forward, and Cora turns to put her hands on his chest, trying to push him back, but Tal ignores her, looking over her shoulder. "Get me in line? That's all we ever do around here, get in line to fight your battles for you, to give you your power back."

"Tal, stop," Cora says.

"Why us?" Tal asks. "I want you to tell me why the beings who corrupted the Line and twisted Fate, the ones who turned Azrael into a fucking walking corpse, are the ones you tasked with protecting the Shadow Queen."

"Cora." The Old God's hands begin to crackle with electricity,

"Tal, stop it now." Cora's voice is strained, pleading, fighting against tears.

Tal's eyes begin to shimmer red. "I want to know why

224

you'd trust us, when we're the very beings that took everything away from you."

"Tallesaign!" Cora grabs his face, forcing him to look at her. "Stop this, please."

"I want to fucking know!" Tal pushes past Cora, out of her grasp, squaring up to the Old God, whose arms are crackling with lightning. "I want to know what kind of plan we're a part of, old man."

"Cora," the Old God says, his voice lethally low. "I told you. I warned you."

"Tallesaign, please," Cora cries. "Please stop!" Her eyes turn to me with alarm as she sees I've summoned my flames too. "Have you both gone crazy?"

"That's my brother," I say, to her, to the Old God, I'm not sure anymore, "and if you hurt him you deal with me."

Tal's back explodes with those towering red wings of flame, and the Old God's eyes widen for a moment, before his mouth sets in a line. He raises his hand.

"Tallesaign!" Cora screams.

It takes me a moment to figure out what's happened. There's a rush of white crackling past us, the smell of ozone, and the Old God goes flying. Tal is still standing there, his wings roaring at his back. The flash of white is on the Old God, red hair flailing in the snapping, crackling lightning.

"You don't touch him!" The voice of the creature on top of the Old God is high-pitched, screaming. "You touch him and I tear out your throat!"

It's Juno.

Juno, with white lightning racing up and down her limbs, emanating from her fingertips, her hand around the Old God's neck, her teeth bared. None of us moves, I think the others are probably as shocked as I am at the sight of a fallen angel holding down the Old God by the throat.

And he looks terrified.

Juno turns to look over her shoulder at Tal. Her eyes are blank white, her teeth sharp. With her attention diverted, the Old God strikes, sending a lightning ball into Juno's chest. Her arms fly up around her face as she's launched into the air, landing with a thud 20 feet away.

Tal's flames roar up his arms, and he sends a strike at the Old God, who deflects the red flames away from him with a wave of his hand. He summons another ball of electricity in his hands as he looks at Tal.

Cora springs in front of Tal, her hands up in front of him. "Stop this!" She cries, her whole body glowing white. "Enough!"

Juno is back on her feet, by my side, her hands clawed as the white volts sizzle within them. My flames are still licking up my arms.

The Old God looks around at us all, and shakes his head. "This is mutiny, Cora."

She looks over at me, and her chest is heaving. "Everyone needs to calm down."

"When he gives us an answer, we will," I say, looking back at the Old God.

His beard twitches as his eyes meet mine. "I don't owe you an answer."

"You know who we are though," I say. "You knew what we were when you chose us."

"I'm bored of this line of questioning," he says, brushing his hands together, and the lightning goes out. He looks back at Tal. "You are not to touch her, do you understand?" He points at Juno, who is still engulfed in white lightning beside me.

"You can go fuck yourself," Tal replies.

The Old God scoffs and shakes his head. "This is unbelievable. Cora, get your house in order." He disappears into nothing.

Tal draws his wings in and rushes to Juno. I take a step back from her as the lightning dissipates, and feel Cora's hand wrap around mine. I look down at her wide eyes, and she exhales heavily, leaning her head against my shoulder.

"Juno?" Tal asks, holding her face in his hands. "What was that?"

"I don't know," she says, clasping onto his hands, "I sensed you were in danger, and I - I just - I don't know what came over me." Her eyes move to Cora. "How the fuck did I do that?"

Cora lets out a shaky breath. "I think we all need to talk."

16
Tallesaign

*M*y cabin is filled with shocked silence. I stoke the fire in the hearth, the crackling of the logs as they burn deafening. I turn back to look at Cora, Amryn and Juno, sitting at my table. They're all staring at nothing. We all know that what's coming isn't good.

"Juno remembered something," I say, breaking the silence.

Cora's eyes rise to meet mine, as though waking from a trance, and she blinks as she looks over at Juno. "And what was that?"

"Gabriel," Juno says slowly, "he is the one who cut off my wings."

Cora's eyes merely widen for a moment. I think she's beyond shock at this point. "The way he looked at you, that doesn't surprise me to be honest." She shakes her head, raking a hand through her curls. "It kind of makes sense. And with what we know about you now, I think we can safely guess you're not just an angel."

"Who do you think I am?" Juno asks.

Cora casts a sideways glance at Amryn, and sighs, her fingers tracing the woodgrain in the table. "The Old God mentioned Arax smoking red once before, in pretty recent history. And since it smoked red again when Tal found you, I think we can guess that you two are linked somehow."

"What do you mean?" I ask.

"Arax spewed red smoke the day you were born," Cora says to me.

I give my shoulders a shake. "I don't get what that has to do with Juno."

"Neither do I, not clearly anyway," Cora replies, looking back at Juno, "but if Gabriel did cut off your wings, and throw you down onto that mountain, he has reason to want you down here, not up in the Halls."

Juno nods slowly, pulling a knee up against her chest and wrapping her arms around it. "I wish I could remember more."

"You will," Cora assures her, "it'll come back."

"So what about the Old God?" Amryn asks, crossing his arms over his chest. "You really think he came all the way down here just to give Tal a ticking off for not keeping it in his pants?"

"No." Cora bites her lip. "It doesn't make any sense."

"The Old God did what?" Juno turns her head towards me.

"The Old God said we violated the Blood Covenant," I tell her. "He knows we -" I break off, my eyes flickering over to Cora and Amryn.

"He knows we fucked," Juno says plainly, and Amryn's face breaks into a grin.

"Sorry." He runs a hand over his face. "Fuck, sorry, I just -" His chest starts to shake as he laughs, and I feel my own mouth twitching as I meet Juno's eyes. The tension in the room dissipates as we all burst into giggles, the nerves and insanity of the day clearly getting to us.

"I need a drink," I say, heading into the kitchen.

"Yes!" Amryn's hand shoots into the air. "Me too."

"Me too," Juno says, then eyes Cora sympathetically. "Oh poor Cora, she can't."

Cora waves her hand. "It's OK, I'll watch you all enjoy it." She smiles at Juno as she reaches across the table to take her hand. "Just water for me, Tal."

I put a glass of bourbon down in front of Amryn and Juno, handing Cora a glass of water. I take a sip of my bourbon as I sit back down next to Juno.

"So, what do we know?" I say, spinning the glass on the table.

"We're half-witch," Amryn says, "and we should probably talk to Elise about that at some point."

"Agreed," I reply.

"We know Gabriel and the Old God are afraid of Juno." Cora's eyes narrow as she stares at the table. "And we know Juno has powers now, unlike any we've seen before."

"Tal's powers have changed," Juno says. "The flames, the wings."

Amryn nods. "Yeah. That's true."

Cora throws her head back and growls. "Fuck, nothing makes any sense, how is any of this connected?"

"Maybe we're looking at this all wrong," Amryn says, "we're looking for connections between everything. Maybe not everything is connected, maybe it's just, I don't know, incidental strands caught up in something bigger. Let's pare it back."

"OK." Cora leans back in her chair. "Pare it back to what?"

Amryn gestures at me and Juno. "OK, let's start here. So Arax smokes red the day you're born and again once Juno is thrown down onto that mountain. So you two are bonded."

"Despite a Blood Covenant?" Cora asks.

"Who made those covenants, baby?" Amryn asks. "The Old God, you heard him, he said it was about keeping the angels' bloodline clean, and himself strong."

"I don't understand." Juno shakes her head, raising her glass to her lips. "You think he has reason to not want angels and demons to mate?"

"It sure sounded like it to me," Amryn says. "What if the Downfall was just a power play? Throwing the demons out because they kept the angels in check? Because we loved humans too much?" He looks back at Juno and I. "He wants you two kept apart, and in my experience there's a very good fucking reason for that."

Cora exhales heavily. "Holy shit."

"Ok, so that's that. Next." I roll my finger in the air. "You, me, and Cora. What's that about?"

"Did the witches corrupt the line?" Cora's gaze shifts to

each of our faces as we stare at her. "What?" She shrugs. "If the angels could lay blame for the Downfall on the birth of a hybrid demon angel baby, what other lies have we been told?"

Amryn nods, taking a sip of bourbon. "Good point."

"We know the witches helped the Alphas, setting the new clan order," I say.

"Under whose direction?" Cora asks. "Michael, working with the clan in Nilau, what reason would he have to ally himself with them? To get to me? He didn't need to do that." She chews her lip for a moment. "No, there's something else going on there."

"You think the witches were working with the archangels to keep the Old God weak?" Amryn asks.

"No." Cora shakes her head. "I think it's something completely different. I think they're all working against something we can't see yet."

Fuck. Everything I thought I ever knew is being torn to shreds in front of me. I reach over and put my hand on Juno's leg, and she smiles at me.

"Can you summon that power?" My eyes flash to her hands.

She lifts her fingers, and as she flexes them, a faint white shimmer runs over them. She sighs. "I guess not."

"So that brings us back to you two being bonded. Your flames changing," Amryn says, then looks at Juno, "and you sensing he's in danger and freight training the Old God with a power you didn't even know you had, I mean, you two, that's meant to be. And the Old God, he looked the same way Lordain did when I came running in to tell them I knew Cora was in Sfayder."

"What look was that?" Cora asks.

Amryn smiles at her. "Dread, baby. He knew that our Bond was getting stronger."

Cora smirks with satisfaction. "Wish I could have seen that."Amryn lifts her hand to his lips, his eyes staying on hers as he kisses it.

I gulp down the last of my bourbon and put the empty glass on the table. "So what else is there?"

"Gabriel playing torturer." Amryn says.

Juno shifts in her seat. "There were more people involved. I remember there were others there. People I trusted." Her brow furrows as she tries to remember. "I feel like, I don't know, a brother?"

"Your brother handed you over to Gabriel?" I ask incredulously and then my stomach turns as I remember what she said the other night, what she remembered about this person and what they did to her. It being her brother just adds another layer of shit to this already awful situation.

Juno shrugs. "Perhaps. But someone did, someone I trusted, they betrayed me."

"The Old God would know that," Amryn says, "and I think the way he was looking at you tells me he knew exactly who you were and what happened to you."

Juno rubs her temples with her fingertips. "OK, is there anything else?"

"At this point, I think that's all the information we have." Amryn stretches his shoulders, wincing a little as his gaze lands on me. "I really am sorry about today."

"Me too, brother. That was... it was stupid."

Juno looks at me questioningly. "What happened?"

"My brother and I got a little heated, and we sort of ended up hitting each other." I tell her, and her eyes widen with alarm.

"Oh you boys," she chides, throwing her hands in the air. "And I suppose poor Cora was out there breaking it up, *da*?"

Amryn and I eye each other sheepishly. "Yeah, she was," Amryn admits.

"That really seemed to bother you," Cora says to me, "the whole being a hybrid thing. You were really heated up about it."

I sigh, pushing the empty glass back and forth between my hands. "The Downfall and all that, it was always a huge deal, they weren't accepted. I don't even know, I mean, I can't believe Dad accepted Mom."

"I wonder how he found out," Amryn muses, rubbing his thumb across his chin. "And I wonder what Elise will have to say about it all."

Cora yawns, and stretches her arms over her head. "OK look, we might need to pick this up again tomorrow. I'm exhausted and we need to go home and get our son off to bed."

Amryn nods and rises to his feet, pulling Cora up with him. "Yeah, I think we could all do with some rest." He gives us both a wide smile. "I'm happy for you two, despite all the shit. I mean it."

"Thank you," Juno replies, entwining her fingers with mine.

Cora plants a kiss on the top of Juno's head as they head out, and Amryn claps me on the shoulder. "Good night, you two," Cora says as they leave.

"Make the Old God angry!" Amryn calls just before the door closes. I hear Cora smack him, and he laughs as she does.

Juno grins at me and shakes her head. "I like your family."

"Yeah, they're pretty great." I pull my cigarette case out of my pocket, lighting two and handing one to Juno. "Now that the pregnant lady is gone."

"Mmm," she sighs as she inhales. "My goodness, what a day."

"Yeah, you can say that again."

"So, I heard right, yes?" She puts a hand on my leg. "You and Amryn, you found out you are witches?"

"Half-witch, half-demon," I say with a nod. "The witch here in the village, Fenella, the one who healed you? She's my grandmother, and I had no idea."

Juno's jaw drops. "No. Oh Tal, it really has been a day for you. Are you alright?"

"No, I was an ass about it. I need to apologize to her." I scratch my cheek with my thumb. "It was just a shock."

"Of course it was."

"And this," I gesture to my chest, "this was from my mother."

"What?" Juno says with a gasp. "But why would she do

such a thing?"

"To protect me." My eyes sting for a moment, and I blink rapidly, pushing away the emotion welling up inside me. "I was running in to save them, to stop them from being taken. I knew..." I clear my throat. "I think I knew I was going to die. But they needed me."

Juno reaches over to take my hand. "She did what any mother would have done, even if it meant hurting you."

I nod, tracing Juno's hand with the backs of my fingers. "Yeah." I give her a smile. "I can't believe you were going to kill a whole ass god for me."

Juno raises her eyebrows and shakes her head. "It was the most insane feeling, I just - I exploded. I was sitting here and then I felt your distress, and I -" She breaks off, raising the hand she's holding the cigarette in, and white volts shimmer up her fingers. "It's the strangest sensation. Like the heat of the sun on my face, but I am in a dark room. I cannot touch it, I can only feel it."

"You'll harness it, don't worry. It was the same for Cora with the Inera, she had to learn to summon it."

"Yes, I suppose I will." She extinguishes the dancing white sparks with a squeeze of her hand. Her eyes move back to me, and she grimaces a little. "What do you suppose the Old God will do now that he knows about us?"

I shrug. "Something tells me that you're more powerful than we know. Otherwise he wouldn't have backed down like that." Smoke billows from my lips as I reach over and trace a finger down her cheek. "I'm not afraid of him."

"Me neither." She takes my hand in hers and turns her

mouth towards it. I expect her to kiss my fingers, but suddenly her teeth have sunk into my thumb, and I jerk in surprise. She giggles as her eyes meet mine. "You like the pain, don't you?"

I don't know what to say. Because she's right. My groin is flooded with heat. I guess I do. I watch as she rises to her feet, stripping off her sweater, peeling her leggings off slowly, her eyes on me the whole time.

"Since the Old God is watching," she says, shaking her hair out, "perhaps we should give him something to look at?" She leans down to run her hands over my chest. "Look at you," she purrs, "waiting for me, hmmm?"

I lick my lips and nod. She chuckles, spreading her hands. My chest ripples under her touch, and she climbs on top of me. Her breath warms the shell of my ear.

"Take me to bed." That tone. That command. It has me hard instantly.

I carry her to the bedroom and lay her down on the bed. She moves back, watching me get undressed, her eyes taking me in.

No one has ever looked at me like this before. No one has ever made me feel like I'm the only thing they've ever wanted, the only thing they've ever dreamed of.

I climb onto the bed, crawling towards her, and she opens her legs. Just as I kneel between her thighs, she puts out a hand and stops me there.

"You need to be patient," she says with a grin.

I watch as she pushes two fingers between the lips of her pussy, bare inches from my cock, and I'm instantly breathing rapidly. I lift my eyes to meet hers, and she moans.

"You watch," she says, "you were bad today, and you need a little punishment."

I suck in a serrated breath at her words and lower my eyes back to her pussy. Her fingers are coated in her arousal, and I dig my hands into my thighs as I watch her swirl over her clit.

I want to watch her face, I want to see her mouth fall open as she moans, I want to see her eyes flutter closed - fuck, I want to make her moan, I want to make her come. But I watch, like she told me to.

This is the sweetest fucking punishment I've ever been subjected to. The most frustrating one, too. My hands are almost shaking with determination, to keep them where they are, to not move to touch her.

Her pussy is glowing and glistening, and her thighs tremble a little, the barest fluttering touch against my skin. I suppress a groan as she pushes two fingers of her other hand inside herself. This is magical, and driving me fucking insane.

I lick my lips again, my mouth is watering so violently as I imagine how she tastes right now. Fuck I want to taste her again. I want her to soak my entire fucking body right now.

"Every time you're bad," she says, almost whimpering, "this is what I do to you."

"Yes."

She raises her feet to hook her ankles over my shoulders, and I can't help the growl that escapes me. Her fingers are moving faster now, and she's fucking served up right in front of me, so wet and beautiful, her scent filling my nostrils.

Her ass trembles against my swollen cock, and I bite my lip to stop myself coming. My nerves are on edge, every single fiber of my being focused on her, on her body as it rises to the climax she's chasing.

"Do you want to make me come?" She asks.

"Yes." *Oh fucking god yes.* "Please let me make you come."

"Tal." She drags my name out on the edge of a breathy moan.

"Please." I want to touch her. My hands are digging so hard into my thighs I'm sure I'm drawing blood and the pain makes everything so much fucking sweeter. "Please let me make you come."

Her back arches as she cries out. "Oh god."

I can't take it anymore. "*JUNO.* Please let me." Oh *FUCK,* let me touch you. Let me look up at you. Fuck fuck *FUCK.* "*Please.*"

She shakes violently, and then she suddenly stops, moving her hands. "Your mouth," she says with a sigh, " now."

The now wasn't necessary. I seize her hips and pull her up to my mouth and sink my lips into her with a loud groan. I look at her face as I lap up all that sweet arousal, and her eyes are fixed on me, her mouth open as she pants.

She's wound so tightly that it only takes a few strokes of my tongue and she's screaming my name. Her whole body shakes, her fingers digging into the bed. But I don't stop. I have to keep tasting her, and I hold her greedily to my face, not letting her go.

"Yeah," she moans, "again. Again."

Her hands feather over her peaked nipples, those perfect breasts rising and falling with every quivering breath. She moans as her eyes meet mine. The high flush on her cheeks is so beautiful, and her lower lip trembles.

"Tal, oh fuck, oh god." The last word is lost as her thighs begin to quake. Her eyes stay on me, drawing me in, keeping me right there with her.

Just as she whimpers I push a finger inside her, and then she's pulsing around me, against me, making a sound almost like a sob as she comes.

I keep licking until a jerk of her hips tells me to stop, and I release her gently, placing her ass on the bed, my fingers caressing her thighs.

Her chest jerks as she tries to catch her breath, and seeing her spread out like this, in a mess because of me, because of my mouth - it's intoxicating.

"Come here," she says.

I crawl over her, and her legs wrap around my waist, drawing me down so my cock throbs against her. She kisses me hungrily, her fingers spearing through my hair. A slight adjustment of her hips and I slide inside her, groaning into her mouth.

I've never needed anyone like this. No one's ever understood what *I* fucking need like this - least of all me. But as she gazes up at me, as she moans, as I feel her body against me, against all of me, everything slips into sharp focus. I'm surrendering everything to her, every part of me. And it's perfection.

I thrust into her, and her thighs tighten around me.

"Slowly," she murmurs, "I want you to take your time with me."

It's agonizing and beautiful at the same time. Her hands are still in my hair, her mouth nipping at mine as she gasps. Her hips roll gently under me, meeting my strokes, letting me sink to the hilt into her heat. Consuming me. Everything about this consumes me.

Her eyes squeeze shut, her back arching under me. I press my lips to her throat, tasting her sweat and her scent. Her hips rock harder against me, and those sobs break from her again. Her body shakes gently, and I feel her pussy fluttering around my cock.

She's breathing heavy as I keep moving, and it takes all my willpower to keep this pace. I bite my lip as she gazes up at me, trying to focus on her. She pulls me back down to her, kissing me, her little moans meeting my mouth. She's slick with sweat, searing hot and trembling.

She wraps her arms around me as I start to shiver against her, feeling that heat in my groin, so good and unbearable at the same time. Her breathing is ragged against my ear, and I clutch her to me, letting her warmth envelop me as I shudder and release deep inside her.

Her fingers caress my back as I subside, gently playing with my hair. She moves one hand to stroke my cheek with the backs of her fingers, and for some insane reason tears spring to my eyes. It's such a small action, but it's so tender, so filled with care.

No one's ever cared for me like this.

241

"That was incredible," she whispers, running her lips along my jaw. "I love you so much."

"I love you too." I rise up onto my elbows, looking down at her, looking into those beautiful brown eyes. "I feel like you know more about me than I know about myself."

She giggles and strokes my cheek softly. "I'm a pretty good judge of character." She leans up and plants a quick kiss on my lips. "Your whole life you've had to look after everyone, you've had to bear this burden, my love. You deserve to be looked after now."

"And punished too, huh?" I smile at her.

"Yes, when you have been very bad." She draws me back down to her and kisses me, slowly. "But even the punishment seemed to please you."

"Everything you do pleases me."

She laughs out loud. "Careful my love, that's a very high standard to hold." She takes a hold of my chin, lifting an eyebrow. "Now, you're going to take me to the shower and do a very good job of cleaning me up."

A shower is just a shower, it shouldn't be anything special. But this feels sacred, like I'm somehow worshiping her, trying to please her. I stand behind her under the hot water and she tilts her head as I lather her hair. I massage her scalp with my fingertips, and she groans softly.

"Have I ever told you how much I love your hands?"

"I had a pretty good idea."

"Well, I love your hands." She lets me rinse the shampoo from her hair and leans back against my chest, turning her face to nuzzle into the crook of my neck. "I love all of you. So big, so strong."

I wrap my arms around her waist, holding her to me, and a sensation settles into my chest that I don't think I've ever felt before. I'm content. I feel whole, and seen, deeply content. It's foreign, but it's nice.

I kiss her temple and move to turn off the taps. "Come on, let's get you dried off. We should try and get some sleep."

We dry off and head to bed, neither of us in the mood to wear anything that would stop us feeling each other's skin. We lie down together, her back to me at first, but she quickly flips over so she can nuzzle those soft lips into the crook of my neck.

"You smell so good," she says with a sigh, her fingertips brushing against my chest. "This is definitely my favourite place to be.

I trace delicate kisses along her forehead, breathing her in. "I wouldn't want you to be anywhere else."

Her warmth is almost overwhelming, and my eyes become heavy quickly. Within minutes her breathing deepens, and she's asleep. I hold her a little closer, as I drift off, sure, for the first time in my life, that I'll never go to sleep alone again.

17
Tallesaign

mryn and Cora are standing on the doorstep
the next morning, smiling widely.

"Good morning," Amryn says brightly, "did
you make the Old God angry?"

Cora looks at me with a heavy sigh and rolls her eyes.

"We did!" Juno calls from the kitchen table, and
Amryn bursts out laughing.

"You two are such squares," he says, looking from me
to Cora.

I shake my head and laugh, stepping aside to let them
in. "You two want coffee?"

"We were actually wondering if you and Juno wanted
to come for a walk with us?" Cora tucks her hands into the
pockets of her coat. "Phoenix wants to go sledding and
build a snowman, do you two want to come?"

"Oh that sounds wonderful!" Juno rises to her feet,
smiling widely as I look over my shoulder at her. "We
would love to!"

"Great." Amryn takes Cora's hand and pulls her along

the porch. "We'll meet you over at our cabin then."

"Sure thing." I wave them off as I close the door.

Juno sidles over to me and puts her arms around my neck, kissing me gently. "A proper day with the family," she says, gazing up at me. "I feel like a part of it now."

"Yeah, you and my brother making sex jokes, you two are going to get on just fine." I stroke her chin with my thumb.

She throws her head back and laughs, and fuck I love it when she does that. I pull her into my arms and kiss her neck, and she puts her hands against my chest with a giggle.

"They are waiting for us. You will have to wait until later to devour me again."

"Is that a promise?" I growl against her neck.

"Oh yes," she says with a sigh, "that I can promise you."

We finally tear ourselves away from each other long enough to get dressed, and head outside to meet Amryn and Cora. Phoenix is dressed in his funny little pointy hood again, all bundled up on his sled, his cheeks and nose bright red from the cold.

"Uncy Tal!" He raises his gloved hands into the air. "We gonna sled downa big hill?"

"We sure are, buddy." I walk over to take the guide rope attached to the front of the sled. "Come on, let's get you moving, huh?"

Cora walks alongside me and I look over my shoulder to see Amryn and Juno walking together, talking and laughing. Phoenix is humming along to himself, and the sky above is overcast but bright.

"Nice day, huh?" Cora says after a moment.

"Yeah, a real nice day."

She looks up at me with a smile. "You know when you're happy I can feel it too, right? Just like how you can with me?"

I nod. "I figured as much."

"Since Juno came I feel a whole lot of happy coming from you," she says with a chuckle. "*All* kinds of happy."

I suppress a laugh as my cheeks burn. "Well, this isn't awkward at all." I give her a side glance. "So I take it you and Amryn had a good night last night too then, huh?"

Cora laughs quietly. "Like he needs any encouragement."

We both look over our shoulders when we hear Juno shriek, and Amryn has thrown her over his shoulder and is running towards a snow drift with her. There's a flurry of white as he dumps her in it, and Amryn ducks as Juno starts throwing snow at him.

Cora giggles and shakes her head. "They're like the same person," she says, and then looks back up at me. "You and me, her and him. No wonder we ended up with them, huh?"

"Guess we both got good taste, kiddo."

Juno and Amryn are throwing snowballs at each other now, and Phoenix leaps off the sled to go and join them.

"Come help me, buddy!" Amryn calls, but Phoenix picks up a handful of snow and tosses it at his father.

Amryn puts a hand to his forehead theatrically, and clutches his chest. "My own son!" He exclaims, sinking to his knees. "My own son has betrayed me!"

Phoenix laughs out loud and launches himself at his father, and hearing my brother and his son laugh so loudly makes my chest swell. I turn to see Cora gazing at me with that dreamy look again.

"What?" I ask.

"When am I going to be an aunty, huh?" She shoves me gently in the chest with her shoulder.

"An aunty?" I laugh incredulously. "Getting a little ahead of yourself there, don't you think?"

She shrugs. "Nope. It's meant to be."

I don't want to admit to the warm feeling that spreads through my body at the thought. It's as crazy as everything else is about this situation, about having this connection to a person I've only known for a short time.

I know that I want to be with Juno, forever. And it's more than just knowing - I feel it. Deep in my soul. I get what Amryn always talked about now, how he feels about Cora. It's more than love. It's meant to be. And maybe having a family together will be a part of that.

Cora's still looking at me when I gaze back down at her. "I told you, you're allowed to want the things you want. You deserve it."

I nod quickly, then gesture to her belly. "I never congratulated you by the way."

Her hand flutters to her stomach, and she shrugs. "Oh, yeah. Thank you. I still can't believe it."

"Amryn's probably thrilled, huh?"

"Yeah." She lowers her eyes to the snow, an awkward smile pasted on her face. "Yeah, he can't wait, he's excited."

I lower my head a little, trying to catch her gaze. "And you?"

Her eyes flash back up to mine, and she shakes her head quickly. "Oh no, I am, I really am. It's just..." She wraps her arms across her body. "I'm just scared. What this whole thing will mean for her, what she'll have to face, you know?"

"She'll be OK." I step closer to put my arm around Cora's shoulders. "She has you, and her Dad, and all of us, OK?" I put a tentative hand on her belly, and she clasps her own hand over it. "We're all together, OK? You don't have to be scared."

Cora leans her head against my shoulder and nods. "I know. I know. I think some days I still can't get it all straight in my head. What this all means."

"I know, honey." I squeeze her shoulders and kiss the top of her head. "We're all still figuring this stuff out."

We stand and watch Amryn and Juno play with Phoenix in the snow, their laughter echoing through the forest around us. Phoenix turns and gestures to me excitedly.

"Uncy Tal, we build a snowman?" He calls.

I nod with a smile. "Sure thing buddy." I look down at Cora. "Come on, let's enjoy the day, huh? Got to celebrate the fact I'm going to have a niece to carry around soon."

Cora rolls her eyes as we start walking. "Oh god, she is

going to be so spoiled, between you and her daddy."

"She sure as hell will be."

The morning flies by amidst building snowmen and running up and down hills with Phoenix. I keep looking over at Juno and feeling a deep sense of being complete. She really was the missing piece in all of this, for me at least. And every time she smiles back at me, my breath catches a little bit. Holy shit I've got it bad.

After a few hours, everyone is suitably frozen through and Phoenix passes out on the sled. We decide to head back, Amryn pulling the sled behind him as he sidles along with his arm draped around Cora. Juno and I follow, my arm around her.

"That was fun," she says, leaning against me.

"Yes it was."

She gives me a sideways glance and grins. "Do you want to have children?"

I try not to be too enthusiastic about the fact that she's asking me this question. I clear my throat and shrug. "Yeah, I'd like to have some. How about you?"

"If they're all as sweet as that little boy," she says, looking ahead at Phoenix, who is sleeping soundly as he's ferried across the snow, "I want at least ten."

I laugh and kiss her temple. "Maybe we'll start with one and see, huh?"

"Start?" Her eyebrows shoot up. "Now?"

"You... You wanna start now?" I ask.

"I was asking if you do." She grins. "Although with how the last few nights have been perhaps it is too late to question that, hmm?"

I flush a little. "Yeah, maybe." I clear my throat. "I guess it wasn't very responsible of me to just, uh -"

"Oh stop it," she interjects, nuzzling into me. "I wasn't much better." Her brown eyes are soft as she smiles up at me. "Let us see what happens, yes? Perhaps we will have our own little one before we know it."

God fucking dammit, why do those words send butterflies rushing through my stomach? I'm insane. We're both insane. But then... if we're that deeply connected, does it matter?

We reach Cora and Amryn's cabin, and Amryn sweeps Phoenix up into his arms. "Let's get this little guy off for a nap," he says softly.

"Why don't you two come over for lunch once he's down?" I say.

"Sure, Ebony and Liall can sit with him," Cora says with a nod. "We'll be right over."

They head inside, and Juno and I sidle back to my cabin, our arms still around each other. I help her out of her coat inside and she shivers. The fire has died down and it's a little cold inside.

"Come on, I'll get that fire going." I strip off my own coat and kick off my boots before I head for the fire, stoking up the glowing embers and throwing more logs on, which begin to crackle instantly.

Juno curls up on the couch behind me. "Tell me about your parents. What were they like?"

I stoke the logs a little, watching the flames lick up the sides of the splintered wood. I turn and sit on the ground with a sigh. "They were... complicated." I shrug when I meet her confused gaze. "My Mom was... she was sweet, but she was weak. She didn't stand up for me, and whatever my Dad said, well, those were the rules. And she didn't go against those no matter what it meant for me."

Juno frowns. "I'm sorry, my love. If you don't want to talk about this -"

"No, no," I say with a wave of my hand. "No, it's fine. I mean, it happened, you know? It's my history. My Dad was... Ummm..." I swallow hard. "He was abusive. It took me a long time to say it, because, you know, I was a kid. It was my normal. But, uh, he was abusive. He beat the shit out of me whenever I put a toe out of line. It was so bad once that Rodelth, Cora's dad, had to step in."

Juno gasps. "Oh Tal."

"Yeah." There's an unpleasant lump forming at the back of my throat. "I was 17, and this girl in the village, she was interested in me. I had to sleep out on the porch to protect Cora and Amryn, and then one night, this girl, she came to find me, and dragged me off to the barn. And we, you know..."

"Had sex?"

"Yeah, it was my first time." I shrug. "I was nervous and excited, and it felt nice and all that kind of thing. She was really sweet and pretty. It was meant to be a special thing, you know? And then when I got back, my Dad was waiting for me, and he was furious. Beat the shit out of me. Broke my arm."

Juno's eyes flare. "He did what?" Her back straightens. "Tal, he did what?"

I nod. I haven't ever really spoken about this before, and hearing the words come out of my mouth, I realize now just how fucked up it all was. And how no one protected me.

"At that point, Rodelth stepped in. Told my dad that it was too much, it wasn't appropriate, and so on. My dad was just angry. Never apologized. Acted like I'd done the wrong thing."

"And what did your mother do?"

I can't help the bitter laugh that passes my lips. "Nothing. Like always. Nothing. Told me she had a fight with him, like that mattered. Like that made a fucking difference." I pick up a splinter of wood from the pile and shred it in half, throwing the pieces in the grate. "His behavior never changed. Not til the day he died. Even though now, it would seem that the last thing he did was save my life. So..." I shrug. Another fucked up, complicated situation I'll never have closure over.

Juno climbs down off the couch and crawls across the floor. She kneels in front of me and puts a hand to my cheek. "I am so sorry, my love. I know those words don't help, but you must know you did not deserve the childhood you had."

"I've always been scared I'd be as shitty a father as he was, you know?"

Juno shakes her head emphatically. "Never. The way you were with Phoenix today, shows me exactly what kind of lessons you learned, and what kind of man you want to be." She leans closer, and smiles as she strokes my cheek. "You would be a wonderful father. And I hope that one day I get to see you with our child in your arms."

Those words take my breath away. I clasp a hand over Juno's. "I hope for that too." For the first time in my life I dare to hope for that. Because maybe Juno's right. Maybe I would be a good father. Maybe I learned the lessons from that childhood, and now I'd ensure no one ever hurt my kid the way I was hurt.

I take Juno's hand and kiss the back of it, before pulling her close and planting a kiss on her lips. "Come on, let's get some food going before Cora and Amryn get here."

She clutches my face in her hands. "I love you."

"I love you too."

"Life can only get better now," she says, nudging her nose against mine, "because we're together."

The lunch with Cora and Amryn turned into dinner with Liall, Ebony and Phoenix over several glasses of bourbon. It only ended when Phoenix crashed on the couch amongst the music and dancing that ensued. Amryn is giggling as Cora leads him home, Phoenix draped over his father's shoulder, snoring softly.

"Good night!" I call after them, met only by more drunken giggles from Amryn and Cora calling good night back. I smile, shaking my head as I close the door.

Juno grins over her shoulder at me as I walk back into the kitchen, her hands elbow-deep in the sink as she washes the dishes. I stand behind her and put my arms around her waist.

"You could have left that til the morning," I say, tracing

my lips along her neck. "You could put those hands to much better use."

She leans her head back against me and chuckles. "Oh is that so?"

"Mmm." I run my hands over her stomach, and grip her hips.

"Are you drunk, my love?" She asks, reaching for the dish towel and drying her hands.

"No." I move to kiss the other side of her neck, "Just a little tipsy." I trace my kisses further, along her collarbone. "Thinking about tearing these clothes off you."

She giggles, turning her face towards me. "I like these thoughts."

"Oh yeah?" I work one hand underneath her shirt, up her stomach, and move it over her breast. I brush my palm over the peak of her nipple, and she sighs. "And what else would you like?"

She shakes her head. "Tonight you tell me what you like." She kisses me, her teeth nipping at my lower lip. "I want you to tell me exactly what you want, and where you want me."

The combination of the bourbon and the thrill of her words has me immediately hard. I turn her around in my arms, and the expectant lust in her eyes is so fucking hot. I thread my hand into her hair, pulling her head back and crushing her mouth under mine. Her hands move under my shirt, running up and down my back as I kiss her.

I pull back from her, grinning down at her. "Get on your knees."

She licks her lips as she obeys, smiling up at me once

she's kneeling before me. "And now?"

"You take my cock out like a good girl." My hand is still in her hair as she undoes my pants, my erection springing forth. The rush of power is made all the sweeter by the fact that she's giving this to me. Like a reward.

Her eyes stay fixed on me as she puts her mouth around the head of my cock, and I can't say I'm not more than a little pleased to see she can't fit much of me in her mouth. But holy fuck, it's enough. Her tongue swirls around me, her perfect little mouth moving up and down my length in perfect rhythm with her hand.

"Your mouth feels so fucking good," I say with a groan. Her other hand flexes on my hip, her nails digging into my skin so deep I'm sure she's drawing blood, and the pain makes those perfect movements of her mouth even more incredible.

She releases me for a moment, her hand still moving up and down. "Where do you want to come, my love?"

What a question. *Holy fuck.* My head is filled with a rush as she keeps moving her hand. No woman's ever asked me this before, and the crazed demon male side of me takes over. I want to fucking mark her.

"Take off your shirt." My fingers flexing in her hair. "I want to come on those perfect breasts."

I release her hair so she can slip the shirt off over her head, and then her mouth is back on me, sucking and swirling and pulling my cock deeper and deeper down her throat. Every tiny movement of taking me deeper makes the heat swelling in my groin more intense.

My head falls back as she sucks harder, and I try not to

thrust, but then her hands are gripping my hips and she's pulling me towards her. The heat of her mouth travels down further and further, everything is so wet now that every stroke of her tongue makes me feel like my goddamn eyes are going to roll back in my head.

With a groan I pull her off my cock, and she holds it between her breasts as I come. I watch as those hot, pumping streams cover her, dripping down her skin. I stroke her cheek with my thumb, and she turns her mouth, nipping at it. I grab her face harder, forcing her to look up at me.

"Uh-uh," I say in a low voice, "no biting yet, or I'm going to have to punish you."

Her eyes flame and she sinks her teeth into my thumb, making me suck in a breath through gritted teeth.

"Oh it's like that is it?" I pull her to her feet, my hand gripping the back of her head. "I'm going to take you to bed now and punish that pussy of yours." I lift her up and she wraps her legs around my waist, her mouth descending on mine.

We make it to the bedroom, hitting a few walls along the way, and I throw her down on the bed.

"Those, off." I point to her leggings, watching as she shimmies them down her legs while I remove the rest of my clothing. Her chest is still glistening with my cum, and the sight of her marked like this, marked by me... *Fuck.*

"Open your legs."

She lies back and does exactly what I told her to. I run my mouth along the length of her leg, nipping the skin of her upper thigh as I go. She's dripping for me, I can feel it,

R D Baker

I can smell it, holy *fuck*.

"Such a good girl," I murmur against her skin, spreading her with my thumb, over the swollen peak of her clit. "Look how wet you are for me."

I sink my mouth into her pussy, tasting all that sweet arousal. She cries out, her back arching as her fingers spear through my hair. I grab her wrists and pin her hands down on either side of her, and I swear I hear a lecherous laugh sound in her throat.

She's loving this. She's fucking loving the surrender.

She writhes and moans underneath me as my tongue strokes her clit. I could fucking die happy down here, between these thighs, feeling them tremble for me, feeling every shuddering movement of her body. It's paradise. She's so perfect.

She comes quickly, and her hips jerk as I keep licking, but I don't let her go. She whimpers, her back arching as she puts her feet on my shoulder blades.

But I don't stop. I want to hear her come again, and again, I want to taste her as she screams my fucking name.

"Tal," she moans, "oh fuck, Tal. I can't." Her thighs are shaking violently, and she's so fucking wet.

I groan into her pussy, holding her down. I look up at her and her head is tipped back on the bed, her chest rising and falling rapidly.

"Yeah," she moans, "oh fuck, yeah."

The cry that leaves her mouth as she comes for the second time is magical. Her hips lift off the bed and I have to push back with my shoulders to hold her down. I'm fucking hard again, and even though I want to keep making her come with my mouth, I need to feel her.

I climb over, between her legs, and plunge my cock inside her. Her fingers claw into the bed as I slam into her, there's nothing slow or tender about it. Juno reaches back to brace her hands against the headboard, her breasts on full display for me, still marked by me.

I collapse onto her as I come, feeling her thighs squeeze onto my hips as she moans. I can barely breathe, she's so fucking heavenly. She's everything I ever dreamed of.

She starts to laugh breathlessly, her fingers feathering up and down my back. "Oh shit," she says, turning her mouth towards me, brushing her lips against my cheek. "That was fucking amazing."

I raise myself a little so I can look into her face. "Yeah, it was. You're... I don't even have words for it."

She wraps herself around me with a satisfied sigh. "Sometimes it is nice to relinquish control." She nips at my neck, rolling herself against me. "It can be very, very pleasing." She's going to send me to an early grave.

I look down at her chest, and grin. "We should get you cleaned up."

She frowns a little, then laughs. "OK, if you insist. But then you are taking me back to bed and maybe marking me again?"

Definitely an early grave.

Once we're both clean we head back to bed. Despite her earlier teasing, Juno just curls up in my arms and snuggles into me. "You feel so nice," she murmurs, her lips brushing against my chest.

"So do you." I stroke her hair gently, my eyes fluttering closed. She's so warm, and my body is still floating on that blissful post-fuck rush.

Rain begins to patter against the roof. Juno relaxes in my arms, and it feels like she's asleep. A shadow passes the window, and I decide from behind my closed eyes that it must have been a cloud crossing the moon.

The moon that should be hidden by rain clouds. The steady drumming continues.

Rain? It's the middle of winter.

My eyes fly open as I realize it's not rain - it's footsteps. Lots of drumming footsteps, racing past my bedroom window. I climb out of the bed, and Juno lets out a sigh.

"Tal?"

I reach under the bed and retrieve my scimitar. "Stay down."

"Tal?" Her voice is suddenly taut with panic. "What is it?"

"There's someone out there. Stay down."

I look out the window, and the footsteps have stopped. I strain to hear anything. The yard is silent, no flitting shadows, no more footsteps.

I turn back to the bed. "I thought I heard -"

An explosion tears through the side of the cabin, and everything goes black.

18
Tallesaign

pening my eyes hurts.

All I can see is my hair, swaying in front of me. My head is rocking back and forth, my chin to my chest. I squint, and pain shoots through my temple. My hair is sticking to the side of my face, I must be bleeding.

My hands are bound behind me. I move them carefully, and the chains binding me clink against the metal floor. I raise my head, slowly, carefully, and look around.

I'm in a truck. Driving on a bumpy road, the throbbing in my head getting worse with every jostling movement.

I clench my eyes shut tightly, replaying the last things I remember before I awoke. I was in bed with Juno. I was almost asleep, but something... Something woke me. What was it? I strain to think as the truck bumps over another painful ridge in the road.

There was.... My eyes fling open as I remember the cabin exploding.

Juno. Shit. Juno.

At that moment, cold, wiry fingers touch mine, clasping on to me.

"Juno?" I ask, trying to turn, fighting against the chains.

She leans against me and sighs. "I'm here, I'm here." Her voice is thick.

"Are you hurt?" I can only see the top of her head over my shoulder.

"No... I'm alright. You?"

I wince. "My head, I think... I don't know. I think I'm bleeding." I feel her writhe behind me, trying to turn. "Baby, it's OK, just stop. You'll hurt yourself."

"What happened?" She asks.

"I don't know."

"We were in bed, and then, there was just fire."

She shivers against me, goosebumps breaking out so heavily over her skin I can feel them. I want nothing more than to hold her close to me, to try to keep her warm. The inside of the truck is freezing, the metal floor burning against my skin. We're both still naked from when we were in bed together.

The truck takes a sharp left hand turn, and the road surface changes underneath us, becoming smoother. The truck slows after a few minutes, and I hear voices outside it, speaking a language I don't understand.

But Juno does. I hear her gasp and mutter something in Russian.

"What are they saying?" I ask her.

"They're saying that we're here, and one of them got in trouble for setting off the bomb too close to the King's house."

"The King?"

"Yes, that's what they said." Juno's voice rises, and I feel her trembling become more violent. "Oh god, where are we?"

The truck comes to a stop.

"Juno, I'm going to summon my flames, don't get scared," I tell her. "Remember, they can't hurt you."

"Yes, it's alright."

The inside of the truck is illuminated as the red flames ignite between Juno and I. There's an exclamation outside, rushing footsteps, and the back of the truck is thrown open.

Floodlights blind me.

"Please, it's alright, we mean you no harm!" A man's voice calls from the glare, his voice thick with an accent, like Juno's.

"You got me chained up naked in a truck," I call back, trying to see in the burning lights. "I got a different idea of no harm to you!"

I can see enough now to see the man turn to someone beside him, and he hits them over the back of the head, scolding them in Russian. He steps up into the back of the truck, his hands extended before him.

"I'm so sorry." He crouches down beside us. He's backlit, so I still can't make out his features. "This wasn't the plan. Please, we will get you inside and get some clothes for you, you must be freezing."

"Yeah, we fucking are," I reply.

"I apologize, please, extinguish these flames and we will help you out." He rises to his feet, shouting commands to the others who rush around the truck.

"I'd like a name before I lower my weapon," I tell him.

He chuckles amicably. "Of course, sir. My name is Petrov, and I assure you, you are both safe here."

"Where's here?" Juno asks. "*Kuda ty nas privel?*"

"*Ya vse ob yasnyu so vremenem,*" comes the reply, and I really wish I knew what they were saying.

I extinguish my flames, and the truck bounces as someone else climbs into the back, the jangle of keys accompanying them. They reach between Juno and I, and the chains fall away from my wrists.

I get to my feet, and Juno's hand clasps mine as we climb down off the back of the truck. "Can we at least get a blanket for her?" I say to Petrov, who I can now see properly. He's shorter than me, clean shaven, pale skin, blonde hair in a crew cut. He looks like military, in a dark uniform.

Petrov turns to a man beside him and barks an order, and the man takes his jacket off. Petrov hands it to me. "Here, please, for her modesty."

Modesty. Yeah, OK. The snow underfoot burns my feet, and I wrap the jacket around Juno, whose skin is now red and blotchy.

"Please, come," Petrov says, gesturing ahead of us.

I look up as we walk. We're outside an enormous old

house, a gothic mansion, almost like a castle. Lights stream from the windows, and we're surrounded by military jeeps and trucks. Someone turns the floodlights off, thank fuck.

The doors of the house open, and we're ushered into a brightly lit foyer. Petrov gives more commands, gesturing from us to the stairs that sweep up beside us.

"Where are we?" Juno asks again. "Who are you?"

Petroc holds his hands up, smiling amicably. "Please, I will answer all your questions once you are warm and comfortable, yes?" He waves forward a young soldier. "He will show you to a room where you may find some clothes and get warmed up. I will send someone to bring you downstairs, yes?" He raises his eyebrows as he looks back and forth between us.

"Yeah, OK." I keep my arms firmly around Juno. We follow the young man up the stairs, and down a long hallway, a thick rug underfoot. Old portraits stare down from the walls, regarding us critically as we pass.

He stops suddenly at a door, and gestures at it sharply, giving us a brief nod.

Juno and I exchange a glance, and I step forward, pushing down on the handle. The door opens to reveal an ornate bedroom, with an enormous four poster bed in the middle of it and a fire roaring in the stone fireplace.

As we step inside the room, the door falls closed behind us, and the lock clicks into place. Junos' eyes widen as she looks at me.

"Where the fuck are we?" She asks, clutching on to me. "Who are these people?"

I go over to the window, covered by heavy red velvet

curtains. I draw them aside, and the windows are dressed with heavy iron bars. "Did you catch anything else of what they were saying down there?"

She shakes her head. "Nothing useful, just talking about the King and making preparations, calling for food, things like that." She puts a hand to her mouth. "Oh god, Tal, the explosion, what if they hurt the others?"

I focus, closing my eyes, reaching out to Amryn and Cora. The shields are down, and I can feel them both. Cora's white threads reach out to me, trying to bind on to me, trying to feel where I am. And then the connection snaps. "They're OK," I tell Juno, and she breathes a sigh of relief. "Something's blocking it though, Cora can't reach me."

Juno hugs her arms around herself, then wrinkles her nose as her hands run over the military jacket wrapped around her. She shrugs it off, throwing it to the floor. "*Fignya.*" She kicks it away from her. "Stinks of pest."

There's a sharp knock on the door, and Juno rushes to my side, hiding behind me. Another soldier steps in, a pile of clothes in his hands.

"*Eto dlya tebya,*" he says, placing them on the floor just inside the room, then locks the door behind him.

"What did he say?" This is going to drive me insane.

"He just said these are for us." Juno gestures to the clothes. "At least we don't have to be paraded around this house naked anymore."

I pick up the clothing, a pile of plain black sweats. Juno is swimming in them, they're way too big for her, and they barely fit me. But we're dressed and warm. Juno finally stops trembling.

"Your head," she says, stepping forward, carefully pushing my hair aside. She sucks on her teeth. "There is a cut, my love, it looks deep."

"I'll heal. With the way that explosion went off I'm surprised I'm still in one piece to be honest. It was right in front of us." I grimace as I think of my house in pieces. Fuck. Not even a home to go back to when we get back from - wherever the fuck we are now.

Juno clasps my hand, her eyes wide as she looks up at me. "What could they possibly want with us?"

I shake my head. "I don't know, but hopefully we find out soon."

Right on cue, the door flies open, and the young soldier who escorted us into the room is there again. "Come with me," he says.

We both hesitate for a second, and I grip Juno's hand tighter.

"It's OK," I murmur, and we follow the soldier out of the room.

Down the stairs, we walk down yet another long hallway. There's a soldier at almost every door, like some eerie guard of honor, watching us as we walk. Their expressions are odd, the soft smiles, the crinkling eyes.

They're almost admiring us as we pass.

We're filthy and bleeding and wearing ill-fitted sweats but we're being watched like a bridal couple walking down the aisle. Juno huddles closer under my arm, trembling.

The hallway finally ends, culminating in a room with heavy stone walls, tapestries hanging from them, a fire roaring in the carved fireplace. A long wooden table stands in the center of the room, 10 chairs lined up down either side of it. Lightning flashes outside the stained glass windows, and thunder rumbles overhead.

Petrov sits at the far end of the table in a black leather chair, and he rises to his feet as we enter the room, bowing his head. "My lord, please, come and sit."

My lord? Juno gives me a sideways glance. Petrov's eyes rove over her as we approach him. Out of instinct I push her behind me as we walk, breaking Petrov's line of sight to her. His eyes are narrowed, almost predatory, until they meet mine, when they are once again friendly and warm. He gestures to the seat beside him.

"Please, sit." He says again, and his jaw tenses as I pull out Juno's chair first, allowing her to sit before I do.

"Where are we?" I ask once I'm sitting.

"Ah, first, food, yes?" He looks over my shoulder and snaps his fingers.

"No, that's alright." My stomach is in such a violent knot I'm pretty sure I wouldn't be able to eat right now.

"*My ne golodny*," Juno says beside me.

Petrov nods. "Of course, you must be feeling rather overwhelmed at all this. But I assure you, it will all make sense very soon."

"I sure hope so," I reply.

"Bring it out!" Petrov calls.

There's movement behind us, and Juno reaches over

for my hand. Footsteps approach the table, and two soldiers carry something in their arms, covered in a black cloth. They place it in front of Petrov, and as it scrapes along the wooden table I hear water sloshing in glass.

Petrov raises his eyebrows as he gets to his feet, looking way too excited.

"What the fuck is that?" I ask.

"It was necessary, to preserve the memories," he tells me.

"What memories?"

He grips the black cloth. "Your memories, Konstantin."

He pulls the cloth away, and my brain doesn't register what I'm looking at before Juno springs from the chair, screaming, covering her eyes.

"*Chto eto za khren*?" She cries, backing towards the fireplace. "*Vy monstry, vy monstry!*"

My own face is staring back at me, through the glass, the eyes half-closed, blank, the lips curled back from the teeth in a grimace. Black hair floats around the severed head, around my face, in the yellowed water.

Juno is crying behind me, crumbled on the floor. "*Vy monstry.*" She keeps saying it, over and over.

"What the fuck is that?" I'm unable to tear my eyes away from the decapitated head. I can't move. I should get Juno, I should comfort her, but I can't move.

Petrov sits down, stroking the lid of the glass jar affectionately. "This is you, my lord. At least, it was once, many centuries ago. Magic has kept the head preserved so well, and your armies have guarded it so closely, all this time."

"How did I - I mean, how did he die?"

Petrov sniffs heavily, hands clasped before him, and he looks around me, to Juno, who is still crying on the floor. "That is a rather long story, my lord."

Juno. I can finally move, can finally get out of my chair, and move to take her in my arms. "It's OK, baby." I hold her close to me. "Come on, baby. It's OK."

"I'm not going near that thing again!" She cries, her hands still covering her face. "Oh god, get it out of here."

Petrov snaps his fingers, and the two soldiers come rushing forth, putting the black cloth back over the glass jar, carrying it out of the room carefully. "I did not mean to cause distress my lord," he says without a hint of sincerity in his voice. "I had to show you, you understand, it was necessary."

"You said -" I break off, Juno quivering in my arms as her sobs subside, "You said it was to preserve my memories. What do you mean?"

"Please, come and sit." Petrov gestures to the chairs again. "As I said, it is a long story, and I want to tell you everything."

Juno slumps down into the chair, facing away from Petrov, her hand still in mine.

"Go ahead," I say.

Petrov glances out the window to my left as lightning flashes again. "Many centuries ago, there was a rebellion," he begins, "an uprising against the new ways, against all that was set to destroy us, destroy our way of life."

"And who is we?"

"The witches, my lord," he says, "the witches and the Royal House of Donathion. Your royal house."

"I don't understand."

Petrov nods. "As I said, my lord, you will." He rises to his feet, walking to the window. "The new God, the one who appointed himself ruler of the Halls, he had already corrupted our way of life by appointing our King to be the Draw of his bastard Queen. He had no right to do this, but by then it was too late. Our King had fallen in love with this bitch, with this woman set to destroy everything we worked for, centuries of tradition, centuries of rule and peace."

Juno's hand grips mine harder, and she gasps.

"This was the first Shadow Queen?" I ask.

"Indeed," Petrov answers, watching the storm close in through the window. "Jeneuer, the hybrid. The result of the demon who seduced an angel."

Uneasiness flickers through me when he says the name. Fuck. My fingers wrap around Juno's tighter, and the distant echo I've been fighting since I flew her down off that mountain gets louder, creeping to the edge of my consciousness, like a ghost lingering by the doorway.

"Luckily, the King grew tired of this new God and his ways, his use of the woman he so loved, his very own bride." Petrov snorts. "She and her dual Draws were unstoppable, razing villages and destroying entire armies for the new God, all in his name. Our own people fell under their swords, decimated by their powers."

"Who was the other Draw?" I ask.

"The Queen's childhood friend," Petrov says with a disgusted scoff. "She had them both in her bed, can you imagine?" He turns back to me as thunder rumbles overhead. "But as I said, the King grew tired of this, grew tired of his woman being the conduit for the new God, violating the old ways, forsaking Mother Gaia."

I try not to let any shock register on my face. "Gaia?"

"Indeed," Petrov responds. "Her power was so weakened by the new God, she lost all hold on the world. And we had to do what we could to bring her back, at any cost."

"So your King, he turned the Shadow Queen away from the old.. I mean, the new God?"

Petrov's fists pound into the table. "Turned away? No. He freed her. He freed her from the shackles of the Halls, the place that had cast her out, that had slaughtered her parents. He loved her." His eyes are filled with fury. "He loved her, and he paid the ultimate price for it. They begged of him to leave her, but the bond that had been created by this new God, it had ruined him. It had corrupted him completely."

"Look." I lean forward in my chair. "This is all very fascinating, but I don't see what this has to do with us."

"You don't?" Petrov asks, the fury dissipating and giving way to something almost akin to amusement. "Well, I must say I find that hard to believe, my lord."

"Why do you keep calling me that?"

"We've been looking for you for so many years, Konstantin." Petrov says. "It wasn't until we finally detected the signal, the sign that her powers had come back to life, that your Queen was protecting you, that we knew where to find you."

My eyes move over to Juno, and she turns back slowly to face me. Dread trickles down my back as her gaze meets mine.

My Queen.

My memories.

My head in a fucking jar.

Her dreams where she stabbed me, when I asked her to do it.

The ghostly echo drags through the doorway, into the room, breathing down my neck.

I look back at Petrov. "How did he end up with his head in a jar?"

Petrov moves slowly, raising his hand to point at Juno. "She. Killed. Him."

Juno cries out, burying her face in my shoulder.

"What the fuck are you talking about?" I snap.

Petrov rises to his feet. "Come, we must meet with someone, it will all make more sense if I show you."

Juno's fingers cling to my arm as we're ushered down yet another fucking hallway. We reach the end of it, and there are rough-hewn stone stairs leading down into the dark.

"Where are we going?" I ask Petrov.

"Into the dungeons."

I laugh bitterly. "I don't fucking think so."

"Not for you, my lord. To visit a prisoner." He says in a

tone that I'm sure is meant to be reassuring but does nothing to assuage any of the prickling panic coursing through me.

I'm tempted to fight back, to throw up my flames and make a break for it. But something tells me they're very much ready for me to do exactly that, and I'm badly outnumbered. I'm not in the mood to die today, and I'm not putting Juno in danger.

Petrov seems satisfied that I'm going to follow him as he starts down the stairs. The stone is cold under my bare feet, the light from the hallway fading as the stairs turn in on themselves, winding further and further down, the air becoming hot and thick. Juno's breathing is ragged behind me.

It feels like we're going to be spiraling down into the darkness forever, when suddenly there's flickering light. We emerge into a dungeon, arched iron gates lining the wall to the left, torches interspersed throughout the room. There are more men in military uniforms down here, standing to attention as we walk past.

Petrov guides us to a cell at the very end of the dungeon, and gestures grandly. "Minerva, look who we found." He grins at me, his eyes shimmering an eerie shade of purple in the semi-darkness.

I look into the cell, and can only make out a black pile in the center of it. It starts to shift, shuffling slowly upright. It groans as it moves, and I swear I can hear bones creaking. It limps towards the iron bars, and one spindly, bony hand wraps itself around them.

A gray face is pressed against the bars next, and the other twisted hand stretches through the bars, pointing at me. The figure shakes, and a growling sound comes from it, which builds until I realize it's a laugh. This thing is laughing.

"Look at you." The voice is rasping, croaking. "I never thought I'd see you again."

"You failed, Minerva." Petrov says triumphantly.

The figure keeps laughing, keeps cackling. "Did I, Petrov?"

"Who is this?" I ask.

"This sad and worn old bag of bones is Minerva," Petrov says, "the very witch who helped the King's beloved murder him."

Minerva cackles again, sounding like she's about to choke or die. Her face is so wrinkled I can't see her eyes.

"That's not possible," I say, "she's centuries old, how is she still here?"

"Magic," Petrov says with a shrug. "She was kept alive as penance for her crimes, sworn to service."

I take a step closer to the bars, leaning down to look at the witch's face. Her cackling stops, and her breath is rough, like a saw through wood.

"Hello, majesty," she says quietly.

"You know me?" I ask.

"Oh yes," she replies, "I remember your pretty face very well, Konstantin."

"He needs some help remembering, Minerva," Petrov says, "they both do."

Minerva curls her finger, beckoning me to come closer.

When I don't move, she sighs. "Oh come now, I'm an old woman, what can I possibly do to you?"

"In my experience, a whole lot of damage can come from a witch." I reply.

Minerva's wrinkles shift, and I see the black flash of her eyes. "Shall I see to that, my lord?" She gestures to my cheek. Her finger glows purple, and she flicks it in my direction.

I jerk backwards, but the magic lands on my cheek, searing hot. I stumble backwards, and my hand flies to my face, but instead of a wound, there is smooth skin. The scar from Morgan's magic is gone.

"How did you do that?" I ask.

Minerva shrugs - or at least I think she does. "I am bound only to do good, majesty. It is a condition of my capture. And you do have such a nice face, that scar had no business being there."

Juno whimpers beside me, and I look down to see her clutching her forehead. "What's wrong?" I ask her.

"The memories, they return," Minerva says. "So, Petrov, you say you want them to remember?"

"Yes, they must see how it was, and understand where they come from." Petrov snaps his fingers, summoning two of the guards over to us.

They shove us to our knees, right in front of the cell.

"What the fuck are you doing?" I try to get back up, but Minerva's hand is on my head, and a flash of light renders me immobile. I collapse against the iron bars, seeing Juno crumple beside me, her eyes wide as they stare at me.

"I'm sorry, my lord," Petrov says, "but you have to understand what it all means."

19
Juno

*T*he walls shake as yet another strike hits the fortress. Konstantin takes my hand as we run, the roof crumbling above us, showering us with debris.

"Come, my love!" He calls. "Come, we must hurry."

My feet ache as they pound against the hard stone floor, my lungs feeling as though they are about to burst. We are running, running, the ground shaking as more explosions rock the fortress.

"They're getting closer!" I cry.

"It's alright, my love." He pushes open the door to the tower, and pulls me up the stairs behind him. "It's alright, we know what we must do."

His words fill me with dread, and my feet become heavy. I know what they've said, I know what they've told me to do. The witch has assured me it will work. Alexei has assured me it will work, that he will protect me. But tears sting my eyes all the same. It feels wrong.

"Juno, come." He yanks on my hand as I slow my

pace, my skirt getting caught around my feet as we climb the stairs, up, up, into the tower.

Alexei is waiting for us, and rushes to me, his hands seizing my face, pressing his lips to mine. "Oh my love, you are safe."

"Yes." I clutch on to his hands. "But they are getting closer."

"We must hurry." He pulls away from me.

It is then that I spy the witch standing in the corner, looking out the window, over the battlefield.

"Three thousand Donathian soldiers, and not even they can hold back the angels." She turns to face me, her skin gray, her eyes so dark they are almost black. "We must hurry."

"I do not want to do this." All eyes in the room turn to me.

"My love," Alexei says, taking my hands in his, "you know why we must."

I look over at Konstantin, whose hazel eyes are soft and warm as he smiles at me. "It will be alright," he assures me, "I can only protect you at my full power."

"How do we know this won't just kill you?" I ask.

The witch scoffs. "My Lady, this dagger is not for the purpose of death." She holds it aloft, the black blade gleaming, the amber set in its hilt glowing warmly. "It is not possible to kill with this dagger, for it may only give new life, and new power."

A cry carries on the wind, from the Donathian forces battling below, trying to fight off the advancing angels.

Alexei's face is desperate as he looks at me. "My love, come, we must hurry."

My hands won't stop shaking as I walk towards Konstantin. He smiles down at me, and takes me in his arms, kissing me tenderly. "Zhizn Moya," he murmurs, "I will protect you. Help me protect you."

I nod. "I love you."

"And I love you."

The witch is beside me, pressing the dagger into my hand. "Quickly, majesty. Do not hesitate."

I draw the dagger along my hand, cutting it open, as I was instructed to do, wincing as my skin breaks open. I run the blade back and forth in my blood. Droplets fall to the floor between Konstantin and me.

The blade thoroughly covered in my blood, I look up at Konstantin. He opens his shirt, laying his chest bare for me. Tears blur my vision as I look at him, the chest I have laid my head on so many nights. Hearing his heart beating in those moments when it was just us, just him and me.

His hands move to mine, on the hilt of the dagger, and I gaze up at him. He smiles warmly. "My love, it is alright."

"Hurry, majesty!" The witch cries, as the ground beneath us quakes again. She begins to chant, words I do not understand.

Alexei is pacing back and forth by the window. "Juno, hurry!"

Konstantin nods, his eyes fixed on mine. "I will be back with you in only a moment."

Only a moment. Yes. Only a moment.

I take a deep breath, and then plunge the knife into Konstantin's chest.

His eyes widen, and he sucks in a breath. Blood springs from the wound, dripping down his torso. His hands fall from the dagger, and he wavers, his legs buckling from underneath him.

"Konstantin?" I try to hold him up, but he is so big. He drops to his knees, and I hold his face in my hands. "My love?"

He smiles weakly. "It is alright, I promise you."

"It will look like death, majesty," the witch says, "do not be fooled."

Konstantin grimaces, his hands on mine, and he pulls the dagger from his chest. Blood rushes out of his mouth, and he collapses against me.

"My love?" I cradle his head in my lap, his long black hair trailing on the floor. "Zhizn Moya, oh what have I done?"

"Nothing," he tells me, even as his voice begins to falter. "My love, this is all, we knew what would happen. I must -" His breathing fails him for a moment. "This was all the plan, to help me be stronger. To - to protect you."

His head falls against me, and I feel his breathing slow. "How long will this take?" I ask the witch. "How long until the enchantment works?"

"But a few moments," she says, and her eyes flash over to Alexei, who is watching from the other side of the room, his arms crossed over his chest.

Konstantin shudders, and his eyes fix on my face. "I love you so much."

It is starting to feel like a farewell. I press my lips to his, and I do not care that I can taste his blood. He strokes my cheek with his hand, and then he grits his teeth.

"What is happening? Why is it taking so long?" I watch as Konstantin's eyes begin to flutter closed. I look up at Alexei. "What is happening?"

Alexei and the witch exchange a glance, and he moves towards me. "My love, it will not take much longer." He extends a hand to me. "Come, you must trust the magic."

I clutch Konstantin to me. "I am not letting him go until it has worked, until he has returned to me."

"My love," Alexei says again, his tone becoming more commanding, his hand moving closer to me, "You heard what Minerva said, it will look like death. You should not distress yourself so."

"No!" I bury my face in the crook of Konstantin's neck, and his fingers trace over my cheek.

"My love," he whispers, "it is alright."

Suddenly a hand is in my hair, dragging me away. I flail and scream, reaching out for Konstantin.

"Alexei," Konstantin gasps, reaching across the floor, blood pooling around him, "what are you doing?"

I reach up and try to free myself from Alexei's grasp, but it's like iron. He will not release me. He drags me across the room, then throws me down on the floor. My head strikes the hard stones, and I blink, trying to see, willing my vision to clear.

"Alexei." Konstantin's voice is becoming weaker. "What are you doing to her? Stop!" He braces a hand against the ground, trying to move, but falters, collapsing to the ground. "Juno."

I try to push myself up off the ground, but Alexei is on my back, pushing up my skirt. "Alexei, get off me!" Raw panic creeps up my neck as I feel his naked thighs against mine, and I begin to scream. I try to unfurl my wings to throw him off me.

He slams my head into the floor again, rendering me silent, holding my head down with his hand. Through the white spots dancing in my vision, I see Konstantin trying to drag himself towards me. I reach out a hand to him, the distance between us impossible to guess as the floor tips away from me in a blur.

"Konstantin," I murmur. "Please."

My hand claws into the stone ground as Alexei rapes me, my eyes fixed on Konstantin, seeing the light fade from his face, his expression tortured.

"Juno." He tries one last time to move towards me. His shoulders heave with a final breath, and then his eyes stare at me blankly. His hand is still reaching for me.

I feel within myself, I feel him die. Ice floods my chest, and then with a painful wrench there is nothing but a wide, gaping hole.

I cannot even scream as Alexei continues to violate me, the witch chanting behind us.

Konstantin does not rise. He is dead. There was no enchantment. They tricked me. They lied to us. I killed him. I killed my only love. I murdered him. I clench my eyes shut, grief tearing through me.

Alexei pants and grunts behind me, and then I feel him shudder as he finishes inside me. Something tears in my chest, and I feel the bond to him begin to fray, begin to break, begin to pull away from me.

"Why?" I whimper. "Why did you do this?"

"How long will it take?" He asks, but he is speaking to the witch, not to me.

"My lord, it should be instant," the witch says to him.

Alexei climbs off me. "I don't feel anything."

"Why did you do this?" I ask him again, my cheek still pressed to the stone floor.

"Shut your mouth," he hisses down at me.

"Alexei." Sobs begin to bubble up in my throat. I push myself off the ground, my arms shaking violently. "Alexei, how could you do this to me? I love you."

"You love me?" He leans over me, his eyes wild. "You love me? You loved him!" He points at Konstantin's dead body. "You loved him, and I was merely the second. I've loved you my whole life, and then the fucking Witch King of Donathian comes along, and I am forgotten! I meant nothing to you!"

I rise on to my knees, trembling, pushing my skirt back down around my thighs. "Alexei, how could you do this to us?" I hug my arms around myself, shaking my head as I look at Alexei's face, overcome with fury. "Why? I don't understand."

Alexei lashes out, slapping me hard across the face, sending my sprawling onto the floor again. "You fucking bitch!" He screams, standing over me with clenched fists. "You have no idea, none, what I have suffered, the humiliation, being second to a half-breed cunt like you, and your fucking coal-haired King." He turns away from me, back to the witch, turning his hands over, back and forth, in front of his face. "I feel no different! How long will it take?"

"I told you, it should be instant, once you have claimed her!" She says, consulting the enormous grimoire on the table before her.

I drag myself along the floor, to Konstantin's side. His hand is still warm as I reach him, and I clutch him to me. "Oh my love, I'm sorry, I'm so sorry. Please, forgive me, forgive me."

He is so limp in my arms, my love, my protector. He was so strong. He loved me so much. And I killed him. I killed him. I stroke his face, his beautiful eyes half-closed. I press my lips to his, willing him back to life.

Maybe my tears can grant immortality, maybe my breath can bring the dead back to life? I'm the Shadow Queen, what good is it if I cannot bring my Draw back to me. But he remains limp in my arms.

Please Konstantin, do not leave me alone.

"Take me too," I whisper to him, "take me with you. Take my immortality. Take it away. Do not go where I cannot follow. Let me come with you."

But breath remains in my body as the life drains from his, carrying him away from me.

"It hasn't fucking worked!" Alexei screams, his hands clawed before him. "Fuck!" He picks up the grimoire and *throws it across the room, pages fluttering to the floor before it hits the wall and lands with a loud thud.*

The ground beneath us shakes as the angels advance, and I wrap myself around Konstantin.

Let them come. Let them kill us. I don't want to live without him. I want to die with him, right here.

But Alexei grabs a hold of me again, dragging me across the room. "I have someone who wants to see you."

I scream, thrashing, trying to reach out to Konstantin, trying to hold on to him. "Don't leave him here!" Do not leave him here alone. "Konstantin!"

I unfurl my wings, trying to fly out of Alexei's grasp, trying to knock him away from me, but the witch is too fast, and sends purple bolts of lightning after me. My wings fall uselessly to my back. My back burns and smokes as the volts course over my skin.

Alexei seizes me, half-dragging, half-carrying me down the stairs of the tower.

"Let me go!" I can feel the Inera clawing in my chest, trying to escape. I try to summon it, but I am too weak. The witch's magic or Konstantin's death or Alexei's violation - I don't know which has robbed me of my power, maybe all of it has. I summon my lightning, and Alexei cries out as the volts course up his arm.

"You fucking bitch!" His fist hits me square in the face.

My vision goes gray, and I can't hear anything. I slump against Alexei, and I am only aware of being dragged down the stairs, then along the ground, my knees scraping against the stone floor. He drops me, and begins to drag me by my hair.

"Alexei," I murmur, trying to hold on to his arm, trying to stop the pain in my head and my shoulders. "Alexei, please..."

Suddenly, I'm hurled across the room, landing at someone's feet.

"Eto ne srabotalo!" Alexei screams. "It didn't fucking work, look at me!"

A laugh sounds above me, and a pair of feet shift right beside my hands. "Oh you are a stupid little man," a voice says. "It is working exactly as I told you it would."

"You said I would have power!" Alexei is pacing now, back and forth, heavy footfalls on the ground.

When I see who is standing above me, I suppress a scream.

"Hello, Jeneuer." Gabriel grins at me. "Looks like you've had a rather rough day."

"What are you doing here?" I push myself up onto my hands, trying to crawl away, but Gabriel seizes me by the back of the neck and pulls me into the center of the room. "What are you doing?"

"What do you mean it's working as you said it would?" Alexei is following us, and I see through the haze shrouding my eyes that his skin is turning gray, sallow. "You said I'd have power!"

"I said you'd have immortality," Gabriel says as he throws me down on the floor, and hauls two heavy chains up out of holes in the stone, their rattle deafening. He grabs my wrist and fastens a heavy iron cuff around it, letting the chain drop back into the floor, the weight dragging me down with it.

"What are you doing?" I scream.

"Shut your fucking mouth, Juno!" Alexei is standing beside Gabriel as he works, as he continues to secure me down to the floor. "What good is immortality if I have no powers?"

"I don't know," Gabriel says nonchalantly, "you probably should have thought about that before you agreed to betray your queen." With both my arms now bound, Gabriel moves to my feet.

I draw on the last of my strength and lash out, striking him in the jaw, and he stumbles sideways.

"Oh, feisty, aren't you?" He laughs bitterly. "Fighting back won't help you, so just give it a rest, you half-breed bitch." He fastens both my feet to the ground, the weight of the chains feeling like they're going to tear me into pieces.

"What do I do?" Alexei asks. "What do I do now?"

I turn my head and see Gabriel pulling a long curved sword from its sheath, the golden blade shimmering in the harsh sunlight that pours in through a hole in the roof. He turns to look at Alexei, his gaze venomous. "I would run off before the Donathians figure out you killed their King, you stupid shit."

Alexei's mouth gapes. "What do you -"

"Fuck off, you traitorous ingrate!" Gabriel swings the sword at Alexei, who springs out of the way. "Run off and enjoy your new gift, an eternity spent in peace, just as you wanted it."

Thunder rumbles overhead, lightning flashing from the clear sky.

287

Gabriel grins at the ceiling. "It is time then." He looks down at me, his white teeth on show. "Are you ready to meet your Fate, my dear Queen?"

I hear footsteps behind me, entering the room.

"Oh, still here are you, sweetheart?" A serpentine voice sounds, followed by a breathy laugh. "The Donathians are coming back, you should run."

"What are you going to do with her?" Alexei asks.

"Don't worry about her," the other voice says, moving closer to me. "She won't be a problem any longer."

I hear scuffling, retreating footsteps, and the last of the bond between Alexei and me tears and withers away, ripping away with a sharp snap deep below my ribs. The sudden rush of emptiness takes my breath away. I'm alone, all alone.

"Alright, Queenie!" Gabriel says brightly. "Michael, come and help me would you? She needs to have her wings clipped."

"No!" I scream and try to thrash, the chains in the floor holding me down as Michael seizes hold of one of my wings. "Please, no! Don't do this!"

"Ah come now." Gabriel throws the sword's hilt back and forth between his hands playfully. "Where you're going, you won't need these." He swings the sword, and slices one of my wings off.

I'm sure I'm screaming, but the searing pain numbs everything, my sense of hearing and sight as well. My vision goes stark white, followed by the burning wrench of my other wing being cut from my back. My throat is raw.

The cacophony of sound around me dies down. No

more sound escapes me. Just a silent stream of tears that pools between my cheek and the stones. The cavernous void in my chest grows, and I hope it stops my heart. I hope it consumes all of me.

Gabriel stands beside me, holding up my wings, my beautiful wings, splattered with blood. "Ah, these will look fantastic on my wall!" He waves them around theatrically.

"Gabriel." There's a third voice, another man, a low voice, stern. "That's enough."

Gabriel rolls his eyes and sighs heavily. "Oh yes, alright, I'm just trying to have some fun."

"Please kill me," I whimper.

Gabriel leans down to me, his brow furrowing. "What did you say, dear?"

"Please kill me. Please, just kill me." I heave in a breath, hoping it is one of my last. "I want to die."

Gabriel laughs out loud. "Did you hear that, Michael?" He straightens, his sickly grin still fixed on me. "Queenie wants to die."

"Oh well, that would be too easy." Michael says, his voice a taunting drawl. "No no, we have something so much better planned for you."

"Let me know when it's done." There's the third voice again, and footsteps retreat.

"Right you are, Daddy!" Gabriel calls, then turns back to me. "Now, dear one, we've found a rather lovely mountain for you to spend eternity on."

"Oh, Gabriel, not on, sweetheart." Michael corrects him.

Gabriel slaps himself in the forehead and laughs. "Of course, silly me, what am I saying? A lovely mountain for you to spend eternity under, is what I meant."

"Please. Please kill me."

Gabriel crouches down beside me. "Oh dear one, no. You're going under the ground today. And your immortality means you will be trapped under the earth forevermore, screaming, clawing to get out, desperate for air, and sunlight."

He and Michael release me from the shackles on my arms and legs. I try to get to my knees, pushing against the stone floor.

Suddenly there is a flash of green and it is as though my skin is on fire. I scream, looking down to see sickly green bonds on my arms, sticking together like burned raw flesh.

Gabriel seizes my hair, pulling my head back, leering down at me. "Now, Queenie, let's get you to your mountain, shall we?"

Everything is hot, and all I can taste is dirt.

"PLEASE DON'T DO THIS!" I want to die. Please kill me. Don't leave me down here.

It's dark and I can't breathe.

"LET ME OUT!"

My fingers flail at stone, my nails tearing from the flesh.

"LET ME OUT! PLEASE!"

I drift in and out of consciousness.

I want to die. Please let me die. But I can't die.

A face drifts before me, a dream. It's Konstantin.

No. It's not. This man has a white streak in his long black hair, and a dimple that settles in the corner of his mouth when he smiles at me.

Who are you? Why am I dreaming of you? I am losing my mind. I already have. I went insane hundreds of years ago. I know I did.

"It's OK, honey," a voice says, and fingers stroke my cheek. "I'm here, and you're safe. No one will hurt you. You're safe with me."

The empty space in my chest, the cavern Konstantin and Alexei left behind, is suddenly full, so hot and roaring I feel I'm going to burst.

My eyes fly open.

My fingers flail at the rock.

The mountain around me begins to quake, the rock splitting above me. Fresh dirt pours in.

I have to get out of here.

He's coming for me.

20
Tallesaign

gasp, my lungs filling with air.

I retch on the ground as the sick feeling of bleeding out overwhelms me, and the blooming sting in my chest where a dagger was only a few moments ago remains. I suck in a breath, and another, and another.

Where the fuck am I?

I try to lift my arms, but I'm paralyzed. It takes me a moment to realize it's not just from the magic Minerva used on us. I'm shackled to the ground in a stone chamber.

Petrov is standing by a table, where the glass jar holding Konstantin's head sits. He watches me calmly, his eyes narrowed, his arms crossed over his chest.

"Where's Juno?" I try to move my fingers, my toes, anything. "What have you done with her?"

"Retrieving a soul is a process, my lord," Petrov replies, "and showing you the day you died was only the first step. Now we must reawaken the part of you that is Konstantin, the memories he holds."

"Why did you show me that? What are you hoping to achieve?"

Petrov inhales through his nose, his eyes straying to the ceiling. "I needed you to see what kind of woman Jeneuer really is. *Juno.*" He scoffs. "Juno indeed. Konstantin was obsessed with her, she could do no wrong in his eyes. He killed his own for her, without question."

"You said he turned her from the Old God. Sounds like there was a lot of questioning going on there."

"And yet she still killed him," Petrov replies.

"She was tricked. Betrayed by people she trusted."

Petrov laughs out loud. "Would you run a knife through her chest right now if I told you to? How stupid must one be to believe such a thing."

"Konstantin believed it too."

"Enough." Petrov waves his hands dismissively. "You had to see who she really was, so that when your memories are restored, you will know exactly what to do."

"So you want me to be Konstantin again, is that it? I won't be me anymore, I'll be him."

"Oh no, no, my lord," Petrov says, pushing himself off the table. "No my lord, you misunderstand. You will still be you, we need your knowledge and your abilities. Konstantin's memories will merely meld with yours, it will be as though you lived two lives at once."

" *Where's. Juno?*" My hands and feet tingle as the feeling slowly returns to them.

"She's safe," he assures me, and I don't believe him.

"She is necessary to this process too."

"You keep talking about the fucking process, what the fuck do you want to achieve?"

Petrov rushes at me, his eyes wild. "Power." He spits the word at my feet. "You demons, you lived your lives, you hid away from the world and let it fall into ruin, blaming the angels, blaming the witches, blaming the absence of the Shadow Queen, blaming the absence of the Old God. Oh, you so loved the humans, but you did nothing to protect them, to help them. No, you split off into your clans and protected your own interests."

"Because they hated us. Because they made us into things to be feared."

"Oh, much like the witches then?" He sneers at me. "Yes, the terrible witches who corrupted the Line, that's the story you've been told, isn't it?"

"If you know something I don't then I'm all ears."

Petrov smiles bitterly, shaking his head. "The witches were slaughtered in the name of the Old God. They had every reason to want to corrupt the Line, to weaken the earth's connection to him. But no, you demons believed the stories, even as you were all cast out of the Halls, abandoned, robbed of your powers, condemned to a life of humanity."

"So if Konstantin comes back, what will happen?" I ask.

"We will reclaim this realm for Mother Gaia," Petrov says. "We will restore the order of things. And we will finally see the Halls destroyed, along with all they stand for." He walks back to the table, opening a satchel beside the jar, withdrawing a needle from it.

My legs ache as I push myself up onto my knees. "What are you doing?"

"The next step of the process." He sounds impatient. He dips the needle into the jar, and stabs into Konstantin's skull with a sickening squelch. He pulls up the plunger, and fills the needle with black liquid. "It will be uncomfortable, but it will pass quickly." He flicks the needle with his fingers and advances towards me.

The iron chains clank as I try to move away from him. "Get that shit the fuck away from me."

He stands over me and sighs. "Enough now." His hand glows green, and he holds it to my head, rendering me immobile again. I can't make any sound as the needle is shoved into my neck, and the black liquid courses through my veins like acid. "Now, try and relax."

Yeah sure. I drop to the floor, and I can't breathe. I can't see. Everything is dark and burning. I suck in a breath, but can't breathe out. My limbs shake as I begin to convulse, and I feel like a thousand needles are being pushed into the base of my skull.

"Just accept it, Tallesaign." Petrov says. "Let the memories align with yours."

I'm blinking, but everything is black. My fingers clasp onto the stone floor beneath me. Then a man appears before me, in the darkness. He looks like me, like Amryn.

His brow is furrowed, and he lifts his hands, looking at them as though he's never seen them before. He tilts his head as he gazes at me.

I realise then that it's Konstantin. His eyes darken, his teeth gritted.

"Where is Juno? Is she alive?" He asks.

"Yes. I found her."

"Protect her. They want to kill her."

"I know."

"I will do what I can." He says.

With a flash, my vision comes back, the feeling flooding back into my limbs all at once. My chest pounds with the exertion of trying to fill my lungs. *Fuck. What the fuck?*

Petrov stands over me, one eyebrow cocked. "Well, that was slightly less dramatic than I had hoped." He leans down to inspect me with narrowed eyes. "And how do you feel?"

"Fuck you." I respond, pushing myself back up on my knees. "And get these fucking chains off me, now."

Petrov laughs. "Oh not quite yet, my lord. As I said, it's a process."

"I've had enough of your fucking process. Now, unchain me and tell me where Juno is."

Petrov looks over his shoulder. "So, you say it will be necessary to unlock his powers with force, yes?"

A quivering pile of black in the corner begins to move, and Minerva's head rises from it, her neck cracking as she moves her head towards me. "Oh yes, she is his only weakness, and will therefore be what unlocks his strength."

Panic and fury course through me. "What the fuck are you talking about?" I strain against the shackles. "Where the fuck is she? Tell me now."

Petrov is still looking at Minerva. "And you are sure?"

"Oh yes," she says. "She is all he cares about."

Petrov gives her a short nod, and claps his hands. "Bring her in!"

I hear Juno's cries and whimpers echoing, and my body erupts in shimmering heat, my veins glowing red. "What the fuck have you done to her?"

Petrov meets my eyes with a smile. "Nothing." His gaze becomes threatening. "Yet."

The wooden door flies open and two soldiers walk in, Juno between them, her hands chained, secured around her waist. Her lip is bleeding. She sees me and her face crumples. "Tal?"

The chains holding me down clatter violently as I strain against them. "What have you done to her? Let her go."

"My lord, you must understand some things about Konstantin." Petrov slowly and methodically pulls on a pair of black leather gloves. "Jeneuer was his obsession, he gave up his throne for her, his people, everything. He killed his own, for her. Now, as such she is the only one who will be able to activate his powers."

Juno's face twists with fear as the soldiers drag her to Petrov. "What are you doing?" She cries, her feet catching on the floor, sending her stumbling. "Let me go!"

"Don't you fucking touch her!" My flames won't do anything to these chains. "Petrov, I swear to you, I will end you if you -"

"Calm down!" He snaps, pressing a fist into his palm. "You will see, it was all necessary in the end." He turns to Minerva. "How much do you think?"

"Do not hold back at all," Minerva croaks. "It is not as

though you can kill her. She can only feel pain."

Juno's eyes widen, and then Petrov's fist slams into her face, blood spurting from her nose. She coughs, her head tipping back.

"Juno!" I cry, the shackles biting into my skin as I pull against them. "You're fucking dead, Petrov!"

Petrov raises his fist and punches Juno in the stomach, and she doubles over. His knee snaps up to hit her in the face, the soldiers on either side of her holding her steady. Her head lolls back, blood gushing from her nose and mouth.

"Juno!" My whole body erupts into red flames, roaring and snapping to the ceiling of the chamber. "Petrov, don't touch her!"

Petrov pulls a knife from his waistband. "Don't worry, this is all a part of it." He says, plunging the knife into Juno's thigh. She screams, blood bubbling from her mouth.

Something is thumping at the back of my skull, and black spots dance in my vision. "Juno!"

Her eyes move to me, her head hanging against her shoulder, snapping back as Petrov runs the knife into her other leg. She gurgles sickeningly, blood rushing out of her mouth, and she spits it up on the ground. "Tal." She whimpers.

Electricity courses down my arms, and black sparks dance across my fingertips. The heat running up my spine is so intense it makes me dizzy. "Petrov, let her go." My voice isn't my voice, it's deeper, roaring, echoing around the stone chamber.

Petrov raises his eyes to the ceiling as the light begins to dim, lightning flickering overhead. He looks at me with a grin. "It's working." He says, and turns to slash the knife across Juno's chest.

I pull against the chains, and the soldiers look alarmed as a loud crack sounds, the iron snapping from around my wrists. Petrov regards me with delight.

"Yes, my lord!" He cackles maniacally.

With a final heave, the chains crumble from my arms, and the soldiers let go of Juno, stumbling backwards. She slumps to the floor, unmoving.

"Do not be afraid!" Petrov cries as black lightning engulfs me. "He has returned."

I'm aware of the breath on my ear. "*Kill them all.*" Konstantin says to me. "*Kill them now.*"

The two soldiers are backing towards the door as I summon my flames, but instead, a ball of black lightning forms in my palm. My skin tingles with electricity. I gaze at it for a moment, surprised. One of the soldiers makes a sound, like a squeak, like a terrified little mouse.

"Are you scared of me?" I ask.

Both soldiers' eyes widen as I launch the ball of lightning at them. They dash for the door, but are caught in the lightning storm before they can reach it.

Petrov cheers with delight. "Yes, my lord! Brilliant!"

I stalk towards him, and his face changes from delighted to uncertain. "My lord, I am your loyal servant," he says, his stance faltering somewhat.

I have the sensation of someone rushing in front of me,

taking control. I can feel that it's Konstantin, pushing forward.

"You call yourself a loyal subject, and yet you have the blood of my Queen on your hands?" Black lightning crackles up my arms. "You summon me and expect mercy?"

Petrov puts his hands up, backing away. "But my lord, we have awaited your return, to lead us, to return us to the old ways."

"And so it shall be," I reply, advancing on him, "but you will not be here to see it."

"My lord." *Simpering fucking fool.* "My lord, I only did what was necessary to summon you. We had to do -"

"Oh, then let me assure you, what I am about to do is also incredibly necessary." I seize him by the throat, lifting him off the ground, the lightning flashing around his head, illuminating the very visible whites of his eyes. "For what better way to test my powers than on such a loyal subject?"

Petrov opens his mouth to scream, but the deafening crescendo of the lightning tearing through his skull drowns out any sound he may have made. Blood pours from his eyes and ears, and his lips slacken. His eyeballs burst in their sockets, and a dam breaks in his nose, blood gushing forth.

He goes limp in my hand, and I throw his body to the ground where he slumps like a rag doll.

My shoulders are heaving as my vision clears, my bloodlust abating. I feel Konstantin step back, retreating to a dark corner of my mind where he lies, silent.

Juno.

She is lying still on the floor as I rush to her side, taking her in my arms.

"Juno?" I clutch her to me, my veins glowing in a haphazard pattern of black and red. "Juno, can you hear me?"

Light travels over her body, inch by inch, and her shallow breathing deepens, becoming more even. I'm her Draw. I can heal her. Her wounds knit together, and slowly, she begins to open her eyes.

"Tal?" She weakly lifts her hand to my face. "Tal? Is it still you?"

"It's me, baby." I clutch her to me. "It's me, I'm here."

She presses her face into my chest. "Oh god. I was so frightened."

I stroke her hair, feeling her body warm against mine. "I know, I know. But it's over now."

A wracking cough sounds from the corner of the room, and I remember Minerva. She pulls herself up, the heavy wrinkles in her face hiding her eyes.

"Well done," she says, her voice raspy. "You have returned."

"*Chertova ved'ma*," Juno hisses, grasping my hands as I help her to her feet. "You betrayed me. You caused me to kill my love."

Minerva cackles, her jaw clicking audibly as her toothless mouth falls open. "You were a fool, so easy to trick. Both of you, fools."

I stand over her, and her head tips back against the wall. "Why did you do it? You're a witch, why did you ally yourself with the angels, against Gaia?"

"Gaia?" The witch spits, another hacking cough shaking through her creaking body. "Under Gaia we were all free. Gaia believed in a world of peace, a world of equality. She underestimated the desire of power."

"That was all?" I ask her. "You sought power?"

"I was offered power, and I wasn't going to pass up the chance." Her head turns, and she must be looking at Juno. "You, my lady, you were so easily swayed by everyone. The Old God slaughtered your parents, and you still became his Shadow Queen. You still did his bidding, killing witches, killing anyone who defied him."

Flashes of memory bite at me, clouding my vision. Bloody scenes of bodies scattered all around me. I squeeze my eyes shut for a second, as the static images blur in and out of focus. Faces twisted in terror. Men, women - oh *fuck*, children too.

There's a sudden image of Juno standing over the body of a child, she's staring at the blood covering her hands. Such a tiny body, empty eyes staring at the sky.

I look at Juno now, the Juno that stands before me. I can see from the pain contorting her face now that the same memories are flooding back to her. I feel her pain and regret so sharply, mingling with my own, that for a moment nausea washes over me.

"But I had turned away from him," Juno says, looking back down at the witch, "I had seen the error of my ways, because of Konstantin."

Minerva laughs, clasping her bony, gray hands together. "Yes, your great savior, Konstantin. The Witch

King of Donathian. Together, you would have brought Gaia back, given her back her strength, and I was tasked with preventing this from happening."

"There was no enchantment, was there?" I ask Minerva. "You simply had her murder her lover."

She shakes her head. "You misunderstand, my lord. There was, certainly. It just did not work the way I expected."

"Why not?"

"Love." Minerva spits the word out from between her white lips. "Love is the most volatile of powers, and her love for you made the enchantment work in a way I did not expect." She laughs as my veins glow brighter. "She was a whore, taking both her Draws to her bed. Disgusting. I was sure I would be able to condemn your soul to eternal purgatory, eliminating you completely. But no." She sighs, shifting on the stone floor. "Her love simply sent your soul into the ether, flying about the universe, waiting to be reborn."

Juno's hand clasps mine, and she begins to cry quietly. "*Ty zlaya ved'ma.*"

"The Donathian forces seized me as I tried to escape the fortress," Minerva goes on, "and they retrieved your body from the tower to preserve your memories. I was kept alive, because I was the only one who could see your soul, the only one who could see when you would be reborn. For centuries, we traveled, waiting for a child to be born, but it did not come. And then, one day, after the battle of the Lowlands, I managed to escape into the forest."

The Lowlands. The battle Fenella spoke of.

303

"The Donathian forces wanted me to ensure your rebirth, but now I was free, and Fate gave me a chance to prevent your return." Minerva says.

"How so?" I ask.

She smiles. "I was on the road, and there was a woman, with two little girls. Long black hair. And I saw the thread, the white cord binding your soul to these children. I knew I was looking at your mother."

My throat tightens. "You attacked them."

She nods. "But the witch, she bound me in place, telling her girls to run. They were getting away from me, your soul tethered to them, following them. It was all I could do to summon a spell, to send after them. An infertility spell."

Juno gasps beside me. "You monstrous bitch."

Minerva cackles. "You hold his hand now, do you not? I failed. I could only hope I hit the right girl, that I could prevent your birth. The Donathian forces captured me again, barely a day later. And all I could do was hope. But then -" She coughs heavily, and a trickle of blood runs out of the corner of her mouth. "Then, 15 years later, Arax began to spew red smoke. And I knew, I knew at that moment, I had failed. I knew you had returned."

"And now what?" I ask. "You helped them retrieve my memories, you helped them activate my powers, what has this all achieved?"

"I can finally die," she croaks. "Until you returned, I was bound to live. Now I can finally rest, after centuries."

"That's it?" I ask.

"Oh no." More blood begins to trickle out of her

mouth, and she seems to shrink in on herself, the black pile melting. "You are the Earth and the Flame, and now you are together again, they will be set to destroy you."

"Who?"

"The Halls, you fool." Minerva snaps. "The Halls will never let you two be together." Her skin begins to crumble from her face as she turns into dust. "You will be destroyed again, believe me. I am only sorry I will not be here to see it."

"Alexei." Juno says suddenly. "Where did he go?"

Minerva cackles, her jaw disconnecting from her skull, her mouth falling open to reveal a blanched tongue. "Back to his castle, to live out eternity." Amid creaking, and snapping, Minerva collapses in on herself. There's a rush of dust flying upwards, and then she's gone.

Juno collapses against me, breathing heavily. "Oh god, Tal. What have they done to us?"

I clasp her to me. "It's alright, we just need to get out of here now." Her eyes gaze up at me. "I'm sorry I'm not him."

Juno frowns. "What do you mean?"

"You wanted him back, didn't you?" I say. "Konstantin. That's what you hoped for, didn't you?"

Juno pulls me down to her, kissing me deeply. It's the strangest sensation, memory prickling across my skin. I suddenly know her in a way I didn't before, and I feel Konstantin extending a hand, running his fingers down her back. He shivers, and shakes his head, retreating again. I can sense his pain, his longing.

"My love," she murmurs, her eyes closed as she

pressed her forehead against mine, "I am yours. I love you. I love you, Tal. I am bonded to you, to your soul." Her brown eyes open, and she smiles. "I loved Konstantin, and I always will. But I love you too."

I nod. Another weird, complicated situation. And we don't have time to think about it now.

"Come on." I take her hand, lightning flashing up my arm. "We have to get out of here."

The soldiers seem to have sensed what had occurred and fled, because the corridor outside the chamber is deserted. Juno and I move slowly, my ears straining for any sound, any sign that the soldiers are still here.

"For forces loyal to you, they certainly made a hasty retreat," Juno whispers scornfully. "What did they think would happen?"

Suddenly we hear gun fire and shouting. I break into a run, pulling Juno along behind me, and I feel a flash of something, a thread snaking out towards me.

Amryn.

An explosion quakes through the ground, followed by more gunfire. We reach a stairwell, and hurry up as another explosion rocks through the floor beneath us. At the top, there are floor to ceiling windows, and outside the flash of gunfire and flames.

Something swoops past the window, and I see it's Elise, her yellow flames raining down on the Donathian forces in front of the mansion.

I turn to Juno. "Can you summon that power?"

She holds up a hand, white lightning crackling in her palm. "I will try."

"You stay right here, we need to clear this place out so we can get safe, OK? If there's trouble, I'll know."

She nods, even though I can see the fear in her face. "Yes. Be careful."

I jump out the window, sending black lightning down into the forces below. I swoop over them amidst more gunfire, but as my lightning sweeps over them, the soldiers begin to drop to their knees, like a house of cards collapsing.

Amryn appears at my side, a gun in one hand, his flames roaring in the other. He looks down at the troops beneath us, then regards me with a furrowed brow. "What the fuck is going on here?"

"I have a lot to tell you."

He raises his eyebrows as black lightning crackles in my hands. "Yeah, I can see that." He regards me hesitantly. "Are you OK? Did they hurt you?"

"Like I said, I have a lot to tell you. For now, let's just get the fuck out of here."

Amryn nods. "OK, let's go."

I fly back to the window and retrieve Juno, who clings to my neck. Elise swoops down beside me, her face twisted with concern. "Are you OK?"

"We're fine," I assure her, "let's go home."

The troops remain there, on their knees, their heads bowed, as we fly away. I wonder just how long they'll stay there, and if they'll ever try to find me.

Their King.

21
Tallesaign

We fly for hours, the twinkling lights of Ocario finally coming into view.

Cora, Liall and Ebony are waiting for us when we land. Cora stumbles into Amryn's arms.

"Oh god, I was so scared," she says. I place Juno on the ground, and Cora throws her arms around me. "Tal." She starts to sob. "Oh my god, you're OK."

I stroke her hair gently. "I'm here, I'm OK. We're OK." I look around the village, seeing the damaged houses around us. "Is everyone here alright?"

Cora pulls back from me and nods, wiping her face with the back of her hand. "There were some injuries but no deaths, thankfully." Her eyes move to Juno, and she gasps. "Oh my god, what happened to you?" She throws her arms around Juno, and the two women cry as they hold each other. "Are you alright?" Cora asks, taking Juno's face in her hands.

"I'm alright, I am." Juno smiles weakly. "Tal saved me. He healed me."

Amryn's eyebrows shoot up. "He did - he did what?"

I shake my head. "Too much to talk about here." My eyes turn to Elise, whose face is twisted with anguish as she looks at Amryn and me.

"I'm so sorry." Her lip quivers. "I'm so sorry I never told you."

I take her in my arms as she covers her face with her hands. "Come on now, it's OK. We'll talk about it all."

She looks up at me, and her eyes widen for a second. "Tal - Tal, it is you isn't it?"

"Of course, what are you talking about?" I look up at the others, and they're all staring at me too.

"Konstantin?" Juno murmurs, covering her mouth with her hands.

I look around at them all as Elise backs away from me. "What? What's wrong?"

Cora points to my head. "Your hair."

I take my hair in my hands, and the white streak, the one that's been there since the day Amryn and Cora were taken away, is gone. I look at my hands, and they don't look like my hands. They're wider, calloused underneath the fingers. I put my hand to my chest - and the fucking scar is gone. It's gone.

I lift my shirt, to check I'm not imagining things, and Juno cries out. There's a tattoo on my chest. I don't have a fucking tattoo on my chest. But it's there, four stars rising above a spire.

I meet Amryn's eyes, and he shakes his head. "What the fuck is going on?"

Juno is crying, and Cora puts an arm around her.

"Come here," I say to Amryn. I wave him towards me when he hesitates. "Just come here."

He approaches me hesitantly. "Tal, what the fuck is going on?"

"Burn me." I hold out my arm to him. I have a strange feeling about something, about all of this. And I want to test my theory.

Amryn holds both his hands up. "I'm not doing that, brother, what the fuck?"

I shove my arm at him. "Try and fucking burn me."

Amryn looks over at Cora, whose brow is furrowed. With a sigh, he turns back to me, igniting a flame. He shakes his head, then lays his hand on my arm.

Nothing happens. It doesn't burn. I can't even feel it.

Amryn stares at me, wide-eyed. "What the fuck is happening?" His head snaps over to Juno, then back to me. "OK, if you two don't tell me what's going on right now I'm going to lose my fucking mind."

"Juno's the first Shadow Queen." I say. "And I'm the Witch King of Donathian apparently."

Everyone falls into shocked silence, the only sound is Juno's weeping. Cora and Amryn don't know where to look. Cora releases Juno and approaches me slowly, a flame springing up from the palm of her hand. She walks right up to me, her green eyes questioning as she gazes up at me. She turns her hand slowly, and places it against my face.

It doesn't burn me. It doesn't hurt. She collapses

against me and lets out a shuddering breath. "I thought - I thought it would be gone." She wraps her arms around me, and shakes her head. "I thought our bond, it would be..." She trails off as she begins to cry.

"Now, Juno." I say to Amryn.

Amryn and Juno look at each other, then back at me. "Juno what?" Amryn asks.

"Try and burn her."

The protest leaves his face almost immediately. He turns to Juno, and she wipes the tears from her face before laying her hand in front of him. Amryn shakes his head, then ignites an orange flame in his hand. He grasps Juno's hand.

"Nothing." Juno clasps Amryn's hand. "I don't feel anything."

Amryn spins back to face me. "What does this mean?"

"I don't think the Old God picked us to be Cora's Draws," I say slowly, holding Cora as she continues to sob.

Liall shakes his head. "So, then who did?"

"I don't know." I look down at Cora's tear-stained face. She raises a hand to my cheek.

"It looks like you," she says, "but...it doesn't."

I look at Elise. "That day, on the road from the Lowlands, when the witch hit you with a spell."

She nods. "Yes, I was 9 years old."

Fuck it all to hell. "It was an infertility spell. She was trying to stop my soul from being reborn."

Elise's eyes widen as she clutches her hands to her

stomach. She stumbles backwards, her mouth opening but no sound coming out. Liall turns to put an arm around her, but she pushes him away.

"No," she says, shaking her head, her eyes not meeting anyone else's, "this isn't important right now, I - I'm OK."

Amryn explodes, tearing his leather vest off and throwing it aside in frustration. "Juno, hit me." He says. "Go on, hit me. Throw that lightning at me."

Juno's eyes flash to mine. "Why?"

"I wanna test this theory too. If there's a bond here, I wanna know about it." He widens his arms either side of him. "Go on."

Cora steps out of my arms, holding a hand out. "Amryn, this isn't a good idea."

"It's fine," Amryn says, keeping his eyes on Juno, who summons a white ball of lightning in her hands. "I've dealt with worse than this."

Juno's lips purse as she exhales, her gaze fixed on Amryn. "I'm sorry if I hurt you."

"You won't." Amryn sounds so certain.

Juno fires the white lightning at him, and we all jump involuntarily. When the flash clears, Amryn's standing in exactly the same place, like nothing happened. Juno looks down at her hands as Amryn approaches her.

"I don't understand." She looks back over at me. "Why? Why have you two been chosen?"

"The Old God said something," Cora says suddenly. "It was weird, cryptic. But he said the Earth and the Flame are going to meet again, and their memories are going to change everything."

Fucking shit. "The witch said the same thing to us in that house." I shake my head. "OK, there's no point going over this tonight, we need to talk tomorrow." I want to get this fucking blood off me.

Amryn nods. "Yeah, let's all get some sleep. This is... It's too much." His face is questioning as he gazes at me. "I don't know where we're going to get answers on all this from."

"We need to talk to Zadkiel and Azrael," I reply. "I think something's going on here that none of us ever saw coming."

Elise offers us her cabin, since mine is in pieces now. She goes to stay with Fenella, and I hate that she's still unable to face me properly.

I look at my face in the mirror. It's my face, but it's not. It's younger. I press my hands against the counter, and it's almost like I can feel it twice. I look back up at my reflection, and I jump when I see it's already staring at me.

"I'm sorry." Konstantin says. "I can't control it. I didn't mean to take over."

"I guess neither of us asked for this." I shake my head. "What does this all mean? The bond with Cora and Amryn, and Juno?"

"I don't know, perhaps the angels will have answers, as you said."

"Yeah, maybe." Footsteps are coming towards the

bathroom.

"We need to do something first." Konstantin leans closer. "We need to find Alexei."

"Alexei?"

He nods. "I need to kill him."

"Yes, we do." I want to skin that motherfucker alive.

The door opens behind me, and Juno walks into the bathroom. When I turn back to the mirror, Konstantin is gone.

Juno puts her arms around my waist, her naked skin warm against mine. "My love?"

I run my hand over her arm. "It's me. I'm here."

"I don't know what to think anymore." She clutches me tighter. "It's you, both of you, isn't it?"

I turn around, and her face is filled with confusion as she gazes up at me. "Come on." I pull her towards the shower. "We need to wash that blood off you."

We step under the warm water, and I run my hands over Juno's back, her shoulders, washing the blood away. I pick up the soap, and lather it in my hands, running them over her again. Her eyes stay fixed on me, and I'm overcome with longing, my whole body taut with desire - not just mine.

"Konstantin?" She murmurs, taking my face in her hands.

I look into her eyes. "He's here."

"Can I - can I talk to him?" She asks. "I'm sorry, Tal, I love you, I do."

I push away the stab of envy that claws at my chest. Of course she wants to talk to him. She loved him. Loves him.

"It's OK. I get it."

Konstantin emerges from the dark corner of my mind he now occupies. He moves forward hesitantly, until I signal to him that it's OK, that he can take over. It's the strangest sensation, being pushed back in my own body. I stand by and watch as Konstantin reaches out for her.

My hands trace over Juno's body, and I let out a sigh of relief. Centuries worth of agony, and now she's here, in my arms. I clutch her to me.

"My love." I bury my face in her hair. "Oh my love, I'm sorry. I'm so sorry."

Juno cries softly. "I was so stupid."

"No, you weren't."

"I killed you." She clings to me. "I killed you."

I seize her mouth with mine, and the relief has tears burning my eyes. She's alive. Her arms move around my neck, and I crush her against me, wanting to feel all of her, feel that heartbeat against my chest, her soft skin under my fingertips.

"I'm going to kill him," I murmur against her lips, "I'm going to kill him for what he did to you. I'm so sorry, I'm so sorry, my love, my only love."

She's crying harder now, clasping on to me. "I watched you die, and I wanted to die with you. I begged you to take me with you. I would have given up everything, my immortality, all of it, for you. I just wanted to follow you."

I shake my head, smiling at her, just looking into her eyes. "We're together again, I'm here." I stop, and realize what I'm saying. "I mean, I'm not. I know that. But..." I nuzzle into her neck, feeling the warmth there, the warmth I've waited centuries to feel again.

I want to... I want to do more. But this isn't my body. He loves her, I can feel his anguish as he watches us together. This isn't fair.

"I'm sorry, my love." I whisper. "I'm so sorry."

I blink a few times, trying to get my bearings. Konstantin is dormant somewhere, and I'm leaning over Juno, whose brown eyes are gazing up at me uncertainly.

"I don't know how to feel about any of this," I say to her.

She leans against my chest with a sigh. "Neither do I."

"He - he wanted to do more. But then he stopped himself." Weird fucking feeling. Being in my body while another man wants to use it to fuck the woman I love. I feel sick. I get out of the shower, and Juno follows me quickly.

"Tal, I love you."

"Yeah, but him?" I shake my head. "There's a whole history there, years, not weeks like it is with us."

"I am bonded to your soul," Juno protests, "that is not a matter of time, it's a matter of Fate."

"So it's just the soul connection, it's not - not me, right?"

Juno scoffs. "Don't you dare do this again." She pushes past me, out into the hallway, still dripping wet.

I grab a towel and wrap it around my waist. "Do what again?"

"Tell me I don't know what I want, or what I know," she replies without turning around, storming into the bedroom.

"I don't fucking know anything right now." I stand in the doorway of the bedroom, watching her stalk back and forth. "All I know is that I just watched you get raped and fucking *tortured*, and now there's some witch king sitting in my head wishing he could fuck you while I watch." I laugh bitterly. "So yeah, right now I'm struggling a little, OK?"

"Well, I'm sorry this is such a struggle for *you*," she cries. "You haven't even asked me how I am, how I'm feeling about all of this! I just had to relive everything and then get beaten and stabbed, so thank you for thinking of me, Tal, when I'm confronted with two men I love more than my own life and now they're bickering over who gets to fuck me in the shower!" She growls in frustration. "It's like Konstantin and Alexei all over again! I cannot escape you stupid fucking men and all your fighting." Her eyes meet mine, and her chest is heaving. "What do you want me to say?"

"I - I don't fucking know."

She rushes up to me, her eyes blazing. "Then hear me say this - I love *you*. I clawed my way through stone and earth for *you*. I heard *your* voice."

"Juno, it's not the same."

She slaps me, hard. "I will say it again since you didn't seem to fucking hear me the first time." She clutches my face in her hands. "I clawed my way out of the fucking ground, *for you*. I heard your voice. *Yours*. Not his. I saw your face. *Yours*. Not his. I will keep saying it until you understand me."

I put my hands over hers. "Juno -"

"Do you understand me?" Her eyes are almost wild.

I sigh heavily, and nod. "Yes."

"Do you doubt my love for you?"

I lean my forehead against hers, even though she's still tense with fury. "No."

"Good. Don't." She pushes my face back up so she can look into my eyes. "*Never* doubt my love for you. I laid under the ground for centuries waiting for you."

The thought has tears biting at my eyes. "I'm sorry."

She softens and melts against me with a sigh. "Please don't be sorry. I'm here now, with you."

I hold her for a while, because there's nothing else to do. Nothing can take away what she went through. Nothing can make that better. She shivers a little, and I feel goosebumps breaking out over her skin. I rub my hands up and down her arms. "Come on, you need to get dry and dressed before you get any colder."

I pull on a pair of sweats, and sit on the edge of the bed, watching Juno dry off and slip on a t-shirt. She begins to brush her long red hair, her eyes flicking to mine every now and then in the mirror.

"How did it all start?" I ask. "With you, and Alexei,

and Konstantin?"

She sighs heavily, and puts down the brush. She stays in front of the mirror, looking down at her hands. "My parents fled the Halls when they discovered my mother was pregnant," she begins, "and Samael hunted them down and killed them, but Eurielle intervened and rescued me. I was only a few days old." Her brow furrows, and she rubs her fingers across the palm of her hand slowly. "She took me to the Halls, to the Old God."

"So I guess the stories we were always told about all the angels being against the Old God weren't true, huh?" I lean back on my hands, keeping my eyes on her reflection.

Juno shakes her head and turns to perch on the bed beside me, one leg curled underneath her. "It was the three brothers, Michael, Gabriel, and Samael. They were the ones who wanted power, who wanted to destroy the Old God's bond to the earth. And when I was born, the ultimate bond suddenly existed."

"So then you grew up in the Halls?"

"No." She traces a finger over the bed, pressing a line into the linen with her nail. "I lived there until I was maybe 5 or so, and then the Old God deemed it too dangerous for me. He sent me to live with a demon clan, in the Earth Realm." She sighs, and her gaze wanders to the ceiling. "And there I met Alexei."

The hairs on the back of my neck stand up at the mention of his name, and I feel Konstantin's rage burning in my face. I reach out and take Juno's hand, and she entwines her slender fingers with mine.

"Alexei was, well, I suppose it was much like Amryn and Cora," she says slowly, "we were friends as children,

and then we grew to love each other deeply. At least -"
She breaks off suddenly, and swallows hard. "At least, I
thought we did."

I circle my thumb over the back of her hand gently.
"We don't have to talk about this if you don't want to."

"No, no, I do." She sighs, and her shoulders slump a
little. "One day, I must have been 21 or so, a war broke
out. The Donathian Forces raided the village, and we had
to flee." She runs a hand through her hair. "I was running
from a figure on horseback, and turned to use my flames
on him." She lifts her eyes to smile at me. "And they did
not hurt him."

"Konstantin."

She nods. "He stopped immediately, threw himself off
his horse and tore off his helmet." She reaches out to touch
the back of her finger to my cheek. "And as soon as our
eyes met, we knew. We both knew. It was instant." Tears
fill her eyes, and she gives out a small laugh. "He ordered
his forces to stop advancing, and from that day on, it was -
oh, my life was not the same."

"You loved him?"

"Oh yes." She inhales deeply through her nose,
blinking rapidly. "I did. Very much. We lived for each
other."

"And Alexei got jealous? From what he said in the
tower, he was pretty pissed about Konstantin."

Her face crinkles a little as she considers her words.
"He never... I don't know." She sighs, tucking her hair
behind her ear. "He was shocked, I think, that there was
another Draw. I tried to be understanding, but..." She

shakes her head. "With Konstantin, it was like my world tilted on its axis. In every way. I loved Alexei, but with Konstantin, it was more than love, he was..."

"Everything." I finish her sentence for her, continuing to stroke her hand. This whole situation is giving me a headache, but I don't want her to stop talking. She needs to get it out.

"Alexei asked to join us in... in the bedroom." Her eyes move to meet mine, and she shifts on the leg folded under her. "It made me uncomfortable, but I didn't want to make him angry, or think I didn't love him. But it..." She presses her palm to her forehead. "It led to a huge argument between him and Konstantin, because I told Konstantin I didn't want to do it anymore."

I puff out a breath. "That's kind of fucked up."

"It was. I felt so... so torn in half. And Konstantin just wanted to protect me. And then..." She clasps my hand firmly. "One month, my bleeding was late, and I was inconsolable, because I realized that if I had a child, I wouldn't even know who the father was." She brushes a hand against her cheek, dashing away a tear. "I told Alexei that I was going to marry Konstantin, and only he would share my bed."

"I guess he didn't take that well."

Juno sniffles and laughs bitterly. "He didn't even protest." Her eyes are sad as they meet mine. "I think that was the beginning of the end. He'd hatched his plan. He knew what he was going to do to us." The end of the sentence is lost in a hiccup, and she pulls her hand from mine to cover her face as she begins to sob. "I was so stupid, so so fucking stupid!"

I pull her into my lap, and hold her as her body quakes with grief. Konstantin's anger swells at the back of my neck, fuelling my own, and we silently agree that Alexei is going to suffer. He's going to die slowly, and in agony.

Juno looks up at me, her face puffy and red. "I'm tired," she murmurs, "please hold me while I sleep?"

"Of course, baby." I gently kiss away her tears.

We lie down together in the darkness, Juno's head on my chest, her breathing finally steadying as her body warms against mine. I caress her back, and then I feel Konstantin. He's emerging tentatively from the darkness, and his sadness is so overwhelming tears bite at my eyes.

Just one night. He pleads with me. *Please, I just want to hold her. I want to feel her head on my chest. I won't ask again. Just one night. Please, Tallesaign.*

Juno looks up at me as my chest quivers. "Tal?"

"It's OK, I'm OK." My voice fucking breaks as I say it.

Please, Tallesaign. Just one night.

I lay my head back on the pillow, and sigh. *OK.*

A tear tracks down the side of my face as I tighten my arms around her.

"My only love," I murmur, and I feel her body tremble again as she cries. I draw her closer, and she buries her face in the crook of my neck. "Come now, don't cry."

The image of her being raped, being brutalised and beaten by Alexei, swims before me when I close my eyes, and bile rises in my throat. *No, don't think about that now.*

R D Baker

Don't ruin this for yourself.

I draw her up to me, her face close to mine. I stroke her hair, her beautiful red hair, away from her cheeks, where it is sticking to the saltwater of her tears.

"All I wanted," she whispers, "was a life with you. A home, and children."

"I know." I brush a kiss against her lips. "I'm sorry that life was not meant for us." I give her a sad smile. "But perhaps now, with him, you can have that." She begins to protest, and I quiet her with another kiss. "He is a good man, you deserve to be happy with him."

"He is a good man." She strokes my cheek. "I love him so much."

"Good." I sigh as she lays her forehead against mine. "That is good."

Her lips quiver as she kisses me, becoming more forceful. My lips part for her tongue, and she climbs on top of me, clutching my face to hers.

"I love you," she says, her breath catching in her throat as she begins to sob. "I love you so much."

My hands run under her shirt, over her naked skin, and then I remind myself of the promise I made. I would only hold her. I just wanted to hold her for one night. This was a mistake. I should have known better than to think I could lie in bed with the woman I love, barely clothed, and not be overcome with desire. I'm a fool.

"My love," I murmur, "please, we need to stop."

She shakes her head, grinding against me. "Why?"

"I promised -" My words are smothered by her mouth

as she kisses me again, passionately, my resolve faltering with every warm stroke of her tongue. I almost give in, I almost surrender to every desire I have to feel her completely. But I tear my mouth from hers. "I promised him. I promised him."

Juno lets out a shuddering sigh. "Oh." A small sob escapes her. "Yes. You're right. We should stop."

"It wouldn't really be me," I say, running my hands through her hair as she lays her head back on my chest. "And you wouldn't want it to be either."

She looks into my face, her brow furrowed. "I'm sorry."

I shake my head. "I understand. I do. Don't be sorry. I want you to be happy, and you can be, you will be. With him." I kiss her, the ache breaking out over my skin as she begins to cry again. Hasn't she cried enough in her lifetime? "Come now, let me hold you. I want to hold you, like I used to."

She arranges herself next to me, laying her head on my chest. Her fingers trace small circles on my skin, slower and slower, until her fingers lie still, and she falls asleep.

I am desperate to stay awake. I'm desperate to hold onto this. To feel her in my arms as long as possible. I stare at the ceiling, willing my eyes to stay open. Don't sleep. Don't waste this.

But her warmth is seeping into me, and my eyes become heavy.

As I drift off, I hear Alexei's voice - furious, accusatory. "Where the fuck have you been all this time?"

22

Amryn

*J*uno crosses the yard, her arms wrapped around her against the cold. Snow is falling softly from the luminous sky, the cup of coffee in my hand steaming heavily in the frigid morning air.

"Morning," I say to her. Our eyes meet and we both balk a little.

We can feel the bond. It's fucking weird. This must be what it's like for Cora and Tal. There's a sensation there, one I can't explain, and I haven't had before, not like this, not for Juno.

Love.

Not romantic love, not sexual, not like how it is with Cora. But something else. The instinct to protect her. The drive to tear anyone who hurts her into tiny pieces. The knowledge that she's a part of me, and I'm a part of her.

She sits down beside me, and I hold my hand out to her for some reason. She takes it hesitantly, then my hand closes around hers, and she looks up at me.

"This is a little odd."

"Yeah, it fucking is." My hand glows as it holds hers. "Are you still hurt?"

She shakes her head, but my hand keeps glowing.

"Where's Tal?" I ask.

"He needed sleep. He - he gave his body to Konstantin for the night." Her eyes widen when she sees me flinch. "Oh no, no, no, Amryn, not like that. Just to - to let him hold me. But it exhausted him, so he is sleeping."

I nod. "OK." I look down at our joined hands. "Cora's sleeping too. The pregnancy, and all this, it's, well, it's worn her out."

The pregnancy.

A thought begins to form in my mind. Something Gabriel said. Something that's been staring us all in the fucking face.

My eyes meet Juno's, and she frowns. "What's wrong?"

"Gabriel said this Shadow Queen thing, it gets passed from mother to daughter. I mean, not always, but the gene is there." I lift her hand, and look at the white glowing in her veins. "So, how did it pass from you to Cora?"

"I - I don't know," Juno stammers, shrugging, "it must have been a blessing from the Old God."

I shake my head. "Nah, that can't be it."

"Of course it can be," Juno replies, clutching my hand tighter. "You think Gabriel has any idea what he's talking about? He was trying to scare you. He was using whatever he could to frighten Cora into relinquishing her power."

"You sure about that?"

Juno nods emphatically. "Of course."

"And how do you know?"

She rolls her eyes and sighs. "Because I never had a child, Amryn."

Yeah. Well.... That is a point. I chew my lip as I stare at the snow. "This still doesn't make any sense."

Juno sighs, and leans against me. I put my arm around her, and she lays her arm across me. It feels so natural.

It feels so *nice.*

Fuck, this is so weird. I always admired Tal and Cora's relationship, the tenderness they have for each other, the pure love that's there. It's beautiful. And now, I have that too, with someone I barely know, but would be willing to fucking die for.

"Amryn?" Her voice is small.

"Mmm?"

"Do you think the Old God can sense that I'm back? That *I* am back?"

I take a sip of my coffee as I consider this question. This could be dangerous, for all of us.

"You don't need to worry about that right now," I say, and squeeze her shoulders. She turns her head to gaze up at me. "I mean it. No one's going to hurt you, OK? Besides, after last time, I don't think the Old God is going to try you again."

Juno gives a small chuckle. "Ah yes, something to teach Cora."

I raise my eyebrows. "And what's that?"

"Internalizing the Inera," Juno replies. "That's how I moved so fast that day. The Inera isn't just shockwaves and white blasts of lightning. It can be harnessed to increase your natural abilities. That's why it's the Shadow power - within and without. In the light and in the darkness, too."

"You're telling me Cora could move as fast as you did that day?" I can't help but chuckle. "Well I'm definitely never getting into an argument with her again."

Juno giggles, and snuggles in under my arm as a cold breeze blows across the porch.

I hold her tighter and rest my chin on the top of her head. "I'm sorry you were under the ground that whole time. So close." I look across the valley towards Arax, barely visible in the mist. "You were right there, all that time, and we didn't even know."

"Tal's going to kill Gabriel if he ever sees him again," Juno says with a sigh.

Yeah, him and me both. "He'll get what he deserves." I exhale heavily. "So, who is this Witch King that Tal was talking about?"

Juno sits up, turning to face me. "He was my Draw, one of them. The one I killed." Her voice falters a little. "I was tricked, and I was stupid."

"Is that why Tal doesn't look like completely like Tal anymore?"

Juno nods. "Konstantin is in there, somewhere. In a way. It's not easy for Tal right now."

The soul of your girlfriend's lover spooking around in your head - yeah, that wouldn't do anyone much fucking good. "So, why? Why is he back?"

Juno shrugs. "The Donathian witches, they still exist.

They seek the destruction of the Old God and a return of Gaia."

I'm only surprised for a moment. This whole situation is going to get a lot more complicated than we think. And a whole lot more dangerous.

The door to our cabin opens, and Cora comes out, with Phoenix in her arms. She smiles at us softly. "Good morning," she says, her voice still heavy with sleep. "Are you OK?"

Juno nods. "I am, thank you."

Phoenix wriggles in Cora's arms, so she puts him down, and he pads across the porch in his little furry slippers, right over to Juno. He climbs into her lap without even a second's hesitation, leaning his head against her chest. Juno eyes me with surprise, and I laugh.

"Guess he likes you."

"Love Juno," Phoenix says, looking up at her.

Juno smiles down at him, stroking his curls. "Oh, you sweet boy." She plants a kiss on his forehead. "I love you, too."

Phoenix puts his little arms around her neck and cuddles her. "I sorry."

Juno frowns. "What are you sorry for, little one?"

"Aria."

Cora and I glance at each other. "Who's Aria?" Cora asks.

Juno shakes her head. "I don't know, I don't know anyone by that name."

Phoenix looks at us and I can see his little brow moving

as he tries to find the right words. "Aria was special." He shrugs, as though that's all he can say. He climbs down off Juno's lap and grabs Cora's hand. "Come on Mama, Allie's hungry."

Cora's eyes meet mine and she smiles. "He's picked a name already." She runs a hand over her stomach. "We were reading a book and the name was Altaira, and he thought that was pretty. So our daughter is called Allie now, just so you know."

I laugh. "Well, that is a pretty name, and since we have a tradition of older siblings naming the younger ones, I'll allow it." I turn to look down at Juno, and gesture for her to follow us. "Come on, have some breakfast with us."

She smiles at me. "OK."

As we head into the kitchen the floor begins to quake. Phoenix throws his arms around my leg and shrieks. Cora and Juno cling on to one another, and we look at each other anxiously waiting for it to stop. A vase trembles its way off the mantlepiece, and a photo of Astrid and Rodelth tips over, the glass cracking from side to side with a loud clink.

It feels like it goes on forever, but it's probably only 30 seconds or so. We all jump when the door flies open, and Tal rushes into the cabin. I jump a little, because he somehow looks even more like me now that he looks like Konstantin. It's like looking into a mirror.

"Are you all OK?" He asks.

"Yeah, we're good." I look around the cabin. "That was fucking weird."

"The earthquakes, I thought those were you," Cora

says to Juno. "What's causing them now?"

"Aftershocks?" I say, but from everyone's expressions I can see they're not convinced and know I'm not either. "I mean, maybe it's just a regular old earthquake?"

There's a thud on the front porch accompanied by a rush of wings, and the door opens to reveal Zadkiel's enormous form. He bends to fit through the door, and when he rises, his eyes move straight to Juno.

"Zadkiel," she says, "you're pretty brave showing up here."

Zadkiel lowers his eyes sheepishly. "Hello Juno."

Tal looks like he's about to tear Zadkiel's wings off. "You knew who she was and said nothing?"

Zadkiel holds up his hands. "In my defense, I was hoping she wouldn't sodding remember, alright? It would have saved us all a lot of trouble if she'd forgotten everything for good and just stayed here and gotten married and had babies with you, Tal."

"Oh I'm sorry to cause trouble," Juno says indignantly, "goodness knows I wouldn't want to bother any of you angels with my problems." She crosses her arms over her chest. "Where is Eurielle?"

"I don't know," Zadkiel replies.

"Bullshit." Juno spits out the word, before looking down at Phoenix apologetically. "Sorry, little one." Her eyes move back to Zadkiel. "You all know where the other is at any given time, where is she?"

"I swear to you, I don't know." Zadkiel takes a step towards Juno, flinching when she in turn takes a step back.

I move into the middle of the room, Phoenix still attached to my leg, and hold out my hands. "OK, alright, stop it now. Everyone needs to calm down." I look at Juno. "Why do you want to see Eurielle?"

"She was like a mother to me," Juno says, her voice catching in her throat as she blinks away tears. "She rescued me from Samael, and she protected me from him in the Halls." Her gaze moves back to Zadkiel. "At least one of them cared."

Zadkiel's face is contorted with pain. "I cared, Juno, I swear I did. I did everything I could to protect you, protect the bloodline, protect -" He stops himself quickly, his eyes widening.

"The bloodline?" I ask. "The bloodline of the Shadow Queen?"

Zadkiel is shaking his head. "I've said too much, oh goodness I've said too much now." He begins to pace back and forth. "Oh no, I've said too bloody much. Azriel is going to take that scythe to me now."

Phoenix lets go of my leg, and I jump, I almost forgot he was there. He pads across the floor to Zadkiel, and tugs on his long robes. Zadkiel looks down at him , and the expression of exasperation fades in an instant.

"Hello little prince," he says with a smile, lifting Phoenix up when he stretches his arms towards him. "Come to say hello to Uncle Zad, hmm?"

"Aria." Phoenix puts his chubby hands on either side of Zadkiel's white face as he says the name. "Do you member Aria?"

Zadkiel's mouth drops open, and his eyes flash to Cora.

"Has he mentioned this name before?"

Cora nods. "This morning, he apologized to Juno, and said it was because of Aria. He said she was special."

Zadkiel sighs heavily. "Oh no."

"Who's Aria?" Tal asks.

Zadkiel cuddles Phoenix tight, and kisses the top of his head. "No one, she died a long time ago."

"But Phoenix said she was special," Cora says.

"She was." Zadkiel sighs heavily. "But she's long gone now."

"Granma?" Phoenix's little face is quizzical. "Like granma?"

Zadkiel clears his throat. "Your granma?"

Phoenix shrugs and wriggles. "Down, pease." As soon as Zadkiel puts him on the ground, he totters off to his room.

Juno rounds on Zadkiel again. "Who was there the day Gabriel and Michael buried me?"

"I don't know, Juno. I swear -"

"Gabriel called someone daddy," Tal says, and Cora gasps. "There was a voice, an old man. And it sounded a hell of a lot like the Old God."

Cora's hands are clasped to her mouth, and she shakes her head. "That's not - no. It's not possible."

"Yes it is," Tal interjects, "because Konstantin had turned Juno away from him. Maybe he knew. Maybe it was his plan all along."

Zadkiel scoffs in outrage. "That is absurd, Tallesaign."

"Is it?" I ask, and Cora's eyes widen as they meet mine. "Baby, it's possible right?"

"No!" She cries, looking around at us all. "That's ridiculous! Burying the Shadow Queen weakened him, he lost everything when they hurt Juno. Why would he have had any part of that?"

"Exactly!" Zadkiel points a talon in Cora's direction. "What could possibly be gained from the Old God destroying his own conduit, his most powerful asset?"

"The Old God was here," I say, "he saw Juno. He knew who she was, and said nothing. He only warned Tal to stay away from her. Why would he do that?"

Zadkiel splutters, wringing his hands, and Cora looks like she's about to burst into tears. Juno's eyes meet mine, and she nods.

"He knew who I was. And it sounded like him." She looks at Zadkiel. "He knew, Zadkiel. He was a part of this."

Zadkiel shakes his head. "No, I refuse to believe that. It's, why it's -" He throws his hands up as words fail him.

"Well there's only one way to find out." Tal says, rolling his shoulders. "We gotta go find that fucker, Alexei."

"I'm coming with you," I say quickly.

Tal shakes his head. "Nope, you stay here, it was dangerous enough for you to come find us and leave Cora here without a Draw. We can't run that risk, especially now we don't know who we can trust."

"Tal, I can look after myself," Cora says, "if Juno's heading out there with the fucking Halls potentially coming after you, she's going to need you both. We don't need a repeat of Nilau."

I feel sick as she says it, and my hands are heavy with the weight of Cora's blood for just a moment. "Cora's right, if anything happens to Juno you're going to need help."

Tal looks at Zadkiel. "Do I have Konstantin's power at the moment? With him floating around in here?" He gestures to his head.

"I don't know." Zadkiel shrugs. "I have no idea how a dual soul works, it's not particularly common as you can imagine. This is Azrael's field of expertise."

"We can't risk it," Cora says, stepping forward. "I'm protected here, and I'm powerful enough to defend myself. Zadkiel, you can stay here with me while they're gone, right?" She gazes up at him and he nods. "I'll be fine, I promise."

Tal sighs, but he knows there's no arguing with Cora. "OK, the three of us go. We'll be gone for a while, it's a long way to fly."

Juno shakes her head. "No, we don't need to fly." She waves her hand at the door. A shimmering mirror forms, no bigger than a basketball, and then it grows and grows, until it's almost as big as Zadkiel. We all turn to stare at her, and she shrugs. "It's a shame no one explained the Inera to you all properly, there's lots to learn."

"I can summon portals?" Cora asks incredulously, putting a hand to her head.

Juno nods. "I'll teach you everything I know, I promise."

"OK, we'll leave tomorrow then," I say. I meet Tal's eyes, and we both feel a flare of bloodlust. We're going to tear this motherfucker into pieces, and I hate the twist of satisfaction I feel at the thought.

"Now, I think we need to go and talk to our aunt." Tal jerks his head towards the door. "Come on. There's some things we need to know."

23
Amryn

The look on Elise's face as she opens the door to Fenella's cabin breaks my heart. The bags under her eyes are deep purple, and she's pale. Her cheeks are even a little sunken in.

"Hello, my boys," she says softly, and steps aside to let us in.

Tal grabs her in a bear hug without another word, and Elise lets out a sob.

"It's OK," he says softly.

"I'm so sorry." Her voice is muffled as she clings on to him, and the scene makes my stomach wrench. "I'm so sorry, Tal."

Tal shakes his head. "Nope, none of that." He pulls back a little and smiles at her. "You're like my second Mom, OK? I'm not mad. I promise I'm not."

"Me neither," I say quickly, and Elise's tear-filled eyes move to me. "I swear, I'm not."

"I should have told you," she says, shaking her head. "I

wanted to, so many times." She steps away from Tal and gestures to the kitchen table. "Come on, come and sit down and let me explain it all to you. I owe you that much."

Tal and I look at each other as we take our seats. Elise fidgets for a moment, clasping her hands on the table then on her lap, blinking rapidly.

"Fenella... *Maman* told me," she begins slowly, and the way she says *Maman* makes my chest ache. The word she hasn't been able to say for so long. "*Maman* told me that you had remembered what happened the day everyone was taken."

Tal nods. "I remembered Mom screaming that she didn't want to hurt me, and Dad urging her to do it."

"You were so brave," Elise says, her eyes fixed on her hands in her lap. "So strong." Her eyebrows twitch as she tries not to cry. "You went running in there, ready to kill anyone who tried to stop you." She raises her eyes to look at Tal, and shakes her head. "Your Mom, she could feel you getting closer. She knew they'd kill you. Your Dad knew they'd kill you. They had to stop you." She reaches across the table, taking Tal's hand. "Your Dad urged your Mom to do the only thing they could, even if it meant hurting you. They saved your life that day."

"So, Dad knew." Tal says.

Elise wipes her tears away from her cheeks, and nods. "He did. When your mom found out she was pregnant, she told me, she couldn't bring a baby into a family built on lies."

Tal exhales heavily. "I can't believe Dad knew, and accepted her."

"I didn't think he would, to be honest," Elise says with a shrug. "I'd packed my bags. I told Elspeth, I said to her, he's the Striker. There is no way, no way in Hell he'll accept it."

"But he did," I say quietly, and Elise gives me a weak smile.

"He did. He adored your Mom. And he loved you, Tal. So much."

Tal's brow furrows, and he crosses his arms over his chest. "Was he... was he... the way he was, because he knew I was a half-breed?"

"Oh sweetheart, no." Elise reaches across the table. "He loved you, he just... he didn't know how to show it. Your grandfather had been a hard man, and your Dad just didn't know any different."

"Yes he did," Tal says quickly, his eyes darkening. "Amryn didn't get the treatment I did. And everyone knew he was Cora's Draw. Why did I -" He breaks off quickly, shaking his head. "It doesn't matter. It's not important right now."

"Tal," I say, but he shakes his head emphatically, not looking at me.

"Brother, not now." His tone tells me there's no point arguing.

Elise sighs. "I'm sorry, Tal. You deserved better. You did."

"It doesn't matter." Tal's voice is almost a growl.

Elise and I exchange a glance. Tal's pain is overwhelming, and I know there's nothing I can do to help him. I'm so mad at my father for a moment, and my mother too. Why didn't she do anything? Another one of those things we'll never have closure on, never have anyone explain to us. More secrets.

"So, do we have powers?" I ask Elise. "Like, can you sense that?"

"I can't sweetheart, no. But there's something there, because you're both immune to the blood magic. It can't kill you."

Tal chews on his lip. "Is that..." He doesn't complete the thought, and he lifts his eyes to mine slowly. "We're Cora's Draws, and we're immune to blood magic."

I nod. "Yeah, I mean, that makes sense. If you have the Halls after you."

Tal's eyes narrow, and I can practically hear the cogs turning in his head. "There's something weird going on here."

"What are you thinking?" Elise asks.

"I don't know." Tal shakes his head. "I just can't shake this feeling that the Old God didn't pick us as the Draws."

"So who did?" I ask.

Tal leans on the table, looking at Elise. "Did anyone else know I was Cora's Draw?"

"Astrid did," Elise replies, "Cora told me that Zadkiel admitted it to her after Nilau."

My throat constricts. "What?"

Tal quickly reaches across to me, putting a hand on my arm. "Amryn -"

I shake him off and look back at Elise. "Zadkiel knew? Cora was dead in my arms, I had to feel the woman I love *die* and he fucking knew?"

Elise shakes her head. "Sweetie, he had no choice, he can't interfere, you have to understand -"

"*Understand*?" Rage swells in my chest and I jump out of my chair. My hands are heavy again, heavy with blood. Her blood, everywhere. I'm overwhelmed with grief as I remember holding her in my arms, feeling her die, feeling that sick fucking icy feeling flood my chest as she slipped away. "I'm going to kill him. I'm going to fucking set him on fire."

Tal rises to his feet. "Amryn, hey, come on."

"No, Tal, I won't fucking come on." I'm shouting now. "What would you do, if it was Juno? You ever held the woman you love in your arms and *feel* her die? What if you hadn't put your hands on her, huh? She'd be fucking *ash*, and Zadkiel would have known the whole time!"

"I get it," Tal says, holding out his hands to me.

"No you don't!"

"I do." His voice is suddenly different, and his eyes darken. It's not Tal anymore. It's Konstantin. He holds out a hand, and I can feel his sadness through the blood bond. "I do, Amryn. I understand. I watched the woman I love be brutalized, right before my eyes, and I could do nothing. I was dying, the last thing I saw was her pleading, begging me to help her."

Elise gasps. "Oh god."

Tal - Konstantin? - takes a step towards me. "I understand. I do. I understand your helplessness, and your fear. And you are right to be angry. But there is more at play here than you or even I know. And Zadkiel has played his part in that."

"So I just have to let it go, huh?" I ask bitterly.

Konstantin shrugs. "No, you don't. But right now we need to keep our allies close. The time for questions will come." He looks over at Elise. "We don't know what's coming, and we have to be prepared. Together."

I watch Cora get undressed for bed, her eyes flashing to mine every so often.

"What're you thinking?" She asks with a crooked smile.

I shake my head and give her a smile. "I'm watching my wife get undressed, what do you think I'm thinking?"

She sits down beside me on the bed, and cocks an eyebrow. "I know that look, and *this* -" She gestures to my face. "Is not *that* look. What're you thinking about?"

I reach out and take her hand, and exhale heavily. "Konstantin, he had to lie there, dying, and watch some fucker rape the woman he loved. He couldn't do a thing about it. He just had to watch." I lift my eyes to meet hers. "And all I keep thinking is that I didn't have that excuse."

Cora sighs and grips my hand tighter. "Oh Amryn."

I pull her closer, stroking the hair off her forehead. "I will never forgive myself for letting that happen to you. I should have stopped him."

"And then what?" She raises her eyebrows, cradling my face in her hands. "What would have happened then? To you? To me? Hmm?" She kisses me tenderly. "They would have killed you, baby. They would have killed you, and I would have lost you, forever. And I'd still be in Nilau, married to Finn."

"But -"

"And you'd be right where Konstantin is now," she interjects. "I do not blame you. I never have. I never will. And I will not have you blaming yourself. We were both trapped."

I take her in my arms, breathing her in. "I'm still sorry."

She turns her head to gaze up at me. "We're alive, Amryn. And that's what matters. We're alive. You and me. We're both here. We have a beautiful baby boy, and soon we're going to have a little girl to love."

She kisses me, and fuck she's so sweet. Still, forever, I know I'll never feel this way about anyone else. "I'd walk through Hell for you, to have you." She whispers.

"Me too." I hold her to me, feeling her warmth and her breath.

"And we did." She nuzzles into me. "But it's done now. We survived."

"I know." I rub her shoulders gently, and she flinches a little. "You OK?" I look down at her and she shrugs.

"Just tense," she replies, "with everything going on, you know?"

"Mmmm." I rub a little harder, feeling the knots in her shoulders. She hums low in her throat and her head falls back a little. "Does that feel good?"

"Yeah," she murmurs.

"Maybe you need a massage, huh?"

She chuckles and shakes her head. "You need to

sleep."

"Ah, plenty of time for sleep." I kiss her forehead before climbing off the bed. "Come on, get on your stomach. I won't be able to do this much longer."

She giggles as she spreads out face down on the bed. "No, I guess not, once I have a big belly in the way."

I retrieve a bottle of oil from on top of the dresser and climb back on the bed, pouring a stream on to her back. She jerks a little.

"You're meant to warm that up first, you know!"

I grin at her as she glares over her shoulder at me. "I like seeing you flinch."

"Asshole."

"You're meant to be relaxing," I say, and she lays her head back down on the bed with a sigh. I rub the oil over her back in long strokes, then begin to massage her shoulders. "You really are tense, baby."

"Kinda got a lot on my mind, you know?"

"I know." I work my hands down her back, and fuck her skin looks beautiful. "You look like you should be on a beach somewhere when you're all shiny like this."

The corner of her mouth turns up in a smile. "The beach sounds nice."

"Maybe we should take Phoenix before the baby's born, huh?" My hands work over her lower back. "Get away for a while, just us."

"I'd like that."

I keep rubbing her lower back in sweeping circles, and she sighs. She's so warm under my hands, and the sight of her spread out like this...

Once her back is covered and slick, I move to her neck and shoulders. My hand works the base of her neck, gently clawing into her hair, and she moans softly each time I release. I work my knuckles down either side of her neck, smoothing out those tight muscles bit by bit. I sweep my hands over her shoulders, and when I press my thumbs in she lets out the most delicious groan.

"Does that feel good, baby?" I murmur against her ear.

"Yes." She lifts her head a little, and she's panting. "So damn good."

"You look so fucking beautiful like this." My hands trail back down her body so smoothly, and I'm lost in the motions now, distracted by her quickened breathing. She's begging to be devoured, I can feel it.

When I reach her hips, I reach underneath her, so close to where I want to touch. She rolls her hips against my hands, and I know she's already wet for me. But I want to drag this out a little longer.

I dig my fingers into her hips then sweep my fingers down, so close to her center, then drag them back over her lower back. Her answering growl makes me so fucking hard.

I pull her leg towards me a little, making space for me to kneel between her thighs. My thumbs work over her ass, further and further down. She gasps as my fingers trace over the lips of her pussy.

"Good?" I ask quietly.

"Yeah."

My fingers push her open, working down into her heat,

and she moans softly. I circle her clit and her hands flex on the bed, the muscles in her back rippling. Her legs open a little further as her hips move, and I love that she's so needy for me. I love that I do this to her.

She gasps as I push two fingers inside her, and she's so hot my mouth goes dry with lust.

"You feel so good, baby." I lower my mouth to her back. I move my fingers back over her clit, my lips moving over her ribcage as a breathy moan leaves her. Fuck, she's so slick and hot and sweet.

Her hips jerk as she moves back against my hand, raising her head from the bed. "I wanna feel you," she says, "Amryn, please."

I move my mouth further up her back, my fingers staying on her clit, swirling over it as she gets wetter. She begins to tremble a little, all her little gasps and moans just making me harder.

"I'm here baby," I murmur in her ear. "I'm right here."

"I want you to fuck me." She turns her head towards me, her mouth seeking out mine.

"Slowly, baby, you're going to come for me first." I move my other hand underneath her, smoothing oil over her breast, her nipple grazing against my palm as it peaks at my touch.

She's breathing hard against my mouth, her hips grinding I fuck her with my fingers. She whimpers, her eyes clenched shut, and then she goes still, pressing her lips against my shoulder. She cries out against my skin as she trembles.

Before she can do anything, before she's recovered or

subsided, I move back down her body, my hands angling her hips, and sink my mouth into her pussy. She cries out, bucking against me.

"Amryn, oh fuck." Her fingers claw into the bed, and she throws her head back. She's still shaking from her climax, and I have to hold her steady. I drag my tongue over her clit in long, hard strokes, groaning as I grind my throbbing cock against the bed.

I want to fuck her right now, but I also want to taste her as she comes again, just for me. This is mine. *She's* mine. Some nights it's like this - I want to claim her. Remind her who she belongs to. Remind myself that I belong to her. All those years of thinking she'd be someone else's... I'm not ashamed to say they left their mark.

And some nights, I want to take my time with her. Not have to be quiet, not have to sneak around and be quick. Each touch of her skin, each whimper and moan reminding me that it'll never be like that for us again.

She's mine. This is only for me. It always was, and it always will be.

Her hips jerk against my face, her arousal dripping from my lips as she hisses out a sharp breath.

"Oh god," she gasps, and then she's coming again, pushing her mouth into the sheets to suppress her cries. She shudders as I give her pussy one last, long lick, then crawl over her. I trace kisses up over her shoulders, up the back of her neck into the wild disarray of her hair.

I guide my cock inside her, and she's still fluttering delicately as I start to grind myself into her. The angle of her hips as she raises herself up on her elbows makes everything so fucking mouthwateringly tight. Our moans mingle as I bring my mouth down on hers.

Her veins are glowing bright white, and a thin layer of sweat has broken out, mingling with the oil that's making her slick underneath me.

"Harder," she pleads, "do it harder."

I roll my hips, letting her feel every inch of me. "We're doing it my way tonight."

Each one of her ragged breaths is almost a sob. She gazes at me with hooded eyes, her lips full and red.

"Is that good?"

"Yes." Her breath hitches in her throat. "Oh fuck. Please do it harder. Please, Amryn."

She feels so good around me, and hearing her beg sends my desire spiraling. I abandon any thought of drawing this out any longer, and I slam myself into her. I put my hands over hers on the bed, and her hips buck to meet my strokes.

I groan into her hair as I release inside her, and she meets me there, coming for a third time. There's nothing delicate about this climax, and her pussy contracts violently around my cock. Her scream is smothered by the bed, and then I feel her body slump underneath me, spent and weak with pleasure.

I roll off her and lie next to her as the sweat cools on our skin, and after a moment she shifts to lay her head on my chest.

"Holy fuck."

"You're so easy to get off when you're pregnant." I laugh breathlessly as she slaps my stomach.

"Like you've ever had a problem getting me off," she scoffs.

I tuck a hand behind my head and stroke her hair. "That's true."

She chuckles softly, tracing small circles on my chest with her fingertips. "Makes me think, you know." She shifts to look up at me. "All those times, when we were younger."

"All the times we fucked?" I ask with a laugh.

"No, just..." She sighs as she trails off. "I had to think about my birthday party, you know, when Lordain slapped me."

"Mmmm." I growl in my throat at the memory. "That fucker."

"I remember you walking across the field, after you'd come down off the mountain, and..." She trails off again. "It's always been you, you know?"

"I know, baby."

She raises herself up and moves closer to my face, bringing her mouth close to mine. "You come back to me tomorrow." Her face is suddenly earnest. "I need you, OK?"

"Baby, I'm not going anywhere, OK?" I stroke her cheek. "I'll always come back to you."

"Promise me." She looks freaked out, and her eyes shine with tears.

I sit up and pull her up with me. "Of course I promise. You know I will. What brought this on?"

"I'm scared." She leans against me, and takes a deep

breath. "I just - I'm scared."

"It's going to be OK." I put my finger under her chin and tip her face up to mine. "I'm going to be fine. And I'll be back before you know it. I will always come back to you."

24
Tallesaign

I t's barely dawn when I wake. I watch from my bed as the sky changes, glowing pink, illuminating the snow on the ground. A flock of crows flies overhead, and I wonder for a moment if the shifters have come back. But they fly off into the distance silently.

I'm going to kill a man today.

I've killed before. That doesn't bother me. What bothers me is that I'm going to torture this man, I'm going to make him hurt and suffer, just like he made Juno hurt and suffer.

And I can't fucking wait.

Juno's wrapped in my arms, warm and soft. I draw her closer to me, burying my face in the crook of her neck as though she's an anchor, tethering that good part of myself securely. I don't want that darkness to overtake me.

"It's time to wake up," I say softly.

She stretches and brushes her fingers along my arms. "I know." She turns her face towards me. "Can you look at my back?" Her brow furrows as she looks over her shoulder at me. "It feels strange."

I move back and look down. In the half-darkness it's hard to tell, and I blink, trying to focus properly.

There are two gentle ridges growing on her back, soft and delicate. I run my fingers over them, and Juno gasps a little.

"What is that?"

I lean over her shoulder and kiss her cheek. "I think your wings are growing back."

She throws herself over on the bed to stare at me wide-eyed. "Are you joking?" She clutches a hand to her mouth as tears well in her eyes. "Tal, do you really think so?"

I give her a wide smile and nod. "It looks like it to me."

She laughs through her tears and nuzzles into my chest. "Oh Tal, I can't believe it!" She shakes her head and looks up at me. "How? How is this possible?"

"Maybe with two Draws, you have the strength to heal now?" I say, stroking her cheek gently. "You'll be flying over this valley before you know it." I kiss her, and she can't stop smiling. I hate that she's so happy now, when we're about to go where we're going, and do what we're going to do. I hold her for a few more minutes, just letting her be happy, before I tip her face up to meet mine. "We have to get ready now."

Her face only drops a little, and I see that steely determination settle in as she nods. "Yes, let's go." She swings her feet to the ground, and I reach out and take her hand. She looks at me questioningly.

"I'm going to kill him, you know that?"

"I do."

"I don't want to do anything you don't want me to do." I run my thumb gently over her knuckles.

"I want him to suffer," she says, the neutrality of her expression more terrifying than if she turned into that shrieking, fanged creature that held down the Old God. "I want him to bleed, and to suffer, and die in pain."

"Then that's what'll happen."

I dress in my leathers and tie back my hair. I swing the sheathed scimitar onto my back, and turn to watch Juno braid her long red hair. She's dressed in the black flex-armor Elise lent her, and she looks lethal like this. She turns to retrieve a small leather belt from the table, and she straps it to her thigh, sliding two long, thin daggers into it.

"Good with a knife, huh?" I ask with a grin.

Juno smirks as she looks back at me. "Very good, in fact. In all kinds of situations." Her gaze wanders up and down my body, and I can't help but laugh.

"I have a feeling you and I are going to have to do a whole lot more getting to know each other when this is over."

She raises her eyebrows. "I would like to think so." Her face drops at almost the same time as mine.

When all this is over. What this is, well, that remains to be seen. It feels like we're just heading straight into another war.

Cora and Amryn are waiting outside for us, Cora wrapped in a heavy red coat, Amryn dressed in leathers, his long black hair pulled back into braids.

"Dressed up for the occasion, huh?" I joke, pointing to his hair.

He smiles at me, then his gaze turns to Juno, who is hurrying across the snow towards him. She clutches onto him when she reaches him.

"Amryn, my wings, they're growing back," she says, her voice cracking.

Amryn's eyes widen, and he takes her face in his hands. "Really? Juno, that's incredible!" He takes her in his arms, smiling widely.

Cora and I look at each other, and Cora shrugs, smiling softly. "They're as bad as you and me." She jerks her head in Amryn and Juno's direction.

My heart swells a little. This Bond is weird, but it's nice. It's so fucking *nice* to be surrounded by so much love.

Amryn releases Juno as Zadkiel and Elise cross the snow towards us.

Cora's face tightens as she looks up at her husband, and she puffs out a breath through pursed lips. "Remember what you promised me?" She says, putting her hands on his chest.

Amryn nods and smiles. "I told you." He leans down and kisses her tenderly. "I'll always come back."

"She'll be perfectly safe while I'm here," Zadkiel says, "I swear to you."

Cora turns to me and puts her arms around my waist, hugging me close. "You take care."

I wrap my arms around her tight. "I always do, honey." I kiss the top of her head, and she looks up at me, smiling even though I can see tears in her eyes.

I don't like how this is feeling so much like a goodbye, and that old ghost is echoing at the periphery again. I push it away. This is no big deal. We're just going to kill some guy and then we'll be back - right?

Cora and Juno embrace, and Zadkiel presses a hand to his mouth. "It's so wonderful to see you two like this," he says, "two Queens, together. I never thought I'd see this moment."

The two women smile at each other, and I think it settles on all of us that this really is a bit of a moment. Amryn's eyes meet mine, and he grins.

"Guess we both have good taste in women, huh?" He says.

"We picked you, don't take the credit," Juno quips, and we all laugh softly. Juno walks over to Amryn and me, and her face becomes earnest. "The house he lives in, it is riddled with traps. You will have to keep your eyes open, and don't move too fast, no matter what he does."

"Does he still have his powers?" Amryn asks. "He's a demon, right?"

Juno nods. "Yes, he is a demon, and he should still have his powers. I don't know what immortality will have done to him. He may be weak, he may be more powerful."

"He looked weakened to me," I say, and I hear Konstantin agreeing in the back of my mind.

"Even so, we cannot assume anything," Juno says, "so we stay close, and we move carefully. I know where to find him."

"Do you still have a connection to him?" Amryn asks.

Juno smiles sadly, and shakes her head. "That broke the second he left me on the floor in that chamber."

Amryn and I glance at each other. This fucker is going to pay.

Juno extends a hand, sending out that small ball of undulating white light again. We watch as it grows and grows, and there's a portal in front of us. Beyond it lies a blurred landscape, as though we're looking out of a rain-drenched window.

"Ready?" Juno says, looking at each of us in turn.

"Ready." Amryn casts one more glance over his shoulder at Cora before he turns back. "Let's go."

Juno walks through first, the portal rippling like a disturbed puddle as she does. Amryn and I look at each other, and I hold out my hand.

"After you," I say.

He walks through, and I can see his back through the blur. I look back at Cora, who is under Zadkiel's arm. She's not crying, but I can see the worry etched on her face.

"We'll be right back, honey," I say, and she nods.

Walking through the portal is strange. It feels wet, but it's not. It's not even really cold. Just a strange sensation, and a soft popping noise as I emerge on the other side. Something crunches underfoot, and I look down to see dead, thorny vines tangled on the ground.

Juno and Amryn are gazing up at a fortress, shrouded in mist. Dark green-gray clouds roll behind it, and as lightning flashes I see the silhouette of an immense mountain range. The thorny vines clamber up every wall, every tower.

"Pretty sure the humans wrote a fairy tale about this place," I say as thunder rumbles overhead.

"Yeah, except there's a sleeping princess in that story, not a demonic zombie," Amryn says with a chuckle.

"Come on." Juno stalks ahead, her long wine-red braid the only streak of color in our gloomy surroundings.

Amryn and I follow, and I look down to see the veins in Amryn's hands are glowing. But they're not orange anymore. They're a deep purple, almost black. I want to say something to him, ask him when they changed, but now isn't the time. We have other things to focus on.

Juno's steps slow as we approach a lowered drawbridge which hangs over a moat. Well, what was once a moat. The few feet of water that remain are black, a strange green foam pooling where it meets the bare soil banks. There's a skeleton half-submerged, it looks reptilian, like a crocodile, and for some reason it weirds me out.

"Where the fuck are we?" I murmur.

We cross the drawbridge, and lightning flashes as we enter a large stone courtyard. We all look up at the surrounding towers, covered in those tangled, sharp vines. The windows have been smashed, most of the roofs have caved in. The top of one tower to the north of the fortress has crumbled completely, the stones of its remaining spire jutting into the darkening sky like crooked teeth.

"Are you sure he's here?" I ask, looking for a door, some entrance into what remains of the fortress. "It doesn't look like anyone's lived here in centuries."

"He's here," Juno says. "Alexei wouldn't go anywhere else." She moves towards a wall covered in brambles, and gestures to it. "Burn these away would you?"

Amryn steps forward and sends his flames into the thicket, and his face flashes to mine. His flames are the same dark purple I saw in his veins. "Uh, what the fuck?"

"Your powers are shifting too," I reply. "It makes sense. Everything's changing for us, all of us."

Juno looks surprised as well, but nods. "Yes, that's right. Our powers will align with each other's."

Smoke rises as the vines burn away, and a broken oak door comes into view. It's barely hanging onto its hinges, and as the heat from the fire touches the metal, it buckles and falls forward. A shower of embers rains over us.

Juno steps forward first, her right hand flexed, small volts of white dancing across her fingertips. Amryn and I follow her into the dark passageway where an overwhelming scent of mildew meets us. Water runs down the walls, the trickling the only sound besides our footsteps.

I ignite my flames to cast more light as we move further into the fortress. The floor is uneven, pebbled with fallen rocks, what looks like old furniture, and then - I lean closer. Yep, that's a skull. Lots of skulls. Animal, human, it's hard to tell. But they're littered all over the ground.

"This is starting to feel like the start of a horror movie," Amryn says quietly.

"Starting to?" I ask, and his eyes meet mine.

Juno stops suddenly, and draws one of her daggers

from her thigh. She crouches down, running the tip of the blade along the stone floor, and we all jump back as an iron door springs up from the floor, slamming spikes into the ceiling. Dust showers down on us, and the walls reverberate around us.

"Well I guess that's a quiet approach done now, huh?" Amryn says, coughing.

"Who's there?"

The voice comes from up ahead. We weave our way through the iron spikes, and keep moving slowly behind Juno. I look back down the passageway we just moved up, and I can't help but think that this was too easy. Juno had said there'd be traps...

Maybe Alexei is tired. Maybe centuries of immortality have worn him out. Maybe he doesn't feel the need to be protected anymore. Maybe a part of him was hoping, praying for this day. But the sneaking feeling that maybe we're missing something won't leave me alone.

There's a stone archway up ahead, and I can see light filtering through it. Thunder rumbles loudly. Juno walks through the archway, and we follow her into a stone chamber. There are candles everywhere, on every surface. Water runs along the gaps in the stone floor as rain falls through the smashed windows.

In the center of the room, there's a wooden chair, like a small throne. There's a figure sitting in it, wrapped in what looks like an old flag, faded blue and yellow with a crest on it. A lion and a rose? It's hard to tell, it's so faded now.

The figure raises its head, and we're met with a gray face with sunken cheeks. Thin lips quiver as Juno approaches.

"Hello Alexei," she says quietly.

Alexei's eyes are a weird shade of pale pink, like they've been bleeding. They move from me to Juno and back again. He doesn't seem to notice Amryn at all. His shoulders begin to quake, and at first I think he's crying. It's only when I see one corner of his mouth turn up that I realize he's laughing.

"You're back," he rasps. "I wondered if you'd ever claw your way out of there."

I feel a sudden rush at the back of my mind, Konstantin rising, full of fury. I tell him to stay back - not yet. We need answers first.

"I did," Juno says. "You look terrible, Alexei."

Alexei laughs, his thin lips pulling back to reveal brown teeth. "Immortality isn't what I thought it would be." He shifts mechanically in the chair. The flag falls from his shoulders to reveal the torn rags he's dressed in. The man looks like he just rolled out of a coffin. "I've spent centuries here, alone, watching the world around me fall apart."

"It didn't have to be this way," Juno says, "you chose to betray me."

"Betray you?" Alexei scoffs. "You betrayed me first. Disappearing like that, I was frantic, searching for you for two years, two fucking years!"

Juno's gaze flickers over to me for a moment, her brows knit together in confusion. "I don't know what you're talking about."

"Of course you don't," he sniffs, sinking back down into the chair. "You and him, you came back, like nothing had happened. Like you'd been gone an hour."

I reach back into my mind to Konstantin, but he shakes his head. What the fuck is this guy talking about?

Alexei's gaze shifts and lands on me. He raises a bony finger. "But how did you come back?"

"The Donathian forces took Konstantin's body and injected me with his memories." I gesture to my head. "He's in here, and he wants to tear you to pieces."

"Of course he does," Alexei says with an exasperated sigh. "Fucking coal-haired degenerate. How he ever became King is beyond me. All he cared about was killing and fucking."

Konstantin's anger flares, and I struggle to keep him contained. *Not yet. Not fucking yet.*

"Who was there that day?" Juno asks. "Who was there the day you threw me to the angels?"

Alexei throws the flag aside, grasping the arms of the chair with his wasted fingers, and shuffles forward. He raises those weird pink eyes to look at Juno, licking his lips with a tongue that looks like it's made of sandpaper.

"You still don't understand, do you?" He sneers at her.

"Tell me who was there," Juno commands, her hands glowing bright white.

"You know who was there," Alexei spits back. "You saw them, Michael, and Gabriel. They cut off your wings."

"There was a third voice," Juno says, "a voice that sounded like the Old God."

Alexei throws his head back, his neck creaking loudly, and he laughs. "Ah yes your precious Old God, the one who slaughtered your parents for their betrayal." He shakes his head. "Oh Juno, I never understood you. How could you be the Queen of the man who killed your own parents?"

"I didn't know," Juno replies indignantly, though I can hear her voice strain a little. "I was lied to. I didn't know for years what had really happened."

"And then when you did, how long did it take you to turn away from him, hmm?" Alexei gets himself too worked up, and coughs, holding a withered fist to his mouth. He takes a deep breath, leaning back in his chair, his pale pink eyes narrowing as he leers at Juno. "You're a fool, Juno. You did his bidding for so long, and then when you finally turned away you were shocked the Halls wouldn't let you go."

Juno rushes at him, pulling a dagger from her thigh in one fluid movement, bringing it up underneath Alexei's jaw. "Was he there or not? I want to fucking know."

Alexei licks his lips and leers at her. "You know, I felt deep satisfaction knowing my cock was the last one you had before they put you in the ground." He chuckles as he looks over at me. "Check mate, brother."

I expect Juno to take his head off, tear his throat out. Instead, she straightens up and re-sheaths her dagger. As though she can sense the rush of fury as Kostantin explodes out of the corner of my mind, she looks over her shoulder at me with a lifted eyebrow.

She nods, and steps back. She wants us to handle this. She wants her *Draws* to handle this. She can sense that we need to - all three of us. The bloodlust is so thick in the air it's practically dripping down the walls.

I rush at Alexei, pulling the scimitar from my back. I hurl it towards his throat, stopping just short enough not to sever his spine, but far enough to begin drawing a stream of thick, black blood.

I look up to see a hand at the top of Alexei's head, holding on to the scrap of hair that remains, and I turn my head to meet Amryn's eyes. Amryn's iridescent, violet eyes. He bares his teeth as he looks down at Alexei.

"You gonna tell us what we want to know or not?" Amryn demands.

Alexei laughs sickeningly, sending a cascade of blood down his chest. "You can go fuck yourself."

"I'd like a word with this fucker before you finish him, if it's all the same to you," Amryn growls.

I draw the scimitar from Alexei's throat, and he gurgles a little. "Certainly." I step back from the chair.

Amryn holds out a hand to Juno, his eyes staying on Alexei. "Juno, may I have one of your fine daggers?"

Juno steps forward and hands one to him.

Amryn paces back and forth in front of Alexei, twirling the knife in his hands. "You know, you remind me of someone." He shakes the dagger in Alexei's direction. "He was a smug son of a bitch, thought he was a king, thought he was an alpha. He was a useless piece of shit, just like you."

"Is that so?" Alexei's voice is barely audible as it fights the seeping gash in his throat. "And where is he now?"

Amryn slams the dagger into Alexei's arm, and the withered corpse of a man cries out. Amryn yanks the dagger out, tilting his head. "He's dead, turned to ashes."

He leans down and gestures to me with the blood-covered blade. "You know, I get what Konstantin felt. Because I had to go through something like that too, watching the woman I loved get raped by some fucking diseased piece of maggot shit like you."

The dagger goes up again, and with a flash it's lodged in Alexei's sternum. Black blood pours forth from his mouth, and he splutters, sending inky droplets flying. His pink eyes are torn wide open as he gasps. I look over at Juno, to check she's alright, and see her eyes glowing white as she watches the scene unfold before her.

Amryn crouches down in front of Alexei and pulls the dagger from his sternum with a loud snap. "Now see, I never got to have my revenge on the fucker who did that to my woman. I mean, *she* did, she got her revenge, and I'm glad she did. But me? I never got to have that satisfaction, that..." He snaps his fingers, trying to find the right words. "That closure. I dream of it. I dream of slicing that fucker's dick off and making him eat it." Amryn laughs, and the sound is so chilling it almost makes me shift on my feet.

He rises again, rolling his head on his shoulders, closing those violet eyes for a moment. He takes a deep breath, and looks back down at Alexei, whose eyes are wide now, black blood seeping into the tattered rags he's wearing.

"But now," Amryn says, his voice dropping to a low snarl, "I get to take all that rage out on you."

It takes my brain a moment to register what happens, because suddenly wings explode from Amryn's back. Not black smoke. Towering black wings, feathered wings, shining like those of a crow. The edges sizzle with purple lightning, and volts of that same color run up and down his arms.

"I'm not going to kill you," Amryn says, flexing his hands in front of him, "but I'm sure as hell going to make you hurt."

He grabs on to Alexei's shoulders with a roar, and there's a blinding flash of violet light. Alexei screams, the sound slowly cut off as it dissvoles into a sick gurgling. When the light dims, Amryn is standing in front of Alexei, holding his severed arms in his hands.

Alexei's eyes bug out like they're about to roll straight out of his skull. His mouth is torn open in a silent scream. He watches as Amryn throws the severed arms aside.

Amryn steps back, black blood sprayed across his face. He turns to me with heaving shoulders, seeming to notice the black wings at his back for the first time. His face barely moves though, and he merely claps me on the shoulder as he passes me.

"He's all yours, brother." He wipes the blood from his cheek with the back of his hand. He walks to Juno's side, and he grabs her, taking her in his arms. She holds onto him tightly, laying her cheek against his chest.

"Thank you," she murmurs.

Amryn presses his lips to her forehead. "Any time."

They both watch as I turn to Alexei, who is whimpering now.

"I'm immortal," he garbles, "how are you going to kill an immortal?"

I look over at Juno, whose brows are drawn into a frown as she looks at Alexei. Her eyes slowly raise to meet mine, and I pause. I'm asking permission to do this. She gives me a brief nod.

I turn back to Alexei, swinging the scimitar in my hand.

"I cannot kill you, Alexei, since you are immortal, you will survive anything I do to you. You will feel pain, certainly, but you will never die."

"Exactly!" Alexei tries to laugh, but it catches in his throat. "I will heal from anything you do."

I point at his severed arms. "Unless I finish what my brother started."

Alexei looks uncertain for a split second. He tries to sit up, but without the use of his arms he struggles in the chair, his feet slipping in the blood that has pooled on the floor. "What do you -"

"I'm going to take you to pieces," I say, pointing the scimitar at him. "I'm going to take you to pieces and then I'm going to scatter those pieces all over this castle. You will feel every cut for all of eternity, and your suffering will never end."

"Konstantin, wait." Alexei's feet find no traction in the slippery floor. He looks over at Juno. "I'm sorry, Juno. I was fooled too, just like you. I was told I could be powerful, I would have saved you if I could, I swear -"

I swing the scimitar, and Alexei cries out. His leg falls to the floor, followed swiftly by the other one as I swing the blade again. I grab the tattered clothing and pull him from the chair, throwing the limbless stump of his torso onto the blood-soaked stone floor.

"You raped her while I watched," I roar, "you held her down and violated her. The last thing I saw was the woman I love begging for me to help her, to save her from you. The man she trusted, who she loved."

He sputters a little, and that just makes me angrier.

"You traitorous piece of shit, even *this* is too good for you!"

Alexei is beyond words at this point. His jaw quivers, his eyes rolling back into his head over and over as his body tries to process what is happening to him. I lunge forward and pierce his chest with the edge of the scimitar, and he coughs up rivulets of blood.

"How does it feel to be run through?" I pull the scimitar out of his body in a shower of blood. "How does it feel to suffer what I suffered?"

The scimitar scrapes the stones, sending sparks flying as I cut Alexei's torso in half. His mouth slackens, his eyes becoming more and more vacant. Another cut, and his head rolls across the floor.

His mouth is moving, a huffing breath passing those withered lips. I pick the head up by the hair.

"What are you saying?"

"S - Sa -" His eyes roll back in his head. "Sa-"

I lean closer to his mouth.

"Sa - Samael."

Thunder claps directly above us.

I look over my shoulder at Amryn, and push Konstantin back into the depths of my mind as I hear it.

A shrill scream, coming over the blood bond. Amryn's eyes widen as they meet mine.

DADDY!

"That's Phoenix!" Amryn cries.

Juno gasps and immediately lifts her hands, summoning up the silver ball, watching it grow into the portal. I can see flames through the expanding, shimmering mirror.

Ocario is burning.

The portal is barely bigger than Amryn before he throws himself through it.

DADDY!

My blood runs cold as I hear Phoenix's voice again.

I throw Alexei's head across the room and Juno and I sprint for the portal. We've almost reached it when it slams shut in an explosion of green mist. Tiny prickling shards sweep across my face, like a shower of broken glass, and I'm knocked flat on to my back.

I gasp, trying to breathe, trying to make sense of what the fuck just happened. I reach for Juno blindly, she has to be here somewhere. I roll on to my side and see her, convulsing, grabbing at her throat.

"Juno, oh fuck, Juno!" I crawl across the floor, reaching her side, and she's wide-eyed, trying to breathe. I put my hands on her face, my veins glowing, and her eyes flutter closed as her chest expands, air rushing into her lungs.

"Tal," she sputters, "what happened?"

"I happened, sweetness."

The voice makes my skin crawl.

Gabriel emerges from the corner of the room, smiling widely. He saunters over to us, shaking his head.

"Oh you are predictable, you demons," he chides. "First chance you get, and what do you think of? Revenge." He sighs. "But you did make my job a whole lot easier."

"What have you done?" I demand, clutching Juno to me. She's gone completely limp in my arms. "What the fuck have you done?"

Gabriel laughs. "Why do you always think I'm behind it all, hmm? Haven't you figured it out yet?" He stops a few feet away from me, and tilts his head. "You honestly still don't know what all this is about?"

There's movement in the corner of my eye, and an old man with a long white beard moves out of the shadows.

"It's time to go," the Old God says quietly. "We need to finish this."

25
Amryn

throw myself through the portal, through that strange wet sensation, and it's like I've landed in a war zone. The entire village is up in flames, and all I can hear is screaming.

There's a loud *pop* behind me, and I turn to see the portal close up. Tal and Juno aren't anywhere to be seen. I reach out a hand, hoping to still feel that shimmering wall, but it's gone.

"Tal!" I take a step forward. "Juno! Tal!"

DADDY!

Phoenix's voice tears me away, and I lurch towards the village, trying to reach out to him, trying to feel where he is.

I can't feel Cora, and my stomach churns. She has to be here. She has to be safe.

Cora, where are you?

The rushing sound behind me reminds me my wings are still out - these new, foreign wings - and I draw them in. I don't have time to think about how that's possible.

There are demons everywhere, some dead on the ground, others tending to the wounded. They all meet my face with expressions of terror. None of them is Cora.

None of them is Phoenix. I don't see Elise, or Liall, or Ebony. I feel sick. I don't stop to ask anyone what's happened. My son is screaming for me. He could be hurt.

Please be alive. Please be OK.

Cora, where are you?

I rush to our cabin, and find the door torn from its hinges and discarded on the snow.

"Cora!" I run inside. "Cora! Phoenix! Where are you?"

Zadkiel said he'd look after them, he said they'd be safe. I should have stayed here, I should have fucking *stayed*.

"Cora!"

The couch is turned on its back, and the dining table has been snapped clean in half, lying in the middle of the room like a sunken ship. The kitchen window has been smashed, but from the inside. There's no glass on the floor.

"Cora!" There's no answer, and I can't feel her in the cabin. I can't feel her presence at all. I reach out to see if her shields are down - but they're just not there. Panic grips my throat. I rush down the hallway to our bedroom, and stop short when I see a huge pool of blood at the end of the bed.

Fuck fuck fuck.

"Cora!" I cry.

"Daddy?"

The tiny voice comes from underneath the bed. I drop to my knees and meet Phoenix's terrified little face. I almost cry with relief.

"Hey buddy, oh my god, hi, are you OK?" I reach under and pull him out, and he throws his arms around my neck. "Hey, Daddy's got you, it's OK. It's Daddy, I'm here."

"The big man took Momma," Phoenix says as he cries into my shoulder. "Momma put me under the bed, and the big man hurted her."

I gasp, clutching on to my son. Fuck. What's happened here? I reach out to Cora again, and there's nothing, just *nothing.*

I pull back from Phoenix, holding his face gently in my hands. "Buddy, I need you to try and remember, OK? I know you're scared, but what happened to Uncle Zad? Was he here?"

Phoenix nods, his shoulders shaking, the corners of his mouth pulled down into a frown as he tries to speak. "I - I saw Uncy Zad, and he had a hurted here." He points to his forehead. "Momma told me hide, and the big man hit Momma's face." Big tears roll down his cheeks. "Momma had blood, here." He points to his chest. "And then Momma was sleeping."

Fuck. Fuck. Fuck. Phoenix begins to sob and I hold him to me. "It's OK, buddy, it's OK. We're going to - we're going to get - we'll find Momma."

Cora, where are you? Baby, where the fuck are you?

Phoenix looks up at me. "Daddy?"

372

I try to answer him, try to be strong, try to show him that it's going to be OK. But no words come out. All I can do is nod.

"The bad lady came back."

I frown at him, blood roaring in my ears, trying to understand. "What bad lady?"

I hear footsteps behind me, and I push Phoenix between the bed and the wall. "You stay here and stay quiet, OK?" I give him a smile, which is probably totally unconvincing. "It'll be OK, Daddy's going to protect you, OK?"

Phoenix wraps his arms around his legs and nods. I spin around to face whatever's coming. High heels clack on the wooden floorboards. I ignite the purple flames in my hands, ready to strike.

And then my blood runs cold.

It can't be. It's not possible. I'm seeing things.

"Hello Amryn." Morgan's violet eyes light up as she looks me up and down. "My, my, my, but you're still as handsome as you were the day I fucked you in that cell."

"You're dead," I say slowly. "You're dead. I killed you. Years ago."

"Yes, you did, didn't you?" Morgan laughs lightly, and her eyes stray to the floor behind me. "Such a sweet little kid, he looks so much like his mother, doesn't he?"

"Where is she?"

"Cora?" Her eyes move back to mine. "Oh, she's dead. Samael was more than eager to have a chance to kill the Shadow Queen, so he did."

"I don't believe you." But even as she says it, I reach out, and I can't feel Cora. There's nothing there. Just... nothing. "You're lying."

"Believe what you want Amryn," she says, tossing her red hair over her shoulder and taking a step into the room. "We all knew this day would come. Did you all really think ending Michael would be the end of it?"

I raise my hand, pointing the purple lightning at her. "How the fuck are you alive?"

She giggles. "It's funny, you know, how ignorant you demons really are. We witches were seen as a lesser species, but we can recognise our own kind. You can't tell an imposter when they're right in front of your face. As your family would well know." She throws her head back and laughs. "Oh yes, all those years in Nilau, I knew exactly who you were."

"How are you alive?"

She smirks, putting her hands on her hips. "I'm lucky enough to have a brother with a whole host of powers, Amryn. Not only is he a powerful mimic, he's also incredibly skilled when it comes to necromancy."

There's more footsteps out in the hallway, and Morgan looks over her shoulder smiling widely. Her gaze moves back to me as Elias steps into the room.

"My dear brother flew straight to Nilau to collect my body," Morgan says to me as Elias takes her hand, "and then when the time was right, he resurrected me."

I stare at them both, shaking my head. "Why? Why are you doing this?"

Elias laughs out loud. "Oh you're such a fucking idiot,

Amryn." His lips pull back in a sneer. "Blind, all of you. Blind to what was going on right in front of you. Especially you, so obsessed with your half-breed fucking Queen." He shrugs. "Not that it matters now, she's dead."

I shake my head, and Phoenix whimpers behind me. "I don't believe you. You're lying. You're both liars."

"Samael stabbed her." Morgan puts a hand over her chest. "Right here, sweetie. Right through the heart." She looks at Elias, her eyebrows raised. "She died pretty quick, huh? I think she called out his name before she died though."

I can't breathe.

Cora, please. Please.

But there's nothing. Phoenix is crying behind me, his hiccuping sobs getting louder.

Cora's dead. She's gone.

"She was pregnant too, wasn't she?" Morgan asks, her lips curling into a sickening grin. "Funny thing about infertility spells, they don't always work the way you think. But now that your pregnant wife is dead..." She raises her hand, purple light glowing in her fingers "I'm going to kill your son while you watch."

I raise my hand just as a yellow flame explodes through the doorway and sends Elias flying into the wall.

"Amryn, *run!*" It's Elise.

Morgan spins towards Elise's voice, and I throw my wings out, bending down to grab Phoenix. I clutch him in my arms, curling the wings around us and hurtle through the window. Glass shatters around us as I land on the ground, and then I'm on my feet running across the village.

I sprint into the barn, running to the trapdoor on the floor. I pull it up and put Phoenix into the empty space.

"Buddy, you need to stay here, OK?"

His eyes are wide as he stares up at me. "Daddy you come back?"

"I promise you." Tears bite at my eyes. The last promise I made to her. "I swear it. I'll come right back. You stay here, and stay quiet."

He nods, curling up as I close the door over his head. I can barely breathe as I run back to my cabin. Cora can't be dead. They're lying. Morgans's fucking with my head again. But that blood on the floor, and I can't fucking *feel* her.

No, she can't be dead. She has to be OK. I lost her before. I'm not losing her again.

I run into the cabin, and there's silence. I stop and listen. Nothing. I move slowly, it could be a trap. They could be waiting for me.

Elise? No response. Her shields are gone too. Just gone.

I creep forward, the unfamiliar buzzing of the purple lightning encircling my fingers. There's no sound, except the occasional cry or yell from outside as the other demons move around the burning village.

I reach the bedroom door, and peer around the corner. Elise is lying in the middle of the room, surrounded by blood, the front of her body torn to shreds.

I cry out and throw myself down beside her. "Oh god, fuck, no! Elise, Elise?"

Her entire chest has been ripped open, like they've torn her heart out. Her eyes stare straight ahead, seeing nothing. I clutch her to me, her blood covering my arms.

I hear running footsteps and turn, ready to strike, tears blurring my vision. Liall and Ebony stumble into the room, and Ebony's mouth falls open as she sees Elise's blood-covered body on the ground.

"No, oh no no no," she cries, covering her mouth with her hand.

"I saw them leave," Liall says, shaking his head, leaning on his thighs as his breath rasps out of him. "I saw Elias, and that red-headed bitch, I saw them running, and I knew -" He gasps, covering his face with his hands.

"What happened to Cora?" I ask, and the look Ebony gives me chills me to my core. I don't want to hear it. I can't hear that. I can't hear her say it.

She kneels in front of me, and takes my bloody hand in hers. "She's dead, Amryn." Tears run down her cheeks. "We saw it happen. Zadkiel tried to stop it -"

I tear my hand away from her. "No."

"Amryn -"

"No." I shake my head, clutching a hand to my chest. "I'd have felt it. I would have - I felt her die before, I would have... I would have.... No. No."

"Samael came," Ebony says, "he brought angels with him, like those ones that came with the chimera."

"We didn't stand a chance." Liall is still bent over, his shoulders heaving. "Cora hid Phoenix, and she tried, she tried to hold them off."

No. My mind can't comprehend it. They're wrong. They're all wrong.

"Zadkiel tried to protect her, but..." Ebony puts a hand to her head, unable to look at me. "Samael, he got a hold of Cora, and he... he...." She covers her face and begins to sob. "Oh god, Amryn, I'm so sorry."

"What did he do?" My whole body is cold. This isn't happening.

"He stabbed her," Liall says, his voice cracking, "in the chest. She was - she was calling out for you."

I squeeze my eyes shut. I should have fucking stayed. *Why didn't I FUCKING STAY?*

"And then, she just... she went limp." Ebony lets out a strangled gasp. "She was gone. She was just gone."

"He took her body," Liall says, running a hand over his face, which is red and tear-stained. "He flew off with her, and Zadkiel followed, but he never came back."

Ebony begins to sob loudly as Liall moves across the room to Elise's side, and I look down at my hands. My hands, covered in Elise's blood.

This isn't happening.

This isn't real.

I lost her before. I can't lose her again.

This isn't happening.

Cora, please. Cora. Cora. CORA.

But there's nothing.

Like she never even existed.

I somehow end up sitting in the hallway of the cabin, with no recollection of how I got there. I remember getting Phoenix out of the barn, and taking him to Fenella's.

I know Ebony told Fenella about Elise, but I can't remember if she cried, or wailed, or raged. Both daughters, gone. I'm sure she did. But I can't remember.

After that, there's nothing. And now I'm sitting in the hallway of the cabin, my legs stretched out in front of me. The light is starting to fade as the sun sets. I should be out there, helping. But I can't move. All I can do is stare at the floor.

Cora's dead.

Liall sits down opposite me, resting his arms on his drawn up knees. "I tucked Phoenix up in bed," he says, "he went right to sleep."

I can't speak, so I just nod. At least I think I do.

"Where are Juno and Tal?" Liall asks.

"I don't know." I shift my gaze to my hands. My bloody hands. "They were right behind me. There was thunder, and then I heard Phoenix calling me. And I jumped through the portal, they were right behind me. And then they weren't." I look up at him. "When did the angels attack?"

"It wasn't long after you left." He sighs. "Cora came back to the cabin, and then, there was this roaring sound, we couldn't place it. And then... then there were angels, like those black ones that attacked the night the chimera came."

"And Samael..." I can't bring myself to say it.

Liall nods slowly. "He... He went after Cora immediately. She tried to hold him off, but he was too strong. Zadkiel got hurt, trying to stop him."

"Why did Samael take her..." I can't finish the question. I can't say the word *Body*. That means she's dead. And she's not. She can't be.

"I don't know, Amryn."

"She's alive. She has to be. They wouldn't take her if she wasn't. That doesn't make any sense."

"I know this isn't easy -"

"No." I shake my head. "She's alive. I didn't feel her die. She's alive. I felt her die in Nilau, and I would have felt her die now. And I didn't. She's alive."

If I say it enough it'll be true. If I say it enough, someone out there will hear me and make it true because I believe it.

Liall inhales sharply, clawing his hands through his hair. "Amryn, we all saw it happen. Samael, he's strong. He's, I don't know, he has some power that could overwhelm Cora easily."

"If that was true they'd have sent him to Nilau and not that fucking freak Michael." I look over at him, and shake my head. "She's not dead. She's not."

Liall gazes back at me helplessly. "When Ceili died, I refused to accept it too. I understand. I do. I know you want to bargain your way out of this."

I hold my hands out in front of me again. Covered in Elise's blood. "What do I do, Liall?" Something breaks inside me. I'm cold, and empty. "What do I tell my son? What do I do? What do I do? What do I do?" My hands start shaking as Liall moves next to me and puts an arm around my shoulders. "Liall, tell me what to do."

"I'm here, Amryn."

"Tell me what to do."

He squeezes my shoulders. "I'm here."

"What do I do?" I stare at the blood on my hands. Just like my mother. Just like when Cora died in my arms. Blood. Death. Nothing else. "Liall, I don't know what to do." Tears begin to roll down my cheeks, but I don't know if I'm crying. "I can't do this."

"Yes, you can," Liall says, his voice strained. "You have to. You have to think of Phoenix."

"I can't live without her."

"Yes, you can. Your son needs you."

Lightning starts to crackle up my arms, and Liall jumps a little. "Amryn, you need to -"

I push myself off the floor, ignoring Liall's protests as I stumble out of the cabin. I can't stay there. I can't control this, these new powers. I can't be near anyone right now. I'll hurt them.

I break into a run. I run and run until my lungs burn. I run until the tears are freezing on my face as the icy evening breeze whips around me. I remember running like this, after I watched Finn fucking violate her.

I didn't stop him. I let that happen. I couldn't save her in Nilau, even though I'm her Draw. I held her as she died. And I wasn't here today. I wasn't here when she needed me. I wasn't here when she called out for me. Why have I never been able to save her?

Why have I never been able to FUCKING SAVE HER?

I collapse to my knees and roar. I claw my fingers along my scalp as though I can somehow tear the grief through my skin, as though making myself bleed will make the pain stop.

I reach out again, and again, but there's no shield. Nothing for me to beat against. Nothing for me to tear down. Just an endless void for me to scream into, keening all my loss and pain into the vast emptiness where she used to be.

It's almost dark by the time I come to my senses again. My feet are numb from kneeling on the floor, in the frigid air. The ground around me is scorched black, the snow melted away. I look down at my hands, and the lightning crackles across my palm. Illuminating the blood that I can't escape.

I rise to my feet, stumbling a little as feeling rushes back to my frozen limbs. I look up at the sky, which is now a deep indigo as the last of the sun's rays slip away behind the mountains.

Two eagles circle overhead. Just like they did the day I found out I was her Draw. I didn't know what it had meant then. I didn't know then what I'd have. I didn't know then that one day she'd be mine.

And I lost her anyway. It was all for nothing.

I try to reach out to Tal and Juno. Juno's shields are up and so hard that I decide she must be asleep. Or drugged.

Or passed out. Knocked unconscious. Who knows.

Tal. I claw against his shields. *Tal, please.* I beat against them wildly, and there's a splinter, but they stay up. *Tal, PLEASE.*

Nothing.

They have to be alive. They have to be.

I drag myself back to the village, past the burned out houses. Past the Great Hall where the other demons are assembled, tending to the wounded. Maybe they look at me. Maybe they expect me to stop, and help. Right or wrong, I keep moving. I can't do this today.

Fenella opens the door to her cabin before I even reach it, her face red from crying. She holds out a hand to me, guiding me inside. It's warm in here. There are candles everywhere. She's set up a sort of altar underneath one of her windows, and there are two pillar candles lit on it.

"For my girls." A sob catches in her throat. "For my beautiful girls. They are together again."

I put my arm around her, and we stare at the candles together. "I'm sorry," I say quietly, and then I can't talk, my legs give out under me, and I collapse onto the floor.

I can't breathe. I can't fucking breathe.

I tear at my leathers, trying to get the vest off, and Fenella is beside me, sobbing.

"Amryn, please, let me help," she says urgently, trying to open the buckles on my armor.

I try to breathe but my throat won't open up. I feel nothing and everything. I'm numb and so flooded with pain I can't think. Fenella undoes the final buckle at my side and I double over as I tear the leather from my body. I claw into the hardwood floor and cry out, hot tears running down my cheeks.

Fenella's arms are around me, and I can feel her body shaking as she cries. I become aware of the soft lilac glow of her veins, and she's trying to heal me but we both know that nothing she can do will heal this.

I slump against her and she strokes my head, like I'm a child. She hums that song my Mom used to sing to me when I was little, though it's broken and interrupted by her sobs and sniffles.

Finally, my breathing calms enough that I can think again. My throat opens enough to let me speak. I look at Fenella's tear-streaked face.

"What do I do?" I ask her the same question I asked Liall. Because I'm lost. I don't know what to do. I need someone to tell me what to do.

She takes my hand in hers, her eyebrows flickering a little as she sees all the blood - the blood of her last remaining child - and shakes her head.

"I lost my husband so many years ago, and I still do not know, my darling boy." She cups my face in her hand. "All I know is that you have a son who needs you, now more than ever. You must think of him. Cora would want you to. Cora needs you to."

"He needs his mom." *And I need her too. Fuck, I need her.*

"He needs you," Fenella says softly. "He needs you. And there will be days when you will need all of us to help you, because the grief will be too much. But we are here. We will help you, and Phoenix." She gets to her feet and gently pulls me to mine. "Now, you need to wash off all this blood, and then you need to go and hold your little boy and try and get some rest."

"I need to find Tal and Juno."

She shakes her head. "Amryn, they are too far away for you to be of any help. The others will do what they can. Right now, you need to rest. Now come." She takes my arm. She's right. They're god knows where, through that fucking portal, lost to me for now.

I can't do anything. I can't help anyone.

The shower is meant to make me clean but I use it to punish myself instead. I turn the hot water on until my skin feels like it's almost going to blister. Until I'm bright red and wincing, my fingers clawing against the tiles. At least it's pain. At least it's something. At least it hurts. I deserve it.

There's a fresh pair of sweatpants and a t-shirt lying on the counter when I get out, and I pull them on. My hair is still braided, and I think for a moment of unpicking it all, but I leave it.

Cora did that.

It's so fucking stupid, as if those braids mean anything. But now they do. Because it's the last thing she did for me. Everything is significant now. Every last moment that counted down til I walked through that portal.

Out in the lounge room, Fenella has gone to sleep in the armchair by the altar, and she's clutching two small pink blankets against her chest. My heart aches so badly I'm sure I'm about to pass out. I leave her there to sleep, and go down the hallway.

Phoenix is curled up in bed, his little mouth pushed open against the palm of his hand that he's tucked under his face. His breathing is slow and steady.

My son. The son I never thought I'd have. And now he's all I have left.

I climb into bed next to him, and he shifts a little, snuggling in to me.

"Daddy?"

I put my arms around him, breathing in the scent of the baby shampoo Cora uses on his curls. "I'm here, buddy."

"Granma was here," he says softly, not opening his eyes. "She sad."

"Yeah?"

"Yeah. She got see Leesy, and now she sad."

I clutch Phoenix tighter to me. "Yeah, I bet she is."

With a sigh he's asleep again.

I lie awake for a long, long time, listening to the beat of my heart as it drums through my ears.

My heart. Her heart.

Cora, please.

26
Tallesaign

The pain in my head is so bad that opening my eyes feels like glass splinters dragging across my forehead. Fucking blood magic. And I'm immune to this shit? No wonder Juno is passed out in my arms like a ragdoll.

I keep kissing her temple, putting my cheek to her mouth, anything to assure myself the warmth in her skin and the breath leaving her mouth is real and not just some spell. I squeeze my eyes shut as I remember that green flash. One second Juno was upright running after Amryn and the next she was struggling for breath on the ground beside me.

Amryn.

I can feel him beating against my shields, but I don't want to let him in. I don't know where he is or what's happened, and I'm afraid they'll track him, or somehow corrupt the blood bond. I can feel his pain, like acid. My breath catches in my throat, because I can't feel Cora's shields.

I give myself a shake and shift Juno in my arms, trying

to rouse her from this fucking coma they've put her in. She has to be OK. Cora has to be OK. I won't lose them. I refuse to lose anyone else. No.

"Baby, come on," I whisper, pressing Juno against me. She's so sickeningly limp. Her head lolls back and I remember Ceili's broken, blood-soaked body in Liall's arms. Nausea sweeps over me. *Come on, COME ON.* "Juno, you have to wake up."

I look around the room, and it's so fucking ridiculous. Gabriel has us in some sort of medieval torture chamber - there's even a rack for fuck's sake. This fucker sure has a sense for being as dramatic as fucking possible.

The door flies open, hitting the stone wall with a reverberating clang, and Gabriel strolls in. He looks around the room until his eyes settle on us, huddled against the wall. I summon up a ball of black lightning, and am instantly overcome with a clawing pain at the back of my head.

Gabriel laughs. "Not just yet, my friend. The binding magic is holding strong, and I wouldn't want you to hurt yourself." He gestures to Juno with a jerk of his chin. "Still asleep, is she?" He asks jovially, tossing a small golden dagger in his hand.

"What did you do to her?" I turn so my body is between Gabriel and Juno, keeping my arms firmly around her.

Gabriel scoffs. "Oh, do stop worrying, Tallesaign, she'll be fine. Just caught a somewhat larger dose of the blood magic than you did."

He sits down on the floor a few feet away from me, spreading his legs from him, leaning back on his hands.

He's dressed like he just walked off some college campus, baggy jeans and a tight white shirt. So fucking casual. His appearance makes our surroundings feel even more menacing. His wings rustle as he arranges them behind him.

"Where's the Old God?"

Gabriel grins. "We'll get to all that once she's awake." He jerks his head down in Juno's direction. "It's important for her to catch that part of the conversation. But for now, you and I can have a little chat. Man to man."

"Man to man, huh?" I give a cynical laugh. "And what do we men need to discuss?"

"Well, you see, this whole situation has become somewhat awkward. I was incredibly embarrassed when I saw Juno in Ocario that day. I couldn't believe she'd managed to claw her way out of the ground, and then you go on ahead and find her, despite the shields I had in place."

"What shields?" Even as the question leaves my lips I remember. The quiet in that forest. The lack of sound. The snow that didn't reach the ground.

"I'd put a shield over Arax when I buried our beloved Queen under it," Gabriel says, absently inspecting his nails. "It was supposed to block anyone finding her, anyone from hearing her cries. Because I knew, I just fucking knew one of you Draws would show up again."

"You did huh?"

"Yes," he snaps as his eyes meet mine again, "Draws are a plague. If the humans do ever manage that nuclear apocalypse, all that will be left after the dust clears is cockroaches and fucking Draws. That's why there's no point in killing any of you. Fate always delivers another one."

"So why don't you just kill the Shadow Queen?"

Gabriel rolls his eyes. "You really are the most dense creature you know." He pulls up his knees, resting his arms on them. "Do you think I wouldn't kill her if I knew how? I put her in the fucking ground for a *reason*, Tallesaign."

"I'm not the dense one here." I shift Juno in my arms. She sighs a little, her brow furrowing. "You put her in the ground right next to Ocario, a fucking demon village."

He throws his hands up and shrugs. "OK, that wasn't my best idea, I will give you that. But Michael was always sure we'd be able to deal with her if she came back. And then-" He huffs out a breath through gritted teeth and taps the dagger against the stone floor loudly. "Well, *then* Cora is fucking born. And there's you and your brother. So, we had to make plans."

"Who picked us as her Draws?"

Gabriel looks at me blankly. "What do you mean? The Old God did of course."

He's so earnest in that moment that I have to believe him. Whatever plan there is, whatever is spurring on my constant thought that something weird is going on here, Gabriel doesn't know about it.

"So, I bet that pissed you off, huh? Two witches as the Draws of the Shadow Queen?"

Gabriel shrugs. "It made the situation a little more complicated, certainly. But when Lordain had the plan of taking Cora for himself, it did seem like such an effective way to keep you all apart, to stop Cora from knowing who she really is."

"Yeah, great plan." I shake my head. "Didn't work out for you, did it?"

Gabriel grimaces. "No. Azrael really fucked up with that one."

My stomach drops. "Azrael? This was his plan?"

"It certainly was." Gabriel gets to his feet, giving his wings a shake as he begins to pace back and forth across the room. "Azrael seemed convinced that keeping Cora and her Draws close was essential. But then your mother nearly killed you, and it was decided that perhaps you weren't necessary."

The words slice through me with a sting that leaves me breathless for a moment. "I was meant to go with them?"

Gabriel puffs out a breath through pursed lips. "Yes, but then -" He lifts his eyebrows. "Anyway, Azrael encouraged Lordain to marry Cora off to Finn, to have Amryn as Finn's Draw."

Rage begins to seep into my veins. Azrael. *That fucking zombie.* "Why did he think that?"

Gabriel waves his hand impatiently. "How the fuck should I know? Something about their powers needing to grow through suffering, he's always very mysterious and quite frankly, I don't have the mental capacity for his bullshit most days."

"So what now?" I ask. "Why do you have us here?"

Juno whimpers in my arms, and I look down to see her eyes fluttering open slowly.

391

"Tal?" She slurs, her eyes unfocused. "What happened?"

Gabriel laughs. "Oh goodie, she's awake, we can *finally* get to the good part."

Juno's eyes widen and her head turns to the side. Her breathing becomes more rapid as she looks at Gabriel, and her veins glow bright white. "You fucking motherfucker. I'm going to -" She lifts her hand and immediately winces, letting it fall as she clenches her eyes shut.

"Juno?" I cradle her head against my chest. "Juno, come on, don't move, I'm here."

"Well, that is one thing you inherited from your father, Juno." Gabriel leans back against the wall with his arms crossed over his chest. "His temper. And also his absolute inability to judge any situation. Stay down for now, the blood magic will take some time to wear off."

"What the fuck do you want with us?" I ask again.

"I told you I wanted to tell you a wonderful story!" Gabriel exclaims, rolling his eyes like I'm an insolent little kid. "My word, Tallesaign, do you ever listen?"

"What fucking story?" Juno asks, her head still against my chest. "I hope it's not too long because your voice is fucking irritating."

Gabriel bursts out laughing, his wings rustling. "She's actually rather fun now that she's with you, well done." He lowers down into a crouch, his wings draped on the ground either side of him. "Now, you see, I want to tell you two about a discovery I made, and to be honest I am a little embarrassed because it should have been obvious.

One look at Cora and I should have known, but alas, I am a mere angel, and have my weaknesses."

Juno turns her head slowly to look at him, and I help her sit up a little more. "I really hope you get to the point soon," she says, her voice still a sedated slur.

"Yes, yes, I will." Gabriel holds the dagger between his hands, dancing the tip of the blade across his fingertips. "Now, you see, when we put you in the ground Queenie, we all thought that would be the end of it. The Old God just had to wait for a new Shadow Queen to be born, and we just had to sit around and wait for her to appear so we could do the same thing again."

Juno makes a sound, like a growl, I feel it vibrate through her ribcage, but she says nothing else as her eyes fix on Gabriel.

"Now, you see, we were stupid, we didn't consider that the Shadow Queen doesn't just appear," Gabriel went on, "but we knew that you hadn't had a child Juno, so it seemed like that was the only way." His lips curl into a lopsided grin. "Except, you in fact, had a child, and I didn't figure it out until the day I visited dear Cora in Ocario to offer her a truce."

Juno gasps and her whole body goes rigid. "What did you just say?"

Realization dawns on me. They were gone for two years, for two years Alexei didn't know where they were. Two years.

"Juno and Konstantin had a child?" I ask, and Konstantin erupts at the back of my mind, like he's pacing wildly.

Gabriel nods, and Juno shudders against me. "I don't remember," she whimpers, "why don't I remember? How is this possible?"

"That would be Zadkiel's doing," Gabriel says slowly. "You see, when you and your Draw discovered that you were with child, my dear, you knew the Old God would do to your daughter what he had done to you - slaughter the parents who had turned away from him and violated his Covenant, and then claim the child for himself. The ultimate connection between the Halls and the Earth realm, the Flame with which he intended to set the world on fire."

I feel Konstantin crashing to his knees, trying desperately to think, to remember, to somehow retrieve the memories of his own child. His grief makes my head spin, and I close my eyes to try and fight the pain and nausea he sends washing over me.

"So I turned to Zadkiel?" Juno asks in a small voice.

"You did indeed, my dear." Gabriel scoffs. "Zadkiel, the hatcher of great plans. He knows all and says nothing until it serves a purpose. He ferried you off in the middle of the night to a demon clan in rural Russia, the very clan you had grown up with Juno, under the protection of Matriyona herself."

My head snaps up at the name. "Matriyona? The Mother Saint?"

"Yes, that one." Gabriel rolls his eyes. "The last stronghold of the eastern Demons. The place where the bloodline of the Shadow Queen could be protected and allowed to grow, shielded from anyone who meant her harm. Juno and Konstantin were taken there, and Juno gave birth to her Heir, Aria."

Juno cries out at the name. "Oh god." She looks up at me, shaking her head, tears running down her cheeks. "I don't remember my own daughter?"

"You were there for two years, enough time for you to birth the babe and then feed her." Gabriel sounds almost bored, swishing the dagger back and forth along the hard stone floor where it throws up sparks. "And then Zadkiel insisted you go back, because it would seem Zadkiel had an interest in the Old God being defeated. But to protect the child and the bloodline of the Shadow Queen, he erased your memories of her. You both went back to Alexei like nothing had even happened."

Konstantin rages in my mind, clutching his hands to his chest. I can feel the heat of his tears on my own face. His child. The daughter he was forced to forget. Juno is shaking in my arms as she cries. I hold her tighter.

"So then what happened?"

Gabriel shrugs. "Then Alexei was angry and envious enough for us to bend him and have Juno convinced that she needed to kill her lover in order to strengthen his powers, which, you know." He looks at Juno with raised eyebrows. "I don't mean to be rude but that was rather fucking stupid, Queenie."

I tense with fury, but Juno slumps in my arms. "I know," she says with a small sob. "I know."

Gabriel seems almost surprised by this response, but he doesn't linger in that thought for long. "And then, once one Draw had abandoned you and the other was dead, you were weak enough for us to overpower you and put you underground. Where we'd hoped you'd stay, but clearly true love really does conquer all because then THIS one comes along." He gestures to me with an outstretched hand. "And then, boom. The Earth and the Flame are back together again, and now there's fucking FOUR of you."

The witch's words echo through my mind. *Everything is connected in ways we do not always expect.*

Juno. Me. Amryn. Cora. All of us. All of it. It's all connected.

"Cora is Juno's descendant then," I say.

Gabriel sighs heavily. "I really did hit you with too much blood magic. *Yes.* Cora is Juno's great-great-great, oh god however many *greats*, grand-daughter. The clan was discovered by the Solaris angels when Cora's mother was a child, and then Zadkiel rescued her and brought her to Ocario. Where she turned out to be the Draw of the Alpha, which made no sense to me at all, but what do I know?" He rises to his feet and stretches his arms wide with a yawn. "Anyhow, enough of that. Storytime is over." He spins the dagger in his hand. "Now I have to decide what to do with you."

"Where is Cora?" Juno' eyes burn with fury. "I cannot feel her shields."

"Oh, well then that would mean she's dead," Gabriel says with a shrug.

My blood runs cold. "You just said you don't know how to kill a Shadow Queen."

"I don't know how to kill *this* Shadow Queen." Gabriel points the dagger at Juno. "*She's* immortal. Cora most certainly is not, as you would well remember because you had to bring her back to life yourself, you dense fuck."

No. It can't be. I reach out again to Cora, but as soon as I do, Amryn's there.

CORA'S DEAD.

It's all I let through before my shields fly back up, cutting him off, keeping him hidden so none of these fuckers sense where he is. Tears prickle at my eyes. Not Cora. *No.* It can't be. Juno looks up at me, and I know she heard it too.

"No." She shakes her head. "*No.*"

"Anyway," Gabriel says, swinging his arms and clapping the dagger between his hands as he advances on us, "I've been tasked with torturing you until you relinquish your powers and then the Old God is going to go and collect that delightful nephew of yours and take him to the Halls."

"Phoenix?" My eyes widen. "What the fuck do you want with him?"

"The Prince of Ashes will do just as well as a Shadow Queen." Gabriel says with a grin. "Oh, you demons really are so wonderfully unaware."

Fuck. I throw my shields down.

AMRYN THEY WANT PHOENIX. GET HIM SAFE DON'T LET THE-

The Line is cut off and Gabriel cackles maniacally.

"Uh, uh, uh, Tallesaign, we don't want to spoil the surprise." He wags a finger at me. "Now, if you relinquish your powers to me without complaint, I'll ensure the little tyke has a really lovely room up in the Halls."

"Fuck you." I hiss, rising to my feet. Juno clasps on to my arm, hauling herself up alongside me.

"We're going to kill you." She's still a little shaky but I can sense the fury that's keeping her upright. Gabriel watches us with amusement.

"Going to try and fight your way out, hmm?" He chuckles. "Very well then."

I summon a ball of black lightning just as Gabriel takes a step forward.

Suddenly everything is pitch black. There's nothing, just a suffocating shadow that's so thick I can almost feel it on my face. All sound is sucked out of the room.

It's such a shock that I take a moment to orient myself when the room is once again flooded with light.

Juno is blinking rapidly, her face twisted with confusion. "What was that?" She asks me.

I see movement out of the corner of my eye, and look up to see the door is open. And a man is standing in it.

He's leaning against the door frame with his hands in the pockets of his black trousers, a black shirt tucked into them. He looks like he's just strolled out of a fancy nightclub.

His dark reddish hair is swept to one side, and his face is clean-shaven. His eyes are a light gray, and right now they're fixed on Gabriel, whose expression is one of such violent shock that it's almost comical.

"Hello, brother," the man says, pushing himself off the door frame and taking a swaggering step into the room. "It's been some time."

As he enters the room his wings become visible, drawn close to his back. Black wings, but not feathered, nor are they smoke or flame. No, these look like the wings of a bat.

Gabriel edges away from him, closer to the wall, and slowly raises his dagger. "What are you doing here?"

The man's eyes stray from Gabriel over to Juno and I, and they flash with an expression of... tenderness? His lips twitch into a brief smile before he turns back to Gabriel, and a steely, lethal grin settles on his face.

"I think you know exactly why I'm here." The man takes another step towards Gabriel, his body still relaxed, his hands still in his pockets.

Gabriel bares his teeth in a sneer. "I don't know what you're talking about."

"You really are the most terrible liar, Gabriel." The man says slowly.

Gabriel snorts. "Everyone says that."

"Because it is true." The man takes another step, and tilts his head. "You and I have some unfinished business, and it's time for you to pay."

"What unfinished business, huh? Pay for what?" Gabriel spits, his eyes becoming ever wider.

The man takes two more leisurely steps towards Gabriel, his grin dissolving from his face. Gabriel's fear is betrayed by the shaking of his wings.

"Pay for what, Lucifer?" He asks again, his voice almost shrill.

The man withdraws his hands from his pockets,

spreading them wide, and the pool of darkness that had enveloped the room begins to rise around his feet.

"For putting my daughter in the ground."

R D Baker

Acknowledgements

Mark – as always, this all would not have been possible without you. Taking over all the housework, ferrying away kids, taking days off whenever you could so I could work through another creative wave; you did it all and more. I promise I'll buy you that 22x22 Rubiks Cube as soon as I can. I love you most.

Felica, Rachel, Deana, Bailey – my amazing street team, what would I do without you??? I love you girls so damn much, and cannot wait for cocktails stateside next year!

My ARC readers – y'all are the best. Just like, hands down. The best. No ifs ands or buts. You're all mine for life now, just so you know.

JR Korpa – for once again providing part of the artwork that makes up this cover. Your art always hits the right spot. You're amazing.

Stephen Rocktaschel – your character art has brought the characters I love so much to life in the most beautiful way. I cannot thank you enough for your passion and vision.

And of course, the BookTok Community, thank you - for giving a little indie author a chance, and hyping these books as much as you did. You changed my life in ways I could have never imagined.

R D Baker

R D Baker began writing stories with the encouragement of the amazing Mrs Shooter back in the First Grade. It began with poetry and short stories, growing into full-length novels later in life.
She has always been a lover of all things romance. She has previously published a romance novella and two full length contemporary romance novels.
The Shadow Drawn series was her first foray into fantasy romance, and has now led on to a new upcoming high fantasy series, The Lost Heirs.
She lives in the Blue Mountains, Australia, with her family.

Printed in Poland
by Amazon Fulfillment
Poland Sp. z o.o., Wrocław

31074360R00233